Praise for *The C*

"A wild, exuberant read from a tr
creates an unbelievable world so n ... as to seem real."

— *USA Today*

"A remarkable debut . . . unforgettable scenes and characters."

— Cornelia Funke

"A story that gallops right along!" —Tamora Pierce

"This extravagant first novel . . . offers ample rewards . . . infectious."

— *Booklist*

"A marvelous and multi-species cast . . . has something to please high fantasy fans of every stripe."

— *Kirkus Reviews*

"Laden with vigorous battle scenes, mystical encounters, and humorous domestic exchanges, Thirrin's vibrant story will be pounced upon and eagerly consumed by readers. . . ."

—*The Bulletin of the Center for Children's Books*

SOON TO BE A
MAJOR MOTION PICTURE
FROM FOX 2000!

THE CRY OF THE ICEMARK

STUART HILL

SCHOLASTIC INC.
New York Toronto London Auckland Sydney
Mexico City New Delhi Hong Kong Buenos Aires

ISBN 0-439-68627-X

12 11 10 9 8 7 6 5 4 3 2 1 06 07 08 09 10 11

Printed in the U.S.A. 40

First Scholastic paperback edition, June 2006
Book design by Elizabeth B. Parisi

To Kathleen Hill, the real Thirrin,
and Clare Hardy
for the faith and support

Also to the G and G,
and to TM, TG, and all the Ts

1

Thirrin Freer Strong-in-the-Arm Lindenshield carried her names with ease. She was thirteen years old, tall for her age, and could ride her horse as well as the best of her father's soldiers. She was also heir to the throne of the Icemark. Her tutor might add that she was attentive when she wanted to be, clever when she bothered to try, and had her father's temper. Few compared her to her mother, who had died when Thirrin was born. But those who remembered the proud young woman of the fierce Hypolitan people said that Thirrin was her double.

The soldier riding guard over her didn't care about any of this. They'd been hunting in the forest since dawn and he was cold and tired, but Thirrin showed no signs of wanting to go home. They were following a set of tracks she insisted were werewolf prints, and the soldier was afraid she might be right. He'd already eased the spears in his scabbard and had been riding with his shield on his arm for the past hour.

Werewolves had been banished from the Icemark after the Ghost Wars, in which Thirrin's father, King Redrought, had defeated the army of the Vampire King and Queen at the

Battle of the Wolfrocks. Probably the werewolf she was tracking was just a loner in search of easy hunting in the cattle pastures, but you could never be too careful. With any luck she could capture it, she thought, and take it back to the city as a prize. And perhaps before it was executed it could be made to give useful information about The-Land-of-the-Ghosts.

"Listen!" Thirrin said urgently, waking from a pleasant daydream about winning her father's respect and gratitude. "Just ahead — I can hear snarling!"

The soldier took her word for it and leveled his spear. "Pull in behind me," he said, forgetting all formality in the moment of danger.

But before they could move, the thick undergrowth that lined the path burst open and a huge animal leaped out. It was vaguely man-shaped but extremely hairy, and its face was a strange mixture of wolf and human. For a moment it stared at them, its eyes full of hate, then it charged. It easily dodged the soldier's clumsy thrust and headed straight for Thirrin, but her horse was battle-trained and it leaped forward to meet the attack, lashing out with its steel-shod hooves.

Taken by surprise, the werewolf took the full force of the kick, but it only staggered back for a second before growling with fury and attacking again. By this time, Thirrin had drawn her long cavalry saber and, in one fluid movement, she wheeled her horse around, leaned from the saddle, and hacked deeply into the werewolf's arm.

The soldier had recovered by now and he charged, knocking the werewolf off its feet. Before it could get up, both horses drew in shoulder to shoulder, snorting fiercely and lashing out with their hooves.

The creature scrambled to its feet and retreated into the thick undergrowth where the horses couldn't follow. For a moment it licked at its wounds with a long red tongue, then it emerged from the thorny bush and without warning threw itself at Thirrin's horse, knocking her from the saddle. Her charger blundered away, screaming in terror, and she lay on the path dazed and badly winded. She seemed to be watching a silent and tiny picture of the world from a point high above the action. She was dizzily aware that there was danger of some sort, but what it was exactly she couldn't quite remember. She watched as a soldier attacked a huge wolfman, but the creature broke his spear and the soldier's horse reared and galloped away as he clung on desperately. Now the wolfman was turning back and walking slowly toward her.

Reality crashed back. The world filled her head to the brim again and with a start she remembered where she was. The werewolf was approaching with slow, deliberate steps as though it was enjoying the moment just before the kill, like a cat with a helpless mouse within easy reach.

Her sword lay close by and, grabbing it, she leaped to her feet. The creature stopped and drew back its lips over enormous teeth, almost as though it were grinning. Thirrin didn't hesitate; shouting the war cry of the House of Lindenshield, she attacked.

Before it could react, her blade bit deeply into its shoulder and it fell back, surprised by her ferocity. But then her boots slipped on wet leaves, and she crashed to the ground. Immediately the creature pounced and, wrenching her sword away, it sat astride her, its massive weight crushing the breath out of her lungs. Thirrin's fighting spirit still roared within her, though, and as the creature lowered its jaws toward her throat, she punched it hard on the nose. The werewolf shook its head and sneezed, taken completely aback.

"Make it quick, wolfman, and make sure all the wounds are

in front. I don't want anyone saying I died running away," she yelled, managing to keep the terror out of her voice.

The creature lowered its head toward her face again, but this time its eyes were filled with an almost human expression of puzzlement. It stayed like that for nearly a minute, seeming to scrutinize her. Then, without warning, it threw back its head and howled, its voice climbing to a high chilling note before falling slowly away to silence. It looked at her again, its eyes so human that Thirrin felt she could almost talk to it. Suddenly it leaped away, leaving her to gasp for breath, its enormous weight gone.

Slowly she struggled to a sitting position and watched as the werewolf picked up her sword and drove it point-first into the thick forest litter. Then it did something that amazed her: The huge creature bowed, folding one of its arms across its torso while the other swept out before it in a delicate gesture, like the most fashionable of courtiers.

Despite everything, Thirrin almost giggled. The werewolf threw back its head again and a rough coughing and growling noise burst from its mouth, as though it were laughing. Then it ran off through the trees, leaving nothing behind but shaking branches.

Thirrin climbed to her feet and collected her sword. She was trembling with shock, but fascinated. Why didn't the werewolf kill her? Could such creatures think and make decisions? And if so, did this one actually decide to let her live?

She was astounded. Everything she'd ever been told and all of her beliefs and ideas about the Wolf-folk were shaken by this. She'd always thought they were mindless killers, as unthinking as any other primitive and evil creature from beyond the Icemark's northern borders, and yet the wolfman had shown . . . what? Compassion, perhaps?

A crashing and thrashing in the trees interrupted her thoughts, and she leveled her sword, ready for a renewed attack. But it was only her soldier escort. He'd regained control of his bolting horse and had come charging back, ready to die in her defense. Better that than die as a punishment for not carrying out his duty properly.

Thirrin had to endure almost ten minutes of him checking her over for injuries and a long and detailed explanation of how he'd had no chance of controlling his horse when it bolted. But at last she was allowed to mount his horse, and they started the slow journey home. She thought through everything that had happened. Could she really just reject all she'd ever accepted as true about werewolves? As she continued her journey home, her quick mind continued to puzzle through the amazing possibility that the Wolf-folk were thinking, even *feeling*, creatures.

After a few minutes of Thirrin riding pillion, her own horse reappeared out of the trees, whinnying with relief to see them.

"Some help you were," Thirrin said grumpily. "I should have let the wolfman have you."

They took the most direct route homeward, and eventually the dense tangle of trees opened up into small clearings and woodcutters' camps as they reached the eaves of the forest. Then the trees gave way completely and the land stretched out before them. They reined to a halt and stared out over the wide plain that surrounded Frostmarris, the capital of the Icemark. The land was a patchwork of hedgerows and fields, orchards and gardens, all green and fertile in the country's short summer, while directly ahead the city rose out of the surrounding farmland like a huge stone ship in a sea of golden wheat.

Each of its massive gates faced the direction of each of the four winds, and over the south gate hung the huge Solstice Bell, its polished bronze gleaming in the bright sunshine, seeming to beckon Thirrin and her escort home. At the center of the settlement, she could see her father's fortress dominating the streets from its position high on the hill. The royal banner of a fighting white bear on a blue background was clearly visible as a cool breeze stretched it flat and snapping in the air, as though it were leading a charge of King Redrought's cavalry.

Thirrin spurred her horse on, already recovering from the shock of the battle and anxious to tell her father about the wolf-man. They thundered across the plain, raising a cloud of dust on the summer-dry roads, and soon she and her soldier escort were riding through the gates of the city and up the main street. It was market day, and country people from the surrounding villages and farms lined the way with their stalls, selling everything from vegetables and cheeses to eggs and newly slaughtered meat. It was hot, and swarms of flies had been drawn to the blood and offal, making Thirrin's horse skittish so that it snorted and sidled as they moved slowly through the crowds.

"Make way for the Princess!" her escort shouted, spurring ahead and using his horse to force people aside. Unused to seeing royalty, some of the country folk who rarely came to the city stared as Thirrin rode by. Some even pressed forward to touch the hem of her tunic or her riding boots, as if she were a holy relic of some sort. This embarrassed her deeply, and she immediately unslung her shield and rode along with it on her arm, hiding behind the mask of her status.

"It's the Princess! It's the Princess!" The whisper ran ahead of her through the crowd of country people. Thirrin found herself wishing she'd worn her helmet and not just the simple iron cap she usually wore for hunting. At least in her war gear she had a noseguard that hid part of her face. She could only hope the crowd of bumpkins thought her blushes were simply the high color of a warrior.

At last she reached the outer gates of the upper city, and the guards on duty barred the way, as required. "Who seeks entry to the King's presence?" the soldiers demanded formally. Thirrin stared at them in silent pride and waited for her escort to answer for her.

"His daughter and heir, Princess Thirrin Freer Strong-in-the-Arm Lindenshield."

The guards snapped to attention, and Thirrin rode through into the castle. As soon as she'd crossed the wide courtyard, she dismounted and left the reins of her horse trailing on the ground, knowing that a groom would run to collect the animal. Then she strode into the Great Hall of her father's fortress.

Just inside the yawning archway of the doors, she paused for a moment to let her eyes grow accustomed to the dim light. Slowly the battered shields of long-dead housecarls — the army's professional soldiers — and the banners of old wars emerged from the gloom, and she once again strode forward.

Before her, the flagstone floor seemed to stretch away forever into the shadows, but here and there small islands of light pooled onto the age-scarred stones as sunshine lanced down from smoke vents high in the roof. At the far end of the hall she could make out the raised dais, where a throne of black oak stood. Its arms had been carved to represent the forelegs of a bear, and its feet into those of a dragon. And above it hung the battle standard of the Icemark: a standing polar bear, lips drawn back in a vicious snarl and claws outstretched. This very standard had been carried by Thirrin's father when the army of the Vampire King and Queen had finally been defeated at the Battle of the Wolfrocks.

Nobody was sitting on the throne, and when Thirrin reached the dais, she quickly walked behind it and ducked her head to enter a low doorway. Beyond it lay a small, cozy room where King Redrought Strong-in-the-Arm Lindenshield, Bear of the North, mighty warrior and wise monarch, was soaking his feet in a wide basin of water. He was leaning back in a chair stuffed with plump cushions and his eyes were closed. But Thirrin knew he was awake because he wasn't snoring and a small, wizened man had just finished his move in a game of chess.

"You're cheating again, Grimswald!" the King's voice snapped.

"Oh, was I? I'm sure I didn't mean to. I must have made a mistake. I'll put the bishop back, shall I?" the little old man answered in a reedy voice.

Redrought opened a bloodshot eye and glared at Grimswald.

"Yes, I'll put the bishop back," the little old man concluded.

At this point the King noticed his daughter. "Ah, Thirrin! Come in, come in! Just top up the basin, will you? My corns are really bad today." He nodded to a kettle steaming gently on a woodstove, and Thirrin dutifully crossed the room, picked it up, and poured the hot water into the basin.

"Put some cold in first!" Redrought bellowed, snatching his feet from the water and sloshing much of it across the floor.

"Sorry," Thirrin said meekly, and mixed hot and cold water in a large pitcher before pouring it into the foot basin.

"Ah, that's better!" Redrought boomed again. In fact, the King only ever seemed to bellow, boom, or shout, no matter what his mood. But nobody seemed to mind too much; at least he never had to repeat himself.

As he settled back into his cushions, Thirrin noticed that his huge red beard — which spread across his chest like a fire in a mountain forest — had started to swing and swirl, and she watched in fascination as a small tabby head appeared and blinked at her.

"Ah, Primplepuss, there you are!" the King cried, seizing the kitten in his huge war-callused hands. "I knew I'd seen you earlier. I must remember to comb out my beard before I go to bed. I don't want to squash you, do I?"

Primplepuss gave a tiny mew in reply, and Redrought watched her fondly as she proceeded to wash a paw.

"Father, I have some important news," Thirrin said when she thought she could drag his attention away from the kitten.

"Well, it must be important, Grimswald," King Redrought said to the old man. "She only ever calls me 'Father' when she's done something wrong or a disaster's at hand."

"I've done nothing wrong, Father."

"Then what's happened?"

"I fought a werewolf in the forest this morning."

"A werewolf, eh? You're not hurt, are you?" he asked, grabbing her arms and looking her over closely. She shook her head and, after a few more minutes of careful scrutiny, he nodded his head and went on. "Well, we can't have the Wolf-folk making themselves at home, now can we? Exactly where did you see it? And did you kill it?"

"Just beyond Peninsula Point, near the Black Peak, and no, I didn't kill it. It was only wounded in its left shoulder and upper arm, and it was pretty kicked around by the horses."

"Nothing to a werewolf. I'll have to send out a patrol."

"Yes!" Thirrin agreed, looking up, her eyes alight. "But first I want to ask you something, Dad." She paused as she gathered her thoughts. "Can . . . can werewolves *feel* and *think*? I mean like people do. And can they . . . understand that we have . . . oh, I don't know, *thoughts* and *feelings* and *lives* to live?"

Redrought fell silent as he thought this through. He'd spent most of his life fighting the Wolf-folk and other creatures from beyond his northern borders. He'd had neither the time nor the inclination to wonder if they thought about anything. But he was a good king, and shrewd enough to know that something important lay behind his daughter's questions. "Why do you ask? What's happened?"

Thirrin took a deep breath. "The werewolf could have killed me today, but it didn't. It disarmed me and could have ripped out my throat. But when I punched it in the nose and told it to make it quick, it stopped and let me go. It even stuck my sword in the ground and left it for me to collect. And I don't understand why. If Wolf-folk can't feel and think, why did it let me live?"

Redrought didn't know, and at that moment he didn't care. He just felt an enormous sense of relief sweep over him. Suddenly he gathered his daughter in a bearlike hug that made her gasp for breath almost as much as the wolfman had when it sat on her. "You will not take such risks again! Do you hear me?" he roared, his anger fueled by the terrible realization that his daughter could so easily have been killed.

"But, Dad, I didn't take any risks. Werewolves don't usually come into the forest. How could I have known it was going to be there?"

Redrought knew this was true, but it didn't make him feel any better. He released her from the hug and sat down again heavily. "I'll send out a full patrol immediately."

"And I want to lead it."

"Oh no, young Madam. My daughter and heir will stay safely here in the castle. Let some other hotheads earn their spurs," Redrought said decisively.

"But they'll need me to guide them to the right spot. Nobody else knows the way."

"Apart from your soldier escort," the King said, a hint of triumph in his tone.

"Apart from my soldier escort," Thirrin was forced to agree reluctantly.

"Good! Grimswald, call in the captain of the guard. You can give him details, Thirrin, and then run along to your tutor. Geography today, if I'm not mistaken."

Grimswald piped at the door for the guard, who arrived in a clatter of armor.

"Captain Edwald. The Princess reports a werewolf close to the city. Take details and send out a patrol!" the King boomed, stroking Primplepuss gently. The kitten screwed her eyes shut against the huge blast of Redrought's voice, then as Thirrin and the captain withdrew to confer, she rubbed her tabby face against the King's enormous finger as it tickled her cheek.

Thirrin was furious. She should have led the patrol to find the werewolf, not that dolt of a soldier! And not only that, but the patrol would probably kill the werewolf as soon as they found it, and she wasn't sure how she felt about this. She couldn't help remembering that it could easily have killed her if it had wanted to, and neither could she forget the way it had bowed so ridiculously and had seemed to laugh before it ran off. She stormed angrily along the deeply shadowed corridor to her tutor's room, striding like an avenging war goddess through the sudden bursts of sunlight beneath each window.

Arriving at her tutor's door, she hit it once with her mailed fist, and burst through. Maggiore Totus was just drinking a cooling beaker of water, most of which he spilled down his black gown as he spluttered his surprise. But one look at Thirrin's blazing eyes stopped him from saying anything about good manners being necessary even for a princess. Instead he smiled in welcome and waved her to a seat next to the window. "Perhaps Her Majesty would be more comfortable in a dress rather than chain mail?" he asked, using the stiff formality of his speech as a shield against Thirrin's bad temper.

"No!" she snapped. But relenting slightly, she removed her sword belt and hung it on the back of her chair. It was Maggiore Totus's job to make sure she was as well educated as the heir to the Icemark throne should be. But only the lessons of the horse and weapons masters really held her attention. Everything else slowed time to a sluggish crawl for her, and she'd perfected the art of staring at her books while her mind galloped over the plains or sailed out on the gray Icemark seas.

Now, as Maggiore Totus sorted through his notes, she let her mind drift away once again, imagining herself riding on the back of one of the huge Snowy Owls that lived on the winter ice fields. From her vantage point on the owl's broad white back she could see the Wolfrock Mountains rising steeply from the northern plain, setting their jagged peaks like teeth against the cold blue of the sky, while to the south, the peaks known as the Dancing Maidens rose and undulated gently across the horizon, then slowly descended as low green hills into the lands of the Polypontian Empire. Maggiore had told her that this strange name actually meant "many bridges" and reflected the huge number of rivers that flowed through the rich green country.

From the height on the back of her imagined Snowy Owl she could see the multitude of rivers flowing across the Imperial land like fine silver threads stitched into a fabulous green cloth, embroidered with the regular field patterns of farmland and the dark splotches of forest, marsh, and pasture.

Then she flew over the cities of this wealthy southern realm, their streets sprawling and gray below her. The settlements had grown so large they'd burst beyond their walls and threatened the green land around them with dark factories that sent smoke thousands of feet up into the air as they filled the country's treasury with gold. With this wealth the Polypontus had built a massive army, which over the years had conquered a huge Empire that stretched beyond Thirrin's knowledge to all points of the compass. The army was led by the fearsome General Scipio Bellorum, who had never lost one of his wars of conquest and had won every battle he commanded personally.

Thirrin's owl now flew lower over the streets of the Empire's cities. There she saw the people. Some were richly dressed and walked with a confidence that cleared a path through the crowds thronging the pavements. Many were dressed as soldiers, ready to fight and die in the Empire's wars. But most wore rags, and a large number of these were slaves assigned to the factories that made the weapons the army needed for its wars in distant lands.

This was the reality of the Empire. People were just one more thing to be used by those few who ruled the massive territories. And if Thirrin had wondered if anything was truly different for the peasants of her own society, she might have argued that in the Icemark no one was called a slave and no one was forced to work in factories that poisoned the air and corrupted the land. The fact that the life of a "serf" living on her father's land was little different from that of a slave would not have troubled her. At least their people lived in their own homes and ate some of the food they labored to grow.

Then in the eye of her imagination her owl wheeled north until they flew over the Icemark once again, and below her the forests and pastures flowed like a green sea around the walled islands of its towns. It was only in the winter that the kingdom lived up to its name and truly became the Icemark, white and frozen from the Wolfrocks to the Dancing Maidens for seven months of the year.

Maggiore Totus watched Thirrin as her eyes gazed unseeingly into the middle distance, and he sighed. She was the most difficult pupil he'd ever had to teach, but she was also one of the cleverest. And it was this knowledge that kept him in the palace as royal tutor. Deep down in the recesses of his brilliant mind he harbored the hope that he'd awaken a love of learning in this warrior princess, so that one day the Icemark would be ruled by a scholar as well as a fighter.

But any hope of that seemed a very long way off, and in the meantime he settled to the task of trying to regain her attention. "I think we'll postpone our lesson on the primary income source of the Southern Continent and concentrate instead on the topography of famous battle sites."

Thirrin grunted and nodded her head, her mood slightly improved, and surprised herself by actually enjoying the lesson.

2

That evening, Redrought held one of his State banquets. All of the barons and baronesses could expect to be called to the capital of Frostmarris to eat with the King at least three times a year. Eating and drinking were actually less important than the real business of keeping a close watch on any of the aristocrats who might become overambitious. But despite this cautious approach to his noblemen and -women, Redrought was a very popular king. He wasn't too overbearing, and more important he was a proven general. Not only had he defeated the Vampire King and Queen of The-Land-of-the-Ghosts but he'd also beaten off many pirate raids along the shores of the Icemark.

In fact, that night's feast was officially a celebration of the victory he'd won over one of the greatest threats the country had faced in more than a decade. Exactly one year ago to the day, Redrought had led his army to the field of Sea Haven, where a battle had been fought against the combined forces of the Southern Corsairs and the Island Buccaneers. Their fleet had been more than two hundred ships strong, and they'd landed an army of twenty thousand troops. But after a bloody struggle that had lasted an entire day, the enemy had eventually been driven into the sea and their ships set alight by Redrought's victorious housecarls.

And now the King's Great Hall was loud with celebration as those same soldiers ate and drank at the lower tables and told one another how brilliant they'd been on the field of Sea Haven. The minstrels' gallery that occupied the entire southern wall was packed with the city's best musicians, who played an unending medley of drinking songs and marching tunes. And between the long rows of tables, acrobats tumbled and threw one another around in an odd mixture of clowning and skill.

As Thirrin watched from her place at the High Table, the Great Hall heaved and swirled like a stormy sea. But her view of fine details was limited by the thick haze of smoke that rose from the fire blazing on the central hearth. Even the huge banners of the housecarl regiments that were suspended from each of the roof beams glowed only dimly through the drifting tendrils of smoke that would eventually meander out of vents high in the ceiling. A dancing bear loomed through the haze halfway down the rows of tables so that, to Thirrin, it looked like a miniature mountain with a clumsy sense of rhythm. And every now and then, one of the acrobats would dive skyward, like a dolphin leaping out of a black smoky sea.

She eventually turned her attention back to the High Table and listened as her father chatted, or rather shouted, good-naturedly with one of his barons. She always sat next to the King at the State banquets. It was good for the lords and ladies of the Icemark to get to know the heir apparent, and because she knew how important this was, Thirrin tried her best to rise to the occasion. She made every effort to crush her natural shyness beneath an exterior that was charming and at the same time intelligent. She tried to laugh in all the right places and to speak only when she was totally sure what she was talking about, but she wasn't at all sure whether she succeeded.

Baroness Aethelflaeda, an old woman with long braids and small twinkling eyes, leaned across the table toward her. "I hear the Princess met a wolfman recently," she said, kindly giving Thirrin a chance to join the conversation.

"Yes, only this morning. I wounded it in the shoulder and eventually it ran off."

The Baroness turned to the King. "I think The-Land-of-the-Ghosts may need to be watched, Redrought."

The King shrugged and nodded to show he agreed but thought the problem wasn't too great. "Yes, yes, I suppose. But none of the watchers on the border have reported anything wrong."

He absentmindedly twirled one of his special feast-day braids around his finger as he considered the situation. "I'll strengthen the border garrisons and send out more spies," he said after a moment. "That should be enough for the time being."

"As long as you don't weaken the southern defenses to do it," the old Baroness said. "I trust the Polypontus and its Empire about as much as I do the Vampire King and Queen. I suspect General Scipio Bellorum has an ambition to add the Icemark to his conquests."

Redrought laughed. "You worry too much, Aethelflaeda! Bellorum has an ambition to add everybody to his conquests, and at the moment he's busy in the south. So stop fretting and have a drink."

"I think the Baroness is right," Thirrin said quietly, her mind occupied with a problem she'd been mulling over for some time. "If we watch one border too closely, we put the others at risk. We need more allies."

The King nodded. "Very true. But we're isolated up here in our northern lands. To the south is the Empire of the Polypontus and to the north of us we have The-Land-of-the-Ghosts. We're not exactly spoiled for choice, are we?"

"No, but sometimes friends can be found in the unlikeliest of places," said Thirrin, her mind inexplicably drawn back to the wolfman and how it had looked at her before it finally let her go.

The King winked at his daughter and smiled. "You're right. Perhaps we should start looking as soon as we can." Then he sat back in his seat, stretched luxuriously, and rested his feet on the table. Thirrin watched in amusement as he maneuvered his large fluffy slippers among the plates and cups of the banquet until he found enough space to cross them comfortably. Earlier, when the King's chamberlain had objected to his footwear, he'd argued that his fluffy yellow slippers were far more comfortable on his corns than the polished boots of the state regalia. And the set of his jaw had warned the chamberlain to say no more.

After the King had settled himself, he reached inside the stiffly embroidered collar of his robes and gently drew out Primplepuss, the royal kitten, and placed her on his heroically curving stomach.

"Grimswald!" he bellowed. "Grimswald, where are you?!"

The Chamberlain-of-the-Royal-Paraphernalia appeared at the King's elbow, and Thirrin found herself wondering if he'd been hiding under the table. "Yes, Sire?" said the wrinkly little man.

"Fetch some milk for Primplepuss. She's thirsty, aren't you, my sweeting?" he said, gently rubbing her cheek and telling everyone around him that she was purring even though a saber-toothed tiger couldn't have been heard over the noise of the banquet.

When the kitten started to play with Redrought's braided beard, Thirrin knew there'd be no chance of getting any sense out of her father for the rest of the evening, so she decided to join the housecarls down in the lower hall.

She leaped off the royal dais and made her way toward the sound of throwing axes being hurled at a target, arriving just as one of them split the apple that had been placed in the center of the bull's-eye. The massive blast of cheering almost knocked her off her feet, but she waded through the press of huge sweating men and women and demanded a turn. Shy she may have been in polite company and when facing the demands of well-mannered conversation, but Thirrin had no such fears among fellow warriors. Here she didn't have to be polite or careful of her language; in fact, the housecarls usually spent the first few minutes apologizing for their own lack of manners. But once they got into the swing of things, all of that was forgotten and she was treated almost like the other young warriors, although her status was always carefully acknowledged.

A great shout went up: "The Princess is going to throw!" One of the warriors respectfully placed one of the smaller throwing axes in her hand.

"Give me something of a proper size," she demanded indignantly, and nodded as a full-sized battle-ax was passed to her.

By this time the apple had been replaced on the target, and with a huge effort she hefted the ax, took aim, drew back, and hurled with such force she fell to her knees. When she dared to look at the target, she saw the apple neatly split in two at the foot of the thick throwing board. Laughing in relief, she accepted the cheers of the housecarls and allowed herself to be chaired around the tables.

From high up on their shoulders, Thirrin could see through the swirling tendrils of smoke down the length of the Great Hall. Some instinct drew her eyes to the huge doors just as they burst open and a blast of cooler air flooded in, cutting through the thick bank of smoke like a hot coal through snow. The hall fell silent, and Thirrin breathed deep as the blast of clean air reached her. The smoke had now been almost completely blown away, and she had a clear view of soldiers marching through the doorway, dragging a huge shaggy figure between them.

The troopers were wearing the uniform of the palace guard, and their business was obviously important, so some of the housecarls hurried to drag the trestle tables aside. Soon a wide aisle leading directly to the royal dais had been cleared, and the strange group began to march forward.

"Put me down," Thirrin ordered. The men who'd been carrying the Princess on their shoulders placed her on the floor, and she cut through the crowds to reach the upper table as the soldiers arrived. It was then that she saw exactly what they were dragging between them. It was the werewolf. Its wrists were tied with thick ropes to a pole that lay across its shoulders, and it was surrounded by a ring of sharp steel as each guard leveled his spear and stood ready to strike at the slightest provocation.

The guards saluted the King. "My Lord, we bring the intruder from The-Land-of-the-Ghosts for sentence."

After a fraught few seconds trying to disentangle a terrified Primplepuss from his beard, Redrought's reply was curt and gruff. "You should have killed it in the field! Waste of effort bringing it here." He stroked Primplepuss gently in an attempt to calm her. "And you'll get blood all over the floor!"

Thirrin approached her father. "I claim the right of sentence!" she shouted, her voice echoing around the hall.

The werewolf turned to look at her, its huge face beginning to lose its ferocious frown as if scenting some distant hope but not daring to believe it.

The silence that followed was finally broken by the King. "You! Why?" he demanded, still grumpy after Primplepuss's fright.

"Because I first drew its blood. Its life by ancient law is mine."

Redrought considered for a moment, then said, "You're right. How do you want it killed?"

Thirrin smiled in gratitude at her father and, as usual, he relented and smiled back. "I don't want it killed. I want to escort it to the border and set it free," she said carefully, still smiling through the uproar of protest.

"What?" the King roared in his best outraged-monarch voice. "It's a monster, a freak from The-Land-of-the-Ghosts. The world will be a better place without it. Just string it up and slice it open and then let's get on with the party."

Thirrin waited for the cheer that followed this to die down before kneeling in supplication. "My Lord Redrought Strong-in-the-Arm Lindenshield, Bear of the North, Guardian of the People, grant your daughter, your only child and heir to the Icemark throne, this boon and favor. I would lead the escort to the border and there release the creature to live and tell of this night's doings."

Her father's eyes had narrowed warily as soon as Thirrin had adopted the ceremonial language of the court. She was sometimes too much like her mother, who'd been as clever as a sack of monkeys. But still, he'd loved his wife and she'd never used her intelligence to bad purpose.

"If I'm to grant you this favor, I must first know why you want the werewolf to live," he said at last, in a voice that was quiet for him.

"Because of what we were speaking about earlier. You know that not even the shield-walls of all your housecarls nor the thundering hooves of all your cavalry will be enough to keep out our enemies if they all decide to attack at once. Even if Scipio Bellorum and the Polypontian Empire attacked alone with none of our other enemies in support, we could never hold them. You yourself have said that the Imperial armies are unstoppable. Put simply, *we need allies*."

"Ha, and you think the Wolf-folk would make good friends?"

"Yes."

"And one mangy werewolf will bring about an alliance?"

"Look at his neck, Father. He wears the brass collar of a wolfman chief; he's no ordinary werewolf."

Suddenly a deep growling voice cut in: "I wear the gold collar of the Wolf-folk *King*. Don't underestimate your prisoner!"

A shocked silence followed. Few people knew the wolf-people could speak, let alone use words with intelligence and pride.

Redrought looked at the prisoner. "Then you're an ideal hostage for peace."

"No, Father! The wolfman is mine!"

"My daughter wants to set you free. Would you promise to be an ally of the Icemark if she gets her way?"

"I promise," the deep voice growled again.

"And your people?"

"And my people."

"How do we know we can trust you?"

A strange whining, snuffling noise came from the werewolf, and Thirrin realized he was laughing. "You don't. You'll just have to trust . . . me."

"And what happens if your allies call for war against us? Could you ignore the Vampire King and Queen?"

"Look, if you're going to search for problems, you might as well kill me now and have done with it," the wolfman answered sniffily.

Redrought nodded. "Sometimes you just have to take risks. Thirrin, the prisoner's yours."

She shouted in delight, leaped onto the dais, and hugged her father. "Thanks, Dad," she whispered in his ear. Then, recovering her composure, she knelt before him and said, "I give thanks, my father. May your decision be proved right and true."

"It'd better be," he answered gruffly, and began to stroke Primplepuss, who'd recovered from her earlier fright and was having a quick wash.

Thirrin turned to the guard. "Release the prisoner."

Again a roar of protest went up, but the King nodded his agreement and the bonds were cut.

The werewolf stood rubbing his wrists and staring around the hall, his expression wary and amazed. The Princess had fought for his life and repaid his mercy.

She'd taken a terrible risk and put her trust in a species that had been enemies of her people for centuries. The huge creature was suddenly moved by her bravery. There was something in her fire and fragility that touched him deeply, and as a monarch with more than twenty years' experience of rule, he knew quality and presence when he saw it. This Princess of the human-folk was going to be deeply important in the struggles to come.

With a sudden urge to repay Thirrin's courage, he strode forward and knelt before her. "By the ever-changing phases of the Blessed Moon, I, Grishmak Blood-drinker, King of the Wolf-folk, pledge lifelong friendship to the Icemark and its ruler and particularly to Thirrin Freer Strong-in-the-Arm Lindenshield. Your pain is my pain, your joy is my joy, your war is my war!"

The wolfman's voice echoed around the strangely silent Great Hall, then the creature threw back his head and let out a long, blood-chilling howl, which slowly descended through the scales to silence.

3

Thirrin led the group deeper into the forest. They'd been riding all morning, exercising some of the horses from the royal stables. There was no actual need for her to join the soldiers and stable hands whose job it was to keep Redrought's war stallions fit and well, but it was a great excuse for getting out of the schoolroom.

Standing in her stirrups, she raised the pace to a canter, weaving in and out of the trees and slowly drawing ahead of the others. She breathed deeply, inhaling the rich scent of the leaf mold disturbed by the horses' hooves, and felt the dust of the classroom blowing away. Overhead in the trees, rooks and ravens cawed harshly as they reported the presence of the riders, and on the forest floor, sudden rustlings in the undergrowth indicated where an animal had scurried away. But Thirrin was just happy to be out riding, watching the woodland blaze in its autumn colors and smelling the spicy scent of the damp earth. Among the trees it was surprisingly warm, and sunlight poured through the canopy as though the last dregs of the short Icemark summer had pooled there before the harsh northern winter set in.

But just ahead to the north, the sky was a deep charcoal gray, and an ominous rumble muttered deeply on the air. The storm had been developing all morning, and now it looked as though it was finally about to break. Lightning lit the clouds as they slowly advanced across the sky, and through natural breaks in the dense covering of leaves, Thirrin could see a distant haze of rain. Reluctantly she decided to give the order to turn back.

She turned her horse, reined to a halt, and watched as the others approached. Suddenly, as if from nowhere, a huge animal burst from the trees. Even running on all fours it was as tall as a horse, but then it reared up on its hind legs, towering above them. It was a Greyling bear, massive, powerful, and quick to anger. It struck at the nearest rider, knocking him from the saddle, while the other horses bolted, snorting in terror.

Thirrin took control. Snatching a spear from the scabbard on her saddle and couching it like a lance, she charged. The bear turned to face her, and she hit it squarely in the chest. Roaring, it lunged at her, but her horse nimbly sidestepped and she drew her heavy broadsword.

She was desperate to lure the bear away from the injured man, so she retreated slowly, leading the animal clear. The spear was still stuck in its chest, but it hardly noticed as it struck at her with its razorlike claws. Thirrin fought back with her broadsword, inflicting wounds the beast barely registered as it rampaged after her. Soon she was beginning to wonder if it would be possible to bring it down at all.

Then the other riders burst back into the glade. They'd quickly regained control of their horses, and the battle-trained stallions leaped forward to the charge.

The soldiers shouted as they attacked, distracting the animal from Thirrin, who immediately seized another lance from her scabbard. Two more spears were driven into the bear's chest, and as the soldiers wheeled away, Thirrin thundered in, striking it in the flank.

The bear reared up to its greatest height and roared, its voice echoing throughout the forest, then slowly it pitched forward, crashed to the ground, and lay dead. A deep silence descended, and for a moment they all stared at the huge fallen bear. They were just about to start congratulating one another on actually managing to kill it when a groan reminded them of the fallen man.

They all dismounted and hurried over to him. His arm was torn open from shoulder to elbow and was bleeding heavily. Quickly the soldiers wrapped a cloak around the wound and tied it in place with cloth torn from their tunics. Nothing more could be done until they got back to Frostmarris, so after helping the wounded man back onto his horse, they began to ride for home.

A cold wind swept down on the forest, running before the storm that had continued its advance over the sky like the vanguard of an attacking army. Then the rain struck, hissing through the trees like a nest of angry snakes. The icy spears of water hit them with such force that leaves were stripped from the trees and the path quickly turned into a running river.

Thirrin decided to ride ahead in the hope of finding shelter for the injured man, and soon left the others behind. She was beginning to wonder what else might happen during such an eventful ride, and muttered a quick prayer to the Goddess for guidance. The track wound through the dense trees, giving no sign of any cover other than inadequate leaves and branches, and she was just about to turn back when a sudden explosion knocked her horse flat. She rolled clear of the flailing hooves and drew her sword. But the only enemy was a lightning bolt that had shattered an old oak tree to splinters.

Her horse was struggling to rise, and she grabbed its reins and tried to calm it as it squealed and shook. Thunder crashed around them, drowning her words, and she was still wrestling with the animal when the rest of the party galloped down the path. One of the soldiers leaped down and helped her force her horse to a standstill.

"We'd be safer in the clearing, away from the trees," Thirrin shouted, and quickly she led them back the way they had just come. Better to get soaked to the skin than struck by lightning.

But as they rode into the wide glade, they all reined to a halt in surprise. Ahead of them stood a tall cloaked figure, arms folded neatly, its hooded head bowed. What more would they have to face on this busy morning? Thirrin wondered. She and the soldiers drew their swords, but the figure didn't move. After a moment she fought down her fear and rode forward.

"You stand before Princess Thirrin Freer Strong-in-the-Arm Lindenshield, heir to the throne of the Icemark. Identify yourself!"

The figure bowed deeply, then stood straight and threw back its hood. Thirrin almost laughed in relief. It was only a boy. Tall for his age of about fifteen, but a boy nonetheless. For a moment, in the uncanny power of the storm, they'd all thought another of the creatures from The-Land-of-the-Ghosts had crossed the border. But this boy was obviously human as he wiped the rain out of his eyes and smiled.

"My name's Oskan Witch's Son. Come with me, I can give you shelter."

Without another word he strode across the clearing and took a path through the trees that they'd somehow missed earlier. Coming to the conclusion that the boy could do them no harm and that she and her companions needed help after the events of the morning, Thirrin urged her horse forward and the entire party followed. The path was steep and became gradually stony, making it quite difficult for the horses, but after a few minutes an outcrop of rocks reared up before them.

The way seemed to end at a sheer face of granite, but Oskan Witch's Son beckoned them on. By this time, Thirrin was soaked to the skin and the storm was raging with even greater force, so, deciding to trust the boy, she rode toward the rocks until she saw a wide cave mouth set at an angle that hid it from the path.

The party rode into the cave and dismounted. It was clean and dry, with mounds of dry leaves and grass set against one wall as though the boy had gathered fodder for the horses of expected guests.

"You can bed down your animals here," Oskan said. "Bring the injured man through this way." He led Thirrin and the soldiers, who half carried their wounded comrade, along a narrow passage into a gathering gloom that steadily deepened to pitch-black.

"Wait there a moment," Oskan said, and the soft clicking whisper of a tinderbox sounded. Suddenly light flared up from a central brazier, and fantastic shadows danced around a wide inner cave as Oskan set about kindling more lamps and braziers.

Soon the cave was brilliant with light, and Thirrin looked around her with interest. A smooth floor was overlaid with clean bracken, and several tables placed along the surprisingly regular walls were neatly piled with pots. A strong scent of herbs and spices made the place smell like the palace kitchens.

"Put him down there," Oskan said to the soldiers, pointing to a bed set against one of the walls. They all watched in silence as the boy placed a table next to the bed and then moved around the cave gathering various objects. Once he had done this he fetched a stool, sat down, and unwound the cloak that had been used to bandage the man's arm.

"What are you doing?" Thirrin asked suspiciously.

The boy hardly looked up from the mixture of red wine and salt he was preparing in a bowl, but eventually he said, "I'm going to stitch this man's arm."

"Stitch his arm?" she exploded. "He's not a piece of torn cloth!"

"No," Oskan agreed mildly. "But his skin and some of his muscle *are* torn, and stitching them together again will help it to heal much more quickly."

Thirrin was just considering drawing her sword and driving the crazy boy off when one of the soldiers said, "My Lady, I know this lad. He's the son of White Annis, the good witch who used to live in these parts."

"So?" Thirrin said hotly. "Does that give him the right to torture my servant?"

"His mother was a healer, among other things," the soldier went on. "And I remember her doing just this when one of the housecarls was injured during weapons training at the palace. He'd stepped the wrong way when he should have dodged, and an ax hacked a chunk of muscle from his leg. He bled badly and would have died for sure, but White Annis came and stopped the bleeding, then stitched his leg back together again."

"Didn't his wound get the green rot?" she asked, interested in this tale of weapons.

"No, My Lady, the witch kept it clean with some liquid, and he was healed. When it was completely better, he didn't even limp."

She nodded. The soldier was a veteran she'd known forever and she trusted his experience. "All right. Then stitch his arm," she said to Oskan, as though he'd been trying to avoid doing it.

Thirrin watched as he washed his hands in more of the red wine. Then he took an oddly curved needle and, with a pair of tongs, held it in the flame of an oil lamp until it glowed red. Thirrin again wondered about his sanity, especially when he then quenched the needle in the salt and red wine.

"Your soldiers will have to hold him," Oskan said. "I have no poppy."

"Poppy!" Thirrin exploded again, unable to contain herself. "What have flowers got to do with it?"

The boy watched her anger mildly and said, "Poppy is a drug that would have deadened the pain. But I ran out of it a year ago."

She looked at the veteran, who nodded reassuringly, but all comfort was lost when she saw Oskan threading the curved needle, then drawing it through a large clove of garlic.

"It helps to stop the green rot," he explained.

She threw up her hands in despair. "Just get on with it. I don't want to know any more."

The stitching of the wound wasn't easy. It was deep, and even cleaning it with salt and red wine made the stable hand shout and struggle. By the time Oskan had tied the last knot, they were all exhausted with the effort of holding the man down. But at last the wound was neatly dressed and bandaged.

"Leave him now. Healing Nature will do the rest," Oskan said. "Look, he's already falling asleep. He'll soon forget the pain."

Thirrin stared at him as though he were crazy. "Well, I'm glad for him. Personally, I think it's going to be a very long time before I forget that nasty little wrestling match."

Back in the main cave, Thirrin sat apart from the others, staring into the fire as the rich scents of wet earth and greenery blew in from the forest. The men were quiet, tired after the day's traumas. She'd sent one of them to Frostmarris to tell the King what had happened, and now she was quite content to wait for the storm to pass before riding back to the city herself. The thunder and lightning seemed to have traveled farther out over the plains, but the rain still lashed down with a steady hissing as it forced its way through the dense canopy of the trees.

After a while Oskan appeared from the passage that led to the inner cavern. Thirrin watched as he washed his hands and turned to the fire, where he stirred a large cauldron that had been bubbling quietly to itself. The scents that rose from the pot made Thirrin's stomach rumble, and the men looked interested, too.

"You'll find some bowls on the trestle by the entrance," Oskan said to the cave in general. There was a scrambling as they were fetched, and Oskan ladled out a thick stew.

Remembering their manners and duty, one of the men served Thirrin first, placing the stew, a rough wooden spoon, and a hunk of bread awkwardly on the hearthstone beside her. When Thirrin was in her best "Princess mode," the men knew better than to take liberties. She was obviously trying to impress the young healer, so for the time being, etiquette and proper procedure would need to be followed to the letter. They all knew she'd be her old self at the next weapons practice.

Thirrin sighed. These men were soldiers and stable hands; she couldn't expect the polished skills of Palace Chamberlains. She nodded imperiously, and the man withdrew to the other side of the fire where the others were eating noisily. She gingerly tasted the stew. It was surprisingly rich, being seasoned with herbs and spices Thirrin couldn't identify, and the bread was as good as anything produced by the palace kitchens. After a while she looked up to see Oskan walking over to join her. She was surprised and annoyed. As the Crown Princess, she'd expected to be left in dignified solitude by this stranger while she ate. Not only that, but now she'd have to make conversation, and she wasn't sure she could do so without blushing. Put her in any situation that was even vaguely new and personal and she was lost; her pale, almost translucent, skin and auburn hair seemed to signal everything she was feeling. She might raise her chin in proud disdain and even curl her lip in an emergency, but nobody was likely to be fooled if she glowed the color of a midsummer sunset.

Oskan sat down on the low stool next to hers without even pretending to wait for permission. "Is the stew all right?" he asked, as if he were talking to one of the soldiers.

"Adequate," Thirrin answered with cold dignity.

He nodded as though not surprised by her answer. "I suppose the palace kitchens must produce a feast every day."

Thirrin decided he was too much of a yokel to realize he was being familiar and said, "Not every day. But they certainly produce the best food in the Icemark."

He nodded again. "Naturally."

She looked at him sharply, wondering if he was being sarcastic, but she saw only accepting innocence. "The men said you're the son of White Annis, the witch. Where is she? Even women with the Power should show respect to the Heir of the Icemark."

He glanced at her oddly before answering. "That's true, but not even Princess Thirrin Freer Strong-in-the-Arm Lindenshield can command the presence of the dead. They tend to be deaf to demands for respect."

"Oh!" she said, blushing to a deeper level of crimson than she'd ever managed before. "I didn't know."

Oskan chewed and swallowed before answering. "That's all right. I know you didn't mean to be rude."

Thirrin was incensed. *Rude!* She thought it was probably impossible for royalty to be rude. They said what they felt and the rest of society had to accept it. But secretly she was angry with herself; deep down she didn't want to offend this strange boy who'd given them shelter from the storm, treated her injured stable hand, and now fed them from his own pot. As her father was always telling her, royalty had a duty to those of society who were lesser than they. It should be beneath her dignity to show anger to a peasant, and it certainly should be beneath her to feel embarrassment.

"When did she die?" she asked, determinedly ignoring her flaming face and showing a proper aloof interest in the troubles of someone who would one day be her subject.

"Two years ago."

"And you've lived alone all that time?"

He shrugged. "It wasn't difficult. My mother knew she was dying and taught me all I needed to know before the end."

"What sort of healer couldn't heal herself?" The words were out before she knew she was going to say them, and her toes curled.

Oskan looked at her in a long silence that almost had her

squirming, but then at last he said, "Only the Goddess can cure all disease."

Thirrin felt that she'd been slapped down, but his voice and tone had remained level, and even now he only quietly mopped his bowl with bread and showed no sign of anger.

After that, Thirrin gave up trying to behave like a princess and just sat in what she hoped was dignified silence while the men ate a second bowl of stew and the rain continued to slice through the canopy of the forest outside like liquid blades. Afterward Oskan gathered up the bowls and stacked them neatly on a table.

"It'll soon be dark," he said. "You may have to stay the night."

"Not possible!" Thirrin almost shouted, for some reason horrified at the thought of having to stay with the strange boy overnight. "We've no bedding."

"There are plenty of blankets in the back cave. Perhaps one of your men can fetch them?"

"The King will expect me back tonight," she said firmly, and almost laughed in relief when she heard the sound of approaching horses. She strode to the cave mouth and watched as an escort of ten cavalry were led along the path by the soldier she'd sent off earlier. Obviously she'd been right. Redrought really did expect her home tonight.

"Gather your things and saddle the horses," she ordered the men, suddenly in full command of herself again. Then to Oskan she said, "We'll leave the injured one with you and send a surgeon for him later."

4

Thirrin had a full day of studying to get through. Math, geography, the natural world, and what Maggiore Totus called "alchemical science." She wished her father hadn't decided to educate her and had just allowed her to rely on scribes and others of the "clever ones," as Redrought called them. After all, he couldn't even write his own name, and yet he'd managed to rule his kingdom with intelligence and cunning for more than twenty years. So why did she need to know how to write and reckon and do all of those other bright things that got in the way of her being herself?

"Because the times are changing and I want a daughter who knows her place in the world and how to keep it!" Her father's booming voice sounded in her memory.

Well, perhaps the world was changing, but did it really help her to know the main exports of the Southern Continent? Or how to calculate the area of a cylinder, or how to brew a sovereign remedy against dropsy? She didn't think so, but her father was determined, and so she must learn to be like one of the educated clever ones of the commonality.

"Well, Your Highness, am I to presume that you've completed your mathematics assignment?" Maggiore Totus asked.

Thirrin handed him a sheaf of paper in cold silence, hating the way the little man managed to make her feel guilty even when she had done her homework. She knew she could kill him in a variety of gory ways in less time than it took him to adjust the strange spectoculums that rested on the very end of his nose, but even this distraction didn't seem to help!

Her tutor tutted quietly to himself as he read through the messy sheets of paper. "Well, the answer is correct, but how you arrived at your conclusion remains a complete mystery."

"If the sum's right, what does it matter?" Thirrin asked irritably.

"It matters because it would prove to me that you didn't just guess at the answer."

She privately thought that in the case of math, getting the right answer was all that was needed, but she didn't say anything.

"Now tell me, what exactly does this jumble of lettering mean here?" the little tutor asked, pointing to a blotchy mess of ink. Thirrin shrugged, and Totus began to calculate just how far he could push her before she exploded and stormed out. He decided she was just short of abandoning the world of learning and spending the rest of the day with her father's housecarls, so he retreated with decorum. "Very well, we'll assume that you arrived at your answer by conventional and logical means, shall we?"

She shrugged again, and the tutor walked back to his desk. He looked out the window on to the garden that had so surprised him when he arrived to teach the Princess. Somehow one didn't expect to find such a beautiful haven of peace in the middle of the grim fortress of Frostmarris. Magnificent rosebushes blazed rich and dazzling colors onto the air, and neatly clipped hedges and borders barely contained an ordered tumble of bright flowers. But already some of the beautifully kept plants were beginning to look just the slightest bit jaded, and the leaves on some of the more delicate trees and shrubs had already turned crimson. He felt a sudden dread as he realized the bitter winter of the Icemark couldn't be far away.

"For the rest of the day we'll study geography," he informed her, "concentrating on the Southern Continent." Thirrin groaned. "And in particular on their navy and its role in the defeat of the Corsairs and Zephyrs in the great Battle of the Middle Sea."

His pupil brightened, and Maggiore Totus tried to convince himself that he wasn't betraying his teaching standards more and more with every passing day. Almost every lesson had to have something about the military in it to hold his pupil's attention. Still, he comforted himself, she would one day be Queen of the Icemark and would probably have to lead her troops in battle, too. He couldn't expect a daughter of King Redrought's to be anything other than warlike and uninterested in the gentle arts of learning. He would feel he'd succeeded if at the end of her schooling she could write an understandable sentence, read a letter without help, and discuss the accounts with her quartermaster. In the meantime he'd aim for the stars, in the hope that he could at least get her to the top of a reasonably sized hill.

He drew the battle positions of the opposing fleets on the blackboard, and watched as Thirrin happily copied them into her book. But his attention was drawn back to the garden beyond the window and its signs of the coming winter. If only he could leave before the terrible winds and snows came, before the deeply penetrating frosts etched every window with thick patterns of ice-ferns. At his home on the southern coast of the Middle Sea, the winter would bring a little gentle rain and the days would be warm rather than hot. But the wine would be mellow, and the lilting language of his people would sing and lull his mind to a quietness he'd almost forgotten here in the cold north.

"Mr. Maggiore Totus!" Thirrin's voice cut into his thoughts. "You're not daydreaming, are you?" And she smiled so brightly he couldn't help but smile back.

Thirrin could be charming when she forgot to be a princess. But just recently that happened only rarely, and Totus was beginning to wonder what was on her mind. He thought that perhaps he knew but couldn't be sure. And how exactly would one ask the heir apparent if she was afraid that she'd have to rule the country before she was ready, and if she was frightened that her father would die before she'd had time to experience life properly? Redrought was a strong man, a *very* strong man, but the history of the Icemark was violent, and Maggiore's studies had shown him that of the previous eight monarchs only two had died in their beds and only one had ruled for more than twenty years — and *that* one was Redrought himself!

He could almost feel sorry for Thirrin, even when she was at her most obnoxious. She might be undergoing the best training for her future role as Queen, but the very real possibility that she could be ruling the Icemark before she was sixteen had to be a terrible burden, especially when the country had The-Land-of-the-Ghosts as a neighbor to the north and the formidable Polypontian Empire and General Scipio Bellorum to the south. To rule even a tiny kingdom at such a young age would be pressure enough for anyone, but the Icemark had no one but the most vicious enemies on its land borders and only the pitiless sea, with its pirates and raiders, to the east and the west.

For the rest of the day he was gentle with his pupil, allowing her a little time to relax before she was called away by the weapons master or horse mistress. Not that she seemed to find those particular lessons difficult. She always ran from his rooms with a most insulting air of happy relief whenever she was off to raise a shield-wall with the housecarls or put some fierce war stallion through its paces. Maggiore Totus sighed. He'd have left for home long ago if he hadn't thought Thirrin had it in her to be a good scholar. But he knew that her sharp intelligence would never be used to sift through the complex facts and figures that might reveal some exciting new truth, some previously unthought-of theorem.

A sudden hammering on the door made him yelp with fright, and a huge bearded housecarl marched into the room. "I've orders to take the Princess to the parade ground!" he boomed.

Maggiore glared at him. Why did they always have to shout? And did they really have to carry a shield and spear with them at all times? "I'm not sure that the Princess Thirrin has finished all of her work yet," he answered, deciding to stand upon his authority as Royal Tutor.

"Yes, I have . . . well, at least most of it. I can finish the rest as homework, can't I?"

She seemed so desperate to get away that Maggiore sighed resignedly. "Oh, very well. But I expect it to be neater than last time."

"It will be," she answered, and as she rushed for the door she suddenly stopped and kissed him on the top of his bald head. "Thanks, Maggie!" she said, and ran off down the corridor.

The soldiers had been marching north for more than a month now, and the Polypontian Empire's superb military roads meant that they'd covered more than seven hundred miles. Their regiment, the White Panthers of the Asterian Province, had been fighting in the south less than six weeks earlier, but after the victorious conclusion to that particular campaign, they'd been given a week's rest and had then begun their march north.

None of the soldiers knew exactly where they were going, and neither did most of the officers, though rumors were rife. Some said they were finally going to attack the Icemark, the Empire's immediate northern neighbor, and most thought it was about time. For some reason General Scipio Bellorum had left the Icemark in peace despite making war on all and sundry around its borders, and exactly why remained a deep mystery. But once again rumor provided some clues. The most popular was that the Icemark was a land of witchcraft, which even the formidable Bellorum found daunting. But others doubted that; the general was afraid of nothing; it was even said he'd live forever because death itself wouldn't dare take him.

The troops were approaching the border area now, on their way to join the huge army that was being amassed. The wide, gently undulating plain that nestled beneath the foothills of the Dancing Maidens mountain range was covered with military camps, forges, armories, parade grounds, and cavalry training runs. To the soldiers of the White Panthers regiment, it was all very familiar. Every block of barrack tents and every parade ground was pitched in exactly the same position, so no matter where they were, in the Empire or on campaign, they felt completely at home.

And now they could see their great leader, Scipio Bellorum himself: part man, part god, ruthless and aloof, riding the lines of troops as they presented arms. They awaited his command.

Thirrin spent the rest of her day happily taking weapons drill with her father's elite corps of housecarls. Within a few minutes of hitting a bull's-eye with her throwing ax, she was happy and relaxed and the dust of the schoolroom had been blown away. The huge soldiers, all of them especially picked for their height and strength, treated her fighting skills with enormous respect. She was not only their future Queen but also their mascot and lucky symbol. They cheered every time she hit the target with her javelin and politely ignored her misses, but over the three years she'd been training with the weapons master, there'd been far more reason to cheer than to remain politely silent.

By sundown when the training session ended, she was pleasantly tired and began to make her way back to her rooms with happy thoughts of supper. Then, changing her mind, she headed instead for her father's apartments. There was no official banquet tonight, so the kitchens would be having an easier time before the next round of diplomatic dinners for one or another of Redrought's barons. And the King would be eating as quietly as he ever could in his rooms. Thirrin had decided to join him, knowing he'd be pleased to spend the evening with his daughter. Besides, she had things on her mind and wanted to talk to him.

She crossed the shadowy Great Hall, listening to her booted footsteps echo from the smoke-blackened beams high above her head in the gloom of the roof. As she passed by, some of the ancient battle standards waved lazily, as though some ghost of wind from a long-ago battlefield still stroked the faded regimental colors. Ahead she could see her father's throne on its high dais rising out of the gathering shadows like a mountain made of carved oak. She reached it and quickly skirted around the back, where the door set in the wall behind stood slightly open.

"Grimswald! I said I wanted ale, not brown river water!" Redrought's booming voice lashed the Chamberlain-of-the-Royal-Paraphernalia.

"Well, I'm sure that it came from the same barrel that His Majesty was happy to drink from yesterday," a voice of old leather and dust answered.

"Well, it tastes like river water today! And fish do unspeakable things in rivers, so get me some more!"

"As His Majesty wishes."

Thirrin walked in just as the old chamberlain waved forward one of the servers who stood in the shadows at the back of the cozy room. He handed the man a jug and, with a huge wink, told him to fetch beer from another barrel.

"Thirrin!" her father shouted when he caught sight of her standing in the doorway. "Come in, come in! Grimswald, set another place; my daughter's come to eat with her old dad."

The little chamberlain bustled around fetching cutlery and placing a chair at the plain wooden table where Redrought ate when there were no dignitaries to entertain.

"I hear you equaled my best housecarl with the throwing axes today," he said, smiling proudly at her.

"Yes. And if the weapons master hadn't called an end to the session, I'd have beaten him," Thirrin replied.

Redrought roared with laughter. He often roared with

laughter when other people would have only smiled. "I bet you would have, too! Sigmund's getting a bit long in the tooth. I'll have to see about retiring him soon. His people come from the northern provinces. I'm sure he'll be happy with a bit of land and a pension."

"He's still a better axman than men half his age," Thirrin said in the old soldier's defense. "It'd be a pity to lose his experience from the bodyguard."

"Oh, don't worry, he's still good for another five years or so. I'm just thinking of the future," Redrought bellowed good-humoredly.

The servant returned with the jug of beer, and Grimswald poured a measure into Redrought's tankard. The King took a huge swallow. "That's better! I can always tell when a barrel's past its best!"

"Yes, sir," the chamberlain said, and smiled to himself like a mischievous little boy.

"And don't forget Primplepuss! Where's her bowl of milk?"

"I have it, sir," the wrinkled little man said, seeming to produce a dish from his sleeve.

Redrought grinned, and fishing around inside the chest of his tunic he extracted the little cat. "Ah, there you are, my sweeting!" he said more softly, and the little creature meowed in agreement. The King's huge fingers wrapped themselves gently around the kitten and set her down on the table before her dish of milk. He smiled on her indulgently for a few moments as she lapped, then turned to his daughter. "Well, why have you decided to have supper with me?"

"Do I need a reason?"

"No, but there's usually a favor to ask if you choose to. Otherwise you're in the mess with the housecarls or in the stables with the hands."

Thirrin felt suddenly guilty. Surely she ate with her father for reasons other than asking for favors? "I want nothing at all," she eventually answered, defensively.

"Just the pleasure of my company, eh?"

At that point the food arrived, and she waited for the servants to place everything on plates and withdraw before she continued. "Yes, for the pleasure of your company . . . and to ask a few questions."

"Ha!" the King shouted, as though his suspicions were confirmed, but then he smiled. "What do you want to know?"

Thirrin chewed on her chicken drumstick for a while as she ordered her thoughts. Ever since she'd met Oskan in the forest, she'd been wondering about his mother and father. It then occurred to her that nobody ever mentioned his father. She made a mental note to ask the King if anyone knew who he'd been, once she'd satisfied her curiosity on several other points. Finally she asked, "Why weren't witches banished after the war with The-Land-of-the-Ghosts?"

"The evil ones were," the King answered. "But the good ones were — *are* — too useful."

"How?" she asked.

"They're healers and midwives, they can drive blight from the harvest, and they're a brilliant line of defense against any evil that comes from the Vampire King and Queen. Not only that," the King said, pausing to drain his tankard of beer, "but they've been staunchly loyal, always the first to offer help when it's needed. You'd do well to remember that when you take the throne."

She nodded as she digested the information. "What was White Annis like?"

"One of the best!" Redrought boomed. "Powerful. I saw her draw a child back from the brink of death when all else had been tried and failed. And once, when out hunting, I watched her turn a charging boar with nothing but the threat of her eyes."

Father and daughter chomped in silence as the image of the witch was absorbed. "And I'll tell you another thing!" Redrought continued, pointing at his daughter with a turnip. "She was beautiful. Hair as black as polished jet and eyes like the sea under a stormy sky!"

Thirrin looked at her father in astonishment. She'd never heard anything even vaguely poetic cross his lips before, and yet here he was describing White Annis as though he were a praise singer.

He blushed and cleared his throat. "Of course, she got a little ragged toward the end of her life. Witches always do, but her Power never faded."

"And yet this great healer couldn't save herself," Thirrin said.

Redrought shrugged. "It was her time. Witches always know and leave life with dignity."

Thirrin beckoned to the servant, and he poured her a goblet of wine — three parts water, as was right for her age.

"Her son lives in her cave now."

"Yes, Oskan, I know. He's treating the injured stable hand."

"Will he have inherited his mother's Power?"

Redrought shrugged. "Who knows? Warlocks, male witches, are rare. Men are usually wizards, more mathematics than magic. But they're not beyond drawing down lightning when they need it or making stones walk if it'll serve their purpose."

"He's a healer," Thirrin said, as though this confirmed his supernatural powers.

"Well, yes," Redrought agreed. "So perhaps he has the rest of his mother's gifts, but who can say? It's not certain."

"Has the surgeon brought the stable hand back to the city yet?" Thirrin asked.

Redrought shrugged. "I don't know. Ask Grimswald. GRIMSWALD!"

"Yes, My Lord?" The little man stepped out of the shadows behind the King's chair.

"Oh, there you are. Has the surgeon —"

"No, My Lord. He thought it best to leave him for a day or two to rest."

"When will he go to collect him?" Thirrin asked, knowing that Grimswald would have every detail of the surgeon's plans.

"Tomorrow, I believe, My Lady."

"Good. I'll go with him. My horse needs the exercise."

Redrought looked at his daughter narrowly. Her horse was more likely to need a rest than exercise. But then he mentally shrugged; let her have her friend if she wanted. She was approaching the marrying age for a royal daughter, but she was already far too clever to let anything get in the way of any advantage to the House of Lindenshield that could be sealed by marriage.

"What about his father?" Thirrin asked, interrupting Redrought's thoughts.

"Whose father? The surgeon's?"

"No! Oskan's. Who was he?"

The King shrugged. "No one knows for sure." He almost added that not even White Annis was certain but decided such talk was unsuitable for his daughter's ears. "There are plenty of rumors, of course: wood sprites, spirits, even vampires. But he was probably just a human traveler who . . . um, just . . . you know, happened to be passing."

"She wasn't married, then?" Thirrin asked.

"No. Witches choose who they want for as long as they want. There's rarely anything formal about their arrangements."

"So, Oskan's father could have been anyone or any*thing*?"

"Yes. But a wood sprite is the gossips' favorite at the moment," Redrought answered, adding: "Mind you, he's pale enough to have Vampire blood somewhere in his veins — so to speak! But who knows?"

Thirrin nodded. Her new friend was certainly an interesting mystery.

Thirrin's horse was saddled and waiting in the courtyard, its breath pluming on the crisp sharp air of early morning. The weather was perfect for riding: A sharp frost had scattered a brilliant crystal sheen of white over the rooftops of the houses, as though in anticipation of the coming snows of winter, and the early morning sounds of awakening households echoed with the purity of chiming bells on the cold air.

She'd allowed the surgeon an hour's head start so that she could gallop to catch up, and as she and her escort of two cavalry troopers trotted down through the winding roads of the city, their horses blew and fidgeted in anticipation of the run. Once through the gates, the riders kicked their mounts and took off across the rich agricultural plain that fed the capital. Within minutes they'd reached the eaves of the forest and the Great Road, which sliced through the trees on its journey to the northern provinces.

They caught up with the surgeon and his assistant just as they were about to turn off the road into the tangled network of forest tracks, and reined back to a walk. Thirrin's face glowed with the tingling cold and, not wanting the horses to get chilled, she urged the quiet mules of the doctor and his assistant to a brisk trot as they headed for Oskan's cave.

The forest was darkly brilliant with deep shadow and dappled sunshine, which pooled amid the rich browns and flame reds of the autumnal leaves. The busy sounds of squirrels echoed through the branches as they gathered stores for the coming winter. Thirrin was so intent on trying to catch sight of the little red creatures as they dived through the forest canopy that she was almost taken by surprise when the horses started to climb the steep track that led to the cave.

She forced herself to concentrate on the broken and stony path, not wanting to arrive at Oskan's with a lame horse. As they drew near the end of the pathway, she looked up to see the tall boy waiting in the entrance of his cave.

He raised his hand in greeting, then, catching sight of Thirrin, he bowed his head formally. "Welcome to my home," he said politely as they all dismounted. "Your man is healing well."

"I'll decide that, thank you, young man," said the surgeon stiffly. "Where is the patient?"

Oskan led them into the cave, which smelled sweetly sharp with the scent of drying herbs and spices. The injured man lay on a low cot next to the fire. As they entered, he raised himself onto one elbow and would have climbed to his feet if the surgeon hadn't pressed him back down. "Before you go anywhere, I want to examine your wounds." He stripped away the clean bandages and stared aghast at the neat stitches that held the edges of the deep gash together. "I heard rumors that you'd done this! What gives you the right to endanger this man's life?"

"Nothing and no one," answered Oskan, sounding puzzled. "I stitched his wound to help it heal."

"You think you can cure by adding further injuries?"

Thirrin had watched this clash in silence, knowing that it would come. After all, she herself had been horrified by Oskan's methods until the old soldier had told her he'd seen it done before by White Annis. She looked at the injured man now and was amazed at the difference in him. He was obviously no longer in pain, and from where she was standing, the wound seemed to be healing cleanly. There was also no sign of any fever. All in all, she had to acknowledge that Oskan's treatment seemed to be working.

"He looks well enough to me," she said to the surgeon.

The man glanced at her with barely concealed resentment. "Forgive me, My Lady, but you cannot know that, and neither can this . . . boy!" He spat the last word with contempt. "I studied for five years under the greatest masters of anatomy and surgery in the Southern Continent; I served another four years in their hospitals and for a further ten years after that as a highly respected practitioner before your Royal Father summoned me to Frostmarris to take up the post of Chief Surgeon to the King! Compared to my experience and expertise, what can this young son of a witch know?"

"Enough to cleanly heal one of the deepest gashes I've ever seen," Thirrin answered pertly.

The surgeon's look spoke volumes. "In my vast experience as a medical practitioner I've seen far, far worse *and* healed them!"

"By luck or judgment, do you think?" Thirrin asked, her temper beginning to rise at the man's arrogance.

The surgeon's anger was held in check only by Thirrin's position as his Royal Patron's daughter. "My lady's judgment is clouded by her lack of knowledge in my field. A lack that is only equaled by this boy's." He turned to Oskan with a massive contempt. "Did you even bleed him?"

"I thought the bear had bled him enough already," Oskan answered calmly.

"And how exactly do you expect to purge his body of the evil humors from the bear's claws?"

"I don't know anything about *humors.* I just cleaned the wound and stitched it up." Oskan was visibly controlling his temper now.

"Then it will fester, the man will die, and you will have killed him just as surely as the animal that attacked him!"

Thirrin stepped closer to the stable hand and peered at the neatly stitched wound. "It looks perfectly all right to me. Healing nicely with no sign of any infection." She turned to the two soldiers of her escort, both middle-aged veterans who'd had long experience of battle wounds. "What do you two think?"

They agreed it seemed to be healing well and stared unwaveringly back at the enraged surgeon. "None of you know anything about the process of such injuries. Either he comes back to the city now and is thoroughly bled or he will die!"

"I'd much prefer he stayed here for at least another three days," said Oskan quietly. "With the permission of the Princess, of course."

"It seems to me we should ask your patient what he thinks," said Thirrin. "After all, it's his arm." She turned to the man and raised her eyebrows expectantly.

The stable hand had been staring from one member of the party to the other, completely overawed by the great people who were arguing over him, but at last he managed to stutter, "I think I'd like the witch's son to carry on with his treatment."

"That's *Oskan* Witch's Son to you," said Thirrin sharply.

"This man can't possibly know what's best for him!" the surgeon protested. "He barely knows what day it is, let alone has the ability to make a medical decision."

"I *do* know what day it is," said the injured man, stung to anger. "It's Thor's day. And I know something else, too. Last year I fell off my horse and gashed my knee. It was about a quarter the size of this wound, but it still managed to fester, gave me a fever, and took about a month to get to the state this wound took only a couple of days to reach!" He fell silent, suddenly aware that he had everyone's attention. But then he plucked up courage and went on. "I was out hunting for the King, so His Majesty sent this man — his surgeon — to treat me. My missus said he nearly killed me and that she could have done better with old wine and clean bandages like her mam used to use."

"Oh, this is absurd. I don't have to defend my clinical methods to ignoramuses."

"No, you don't," Thirrin cut in coldly. "The man obviously has chosen to trust the methods of Oskan Witch's Son. So I suggest you leave the ignoramuses here and return to Frostmarris."

"But, My Lady, the King directed me to —"

"*Examine the patient*, which you have done. You've carried out your duty, so I now give you permission to return to the city and your other patients, who are so fortunate in having your vast expertise."

Never having been dismissed by a thirteen-year-old girl before, it took the surgeon a few moments to gather his dignity, but then he turned and swept from the cave, collecting servant and mule en route.

Thirrin watched him go, then turned and warmed her hands at the fire. "Well, shall we get the patient back to the inner cave?" she said brightly, helping the man to his feet. "And you men can attend the horses," she added to her escort, who saluted and went outside. Oskan took his patient's good arm and led him back to the bed along the narrow corridor that connected the complex of caverns.

It was while she was left alone for a few minutes that

Thirrin's mask started to slip. What was she thinking of? She was suddenly and horribly aware that she'd effectively got rid of everyone but Oskan, who would soon return to the hearth where she was sitting all alone! If she had a *situation* to deal with, such as the surgeon and the injured huntsman, she was fine — even domineering — but when she was on her own, or it was something about herself, that's when everything nearly always went wrong.

She almost panicked. Being alone with a boy meant she was bound to blush and stutter and make a complete fool of herself!

If she acted quickly, she'd be able to cross to the mouth of the cave and call the men back in; at least that way there'd be others around her to distract attention. But then she heard Oskan coming back from the inner cave, and she abandoned the idea. Far better to look like a princess in control — even if she didn't feel it — than be caught rushing around and squeaking like a fool.

Thirrin tried to calm herself, and had to call on all her training as a warrior as she prepared to deal with her embarrassment. But in the end she carried it off quite well. She was hardly blushing at all when Oskan reappeared. She took deep, steadying breaths and managed to keep her voice relatively level.

"You'd better hope he doesn't develop fever or the green rot now, Oskan, otherwise our gentle surgeon will do his best to have you driven out."

The boy drew up a stool and sat next to her before he replied. "I'd hope he wouldn't get sick, anyway," he said and, grinning one of the brightest smiles Thirrin had ever seen, he went on, "but especially so now. I want to prove that pompous moron well and truly wrong."

Thirrin smiled in return, slowly beginning to relax again, and decided to forgive him for not asking permission to sit in her presence. "Is there any doubt?"

"Things can always go wrong in healing."

"Do you expect them to?"

He grinned again. "No."

There was something about the boy's calm presence that helped Thirrin to feel unusually at ease, and she bravely decided to ask him about any other skills he might have learned from his mother. "Can you do magic?"

He took so long to reply she thought she'd offended him in some way, but at last he said, "I don't really know what you mean by magic. I can read the weather, but any shepherd can do that; I know the ways of the animals, but again so does anyone who lives in the forest. . . ."

"Can you see the future?"

He shrugged. "The Sight, you mean? Sometimes . . . perhaps. But never to order and never the whole of any situation. There's always a mystery, always something we're not meant to know."

Thirrin nodded, her suspicions confirmed. "Can you draw down lightning?"

Oskan paused, startled by her directness. "I've never tried. Seems like a silly idea to me. You could be hit."

"I never thought of that." Thirrin was now beginning to feel so relaxed in this boy's company that her contradictory nature decided to take control, and she immediately began to feel hot and uncomfortable. Complete social humiliation was now threatening. She stood and made ready to go. Being Princess, with the royal right to ignore conventions of leave-taking, often had its advantages. "How long will you keep my servant?"

"Another three or four days," he answered. Then looking at her standing stiffly in her full Princess mode, he added, "My Lady," and bowed.

She strode to the entrance of the cave and nodded imperiously to the soldiers of her escort, who immediately led up her horse. "I'll return in four days, then."

Oskan nodded. "He should be ready to ride by that time."

Thirrin swung easily into the saddle and, being firmly hidden behind her Princess facade, she felt brave enough to hold out her hand. Perplexed, Oskan just stared at it stupidly, and she thought she was going to have to embarrass herself excruciatingly by demanding that he kiss it. But then he took her fingers and pressed them to his lips — for much longer than she thought was strictly necessary.

"In four days, Oskan Witch's Son."

"In four days, My Lady. I'll look forward to it."

She rode off at the head of her escort, suddenly feeling a need to unsling her shield from the saddle and carry it on her arm.

5

Thirrin sat in her room, staring out her window over the garden below. She was supposed to be doing her geography homework, but a deep sense of excitement filled her to bursting point and she couldn't concentrate. It was the season of Yule. The servants had brought holly, ivy, and the sacred mistletoe into the Great Hall and hung it from the roof beams so that the place looked like a huge indoor forest and the spicy scent of evergreen foliage pervaded everything. The housecarls had selected the biggest log they could find, hauled it through the city, and then stored it safely in the courtyard of the royal fortress, ready for the triumphant procession to the hearth on Yule Night. Everything had that excited, breathless atmosphere that the festival always brought with it. The candles burned brighter, music sounded sweeter, and even the most ordinary of actions were steeped in the anticipation of the season.

But for Thirrin there was an added excitement: Her birthday fell at Yule, and she would reach fourteen, the Coming of Age for girls. Everyone knew she was heir to the throne, but on this day Redrought would present her officially to the housecarls, who would proclaim her their Princess and swear loyalty to her. At fourteen she would be considered old enough to marry, and in the past many royal princesses had been forced to do just that, as a means of sealing an alliance or confirming some great lord in his position of power. They'd had little choice, but Redrought was different, and anyway, times had changed. No one was interested in an alliance with the little icebound kingdom far to the north. For centuries the Icemark's survival had depended on the power of its armies and the cunning of its kings and queens. And in Redrought the country had a happy combination of foxlike guile and the fighting power of a wild boar.

The fact that Thirrin knew he was also one of the softest fathers any headstrong girl could want was a secret she was happy to keep. He might be King Redrought Strong-in-the-Arm Lindenshield, Bear of the North, Defender of the Realm, Descendant of Thor, but to Thirrin he was just Dad, a man with a fondness for cats, a taste for comfy slippers, and a huge laugh that could dent pewter at fifty paces.

A movement in the garden below her window drew her eye, and she watched as one of the massively cloaked housecarls guarding the gate stamped to attention, then marched up and down to keep warm, his breath pluming in the freezing air of the Icemark winter. She felt a slight sense of disappointment welling up under the excitement caused by the nearness of Yule and her Coming of Age. Everything was almost perfect: candles, holly, music, but the garden was a dull, boring gray. At this time of year it should have been bright and crisp with the crystal clarity of fresh snow. But there was none. There was a thick layer of dirty frost over everything, the rivers had frozen as usual, and massive icicles hung like crystal swords and daggers from every roof. But there was no snow. For the first time in her life it looked as though Thirrin was going to celebrate Yule and her birthday without the usual blizzard howling in the darkness beyond the warm, smoky coziness of the Great Hall. It was a bit unsettling that her Coming of Age should fall on the year that the snows were late. Perhaps she should ignore her modern education and see some *message* in this; after all, the Icemark was surrounded by enemies. Perhaps it was a portent of some sort.

Only the oldest folk in the city of Frostmarris could remember the snows ever being so late, and they muttered darkly about bad omens. The last time such a thing had happened, they said, a great illness had come and thousands had died throughout the country. And the time before that, their grandparents had told them, war had laid the land to waste. Many had started to mutter about Scipio Bellorum and his invincible army just waiting for a chance to invade. But Thirrin sniffed disdainfully at this, as Maggiore Totus, her tutor, had done. She finally decided that such superstition was for peasants. As an educated young woman, she knew that weather patterns and wind directions caused the lateness of the snows. But all the same, deep down she couldn't help feeling uncomfortable.

She cheered herself up by thinking of the preparations for the great feast. There was a constant stream of traders from the city into the castle, and servants bustled to and fro carrying baskets full of every kind of foodstuff, from cheeses and dried fruit to eggs and even oranges imported from the Southern Continent. Some of the housecarls had been excused guard duty to help and could be seen stumping along with huge flitches of bacon or entire sides of beef on their shoulders. Delicious smells of roasting and baking wafted along every corridor, and the ghostly sounds of distant musicians practicing

Yuletide carols in the towers and basements stole into the ear whenever there was a lull in the noise.

But even above the Yuletide preparations and her birthday, Thirrin felt an added spice of secret excitement, though she wouldn't admit the cause of it, even to herself. She'd invited Oskan to the Yule Feast. Or rather, she'd sent a royal command ordering his presence on the twenty-first day of Icemas. At least the lack of snow meant that the roads would be clear and he could get there from his cave in the forest with no problems. Even so, she'd decided to send an escort of cavalry to fetch him. The wolves were always hungry at this time of year. She'd also have to make sure that he and the surgeon didn't cross each other's path. Ever since she'd brought the stable hand home from Oskan's cave, and he'd returned to his duties with only a slight scar on his arm to show where he'd been injured, the surgeon had been insufferable.

She stood up from the window seat and fetched her sword. She hated sitting still for long, and she knew that even during the Yule preparations there were always housecarls ready for weapons practice down in the lists or training grounds. As Thirrin strode along the corridor, the bustle and noise swirled about her, filling her eyes, ears, and nose with color and scent and distant magical music. She felt she'd burst with happiness. All that was needed to make the season complete was the snow. But even though the skies were a dull, swollen gray, there was no sign of even the tiniest flake.

The next day was Yuletide Eve, and Thirrin had decided that she would lead the escort of cavalry to collect Oskan later that evening. She thought she'd tell him that she just happened to be riding in the area and so dropped by to see that he reached Frostmarris safely. Of course, the fact that they'd have a spare horse for him to ride would be a bit of a giveaway, but she'd just hide behind her royal persona and no one would dare to point this out to her. In the meantime she would spend the morning with Redrought.

Her father always said she only ever ate with him or visited his private rooms when she wanted something. Partly to disprove this, she'd made up her mind to arrive in his rooms just after the midday meal and not leave until the evening, without asking for a thing.

Crossing the Great Hall on her way to the King's rooms was an exciting obstacle course of decorations lying around the floor, ready to be tacked to the lath-and-plaster walls; trestle tables set at all sorts of crazy angles as servants attached wreathes of ivy to the edges; and harassed-looking chamberlains rushing by on their way to kitchens, storerooms, or the wine cellar. It was less than a day now before the great feast began, and everything must be ready. Several of Redrought's most important barons and baronesses would be staying, and finding housing for their entourages and soldier escorts was the usual nightmare that happened every year. It was odd, thought Thirrin, but no matter how early the household staff started their preparations, there was always this crazy, last-minute panic before everything finally came together.

At last she skirted around the Throne of State and almost fell through the small entranceway hidden behind it that led into Redrought's rooms. She shut the door behind her and leaned against the woodwork for a moment, completely overwhelmed by the excitement of the preparations. When she finally looked up, the quiet and calm of the room washed over her. The King was sitting in his usual chair surrounded by a mountain of colorful cushions, while Grimswald, the elderly Chamberlain-of-the-Royal-Paraphernalia, sat on a low stool next to him reading from a beautifully illuminated book.

Thirrin recognized this as one of her father's personal Yuletide traditions: He had a passage from *The Book of the Ancestors* read to him every day during the two-week lead-up to Yule. And true to form, he suddenly bellowed a huge guffaw of laughter as he happily scrutinized the illuminated scrollwork of the pages and caught sight of one of the mythical animals peering out at him. Redrought had ordered the book from the Holy Brothers of the Southern Continent when Thirrin was still a baby and, such was the work that had gone into its richly decorated pages, she'd been eight years old when it had finally been delivered.

"Ah, Thirrin!" her father boomed when he caught sight of her at the door. "Come in! Come in! Grimswald's just reading about Edgar the Bold and his war against the Dragon-folk of the Wolfrocks."

This was one of her favorite tales, so she quickly crossed the room and squeezed into Redrought's huge chair with him. She threw some of the comfy cushions onto the floor to make extra room, then took Primplepuss, who was mewing a polite greeting, and placed her on her lap. The little cat purred loudly and settled down to a good wash as Grimswald continued the story.

It was one of the longest chapters in *The Book of the Ancestors,* and so by the time Edgar had finally killed the Dragon King at the last battle of the long war, the thin afternoon light had retreated into the shadows of full night.

"Excellent! Excellent!" Redrought bellowed. "Well read, Grimswald. You must be thirsty. Have yourself some ale, and while you're about it bring me a tankard, too, and some small beer for the Princess."

Thirrin stretched, loosening the muscles that had become cramped during the long reading. "Well, Dad, have you made your list for the Fat Old Elf?"

"I have. And if he doesn't bring me a new pair of slippers and a sword belt, he won't get his mead and pies next year!"

She grinned at the King, suddenly feeling an overwhelming love for the man who, apart from Yuletide, spent most of his waking hours running the country and yet could still find time to make the traditional old jokes with his daughter.

"And what about you?" he asked. "Have you burned your letter on the hearth?"

"Yes. I'm hoping for a new sword and war saddle."

"Don't you think they might be a little heavy for his reindeer?"

"They'll see the inside of a venison pasty if they are! We can't have the Fat Old Elf making do with substandard reindeer."

"I like venison pasties," Redrought said wistfully, rubbing his impressively curving stomach. "Grimswald! Food!!"

The Chamberlain-of-the-Royal-Paraphernalia had obviously been expecting the King to be hungry and had arranged for dinner to be ready by the time the story from *The Book of the Ancestors* finished. Soon the table was covered with dishes and platters of game pie, mounds of vegetables, and steaming fruit tarts. It was a simple matter to add a plate for Thirrin and to order some extra dishes just in case the royal appetites managed to clear the table and still want more.

Grimswald seized the opportunity and withdrew with the servants, leaving Thirrin and Redrought to their meal. At Yuletide there was never enough time in the day to get everything done that was needed to make the celebrations run smoothly.

"You're entertaining the barons of The Middle Lands this year, aren't you?" asked Thirrin.

Redrought swallowed the heroic mouthful of game pie he was chewing. "Yes. Lord Aethelstan, Lady Aethelflaeda, and old Lord Cerdic. Aethelflaeda is the only one who's ever out-drunk Cerdic, and this year he's after revenge. I've ordered in extra ale to cover it."

"Won't Baron Aethelstan compete?"

"Not that old fussling! He'll sip a glass of wine and nibble a bit of turkey, if we're lucky. I'd sooner have invited Lady Theowin of the Grassmarch — she's always good for a laugh at Yuletide — but she's worried about the mountain passes into Polypontus."

"Oh yes?" Thirrin was immediately alert to the possibility of trouble from the huge empire to the south.

"Yes. Some of her spies have reported troop movements. Nothing serious, they're probably just carrying out maneuvers in preparation for their next war. That general of theirs, Scipio Bellorum, can never sit still, and it's been three months since his last campaign. He'll be getting restless."

"Are you sure the next war he's planning isn't with us?"

Redrought chewed thoughtfully. "Yes. I've considered the possibility, I'll admit. But I think he'll strike southward first; the last spy reports said there was nothing amiss. Mind you, that was more than two weeks ago, and when Bellorum decides on action, no one's faster. Still, the next reports are due any day now, and I'm confident they'll have nothing new to tell us. He'll come this way one day, though, I'm sure of that — and then we'll see how shield-wall and longbow do against cannons and matchlock."

"The housecarls will smash them!" said Thirrin fiercely.

"Yes," Redrought agreed thoughtfully. "They'll smash them again and again, but the armies of the Empire have a secret weapon, far worse than any cannon."

"What's that?" she asked, eager for any information about a new method of warfare.

"Size," answered Redrought simply. "Sheer size. You can break them time after time and they just keep coming. A single Polypontian host is at least three times bigger than our largest regional force, and they have four hosts ready to march even in the few periods of peace they've allowed themselves. If they're on a war footing, there are usually six full-strength armies, each of one hundred thousand troops, and another four in reserve. In an emergency they can call on another three armies of veterans on top of that!"

Thirrin sat quietly digesting this information. She knew from her lessons with Maggiore Totus that the Polypontians had never been defeated in war. And they'd rarely lost even a battle.

"So, what can we do?" she asked at last.

"Hope the next country they pick on keeps them busy for a long time, perhaps even wears them out and makes them change their minds about the joys of war."

"But we can't rely on that. They've never lost a war yet. . . . And what happens if we really *are* the next lucky country on their list?"

Redrought was halfway through a huge fruit pie and took some time to wipe away the cream and crumbs before answering her. "We can only hope the army reforms I brought in five years ago will be enough to hold them. Every region now has its elite corps of housecarls as well as a professional cavalry regiment, and the period of training in the fyrd has been extended to four months. You know as well as I what that means: Every farmer and field hand, every clerk and shopkeeper, is battle-trained, *and* the new War Tax means they're all armed with shield, helmet, sword, and spear. What more can we do?"

All able-bodied citizens had to serve in the fyrd whenever

there was a military emergency, and they had to train for it every year. But Thirrin knew it wasn't enough. Even with the best training methods and with professional soldiers leading them, the fyrd was still an army of farmers and shopkeepers. Polypontian soldiers spent every waking moment training or fighting or preparing to do so. A soldier of the fyrd spent a few weeks of the year learning to raise a shield-wall and to use an ax. They'd have no hope against Bellorum's professional murderers. "We need to get allies," Thirrin said decisively.

At this point Primplepuss awoke and walked sleepily across to the King's lap, and Redrought took some minutes of cooing and fussing over the little cat before she was happily settled. "Who would you suggest?" he then continued as though there'd been no interruption. "Let me remind you that the Polypontus stands between us and any potential allies to the south; seaward there are only the Zephyrs and Corsairs, who hate us; and way to the south there's the Southern Continent, which is too far away."

"There's always The-Land-of-the-Ghosts."

Redrought's huge callused hand slammed down on the table, making Primplepuss leap vertically skyward and land back on the King's lap. "That again! The Vampire King and Queen want us all dead. Why should they agree to an alliance?"

Thirrin, not at all bothered by her father's outburst, answered quietly. "For mutual benefit and safety. If we fall, The-Land-of-the-Ghosts would be next. Maggiore Totus tells me the rulers of the Polypontus believe in science and rationality. Vampires and ghosts, witches and zombies, would be an affront to their view of the world. They'd have to wipe them out, if only to rid the world of such unscientific creatures."

"Perhaps they'd just ignore them," Redrought answered more quietly, as the truth of her words began to percolate through. "I hear some of their scientists don't even believe in lodestones — you know, those pieces of metal that are drawn to iron — so they refuse to give any credence to them, even if they see their effects with their own eyes. That's a powerful sort of denial, perhaps powerful enough for them to reject the existence of an entire country."

"Scipio Bellorum ignore a possible conquest? I think not. Especially when there's a chance of adding another land and all its wealth to the Empire. He'd be itching to invade The-Land-of-the-Ghosts almost as soon as he'd tidied away the problem of the Icemark."

The King sat quietly considering her words. He was a shrewd ruler, and her argument stood close scrutiny. "You might . . . just might have a point." He absentmindedly stroked Primplepuss, who settled again as he cogitated. Finally he reached a decision. "They'd never agree to an alliance with *me*. We loathe each other equally. But with you, Thirrin . . ." He reached for another fruit pie and demolished it with quiet efficiency. "Of course, you've already made a start by making a friend of that wolfman-king you released. Perhaps it's something you should follow up after Yule."

Thirrin sighed happily. She was enormously proud that she'd convinced her father of the good points of a plan she'd been mulling over for some time. Usually her father would listen with quiet patience to her ideas about the governing of the country, then reduce them to rubble. But this time he'd accepted her arguments. She stored away his instructions to seek allies and chose one of the game pies to eat.

6

A brilliant full moon had risen when Thirrin finally set off with an escort of ten cavalry troopers to collect Oskan. Several degrees of frost had settled over the city, and as the horses made their way down from the castle and through the streets, the rattle of their iron-shod hooves sounded sharp and brittle in the freezing air. The spicy scent of wood smoke filled the narrow streets as people fed their fires with logs and branches, and ice sparkled everywhere over the roofline so that Frostmarris looked like a city of black crystal reflecting the cold, shining beauty of the moonlit night. But still the snows hadn't come, and now the skies were clear of the clouds that had lowered over the city, allowing the temperatures to drop so far below freezing that the horses' breath settled around their muzzles and reins in a fine gauze of ice crystals as delicate as lace.

Thirrin and the cavalry troopers all wore thick furs over their armor, and they trotted through the streets at a brisk pace, hoping to warm themselves and the horses as quickly as possible. The roads were almost deserted, as each household had shut its doors against the bitter cold and was preparing for

Yule. Even the taverns were relatively quiet in these last hours before the dawn. Then, with the first light of the morning, the traditional songs would be sung and the wild celebrations would begin. But now every tiny sound was magnified on the freezing air, so that Thirrin's small escort sounded like an entire regiment of horses.

At last they reached the main gate and were quickly allowed through by the guard. They clattered through the long tunnel of the barbican, then drew rein as they looked out at the land beyond the city walls. Before them lay the plain of Frostmarris, silent and brooding under the cold silver of the moonlit night. Far off in the distance a wolf howled, giving a voice to the quiet, and Thirrin shivered. The packs were hungry and had come down from the mountains to raid the outlying farms. No human being had ever been taken, but people feared for their cattle, and the old legends of wolf attack always came to mind when the packs howled in the cold of winter. Thirrin urged her mount forward down the steep track that led to the flat plain, then, as she reached level ground, she shook the reins and her horse leaped forward. The bitter cold of the night was increased to biting steel by the wind of her speed, and she crouched down behind the stallion's neck as they thundered across the plain. Behind her the cavalry troopers kept pace, spreading out in a wide fan, like a living cloak that flowed behind the head of the Princess. They could have followed the broad road that swept northward to the cities of Pendris and Wearford, which nestled on the farthest northern border of the Icemark. But instead Thirrin led them across the winter fields, leaping hedgerows and ditches in a wild gallop through the night.

In the distance lay the forest, like a dark bank of clouds

threatening a storm. It slowly loomed larger as the horses galloped across the fields, and after twenty minutes or so Thirrin reined back to a canter and finally to a brisk trot as they reached the first outlying trees. As they entered the true eaves of the forest, she stopped and waited while each of the troopers took out his tinderbox and prepared to light a pitch-soaked torch. She sat and stared ahead into the ancient gloom of the trees. The forest at night was very different from the woodland of the day. Not all of the supernatural creatures of the darkness had been banished to The-Land-of-the-Ghosts after the Battle of the Wolfrocks, quite simply because not all of them could be found. And of those that had stayed behind, many had set up home here in the deep shadows of the crowding trees.

After a few minutes Thirrin's eyes grew accustomed to the deeper levels of dark, and the beautiful black-and-white mosaic of moonlight filtering through the trees became visible in all its subtle brilliance. But then the sudden flare of the torches bursting into flame drove back the sight, and darkness crowded around the circle of light they carried with them.

They found the path that would eventually meander to Oskan's cave, and pushed on briskly. The troopers began to sing a cavalry song, but their voices echoed and reechoed eerily through the trees as though a squadron of ghosts were riding with them somewhere just out of sight, and they quickly fell silent. But the forest continued to make its own mysterious comments as they trotted by. Far off, a branch fell; nearby twigs snapped; and every now and then the lonely, mournful wail of a hunting wolf would sound, thin on distance and fat with fear.

Thirrin slung her shield on her arm and held her flaming torch higher, and the troopers did likewise. The familiar weight restored their confidence and they trotted on, guiding the horses with their knees, battle fashion. After a while Thirrin thought she saw the gleam of red eyes away off in the trees. But when she looked directly at them, there was nothing to be seen. This continued for some time, and she'd just decided not to say anything to her escort when the sergeant at arms said, "I think there's something following us, My Lady. I suggest we ride with sabers drawn."

She nodded her agreement and, transferring the torch to her shield hand, she drew the long cavalry sword. "What do you think it is? Wolves don't attack people."

"No idea, Ma'am," he answered briskly. "There are some dangerous things in the forest, but whatever they are, they won't like cavalry steel."

She smiled, cheered by his confidence. "We'll soon be at Oskan Witch's Son's cave. Perhaps he'll have some answers for us."

"Yes, Ma'am. Perhaps."

They rode on, their pace unconsciously increasing as the red eyes slowly drew closer. By the time they reached the clearing where Thirrin had first met Oskan in the autumn, they were cantering as fast as they dared on the treacherous path. But then they surged forward to the far side of the dell and, at a signal from Thirrin, they turned and faced whatever was following them.

Bright moonlight illuminated the clearing, and they clearly saw twenty or so figures emerge from the trees. They were almost human, but their bodies seemed to be covered by shiny holly leaves, almost like armor, and they all carried round shields and long spears made of a gray wood that seemed to glow in the moonlight. Thirrin was close enough to see that their skin was the same strange gray color, and their eyes were the brilliant red of berries.

More fascinated than afraid, she urged her horse forward a few paces and, standing in the stirrups, she called out to them:

"I am Princess Thirrin Freer Strong-in-the-Arm Lindenshield, heir to the throne of the Icemark. Identify yourselves so that I may know if you are friend or foe." Her voice sounded high and fierce in the silence, like the challenging call of a bird of prey, and her escort felt their confidence in their young leader grow even stronger.

Without warning, a dark figure emerged from the edge of the clearing, and a familiar voice said, "These are soldiers of the Holly King, who rules all wild places in the wintertime."

"Oskan!" Thirrin shouted in surprise. "You know them. Soldiers, you say? What are they doing in the Icemark?"

"They've been here since before the land was named by your people, and the Holly King is as old as all tree life, as is his brother the Oak King, who rules in the summer."

"Kings? Who are these rulers that I've never . . ." Her voice trailed away as memories of nursery rhymes and stories came back to her. "You mean the Kings of the Wild Wood are real?!"

"As real as the forest around you, and their twin royal lineage is far older than the House of Lindenshield."

She sat in amazed silence, considering the legends that stood before her, until her acute sense of ceremony and occasion suddenly took over and, standing in her stirrups again, she raised her sword above her head. "I salute you and your royal master, soldiers of the Holly King. Go now and take to him the friendly greetings of Thirrin Freer Strong-in-the-Arm Lindenshield."

From among the ranks of the strange holly soldiers a tall figure stepped forward and raised its spear in salute. Then, stepping back into the trees behind them, they all simply melted away.

"That was well done," said Oskan, walking over to stand at her stirrup. "The Holly King and Oak King are powerful friends to have, and even worse enemies."

"I'm afraid we'll soon need all the friends we can get," Thirrin answered quietly, still amazed by the creatures of legend she'd just seen. Then, suddenly brisk, she said, "And where did you spring from, Oskan? I'd already had enough shocks without you leaping out of the shadows like a skinny ghost!"

Oskan drew his tall, slender frame to even greater heights and said with dignity, "I was waiting for you to arrive. I thought it best to . . . intervene before things got out of hand."

Thirrin almost answered that she'd had the situation very well in hand, thank you very much, when she stopped herself. Oskan was right, who knows what would have happened if he hadn't turned up when he did? "You arrived at just the right moment," she finally said. But somehow the tone was all wrong. She sounded just like one of the elderly lady chamberlains of the palace graciously rewarding a lowly scullion by condescending to talk to him.

She filled the awkward silence that followed by slinging her shield on her back. "Well, have you got your gear with you or do we have to go up to your cave?"

"It won't take me long to get it. Wait here."

He'd gone before she had time to tell him that no one told the heir to the throne of the Icemark to wait anywhere, and he was back by the time she'd realized she was glad she hadn't said it.

She waited while he scrambled clumsily onto the quiet horse they'd brought for him, and then she said, "So, why haven't I seen these holly soldiers before? I've ridden in the forest at night lots of times."

Oskan looked at her and awkwardly urged his horse forward. "You're asking the wrong question. It should be, 'Why did the holly soldiers allow themselves to be seen?' *I* only usually see them a couple of times each winter, and the same can be said for the oak soldiers in the summer. But I've never known them to show themselves to city people before. Something must be bothering them."

"Like what?"

"Who knows? Perhaps they're worried by the late snows."

Thirrin slapped her leg in exasperation. "Not you as well! You'll be telling me next that there's going to be a plague or a bad harvest."

"No. It'll probably be war this time."

She reined to a halt so abruptly that her horse snorted in surprise. "War! What do you mean?"

Oskan shrugged. "These omens go in cycles. My mother told me the last time the snows were late there was famine, and before that, disease. This time it must mean war."

Thirrin turned in her saddle and hastily waved her escort of troopers back to a greater distance. She didn't need any rumors springing from this. "But you don't believe that, surely?"

"Yes," he answered with such open simplicity that Thirrin was both shocked and convinced. It tallied with her own fears exactly, but hearing someone else talk of coming war with such certainty was deeply disturbing.

"When?"

"I don't know . . . precisely."

"Within a year?"

"Yes. And probably before the season changes."

They rode on in silence while Thirrin thought things over. Maggiore Totus would scoff at such superstition, but then again he'd scoff at the idea of the Holly King and Oak King, and she now knew without a doubt that they existed.

She and Oskan were riding well ahead of the escort by this time and, as neither of them had torches, they could see the simple black-and-white beauty of moonlight percolating through the trees glowing mysteriously all around them.

"What should we do?" she asked.

"I don't know. I'm no politician or soldier. Just be ready, I suppose."

She nodded. They were as ready as they could be. The only thing they couldn't prepare for was the direction of an invasion.

"I don't suppose you have any idea who will attack us?" she asked, half prepared to rely on any mystical powers or intuition he might have inherited from his mother.

"Oh yes, that's easy. The Polypontian Empire, of course."

"Of course," she answered with quiet irony. "But why are you so certain?"

"Logical, really. Who else?"

"The Corsairs and Zephyrs. They've been quiet for too long."

Oskan sat in thought for a moment, then shook his head. "No. The Polypontus for sure."

Exactly why she believed him was unclear even to herself, but believe him she did. The only problem was to convince the King and get him to call out the fyrd in the southern provinces and send the Royal Army to help, even if it was only a precaution. She'd have to take it up with him at the Yule Feast the next day: After a few festive ales he was always more open to discussion.

As they rode, the mournful wail of a distant wolf echoed through the forest, making the horses whicker nervously.

"There may be no snow, but it's still cold enough to drive the packs down from the mountains," she said.

"True," Oskan answered. "But that wasn't a wolf, or not completely so, anyway."

"Another wolfman, here in the Icemark?"

"Wolfwoman, actually."

"You can tell that? Then can you understand their language? What's she saying?"

The howling broke out again, descending slowly through the octaves to a deep and strange moan.

"I can understand a little, not everything. She's warning of something and calling a . . ." He stopped and in the subtle brilliance of the moonlight his face looked deadly pale. "She's calling a muster of the Wolf-folk! That hasn't happened in generations! Something big must be going on. Perhaps we should look to the north for war after all!"

Thirrin stood in her stirrups and waved up the escort ready to gallop for Frostmarris. But Oskan grabbed her arm.

"Wait. There's more." He listened as the distant howling continued, weaving a melancholy web of sound over the night sky. "No, I was right. The trouble *is* coming from the south, and she thinks they'll be too late to fulfill their . . . Well, she uses the word *oath* and then says 'to the Princess.'"

Thirrin gasped, then barked orders at the troopers. "Ditch the torches. We ride for the city!"

"She's probably right, of course," Oskan continued as though chatting comfortably by a fire about the price of bread. "The wolfwoman's obviously just part of a relay sending this message back to The-Land-of-the-Ghosts, and by the time it gets there, whatever's about to happen will already have done so, if you see what I mean. I wonder what oath she's talking about. And who's this *Princess*?"

Thirrin cuffed him impatiently around the head. "Shut up and ride!"

With that her horse leaped off through the forest. Oskan urged his mount on and then immediately wished he hadn't as the animal charged after Thirrin and her escort. He clung to the horse's neck, desperately trying to avoid the branches and twigs that whipped overhead as they sped along the narrow forest track. The rich scents of leaf litter kicked up by the galloping hooves of twelve horses reminded him of the Yuletide cakes he hoped to be eating. But he soon forgot all about food as he concentrated on staying mounted on the wildly galloping animal.

In what seemed an incredibly short time they burst out of the trees and fanned out over the farmland that flowed up to the walls of the city like a windswept fertile sea. If anything, it was even colder here without the shelter of the forest, and Oskan tried to draw his cloak around him to keep out the bitter iciness. But it was no good; he'd no sooner risked life and limb to grab an edge when the wind ripped it out of his hand again. He clamped his jaw shut on his chattering teeth and stared ahead to Thirrin and the cavalry escort. He wondered if he looked as wild as they did, all flailing hooves and billowing cloaks, and concluded that he must.

Frostmarris was drawing nearer, looming over the plain like a disciplined mountain range, all right angles and straight edges instead of jagged peaks. But in the moonlight its granite walls glowed slightly, as though it were made of nothing more solid than moonlit cloud, just waiting for a gust of wind to blow it away across the plain. In the clarity of the night air Oskan could see the glint of spears as the guards made their slow circuit of the walls, and he was struck with a sense of the city's vulnerability. A besieging army could starve it, break its walls, kill its people. Was that what the wolfwoman's message was about? But why should the Wolf-folk be bothered about Frostmarris? Before he could give any more thought to these questions, he lost his grip and almost slid sideways from the saddle. With a wildly thumping heart he managed to struggle back upright, and he decided to give all his attention to riding and ask questions later.

7

Oskan had been dreading having to sleep in the Great Hall along with all the other less important guests who would fill the castle for Yule. He was used to the privacy of his cave, and the thought of sharing his space with any number of total strangers was daunting. But he needn't have worried; he had been given his own room. Admittedly it was small, with just enough space for the narrow bed, a chest for the few things he'd brought with him, and a stool to lay his clothes on, but it was a private room and a huge privilege. He knew for certain that there were some quite wealthy merchants curled up around the central hearth of the Great Hall, vying for space with the wolfhounds and trying to guard their property from their fellow guests. He almost felt guilty that an orphaned peasant boy like himself should be given his own room — almost, but not quite.

He stretched comfortably under the warm covers and savored the peace and quiet. Only an hour before, he'd been in the King's private chamber with Thirrin, and Redrought's huge voice had filled everything to capacity, including Oskan's head.

As soon as they'd arrived in the castle courtyard, the Princess had leaped from her horse and waited impatiently while Oskan had climbed carefully down from the saddle. Then she'd led him through the massive double doors that stood before them into the Great Hall. Neither Thirrin nor her escort of soldiers seemed to care in the least that they walked over several guests who'd settled down for Yuletide Eve around the central fire. Oskan had whispered hurried apologies to several outraged figures who had sat up spluttering into the red glow of the fire-lit hall. Things hadn't been helped, either, when most of the wolfhounds, seeing Thirrin and the soldiers, had decided it was morning and time for their run, so they had started to bark excitedly and jump around over the rest of the sleeping guests. By the time they'd reached the massive oak throne on the dais and dodged behind it to enter the King's chambers, the Great Hall was in an uproar with dogs baying, sentries shouting challenges, and woken guests demanding to know what was going on.

Thirrin had thumped once on the low door to her father's private apartments and burst in. A sentry just inside the room had leveled his spear and shouted a startled demand to know their business, and a small collection of white hair and wrinkles in a red nightshirt had hopped out of a low cot with a squeak. "Who is it, Bergeld? See them off! Call out the guard!"

"It's the Princess, sir," the sentry had replied, lowering shield and spear.

"The Princess? At this hour?" Grimswald the chamberlain had then rubbed his eyes and gazed at the party of Thirrin, Oskan, and the soldiers. "Not only the Princess, it seems. You can dismiss your men, Ma'am."

Thirrin raised her hand, and her escort saluted and marched away. Oskan, in the comfort of his bed, remembered how much larger the room had suddenly seemed after the ten heavily armed soldiers had gone. Grimswald had then cleared his throat with deliberate dignity and asked precisely what they wanted.

"I have urgent news for *my* father," Thirrin had replied, with a slight but powerful emphasis on the word *my*.

"Well, since you've woken him up, you might as well tell him what you very well want!" a huge voice had boomed into the room and was soon followed by an enormous white nightshirt that made its way irritably through a door from an inner chamber. Oskan's jaw had literally dropped open before the massive figure of the King. His billowing nightshirt and swirling red hair and beard made him look like a snow-covered volcano in mid-eruption, and the rumbling that could be heard deep in the barrel chest suggested that further fireworks were likely.

"Father, we heard a wolfwoman in the forest. . . ."

"Is that all? Well, hunt her tomorrow! Is that the only reason you woke me?" The King had been outraged, and his face had gone almost as red as his flaming hair.

"No," Thirrin had said hurriedly. "Oskan understands their language, and it seems she was part of a relay of messages back to The-Land-of-the-Ghosts."

By this time the King had marched over to the chair he used during the day and was pummeling the cushions to his liking. He stopped and looked up, his eyes narrowing with interest.

"What did she say?" he'd asked.

"She was calling a gathering! A gathering of the Wolf-folk . . ."

"Odin!" Redrought had boomed in amazement. "What else?"

Thirrin had paused, unconsciously raising the tension. "She

said that she didn't think they'd be in time to fulfill their oath to the Princess."

The King had leaped to his feet and turned to Oskan. "Do you know which direction this message came from?"

For a moment Oskan had quailed under Redrought's fierce gaze, but then he'd answered. "She was calling to others in a relay to the north, so it must have come from the south."

"The Polypontus, then," the King said, and then astonished Oskan by smiling. "It looks like we're going to meet General Scipio Bellorum at last, eh, Thirrin?"

"Yes, Dad. At last." And she'd smiled, too.

In the warmth of his bed afterward, it all seemed unreal to Oskan. With an amazing speed, the King had sent out messages to all points of the compass calling out the fyrd and ordering the regiments of royal housecarls to march south immediately. Redrought, though, seemed to be planning to follow the day after Yule with the cavalry. Obviously he didn't think the invasion was imminent and was coolly determined to enjoy the Yuletide Feast before going anywhere.

"Do you think the Lady Theowin will know what's going on?" Thirrin had then asked.

"Certain to," Redrought had answered. "Her scouts keep a close eye on the border every day of the year. She and her housecarls will keep any invading force busy until we get there. But judging by what your new allies the Wolf-folk were saying, the invasion hasn't happened yet; they were just worried they wouldn't be ready in time to help."

Thirrin had glowed with pleasure. Her insistence on an alliance with at least some of the creatures from The-Land-of-the-Ghosts was already paying off. But then Redrought had begun to doubt the reports of the emergency.

"You are *fluent* in wolf speech, aren't you?" he'd boomed at Oskan.

"Oh yes, sir," Oskan had answered confidently. "My mother taught me before I could even read or write."

"You can read!" Redrought had bellowed in surprise. Picking up his precious *Book of the Ancestors* that still lay next to his chair, he opened it at random and told Oskan to read where his finger pointed. Oskan had done so, and when Redrought had looked inquiringly at Grimswald and the old chamberlain had nodded, he'd grunted in satisfaction and smiled.

"You have a learned adviser, Daughter! Use him well." Both Oskan and Thirrin had blushed at that, and the King laughed hugely.

"Now, Grimswald, bring my cloak and boots! We're going to the lookout tower to see if Thirrin's allies are saying anything else about General Scipio Bellorum."

Oskan shivered in his bed as he remembered the icy cold of the winds blowing about the high tower that reared above the battlements of Frostmarris. The city lay below them, tiny and hard-looking under the moonlight, like an exquisite toy carved out of crystal. He'd stared in fascination at the tangled pattern of streets and alleyways that tied a knot of connections between the four main gates of the city, but then he'd tensed as the thin wailing of the Wolf-folk slipped through the cold night air like a blade.

The voice was torn to tatters by the wind, and Oskan had to wait for the cycle of howling to begin again before he had it all.

"Well?" the King had boomed through a storm cloud of steaming breath. "What are they saying?"

"It's a reply from the north," Oskan had answered. "The muster has begun, but they expect it to take months to gather all their warriors together. They say the invasion will happen before that, perhaps in less than a week, but they'll be ready to help the Princess . . . if she still lives."

"Hmm, optimistic bunch," Redrought had said in a tone that was quiet for him.

"There's something else," Oskan had then said. "The Wolf-folk say they could have warned the Princess directly, but they didn't think they could have reached Frostmarris without being killed by the city guards before they'd even seen her."

"Good point," the King admitted. "Still, we know now, thanks to you, Oskan. The fyrd has been called out over the whole country. My professional housecarls will set off within the hour and begin a forced march south, and I'll lead out the cavalry the day after Yule. We should overtake the housecarls by the following day and arrive together in the Southern Riding the day after that."

"Five days," Thirrin had said quietly. "And the Wolf-folk expect the invasion within a week."

"Well, I don't expect it before the week's up," Redrought had said confidently. "I've heard nothing from Lady Theowin yet, and her scouts will certainly have noticed any buildup of troops below the southern border. So it can only just have started to happen. It's no easy matter maneuvering an army the size of old Scipio Bellorum's, you know. I don't expect anything to happen for a good eight or nine days yet."

"But you yourself have said that Bellorum has won most of his wars by the sheer size of his armies, iron discipline, *and* by doing the unexpected," Thirrin had pointed out.

"That's right. But he doesn't know we're ready for him, does he?"

* * *

Oskan snuggled down under the blankets and continued to mull over the meeting with Thirrin and her father. There was no denying that both were deeply worried by the threat of invasion, but there was something that overrode even that: They were both looking forward to it! Oskan was sure that neither could wait to get out onto the field of battle and test themselves against the mighty army of the Polypontus and most of all against the legendary skill and daring of the great General Scipio Bellorum. Oskan was appalled. The threat of war filled him with an honest terror. When he'd told Thirrin about the omen of the late snows, it had all seemed somehow remote and unconnected with his own reality. But now that the Wolf-folk were mustering and the King had called out the fyrd, it all seemed horribly real. In his imagination's terrified ear, he could almost hear the heavy tread of the Empire's army as it advanced on the little land. But nobody else in the royal household seemed particularly worried; Oskan knew that everyone from the loftiest baron to the lowliest scullion would know every detail by now. And yet he could clearly hear the first stirrings of the castle as the household prepared for Yule Day, as though war and its threat of death and chaos weren't hanging over them all.

But perhaps they were just hiding their true feelings and getting on with life as best they could. After all, when he went over the facts himself, he had to admit there was nothing he could actually do about it. The housecarls had set out and the fyrd had been raised, and no amount of his worrying would alter a thing. Perhaps this relaxed attitude to horrific situations was infectious, he thought, as at last he settled down and drifted off to sleep.

Outside, the Wolf-folk continued to howl, their messages

taking on a note of urgency that anyone could have recognized if they'd been listening, but Oskan slept on warm and, for the moment, safe in his bed. The moon set in a glory of silver, and slowly the solstice dawn lightened the eastern sky. The castle bustled with Yuletide preparations that filled every corridor and hall with delicious smells and an excited hum of activity. But still Oskan slept on, until at last he was awoken several hours later by a hammering on his door and a heavily armored palace guard bursting into the room.

"Princess Thirrin commands your presence in the Great Hall! She says if you look too sleepy I'm to tip you out of bed and drag you along as you are!" The soldier looked at him sharply, and Oskan sat up, his eyes wide open.

"I'm awake! It'll only take me a moment to dress!"

The guard nodded curtly and disappeared. Oskan clambered out of bed and started to throw on his clothes. It was while he was struggling to pull his shirt over his head that the sweet sound of singing slowly reached him through the cloth and filled him with an excited sense of the day. It was Yule! The death of the old year and the birth of the new.

It was a day he'd always loved, and he sat on the bed for a moment as he remembered decorating the cave with his mother. She'd always known exactly where to find the glossiest holly with the brightest berries. And she'd always taken him with her when she'd set off into the forest in search of mistletoe. Once, they'd found a grove of twisted old crab apple trees that were bent almost double under the weight of the strange pale-leafed plant growing on them. But even so, she'd still bowed gravely to the trees and asked permission before cutting a bunch of the mistletoe with a strangely marked sickle.

He could still remember the cave, spicy with the scent of evergreen foliage and the smell of delicious roasting and baking. In fact, Yule was one of the few occasions when his mother would hint at who his father might have been. He knew better than to pester her about it, but he'd stored away the nuggets of information to think about later.

"It was this time of year when I first saw him," she'd said one day while gathering holly. "Tall, he was, and as slender and pale as a silver birch."

"But who was he, Mother? What was his name?"

She'd smiled mysteriously then and said, "His sort never tell their names. Whoever knows their names has power over them, so only the closest of their own kind have such knowledge."

"Then can't you at least tell me who his *kind* were?"

"Oh, they're the oldest ones. The Elders of all thinking beings. Can't you guess? Haven't I given you enough clues?"

Oskan thought perhaps she had. "Was he powerful? Was he good?"

"All of that sort have Power. And as for *good*, well, who knows? They choose between light and dark, that sort — it's a choice they all have to make. A choice you'll have to make one day, too."

So vivid were his memories that he could almost feel the breeze that had been blowing through the forest that day stroking his skin again, and with it came the smell of the pies and pastries that his mother had baked for Yule. But then he came to and realized the aroma was coming from the palace kitchens, and that reminded him he was expected by Thirrin for Yule breakfast.

He finished dressing and hurried out into the corridor, which seemed almost as busy as a road on market day. Servants hurried to and fro carrying trays and baskets of food, and richly dressed guests walked with as much speed as dignity would allow. Oskan had been shown to his room by a guard in the dead of night when almost on the point of collapsing with exhaustion, so exactly where he was in the palace was a mystery. But he noticed all of the guests were heading in the same direction and, guessing the corridor led to the Great Hall, he hastened to follow them.

When he reached the end of the passageway, he almost fell into the massive space that old men still called the Mead Hall. The noise, color, and scents were overpowering as musicians played and choristers sang; brightly dressed courtiers and servants rushed about, and excited wolfhounds barked and chased one another around the tables that were already filling up with guests. At the head of the hall, Redrought sat on his huge throne dressed in a rich deep green robe that exactly matched the boughs of holly that hung from the rafters and lined the walls. He wore the ancient iron crown of the House of Lindenshield, and as King he was the only one allowed to wear a sword under that massive roof. Even the palace guards carried only spears and clubs.

Redrought sat in dignified silence as the servants bustled around. But after watching them for a moment he threw dignity aside and started a bellowed conversation with one of the merchants who sat at the top end of one of the long rows of tables. Judging from the way the King kept stroking his robe and holding his sleeve up to the light so that he could admire the color, Oskan guessed that the merchant was a member of the Cloth and Weavers Guild and that Redrought was more than pleased with his Yuletide robe.

The High Table was set at right angles to row upon row of long trestle tables that completely filled the Great Hall. And as Oskan stood and watched, they were filling up quickly as guests arrived and found a good place as close to the dais and the King as possible. There was a definite order of precedence, with the richer merchants near the top end, the less wealthy in the center, and the peasantry who'd been lucky enough to be invited crammed down at the lower end near the great doors. The nobility sat with the King at the top table and noting this, Oskan scanned it, looking for Thirrin. She wasn't there, but he noticed a smaller throne standing next to Redrought's that not even the most important of the barons or baronesses had tried to sit in.

She hadn't arrived yet, then. So much for threatening to have him dragged out of bed if he didn't hurry, Oskan thought. And he was just turning to make his way down to the bottom end of one of the tables when a huge brassy fanfare blew and the hall fell silent. Into the sudden quiet strode the slender figure of Thirrin Freer Strong-in-the-Arm Lindenshield. She was wearing a simple dress of sky blue and on her head a circlet of silver set with a huge sapphire. Oskan stared; he'd never seen her in anything other than battle dress before. Even her hair, usually braided and tucked up under a helmet, now hung loose in a glorious blaze of red-gold, and her eyes shone with excitement as she looked out over the hall. As it was her fourteenth birthday, she was, in effect, the guest of honor and so had precedence over even the King.

Thirrin would have been surprised if she'd known what Oskan and many other people were thinking. *Beautiful* was a word used for grown women, for her mother and one or two of the young noblewomen who sometimes came to court. She was just Thirrin, fourteen years old today and tired after a bad night's sleep. She thought she'd been restless because of the coming war but didn't really believe it. Far more likely was that it had been Yuletide Eve and the night before her birthday, when she'd be officially presented to the court and proclaimed heir.

She'd eventually fallen asleep only to be troubled by strange dreams. In one, she'd been riding her stallion in full war armor and beside her ran a truly enormous cat, a leopard, she thought. But it was unlike any leopard she'd ever seen in the books of her tutor, Maggiore Totus. Its coat was mainly a brilliant white with spots that ranged from silver-gray to the deepest black. But the strangest of all was the fact that she wasn't hunting it or it hunting her. In the dream she felt an enormous affection for the animal, and she felt proud to be with it and almost humble — a feeling, Thirrin reminded herself, that she didn't often feel! Maggiore Totus would tell her that it was a classic anxiety dream, but she hadn't felt in the least bit anxious, only proud and happy.

She looked now to see if Maggiore was at the top end of one of the tables, skillfully denying to herself that she was actually looking for Oskan. The Yuletide bustle and noise had reasserted itself, and people began milling around again as they jockeyed for space as close to the High Table as they could get. So when Thirrin eventually spotted the witch's son, she was surprised to see him standing directly in front of her, his mouth hanging open in a slightly imbecilic way.

The sight of him annoyed her, and not only because of his sagging mouth. In the chaos that had followed the news of war, she'd forgotten to send the new robes she'd bought him for Yule, and he was still wearing the threadbare tunic and leggings he always wore.

Not deigning to call directly down to him, she beckoned to a chamberlain and spoke quietly into his ear. Oskan watched as the man then walked from her side, stepped down off the dais where Thirrin sat at the High Table, and hurried over to him.

"Her Royal Highness suggests you close your mouth before one of the wolfhounds does something unspeakable in it."

Oskan's jaw snapped shut with a loud click. "She also wishes you to take a place at the head of the central table."

Oskan had been heading for the section reserved for the peasantry near the great doors, but now he shyly made for the table the head of which was directly opposite Thirrin's throne. The fat merchant who already sat there looked at Oskan's worn tunic and was about to loudly tell him exactly where he should go, when the chamberlain whispered something in his ear and nodded at the High Table. Thirrin's coldest gaze was already leveled at the merchant, and he quickly shuffled farther down the bench without another word.

Opposite Oskan sat a small dark man who wore small pieces of glass set in a frame in front of each eye. Oskan was fascinated by this contraption and stared in amazement. The small man returned his gaze, and Oskan noticed that his eyes looked enormous behind the glass.

"Oh, of course! They make things larger, like a bead of dew will magnify the blade of grass it hangs on."

"Exactly right, young man! These are my *spectoculums*, especially designed by myself, to correct my myopia, or 'dim sight,' as you may say." He stood and extended a small and very clean hand. "May I introduce myself? I am Maggiore Totus, tutor to the Princess Thirrin."

Oskan shook his hand gravely. "I am Oskan, known as the Witch's Son . . . er, Thirrin's friend, or should I say friend of Princess Thirrin Freer Strong-in-the —"

"'Thirrin's friend' will do nicely," Maggiore interrupted gently. "Very nicely indeed. And may I say that I'm enormously pleased that she's made the acquaintance of such an intelligent young man. Nobody else has ever rightly guessed the nature of my spectoculums before. I'm very impressed."

Oskan felt himself growing warm with a mixture of pleasure

and embarrassment, but despite this he couldn't help noticing the small man's rich accent. "You're not from the Icemark, are you? Your name makes that pretty obvious, but your voice, too . . . it sings."

Maggiore smiled. "No, I'm from the northern shores of the Southern Continent, where the sun is enormously generous and ice is only ever found in cooling drinks. And soon I'll be going home, now that the Princess is reaching the limit of her patience with schooling." His voice had become wistful, and his spectoculummed eyes stared into a distance of imagined olive groves and small mountain villages honeyed with sun and quiet in their gentle dust. "At least I *hope* to be going home soon, but this rumor of war may mean the ports will be closed and the seas unsafe to travel. We shall have to see."

Thirrin watched Oskan and Maggiore chatting together with approval. There was something very similar about their natures. Both seemed fascinated by the world around them, and both knew so much. She was sure they'd find plenty to talk about. And now, safe in the knowledge that her two favorite guests were entertaining each other, she could concentrate on the High Table and the talk of the coming war. But before she could say anything, a fanfare rang out and the sweet singing of Yule filled the hall.

The hubbub died down, and all eyes turned to watch as the great doors opened and a choir of boys and women paced slowly into the hall. Behind them walked dozens and dozens of servants carrying platters and other containers of every imaginable sort of food, and at the head of the procession walked Grimswald, the chief chamberlain, carrying a huge round loaf of bread. Thirrin couldn't help noticing the lack of the housecarls' bass notes that would usually have been part of the choir. Almost as though Redrought had read her thoughts, he suddenly leaped to his feet and added his own hugely deep voice to the singing. Down the center of the hall walked the procession, skirting the massive central hearth where the Yule log would burn, and traveling slowly up to the dais where the King waited. For a moment or two longer the sweet ancient song threaded into the quiet, slowly wafting up to the rafters and echoing back from the roof, so that the singers seemed to be accompanying themselves in a tumbled choral round. Then at last it died away like a gentle sigh, the King drew his sword, and as Grimswald held up the round loaf of bread, Redrought cut it in two.

A roar rose up from the hall, and the servants scattered to all points of the room and started serving the food. More and more scullions poured through the doors carrying yet more delicious food, and the long minstrels' gallery that jutted out above the great doors was suddenly full of musicians playing a tumbling dance tune.

Thirrin waited patiently for the noble guests at the head table to finish the first course of their Yuletide breakfast, then, as the scullions cleared away the debris, she asked, "What's the news on the calling of the fyrd? Has all gone smoothly?"

"Not a hitch or problem anywhere," Redrought answered, his powerful voice easily rising above the noise in the hall. "I'm more than pleased. Yule's a bad time to call out the fyrd, people want to be with their families, but everything's in order and working as it should."

Thirrin sat back and listened intently as each of the lords and ladies at the table added detail to this, but overall the reports were the same. All was going well. She already knew the disposition and strengths of each regiment likely to engage the enemy, so when Redrought started to fill in details for those with less knowledge, she sat back and let her eyes wander over the hall.

Already the tumblers and acrobats were leaping skillfully around the tables in a dazzle of sequins. One had even managed to leap from the shoulders of his partner and reach one of the dozen or so crossbeams that stretched across the width of the hall. He sat there now, calling down to the crowds below and deftly catching the small morsels of food they threw up to him.

Thirrin smiled. She loved this early part of Yule Day. Everyone was still boisterous and full of energy, but by mid-afternoon most would be sleeping in snoring heaps or holding deeply earnest conversations with people they'd probably just met. Her eyes wandered on, and came to rest on Oskan and Maggiore Totus. They already seemed to have reached that stage. They were bent over the table between them, their heads close together as they talked. She watched them, trying to make out what they were discussing, but it was impossible. Probably the life expectancy of the earthworm, she thought dismissively. But she continued to watch them for several minutes, trying to ignore a growing desire to leave the High Table and join them. She felt inexplicably annoyed with Oskan, and after trying to find a reason for her irritation, she decided it was because he hadn't looked her way once in all the time she'd been watching him. Being far too dignified to throw a bread roll at him, she beckoned over a servant, then sent him off to Oskan's table.

"Her Royal Highness requires that you remember her presence," he announced as he reached the two conversationalists. Oskan looked up in surprise. They'd been discussing the wildlife of the forest, and he'd become so absorbed he'd almost forgotten where he was.

"Um . . . tell the Princess we wouldn't dare forget her."

The servant was just bowing stiffly when Maggiore laid his hand gently on his arm. "No. Tell Her Royal Highness that she has never been out of our thoughts, and we remain deeply grateful that she should remember us."

The servant withdrew and delivered his message, and Thirrin looked on them coldly. She was actually as happy and relaxed as she could be, considering the pending invasion, but she wasn't going to let Oskan know that. And as for Maggiore Totus, she had no doubt that he was watching them both and laughing. The fact that the laughter was friendly and affectionate made little difference to her; she still found it annoying.

After that, both Oskan and Maggiore remembered to look up to the High Table and toast Thirrin on a regular basis, but her face remained an unsmiling mask.

By mid-morning the celebrations had reached their noisy height, and a great cheer arose when the double doors burst open and soldiers of the palace guard dragged the enormous Yule log into the hall. It took several minutes to pull it across the flagstones while the guests sang a noisy song of welcome and musicians escorted it to the waiting hearth. Lesser logs were already blazing there, and these would cradle the Yule log above the deep mound of glowing coals that lined the pit of the central hearth.

Ten strong men of the palace guard then heaved the log onto stout iron bars and slowly lowered it onto the waiting flames. For a moment silence descended on the hall, then a single voice sang praise to the Sun that would begin its long return journey after this, the shortest day of the year. As the last note died away, tankards, goblets, and leather jacks were raised in salutation and drained in one movement, and a huge cheer rose to the rafters.

The Imperial army swaggered along the narrow road through the pass, the stamp and thump of each disciplined step telling the world that conquest was coming and nothing could stop it. In less than an hour the road began to widen, and the soldiers caught their first glimpse of the land they were about to add to the Empire.

Baroness Theowin of the Icemark's Southern Riding watched as the Polypontian commander stepped over the border. She was surprised to see that he didn't match any of the descriptions she'd had of Scipio Bellorum, but soon dismissed the puzzle as she prepared to take action. The Baroness had barely had time to call out the fyrd and send word to Frostmarris, but help would still be days away and she had an Empire to fight all alone. She watched the Imperial army swaggering along as though they'd already won their war and put all other thoughts aside.

Commander Lucius Tarquinus of the Polypontian Imperial forces raised his hand, and the army stamped to a halt. The fife-and-drum units that had been filling the freezing air with stirring martial music fell silent, and an expectant hush settled over the soldiers.

Tarquinus now urged his horse on a few steps and then, standing in his stirrups, he called, "*Veni, vidi, vici!*" — the traditional phrase declaimed at the start of each of the Empire's many invasions.

Theowin smiled grimly. "'I came, I saw, I conquered,' eh?" she said, translating the words to herself. "Well, you've certainly come, and undoubtedly you're seeing, but conquest is an entirely different matter." She raised her hand and chopped it down viciously.

Arrows rained down on the Polypontian army. Several staff officers who were riding with the commander fell to the ground and lay unmoving as their horses bolted. For a moment chaos reigned, but then the rigid discipline of the Imperial troops reasserted itself and they fell back in good order, their shields raised above their heads as they withdrew. Commander Tarquinus trotted his horse gently back to his army, almost as though he were out for a pleasant ride, and immediately took control.

He'd noted the approximate position of the enemy hidden behind an outcrop of rocks, and sent out a detachment of heavy infantry who formed a *testudo,* or tortoise — shields were locked to form a roof and walls all around the unit, protecting the soldiers inside.

Baroness Theowin immediately gave orders for the archers to withdraw, and they melted away into the hills. Then, with a nod at her cavalry, she led them in a smashing charge, screeching and howling the Icemark war cry as they roared down on the infantry.

Horse and rider smashed into the shields, and a rending clang like an unholy bell echoed over the land. For a vicious few moments cavalry saber and infantry sword hacked and stabbed at one another, but then, just as Tarquinus was sending out reinforcements, the Baroness and her troopers withdrew, streaming over the frozen ground to disappear among the gullies and canyons of the borderland.

After another two hours or so, the midday meal was brought in. This was only made obvious by the fact that there was even more food on the tables, and the guests turned to the task of eating with huge sighs and shaking heads. But somehow they managed, after which some of the less able began to slip into quiet sleep amid the uproar of singing, shouting, and laughter.

Thirrin had been discussing the relevant advantages and disadvantages of the longbow over the matchlock musket with the Baron of the Middle Riding when she noticed that Oskan had stood up and was looking toward the back of the Great Hall. She followed his gaze and watched as the massive doors swung open and a warning shout rang out. Silence as complete and deadly as the midwinter chill fell on the hall, and all eyes watched as ten men of the Palace Guard marched forward dragging a werewolf between them.

Its arms had been tied to the shaft of a spear that ran across its shoulders, and a thick chain hobbled its legs, forcing it to shuffle along with ridiculous mincing steps. But the guards kept their distance, pressing their spears so hard into its flesh that Thirrin could see blood trickling over its thick black pelt. Enraged, she leaped to her feet, and before the strange party had reached the dais where she sat, her angry voice cut into the silence.

"Set him free!" The guards stopped and looked at her in amazement. "Set my ally free *now*, and let him approach the High Table."

The Princess seemed almost to blaze as her red hair stood out about her head in a halo of wrath, and the guards hurried to release the werewolf. A sigh went up as the chains fell away and its hands were released from the spear shaft. It stood rubbing its wrists for a moment, then strode toward the dais. The guards immediately snatched up their spears and formed a shield-wall in front of the High Table.

"Put down your spears and stand aside!" Thirrin snapped. The commander of the guard looked at Redrought, who nodded in silence, then as the soldiers parted slowly, the werewolf stepped up to the table and dropped to one knee. The intense silence that had descended on the hall again was broken only by a whimpering and snuffling sound as the creature contorted its face in an effort to use human speech. Then at last a sudden explosion of sound burst out of its mouth.

"Hail, Princess Thirrin Freer Strong-in-the-Arm Lindenshield, heir to the human kingdom of the Icemark. Greetings from My Lord, King Grishmak of the Wolf-folk." The great belch of gruff sound echoed from the stone walls of the hall, and Thirrin nodded in reply.

"Greetings to my ally King Grishmak. What news does his envoy have for us?"

"My Lady, your land is invaded! The Wolf-folk are mustering, but we fear we'll be too late." The wolfman had gained some control over his voice and the volume was a little lower, but still it echoed over the otherwise silent hall. "Already the armies of the Polypontus have marched through the mountain pass in the south, and your people are fighting to stop them."

"They've invaded already?" Redrought boomed. "When? What time? How many?"

"At dawn this morning, and their numbers are more than ten times the army of your people that stand against them."

"Ten times!" Redrought bellowed. "I need precise numbers, details, types of weaponry. But I don't suppose you people can count."

The creature drew itself up to its full height and looked Redrought in the eye. "Nothing escapes my people if they want to see it. I know now my news is not entirely unexpected. You must have known war was coming even if you don't know how many fighters they have. But my people *can* count, so I can tell you the Polypontians have twenty thousand horse soldiers, thirty thousand that carry sticks that kill with noise, and fifty thousand soldiers with long spears. And they also have with them metal tubes on wheels, like the sticks that kill with noise but bigger."

"Cannons!" said Thirrin. "How many?"

"Two hundred."

"One hundred thousand troops and two hundred cannons!" Redrought gasped. "The Lady Theowin and her housecarls will never hold them." He suddenly stood up and called the names of his commanders, and figures began hurrying from all points of the hall. "Cerdic, Gunlath, Eobold, Aethelstan. Call in your cavalry and send out riders to the outlying towns. The muster is brought forward. We ride in two hours!"

"But, My Lord!" Commander Aethelstan protested. "How can we be certain this isn't some trick of the Vampire King and Queen? How can we be sure they're not drawing our best troops to the south so they can attack from the north?"

"Because King Grishmak is my ally!" Thirrin cried. "And because Oskan Witch's Son heard and translated the messages of the Wolf-folk last night. They couldn't have known we would understand their howling."

"So that's how you knew," said the werewolf. "Where is this human who knows our tongue?"

"The son of a witch could easily be an ally of The-Land-of-the-Ghosts. How do we know he's not part of a conspiracy?" Aethelstan persisted.

Thirrin's blue eyes blazed with a hating rage, but before she could speak, a huge shout from the rear of the hall drew all eyes to a travel-stained soldier being escorted to the dais by two Palace Guards. He stopped in front of the King, saluted, and laid an arrow on the table.

"My Lord, I'm from the Southern Riding, sent with the Arrow of Calling by the Lady Theowin. The Polypontus has invaded, and our housecarls are heavily outnumbered."

Redrought gave a bark of laughter. "There, I think, is your answer, Aethelstan. All fears are brushed aside. Now waste no more time, and muster your troops!"

"But what of the numbers of this invading army, My Lord? One hundred thousand must be wrong. How can we expect creatures like this to count accurately?" Aethelstan asked stubbornly.

The King's color deepened and his voice rumbled dangerously as he spoke. "I assume you'll accept the report of this soldier?" Without waiting for an answer, he turned to the messenger. "Well?"

"My Lord, the army of the Polypontus is huge. They have fifty thousand pikemen, thirty thousand musketeers, and twenty thousand cavalry troopers. In addition, they have two hundred cannons. The fyrd and housecarls of the Southern Riding are outnumbered ten to one."

Redrought turned a bloodshot eye on Aethelstan. "I think, Commander, that answers every single one of your doubts. Somehow I think the armies of the Polypontus are the least of your worries. You've earned the disapproval of the Princess Thirrin. You'd better make yourself scarce and muster your force!"

The King now drew his sword and clambered onto the table. "Foes are in the land of the Icemark!" he roared in his loudest war voice. "They kill our people and threaten our cities, they burn our farms and make slaves of our children. Blood! Blast! And Fire!"

The Palace Guard began to beat spear on shield, and a slow chant began in a relentless rhythm that swelled and grew to a crashing noise that beat against the roof of the hall. "OUT! Out! Out! OUT! Out! Out! OUT! Out! Out!"

Everyone in the Great Hall took it up, beating the tables with fist, plate, and knife and stamping the floor so that it sounded as though a great army of giants was marching out to crush the puny soldiers of the Polypontus. "OUT! Out! Out! OUT! Out! Out! OUT! Out! Out!"

And in all that enormous excitement of fighting spirit, only Oskan noticed that the terrible warlike figure of Redrought Strong-in-the-Arm Lindenshield, Bear of the North, Drinker of Blood, was still wearing his fluffy slippers and that Primple-puss the kitten was peeping out of his shirt collar to see what all the noise was about.

8

Thirrin was bitterly disappointed. Her Yule present from Redrought, a new cavalry saddle, lay where she'd dumped it in the corner of her room, and she'd managed to put a dent in her shield-boss when she'd smashed it in a temper against the wall. The King was going to war without her! She was fuming. At first she'd thought it the worst possible humiliation, but after the first moments of rage and disappointment had passed, she'd had time to think, and slowly her attitude had changed. Redrought might not be taking her to fight the great army of the Polypontus, but before the entire assembly of the royal household he'd proclaimed her his Regent and given her the Great Ring of State. The Power of Rule was now hers in the King's absence, and not only that but he'd given her a battle name. She was now officially to be known as Thirrin Freer Strong-in-the-Arm Lindenshield, Wildcat of the North.

Wildcat of the North — she liked it. She liked it very much. She looked at herself in the mirror that had been imported from the Southern Continent and smiled. But she didn't have long to enjoy the moment. There were things to do. The King would be riding with his cavalry in less than an hour and the city had to be evacuated.

A hasty council of war had decided that since the roads were clear of snow, any victorious enemy would be able to sweep north into Frostmarris and capture it and its citizens before any defense could be mustered by the small garrison that would be left behind. Far better for the people of Frostmarris to retreat to the north and seek refuge in the province held by the Hypolitan. This was a separate people of fierce warriors who also lived within the borders of the Icemark and owed fealty to the King. Thirrin's mother had been a member of their aristocracy, and her marriage to King Redrought had strengthened the already close bonds between the two races.

From their province a counterattack could be mounted in the spring. The snows might be late, but they would eventually come, and then not even the mighty armies of the Polypontus would be able to move. Plenty of time over the long months of the winter to make plans for war.

As Thirrin ran over this in her mind, she was arming herself in her best panoply: mail-shirt, helmet, shield, heavy cavalry saber, and short-hafted battle-ax. Its comforting weight and familiarity steadied her nerves and gave her an added sense of purpose, not that she needed much help. She'd already sent out her first commands to the chief burghers of the city to begin the evacuation of Frostmarris. All of the wagons and horses would be waiting at designated muster points, and the citizens would be gathering with the few possessions they'd be allowed to take with them. Redrought had long ago drawn up his war plans, and they'd been practiced time and again by army and citizen. The only difference this time was that it was for real. One of the few advantages of being a small country with many enemies in a dangerous world was the people's readiness to face trouble without much complaint.

Thirrin buckled her belt, fastened the last strap, and strode to the door. She was just turning the handle when an obvious and devastating thought struck her. All of the plans and evacuations assumed Redrought would be defeated and killed! She stood with her head resting against the woodwork of the door as the realization sank in. She was making plans for her dad's death.

Redrought: the huge man with the voice like a storm in the mountains, with a laugh like a rockslide, and with an almost childish sense of fun. Whenever she thought of him as King, she remembered his victories in battle and his ability to run a country. But as Dad, he was the man who'd brought her up, who'd played mountain bears with her as a little girl, chasing her along the corridors of the palace, roaring hugely, and pretending to eat her when he scooped her off her feet. As Dad, he was the man who loved cats and complained of his corns and had a collection of ridiculous fluffy slippers. What would she do if he were killed in battle?

For a moment panic threatened to swallow her up, but then she squared her shoulders and threw back her head. What would she do? She'd be a worthy daughter by avenging his death and leading her people with bravery and style. She was Thirrin Freer Strong-in-the-Arm Lindenshield, Wildcat of the North, and if her father were killed in battle, he would have earned his rightful place in Valhalla and could rest happy in the knowledge of her strength.

She pushed open the door and strode into the corridor. The palace was seething like a kicked ants' nest. Servants hurried backward and forward, soldiers rushed around on last-minute errands, while wolfhounds bayed and howled as they caught the mood. Most of the Yule guests had left already, scattering to their homes to prepare for the emergency. Thirrin was looking for Maggiore and Oskan. Her first act as Regent had been to set the evacuation plan of the city in progress and her second had been to appoint her now ex-tutor and the witch's son as her official advisers.

Oskan had seemed confused when the King had nodded his agreement to their appointment and when the housecarls of the palace guard had roared their approval, he'd flinched as though they were going to hit him. Despite the emergency of the moment, Thirrin grinned. She knew there was more to the Witch's Son than met the eye: something unusual, probably *magical*, though exactly what form it might take she just wasn't sure yet. But whatever it turned out to be, she was determined to make good use of it.

She arrived in her father's quarters to find the King sitting comfortably in his chair while Grimswald scurried around opening chests and snapping at the servants. Oskan and Maggiore stood nearby, the older man sipping from a fine glass of cut crystal while the witch's son chewed his nails. As she strode forward, Thirrin slapped Oskan's hands down from his mouth, and he shamefacedly put them behind his back.

"Ah, Thirrin, good. The muster's almost complete, so we've got ten minutes or so to finalize things," Redrought boomed happily.

"Finalize things?"

"Yes. I'm leaving Primplepuss with you," he said, stroking the little cat fondly. "Make sure she's fed properly and fuss over her, otherwise she'll fret."

"Yes, Dad," Thirrin replied, feeling that such a momentous time in the history of the country needed to be marked by something more significant than feeding instructions for the royal kitten.

"Oh, and I'm also leaving Grimswald with you."

A sudden clatter as the old chamberlain dropped a piece of the King's armor clearly showed he hadn't been told about this.

"But, My Lord, I've always accompanied you on campaign! Who else will attend to your needs? Who else knows exactly how you like your bedchamber set out?"

"No one, Grimmy," the King said kindly. "But I'm moving fast and your old mule will never keep up."

"Even so, the King has a dignity and a sense of estate to maintain," the old chamberlain insisted. "I could follow at my own pace and rendezvous with you later, after the battle."

Redrought fell unusually silent, then said carefully, "I probably won't need your services after the battle, Grimmy."

In the quiet that followed this, Thirrin's eyes filled with tears and Grimswald began to weep, blowing his nose noisily and looking at the King like a small child watching a parent unexpectedly leaving forever.

"Besides," Redrought boomed at something like his usual level, "you're too old. If you were a horse, I'd have put you out to pasture years ago . . . or eaten you."

The old chamberlain smiled at that, as the King had intended him to. "Now, make sure all of the maps and charts are packed. I think some were left in the council chamber."

Grimswald bowed, then almost shyly he took the King's hand and held it for a moment. Then, blushing at breaking the rules of etiquette, he scurried off on his errand. Redrought turned to his daughter. "Keep him by you, Thirrin. There's no one better at organizing a palace, and State occasions are his speciality. You never know, there may be a time again when the Queen of the Icemark will need his knowledge of precedence and procedure. Besides, thirty years of service shouldn't end on a battlefield."

"I'll make sure he's all right, Dad," Thirrin answered quietly.

"Good," Redrought said with a note of finality. Then he added, "The Icemark will be yours soon, Thirrin. You've been groomed and trained for this, so you know what you're doing."

"Yes, Dad," Thirrin whispered, unable to trust her voice.

"With no snows blocking the roads I'm going to have to break this invasion force, if I can. Otherwise the whole of the country's going to be wide open and no one will be ready enough to try to stop them. But if I do manage to destroy them, there'll be nothing left of our army. And then you'll need all the help you can get, because the Polypontus will send another force. Old Scipio Bellorum won't give up that easily. Once the snows have come, you'll be safe for the rest of the winter and you can get ready for the spring offensive. You've made allies of the Wolf-folk; perhaps there are others who'll help."

"Who?"

"I'm not sure. . . . To the north, beyond The-Land-of-the-Ghosts. There are rumors of a people of some sort. But I don't know. Find out. There are friends to be had with the unlikeliest faces."

"And the Vampire King and Queen?"

"Well, they have the unlikeliest faces of all. But if anyone can make allies of them, you can. You're different. Perhaps it's your mother in you; you get more and more like her every day. When you smile, I see her again, my brave young shield-maiden of the Hypolitan." He smiled at her sadly.

A sudden commotion outside the door signaled the arrival of a messenger to tell the King the muster was complete.

Thirrin hurried forward, hugged Redrought fiercely, and kissed him. She was achingly aware that this was probably the last time she'd see her father. "I love you, Dad," she whispered in his ear. Then she stepped back, her face sternly set as the soldier marched in.

Redrought held up his hand and the trooper waited quietly. "Maggiore Totus and Oskan Witch's Son, you both hold the sacred office of Royal Adviser. Are you up to the task?"

"No, My Lord," Oskan blurted out.

"Good!" Redrought boomed, his voice getting back up to its normal level. "I'd have been worried if you thought you were. Just say what you feel honestly and ignore her snarling; it'll make her think all the harder."

"Don't worry, My Lord," said Maggiore in his gentle singsong voice. "We'll look after her as best we can."

The King smiled at him warmly and then picked up his shield. "Well, off we go!" he bellowed at the young soldier who had been waiting quietly. "We've a bit of a scrap waiting for us."

After the door had slammed behind them, a huge vacuum of silence filled the room. Primplepuss, who'd been watching everything closely from her place on Redrought's chair, stood and stared after them. But the door remained shut, and after a while she looked at Thirrin and opened her mouth in a tiny silent meow.

An icy wind kept the battlefield clear of the smoke from musket and cannon fire, so Redrought had a clear view of the fighting. He and the Lady Theowin were sitting on their horses on a hill overlooking the rocky ground locked between the mountain range called the Dancing Maidens and the frozen River Freme, where the two armies were struggling to destroy each other. For a moment the King was struck by the incredible beauty of battle. The pipes and drums of the Polypontian army shrilled and rattled whenever the wind blew in their direction, and the different regiments moved with a precision and grace Redrought found almost moving. The enemy soldiers were brilliant with color, wearing highly polished breastplates over trousers and doublets of red, yellow, or blue, depending on which regiment they belonged to. These, along with the sashes and plumes that were also a part of their uniform, almost shone in contrast to the steel and leather of Redrought's army.

On the left wing the housecarls of the South Farthing were advancing against a line of musketeers and pikemen, while in the center the infantry of the fyrd were holding their own surprisingly well against Polypontian swordsmen. Up on the hill, Redrought found it was almost possible to forget the pain and blood of war. But when the wind shifted, the screams of the wounded washed over them in a huge wave before it shifted again, and once more all became a silent ballet.

He waited for precisely the right moment before giving the signal for the cavalry of the South Farthing to move onto the field, the troopers drawing their sabers as one in a graceful arc that glittered in the sun. Then a clarion rang out, and the horses leaped to a full gallop, feinting a charge at the Polypontian center where their musketeers fired a volley and the pikemen closed ranks, ready to receive the shock of onset. But at the last moment the cavalry swung away in a controlled turn before finally smashing as a solid wall of horse and steel into the enemy's right wing. Redrought could see clearly as the battle-trained horses lashed out with their hooves at the line before them and the cavalry troopers hacked at the Polypontian soldiers. For a moment the enemy line wavered, giving ground before the ferocity of the attack, but then a reserve regiment of infantry swiftly moved up and the position was saved.

Redrought was deeply impressed by the discipline the invaders had shown throughout. At first he'd been disappointed that Scipio Bellorum himself wasn't in command of the army, but whoever this general was, he was wily and determined, if a little lacking in imagination. "Battle tactics by the book," Redrought had commented to the Lady Theowin as the Polypontian army reacted almost mechanically to each problem he sent them. "It'll be an awful shock when they find they've lost."

This was the second day of the battle, and it was almost time for the final throw. The Lady Theowin had fought a brilliant holding action until the King had arrived, using her small force to harry and slow down the Polypontians so that they'd hardly moved more than a mile from the mountain pass they'd managed to force. The terrain was obviously rocky so close to the mountains, and the steep scree slopes and canyons had made ideal ambush points from which Theowin had led almost suicidal hit-and-run raids.

Redrought looked at her surreptitiously now as she calmly watched the battle from her horse. She had the profile of a vicious old eagle, he thought, the nasal guard on her helmet barely managing to cover her hugely hooked nose, and her bright blue eyes showed nothing but cold calculation as the battle swung one way, then the other. She'd tied her long steel-gray hair into two braids and coiled them up over each ear so that it looked like she was wearing two smaller helmets just below the rim of her real one. She'd also painted a black line under her eyes and chewed something that dyed her usually strong white teeth bloodred. Redrought shuddered. How many

Polypontian soldiers had seen her fierce old face as their last view of this world before the final dark had taken them? He was only thankful she was on his side.

He turned back to the battle and began his closing moves. He gave the signal, and the battery of ballistas began their barrage, the huge wheel-mounted crossbows sending flight after flight of steel bolts scything into the enemy ranks. One of the few remaining cannons replied, but its range fell well short of Redrought's position. The numbers of the big guns had been reduced by more than three quarters after the first day of the battle when the King had led his cavalry against their batteries. After Redrought had calculated how long it took to reposition each cannon and how long it took to reload, it was a simple matter of outflanking them and charging between salvos. Of course, if the enemy general had been a little more imaginative, he'd have positioned his cannons in defensive circles or squares and protected them with pikemen, but fortunately this general was no Scipio Bellorum. He already had enough of an advantage with his numbers; if he'd had tactical flair as well, the battle would have been lost on the first day.

Redrought now sent his orders to the regiments of longbows and they, too, began to send devastating flights of arrows into the enemy position. It was a huge pity he'd not had more archers to use against them. Their effective range was more than twice that of the muskets, and they could shoot six arrows a minute as opposed to one round fired by the cumbersome guns. On the first day of the battle the longbows had had a brief but bloody duel with the musketeers, during which the archers had devastated their opponents without even coming into their range.

It hadn't all gone the Icemark's way, though. The invading force was huge and superbly disciplined, moving with confidence and bravery against Redrought's soldiers. And even though their general was no genius, he was at least competent and obviously experienced. The fyrd had suffered badly in the opening stages of the battle, and it had taken all of Redrought's cunning and the steadiness of his veteran housecarls to hold the line and prevent a rout. The Lady Theowin had also been an invaluable wild card, striking terror into the enemy wherever she appeared, leading her cavalry in ferocious charges that smashed through the strongest defense, then swept away before the Polypontian cavalry could strike back. Again and again her appearance in the nick of time had saved the day, and the Polypontians had been slowly ground down.

There was one other factor that drove the soldiers of the Icemark to greater heights of courage than they'd ever reached before: Redrought let it be known that he thought Scipio Bellorum had decided not to lead this invasion himself because he thought victory was assured. Their little country would be a pushover, and his army would sweep through the land destroying all opposition and taking what they wanted. They'd enslave the people — the loved ones of the very soldiers who were fighting now against the invaders — they'd steal livestock and property, and then when they'd bled the land dry, they'd destroy whatever they couldn't use. Bellorum probably thought the Icemark would be added to the huge Empire of the Polypontus in less than one campaigning season.

As Redrought had hoped, his soldiers had been incensed: Personal and national pride was at stake, and the Polypontians would pay dearly for every piece of earth they took.

And now it was time for Redrought to play his trump card. The Polypontian general had no idea that he was prepared to sacrifice his entire army to stop their advance. Thirrin had to have enough time to escape to the province of the Hypolitan, and there must be no enemy soldiers left to take advantage of the late snows.

"This is it, then, Theowin," he said to the fierce old baroness who sat on her horse beside him.

"Yes," she answered calmly. Then she continued in a different tone. "But before we go, there's something I'd like to ask you."

Redrought was shocked to hear what sounded almost like a note of panic in her voice. "Ask away. If I can give it, it's yours."

She hesitated as though trying to find the right words, worrying Redrought even more. Then at last she said, "After the Baron died, no man came near me in twenty years. I seem to scare them, for some reason. So . . . I'd like you to kiss me, My Lord. Let me feel a man's beard tickling my face again before I die."

In the silence that followed, the war chant of the housecarls could clearly be heard echoing across the battlefield. "OUT! Out! Out! OUT! Out! Out! OUT! Out! Out!" The fierce determination in the explosive sound gave the King just the level of brute courage he needed, and he suddenly leaned from his saddle and kissed the grim warrior's mouth of the Baroness. Their helmets clashed and rang like bells as the kiss was firmly planted, drawing the attention of the regiment of cavalry waiting in reserve behind the hill, and a huge cheer rose up from the troopers.

Redrought laughed thunderously, then standing in his stirrups he drew his sword and gave the signal to advance. The cavalry fanned out and set off at a slow walk down from the hill. Before him, Redrought could clearly see how over the last two days of fighting his tactics had ground down the Polypontians and forced them on to the defensive. They stood at bay now, surrounded by the army of the Icemark even though they still outnumbered Redrought's force by at least three to one. Perhaps their general hoped that they'd smash themselves to pieces on his superior numbers and that he could ultimately win the war of attrition by sitting and waiting. But he had no chance of that happening: Redrought was ready to end the battle right now.

The archers were still pouring flights of arrows into the enemy ranks, concentrating much of their shooting on the center, knowing exactly where Redrought's hammer blow would fall. The Polypontians had positioned their remaining cannons at the corners of a defensive square, and at the beginning of the day they had devastated the ranks of the Icemark. But Redrought had reacted quickly to the threat and ordered the ballistas to aim their long steel bolts at the batteries. For two hours the duel had been fought, and as a result the guns had fallen as silent as their dead crews. Meanwhile the housecarls kept up a dogged attack on the enemy's left wing, enduring volley after volley of musket fire, then rushing forward with locked shields to hack at the line and force the Polypontians back. And all around, the fyrd seethed like a sea flowing back and forth and leaving a debris of dead like flotsam behind them.

Redrought judged his moment to the last possible second and then, after leaning across to kiss the Lady Theowin again, he stood in his stirrups and roared out the war cry of the Icemark: "Blood! Blast! And Fire! Blood! Blast! And Fire!"

The troopers of the cavalry took it up in a great roar, and as one they leaped forward in a charge that shook the ground beneath them. The archers stepped up their shooting rate and were soon loosing their arrows over the heads of the cavalry, then they laid aside their bows and, drawing swords, they charged forward to support them.

Redrought could hear the chant of the housecarls as his

cavalry bore down on the ranks of the Polypontian army, the wind of his speed making his hair stream and tumble like flames of fire around his helmet. Even now the enemy's discipline held, and they attempted to redress their shattered ranks as the cavalry of the Icemark roared down on them. A salvo of musket fire erupted on to the cold winter air, smashing into the advanced ranks of the cavalry, but it was as effective as throwing stones at an oncoming tidal wave and the charge thundered on. Redrought bellowed his rage, and his stallion echoed him with a squeal as they smashed into the line of soldiers before them. The enemy ranks broke apart, and the cavalry cut deep into the Polypontian position, the Lady Theowin laying about her with a huge battle-ax and the horses striking out at the Polypontian soldiers before them. The housecarls, too, breached the line and steadily carved their way through, chanting as they came. At the center of the Polypontian host, their general watched calmly beneath his battle standard of a running white horse as Redrought's army smashed through his lines. Then, drawing his sword, he roared out an order, and the remains of his once mighty cavalry force leaped forward to meet the soldiers of the Icemark.

Many of the musketeers used their guns as clubs, having no time to reload in the close press of the hand-to-hand fighting, and even some of the pikemen, the most effective of the enemy troops, threw aside their twenty-foot spears and drew their cutlasses. Standing shoulder to shoulder, the Polypontian soldiers hacked and slashed at all before them, but the steadily locked shields of the housecarls bore them back and the wild rush of the fyrd swarmed forward, screaming insanely as they came.

Redrought and his cavalry still pressed on, driving the enemy before them. Then, catching sight of the Polypontian standard, he turned his warhorse to meet it, the animal rearing and screaming a challenge before leaping forward. King and general met in a ringing clash of sword on sword, Redrought forcing back his enemy in a savage display of fighting rage that ended as the Bear of the North broke the general's arm through his shield and then hacked his head from his shoulders. The Polypontians fell back in dismay, but even now their discipline held as they rallied around the battle standard and prepared a defiant last stand around a small hill in the center of the field.

For a moment all fighting ceased. This was the final phase of the battle, and Redrought prepared his cavalry for their last charge. The Imperial lines bristled like a steel hedgehog as the pikemen leveled their spears, and those enemy musketeers who had reloaded their weapons waited in grim silence. The Lady Theowin sat on her horse beside the King, smiling through a mask of blood that ran down her face from a scalp wound while gently wiping the blade of her battle-ax on a delicate lace handkerchief she'd produced from somewhere.

"They'll die hard, Theowin," said Redrought calmly.

"Yes," she agreed. "Good, aren't they?"

"Very. But we've almost destroyed them, and by the time any reinforcements arrive from the Polypontus, the best general in all the Icemark will be waiting for them and not even Scipio Bellorum will be able to beat him."

"The best general in the Icemark?" the Lady Theowin asked. "Who?"

"Oh, you know him well. We all do: General Snow and his ally, Marshal Ice. No army can march through one of their blizzards or pass any road they've blocked."

Theowin laughed. "No army at all," she agreed. Then, pointing with her ax at the Polypontian lines, she said, "Shall we?"

Redrought nodded, and standing in his stirrups he stabbed his sword into the air and roared out the order to advance. With a great shout, the soldiers of the Icemark swept down on the enemy lines. A volley of musket fire rang out at point-blank range, cutting a ragged swath through the fyrd, but still they came on, the entire army shouting the housecarl war chant: "OUT! Out! Out! OUT! Out! Out! OUT! Out! Out!"

Redrought and his cavalry smashed into the line of enemy pikemen, sweeping them aside with a huge roar, the air rent by screaming as soldiers on both sides fell. Many saddles were emptied by the long spears, but into the breach rushed the housecarls and fyrd, cutting at the Imperial troops until a small knot struggled about the battle standard, which swung one way and then the other as desperate hands reached to take it and Polypontian soldiers furiously defended it. Redrought and Theowin had both been unhorsed and now led the struggle to take the battle standard on foot, raining blows at the stubborn fighters before them.

Soldiers on both sides fell in huge numbers as the King led charge after charge against the enemy defenders, their superb discipline holding out as they continually redressed their line and denied the Icemark their standard. But at last Redrought breached their defense, just as the Lady Theowin fell under a hail of sword blows.

Roaring his rage and grief, Redrought drove forward, sweeping aside all before him with the swinging arc of the battle-ax he'd taken from Theowin's lifeless hand. The last Polypontian soldiers fought with ferocity but fell to the King's ax, until at last he was fighting hand to hand with the standard-bearer, the last man standing of the entire invading army.

The standard-bearer was wearing the plumed helmet and elegantly gilded armor of his office, but his sword was bloody with use and razor-sharp and he fought for the honor of his fallen comrades. Redrought and the standard-bearer traded cut and parry, whirling around the pivot of the flagpole, whose shaft the Polypontian soldier had driven deep into the ground. Every thrust of his sword was powered by desperation and a driving thirst to kill the barbarian king who'd destroyed his army, but he was also a veteran of more than twenty campaigns and he fought with the skill of long experience. Cut and thrust, parry and feint — the economy and measure of his tactics were superb. But Redrought had neither the time nor inclination to admire his fighting finesse and, spotting a sudden gap in his defense, he chopped deep into the junction where neck meets shoulder, and the last Polypontian fell.

Triumphant, Redrought seized the battle flag and held it aloft with a huge cry of exaltation. But at his feet the standard-bearer felt a surge of hatred that drove him through his pain, and with his dying breath he reached up and drove his sword deep into Redrought's belly.

A strange silence slowly descended on the field. Only the groans of the dying and the moaning of the icy wind could be heard.

9

Thirrin watched as the last wagon lumbered through the gates of the city, then gently urged her horse forward. Frostmarris was uncannily silent, and even the usual wintertime scent of wood smoke had gone, leaving the streets smelling unnaturally neutral, apart from the occasional sharp tang of dung where one of the many horses had deposited a pile.

The capital city had been evacuated only once before in its thousand years of history, but with the late snows leaving the roads open, there was no real option. Thirrin had to admit that if the Polypontians were victorious, then Frostmarris would be at their mercy, and withstanding a siege here in winter would be impossible.

Her horse was approaching the archway that led to the long entrance tunnel from the main gate, and reining to a halt she looked back at the royal fortress on its dominating hill. The battle banner of the Icemark still flew from the keep, the rearing white bear standing out clearly in the icy wind against the pristine blue sky.

"I'll be back in the springtime," she whispered. "And I'll have an army that'll drive back any invader, even Scipio Bellorum!"

She turned her horse into the tunnel, closing her eyes against the freezing cold wind that was funneling through from the outside world, but at last she reached the main gate and passed through into the brilliant sunshine of a crisp winter's day. Oskan was waiting for her along with an escort of ten cavalry, but she waved the troopers ahead and, catching the Witch's Son's eye, she pointed imperiously to her side.

He was riding a quiet mule with ears as long as swords and a face like a slightly amused camel, and though she could see that the animal was both strong and willing, she'd have preferred it if one of her most important advisers had chosen to ride a warhorse.

Thirrin looked out over the plain to where the long winding snake of wagons, horses, and cattle was slowly making its way along the North Road. "We'll need to go faster than that if we're to reach the Hypolitan before the snows come."

"Maggiore Totus is seeing to that now," Oskan answered. "He's told the commander of the cavalry to increase the pace and position back markers to drive on the stragglers."

She nodded in approval, then added, "Exactly where did you find that animal?"

Oskan stroked the mule's neck. "The head groom gave her to me. Jenny's kind and gentle and as strong as two horses."

Thirrin looked down on him from the great height of her stallion. "*Jenny?*"

"Yes. Suits her, don't you think? She knows I'm not a very good rider and she makes allowances."

"Does she?" said Thirrin in a voice that was as cold as the wind. "And can Jenny keep up with a full gallop?" And with that, Princess and stallion plunged forward and charged down the approach road to the city and out onto the plain. Oskan followed behind, desperately clinging on as the mule suddenly produced a surprising turn of speed. At one point it even seemed that they were gaining on the tall horse that was thundering ahead, but Thirrin reined to a halt and only just managed to hide her astonishment when the mule quickly drew up next to her with a breathless Oskan hanging on to her neck.

"She'll do, I suppose," Thirrin admitted.

For the rest of the morning the wagon train wound its way along the road, its pace now a little faster as the cavalry escort rode up and down its length, urging on the drivers. At the head of the column rode Thirrin, with her two advisers and the commanders of the skeleton detachments of cavalry and housecarls. The noise of screaming babies, barking dogs, and complaining citizens swelled and rolled over the plain as they slowly plodded forward, but at heart everyone was in good enough spirits. Redrought had always said that the people of Frostmarris were at their best in a crisis, and it seemed he was right. There were no fights, few arguments, and though there was plenty of moaning no one refused to help where they were needed.

All seemed to be going as well as the circumstances could allow. But even so, Thirrin was desperately worried. How could she hope to get her people safely to the Hypolitan in the depths of winter? She was lucky it hadn't snowed yet, but she knew that was only a matter of time, and then what would she do? Her advisers were an old man who knew more about books than the reality of war and a boy who was hardly older than she was. She had no one to rely on, and at fourteen she just didn't feel ready to lead anyone anywhere, let alone the entire population of a city.

Nevertheless, because she appeared to be a strong leader,

the people seemed amazingly confident in her and happy to follow her plans. One of the most important lessons she'd recently learned was that looking strong and confident was sometimes all the people required of you.

Even so, as time wore on and the eaves of the Great Forest drew closer, uneasiness began to grow among the refugees. The route to safety with the Hypolitan in the north passed through the huge expanse of trees, and many of the people stared mournfully at the forest in superstitious dread. Generations of misbehaving children had been threatened with ghouls and monsters from the massive forest, and even adults found their dreams invaded by its terrible image, reduced to children again by their fears. And now those fears were coming to dreadful reality as the stark and naked branches of the winter trees loomed on the skyline like a billowing storm cloud. Only a few hunters dared to walk the forest's strange pathways, and although the army sent fairly regular patrols along the North Road, to most of the people it remained a place of fearful mystery. And now as they approached the forest, it was busily living up to its reputation as the icy wind found a voice, blowing through the miles of wooded hills and valleys, moaning and howling mournfully like the ghosts of wolves. Soon even the noisiest baby fell silent, and the cattle stopped their constant bawling as the shadow loomed ever closer.

"If they're worried by the very sight of the forest, just wait until they realize we're going to be camping in it for the next week or so," said Thirrin.

"Quite," Maggiore Totus said, inexpertly adjusting his grip on the reins of his gentle mare. "I think a reminder of that situation should be passed on to the citizens so that it comes as less of a shock."

Thirrin nodded in agreement and beckoned to the cavalry commander. "Tell the people to ensure that they have everything they need for several nights' camping in the forest."

The commander saluted and cantered off, passing the message on to his troopers.

"Perhaps I should have a word with the people," Oskan said. "Most of them know who I am and that I live in the forest, and they can all see that I've never been harmed by it."

"But my dear Oskan," Maggiore pointed out gently, "you are the son of a witch. A White Witch admittedly, but a witch nonetheless, one of the very . . . creatures the people fear live in the forest. I think it would be best if you didn't remind them of your parentage."

"But my mother was a good woman, a healer. Many citizens of Frostmarris were helped by her."

"True, but I don't think you are taking into account the collective mind of a large group of frightened people. If they remember that a White Witch who helped them once lived in the forest, they'll also be reminded of the possibility of Black Witches who could do exactly the opposite."

Thirrin had listened to the debate, quietly aware that she must seize any opportunity that would help her to keep the people together. After a moment of thought she said, "I think the citizens have already thought enough about the bad things that can live under the trees. It's time to remind them that good can also live there. Go and speak to them, Oskan." All those close enough to hear were struck by how like her father the Princess sounded, and took comfort from it.

Oskan smiled at her and cantered off along the line of wagons, stopping every now and then to talk to a driver or someone plodding along on foot.

"I know you'll probably think it superstitious nonsense,

Maggie, but I'm going to ask Oskan to perform . . ." Thirrin shrugged her shoulders as she struggled to find the right word. "Something . . . a ceremony of some sort before we go into the trees. Something that'll help the people believe they're protected in some way."

"On the contrary, Madam, I agree with the idea," Maggiore answered, and smiled. "It's wise to use everything you can to keep the citizens calm. I'll be there chanting whatever you want and waving around as much incense as you think necessary."

She smiled. "Thanks, Maggie. I hoped you'd say something like that."

The long train of refugees moved so slowly that it was early afternoon before they finally reached the eaves of the forest, and though the sun still stood above the western horizon, night had already gathered under the canopy of the Great Forest. The huge crowd of people stood in silence before the two massive trees — one oak, the other beech — that overreached the road and created a natural archway into a very different world.

Thirrin beckoned to Oskan, who'd just returned from his mission to reassure the people about the forest. "I think it'd be a good idea to conduct some sort of ceremony of protection before we go into the trees," she said.

"Fine, who do you suggest does it?"

"You, of course. You've got White Witch connections and you have the added official status of Royal Adviser. It'll have *weight* coming from you."

"*Me!*" Oskan exploded. "I'm no priest; I have no special powers. And what am I supposed to do exactly, rub two sticks together and mutter some sort of mumbo jumbo?"

"If need be," said Thirrin, far more firmly than she felt. "I don't care what you do, as long as it looks good and makes the people feel better about traveling through the forest."

"So, 'Just get your cap and bells on and perform for us,' is that it?" he protested, feeling as though Thirrin was just using him to further her aims.

"Look, I don't really care what you do, just as long as you do *something* to help these people feel that it's safe to sleep among the trees at night," Thirrin answered, suddenly feeling horribly weary.

"Well, I can't and won't do it," he hissed angrily as the nearest ranks of the refugee column started to look at them curiously. "I'd . . . I'd feel like a fool!"

Maggiore Totus eased his quiet mare over to join them. "Oskan, my dear boy, this war is making us all act in ways we wouldn't normally dream of doing." He smiled gently, and immediately a calming influence settled over them all. "Look at me, I've seen more winters than Jack Frost, and I'm riding horses and leading people as though I were born to it! We need your help, Oskan."

The boy gazed sullenly at the ground for a few minutes. Everyone was making demands of him and yet before he'd met Thirrin, he'd been as free as the beasts of the Great Forest. Was this the price of friendship? Was it worth it? He wasn't sure; this was something he'd need to think about when he had more time.

Eventually he lifted his chin and said firmly, "I can't carry out any sort of rite for protection, but I think we should call on the Oak King and his soldiers for permission to enter his realm in such huge numbers. That call could take the form of a ceremony and might also ensure our protection."

Thirrin sighed with relief, but then, a little confused and remembering he'd dared to argue against her idea, she snapped, "What happened to the Holly King?"

"You've obviously forgotten your nursery rhymes and lore," Oskan answered. "The two kings struggle for rule throughout the year. The Holly King reigns from the summer solstice, when the power of the sun begins to wane, and the Oak King takes the throne of the seasons from the winter solstice, when the sun's power begins its slow return. So if we want to be diplomatic and keep good relations with the present ruler of the forest, we should ask for the right to pass through his realm, especially since you've only sent your royal greetings to the Holly King so far."

Thirrin sat in silence for a moment. She still didn't like the idea of another monarch ruling in the Icemark, but she was aware of their desperate need for allies.

And slowly another idea was forming. "Can you ask the Oak King's soldiers to watch over us while traveling through his lands?"

Oskan looked at her sharply. "Well . . . yes . . . if I choose to."

"Good. Do it. What do you need?"

"Nothing . . . well, perhaps a few barrels of beer and mead, if we have any," Oskan answered, still feeling that he was being manipulated somehow.

"Beer shouldn't be a problem. I'm not sure about the mead, though. I'll order a search through the wagons."

Within a very short time five large barrels of beer and two smaller ones of mead had been found and placed in the center of the road beneath the oak-and-beech-tree archway. The people gathered in the road in a huge expectant crowd. They knew something was happening, and rumors said Oskan Witch's Son was going to perform magic of some sort.

If he'd known he was meant to fulfill the citizens' expectations of him as a wizard, Oskan would have refused to go any further. But fortunately he didn't, and soon his tall, thin figure could be seen standing beneath the arch of trees with his hands raised above his head. Thirrin nodded to a cavalry bugler and a fanfare rang out, echoing through the strangely silent forest. Oskan's voice boomed with surprising power, and Thirrin found herself wondering if this was another trick he'd learned from his mother. But she reined in her thoughts and concentrated on what he was saying.

"Greetings from Princess Thirrin Freer Strong-in-the-Arm Lindenshield, Wildcat of the North, heir to the throne of the Icemark, and Regent of the land as her father, King Redrought, gives battle to invaders from the Polypontus. Salutations to His Majesty the Oak King, Monarch of the Wild Wood and all untamed places. The Princess extends the hand of friendship to His Majesty and asks permission to lead her people through his domain as they seek refuge from the Polypontian invaders and their soldiers.

"These small tokens of her friendship the Princess offers to His Majesty." Here Oskan paused, and with widely sweeping gestures he pointed to the barrels. "And asks that their meagerness be forgiven and requests your understanding in this time of crisis. She also craves the boon of His Majesty that his soldiers watch over her people as they travel through his lands, and herewith promises perpetual friendship and alliance with the Oak King and his subjects."

Thirrin was surprised by the formality of the language Oskan used, and guessed that he'd found time to talk with Maggiore Totus while she'd been searching the wagon train for mead and beer. But more surprising was the impressive presence that the skinny young boy managed to convey as he stood under the forest canopy. His long midnight blue cloak and rich red tunic, both Yuletide presents from Thirrin, seemed to glow in the light of the setting sun, and his thin frame cast a tall shadow deep into the trees. But more extraordinary than all of this was the indefinable aura of power that seemed to flow around him as he waited in the silence that followed his speech. Oskan might deny that he'd inherited any gifts from his mother, but there were times when Thirrin was almost certain there was more about him than even he knew.

After a few minutes the people began to get restless, and a low murmur ebbed and flowed among them like the sound of the sea. But suddenly a blast of wind sprang up, howling through the forest canopy and then dropping completely as though someone had opened and quickly closed a gigantic door on a stormy day. Then into the following silence stepped twenty or so strange figures.

Thirrin leaned forward in her saddle and looked at them closely. They all stood as tall as the tallest housecarl she'd ever seen. Their armor reminded her of the soldiers of the Holly King she'd met just before Yule: Like theirs, it seemed to be made of polished leaves of different sizes and covered their bodies from head to foot. The small amount of skin that could be seen was the color of bark, and their eyes were as brilliantly green as newly opened oak leaves. Hearing movement behind her and instinctively knowing that a cavalry trooper was reaching for his sword, she signaled him to be still.

Oskan stepped forward and raised his hand in greeting. An oak soldier replied by raising his spear, then planting it firmly at his feet. A moment of stillness followed as a slow murmur of hushed awe rose from the crowds of people who filled the road and surrounding land. Then Thirrin spurred forward and saluted the soldiers.

"I am Princess Thirrin. Take my personal greetings to your Royal Master and thank him for his patience and understanding as I lead my people to the land of the Hypolitan beyond the northern borders of the Great Forest. Assure him of my gratitude and convey to him the friendship of the Royal House of Lindenshield."

Once again the oak soldier saluted, and turning to his companions he signaled for them to collect the gift of beer and mead. Then, as the now horizontal shafts of sunlight illuminated the trunks and canopy of the forest in a softly golden glow, the soldiers stepped back into the undergrowth and simply disappeared. Once again a sudden gust of wind rushed through the branches of the trees, stirring up a blizzard of fallen leaves and drenching the watching people in the rich scents of damp earth and leaf litter. Then, as swiftly as it came, the wind dropped and silence returned.

"Well, well, how fascinating," said Maggiore Totus from where he sat on his mare just behind Thirrin. "Unless we are all suffering the effects of mass hysteria, I think I am going to have to reassess my own personal view of natural history. It seems the Oak King and his people and, by a natural projection, the Holly King and *his* subjects, really do exist. Madam, watching you has been an important addition to my education."

"Don't forget the werewolf, Maggie," Thirrin answered.

"No, indeed. How could I?"

"Just name any other animals you think belong in the world of mythology, and I have a feeling that in the next few months we're likely to meet them face-to-face."

Redrought lay back as comfortably as he could. Most of the pain had abated and now he merely felt deathly tired. The view around him was grim. As far as he could see, dead and badly injured soldiers lay where they had fallen, though over the last few hours most of the moaning had faded away and only the flap and flutter of carrion crows disturbed the quiet.

He was beginning to feel light-headed, probably from the loss of blood, he managed to reason. And his eyesight was definitely ebbing away. He could no longer be sure if it really was beginning to get cloudy or not. If General Snow was really on his way, then he could go happily. He'd smashed the first Polypontian army and Thirrin would have time to prepare for a spring offensive. He smiled fondly. She was a formidable young woman and would make a fearsome queen, the mixing of the royal blood of the Icemark with that of the fighting women of the Hypolitan had produced a wildcat! Young Oskan would need all his warlock's power to keep up with her. He laughed aloud, and then suddenly stopped. On the very edge of his fading sight, three figures appeared. They were tall and armored like rich housecarls, but as they came closer he could see they were extraordinarily beautiful young women.

"Hail, Redrought Strong-in-the-Arm Lindenshield, Bear of the North!" one of them said in a voice that was both fierce and melodic. "You must leave all of this behind and come with us!"

"Where to?" Redrought asked, overawed by the young women's presence.

"To Asgard! Your place at the table awaits you in the hall of Valhalla. Come, the Lord Odin will not be kept waiting."

Redrought was surprised to find that he could stand and was free of pain. The stern young women smiled and, taking his hands, they led him toward a beautiful bridge of rainbow light.

* * *

The pass through the mountain range called the Dancing Maidens was still open, and the regiment of Polypontian cavalry trotted through unopposed. They'd been sent by their command as reinforcements for the invading army that had set out three days earlier, and they fully expected to find a comfortable encampment waiting for them, or even billets in one of the captured cities. No messengers had been sent back proclaiming the expected victories, but this wasn't unusual. A small country such as the Icemark wouldn't present any difficulties to a Polypontian force, and to proclaim such a victory would be to state the obvious.

The officer of the cavalry was young and had been bitterly disappointed not to have been included in the first wave of the invasion, but discipline was all and he'd accepted his orders without question. Now he was leading his troop of one thousand horses to join a campaign that wouldn't get properly under way until the following spring, and he happily expected to bring honor to his family name of Cassius Brontus.

The idea to begin the invasion in the winter and secure a staging post for the following year had been proposed by the great General Scipio Bellorum and had undoubtedly taken the armies of the small country completely by surprise. Tucked in his saddlebag, Cassius Brontus had a map of the South Farthing of the Icemark that had been drawn by Polypontian spy cartographers earlier that year. Nothing would have changed, but even if it had, he expected to find the victorious invading army simply by following the path of destruction and death they'd have left in their wake.

The mouth of the pass came into view and he called a halt. The cavalry training manual dictated that troopers ride with sabers drawn and shields enarmed in all unsecured territory, and though he believed the land to be in Polypontian hands, he'd received no confirmation of this and gave orders accordingly. As they rode forward, the broad sweep of the country came into view. Before them lay a wild and fierce land of broken rocks and scree slopes, and under the brilliant blue sky and dazzling sunshine it had an untamed beauty that made the young officer shudder. If the people were anything like the country they inhabited, then the Polypontus would have a worthy opponent.

They rode into the land in battle order and followed the road that swept down from the pass. Soon they came across evidence of resistance to the invading army's advance, with dead horses and broken equipment lying where they'd fallen or been dropped. Cassius Brontus was puzzled. Normal procedure was to clear away debris after a skirmish, unless, of course, the army was under heavy pressure. His troops rode by with hardly a second glance at the flotsam of battle. Their forces had been hard pressed before and always they'd been victorious.

But soon they passed more broken equipment, then the burned-out remains of four supply wagons and even six cannons, their carriages charred and blackened and their barrels broken by what must have been amazingly ferocious hammering. Cassius Brontus called a halt and ordered his command to load their long-barreled cavalry pistols. Each trooper carried two in holsters on either side of their saddles. Once this was done they set off again, but this time the young officer sent out scouts and outriders to check the way ahead.

Within five minutes the outriders were racing back along the road calling out that the battlefield lay ahead. Cassius Brontus was relieved. Obviously the Polypontian army had brought the enemy to bay early, and at least he and his troops wouldn't have far to ride before they were assigned their quarters. But at this point the scouts appeared on the road, riding with great urgency and looking back over their shoulders as they came on. The officer immediately put his troops on alert.

"All dead, sir! They're all dead!" the scouts called as they thundered back to the regiment. They halted wild-eyed before him in a flurry of loose stones and rearing horses.

"Report clearly!" Cassius Brontus ordered sharply. "Who are dead? How many and where?"

"The entire invasion force, sir. Half a mile farther on."

The shock of their words left him numb. An entire Polypontian army wiped out? Impossible! "You're wrong! There may be some soldiers of the Polypontus mixed with the fallen, but you must have seen the remains of the Icemark's army."

"Yes, sir. They're there, too. We saw their battle standard fallen with ours."

"Our battle standard fallen!"

"Yes, sir. It's held by the corpse of a giant red-bearded man in fine armor. Our standard-bearer lies dead beneath him."

In the silence of his shock the young officer reached the obvious conclusion. The two armies had wiped each other out, and the description of the giant red-bearded warrior fit that of Redrought, King of the Icemark.

Recovering quickly, he sent two messengers with news of the disaster back through the pass and then ordered his troops to advance in battle formation. His agile mind was working quickly. The Icemark had probably risked all on wiping out the invading army and most likely would have nothing left to defend the land. It was wide open for the taking, and if he acted quickly enough, the name of Cassius Brontus would live forever in the Empire of the Polypontus. For one thing, he knew the heir to the throne of this little land was a mere girl of thirteen or fourteen. Who was protecting her now? A few of their barbaric *housecarls*? An assorted ragbag of half-trained soldiers of the *fyrd*? He had an entire regiment of battle-hardened and disciplined cavalry troopers with him. If he seized the moment now, he could ride for the palace and capture the girl. A puppet monarch set on the throne of a client kingdom by a mere cohort of the invading army. He'd be made for life! Promotion, perhaps his own army. And in later years maybe even a seat on the Senate.

He ordered the pace up to a canter, the rattle of the horses' hooves echoing in the narrow canyon through which the road now wound. Then the rocky walls fell away, and the highway burst onto a wide plateau, stark under the brilliant winter sunshine. Spontaneously the troopers reined to a halt. Before them lay a sight none of them had ever seen before: a defeated and destroyed army of the Polypontus scattered over the land like the fallen trees of a blasted forest. Even though they'd been warned by the scouts' reports, it was still a terrible shock. No armed force of their country had been defeated for more than three hundred years, and yet here lay an entire invasion force completely smashed.

Cassius Brontus recovered first. He had a plan to fulfill and his driving ambition gave him the impetus he needed. He gave orders to secure the area and sent back more messengers for supplies and the sturdiest tents the quartermasters had. Obviously no cities had been taken yet, and if the Polypontus were to maintain the small toehold they had in this land, they'd need to be prepared to ride out the coldest and longest winter any of them had ever experienced.

His troops rode out in companies, looking for survivors and establishing their control of the site. He was just about to send scouts north along the highway in case the Icemark had another surprise for them and a second army was on the march when he suddenly noticed a group of five or six figures running from a line of hills toward the part of the battlefield where the bodies lay thickest. At first he thought they were human, but then he wasn't so sure. They were running on two legs certainly, but even from this distance they looked huge, and either they were wearing furs of some sort or *they* were furry! A company of cavalry spotted them, and as Cassius Brontus watched, they wheeled around with superb discipline and galloped toward the figures. The five running shapes then stopped and turned to face the charge. A volley of pistol shots rang out, and then a strange howling roar rose up into the air. Horses reared and screamed and cavalry sabers flashed in the brilliant sunshine as a fierce skirmish followed. But it didn't last long. Before anyone else could react, ten horses were bolting riderless across the rocky plain.

With lightning speed the figures then ran to where the fallen battle standards lay and, tearing them from their staffs, they rolled them into balls and stuffed them into a crude sack they had with them. Cassius Brontus sat quietly watching. He was the sort of commander who was quite prepared to "blow with the winds of chance," as the saying went, and having lost ten troopers already, he wasn't prepared to risk the lives of any more. The hairy figures picked up two of the dead from among the hideous tangle and ran off at an amazing speed toward the hills they'd first come from. Several of the cavalry companies scattered around the field gave chase, but their commander waved up one of the buglers and ordered him to sound the recall. The strict discipline of the Polypontian forces immediately asserted itself, and all of the companies turned around and galloped back toward him.

"Commander, those *things* have taken our invading army's standard!" called the officer in charge of one of the companies as he rode up.

"Indeed. And what use would we have for the disgraced flag of a defeated army? Perhaps you thought we could clean our boots on it before tomorrow morning's parade?"

"Well, no, but . . ."

"But?" his commander inquired mildly.

"It's a standard of the Polypontus."

"It's a desecrated rag. Call in your troopers and wait for orders!"

By this time the strange figures had reached the line of distant hills and disappeared from view. Cassius Brontus was more than happy to see them go. He'd heard strange tales about the monsters that plagued the land of the Icemark, and he was beginning to think he'd just had firsthand experience of some of them. Judging by what they'd done to some of his cavalry, he was relieved they were unlikely to have either the brains or the discipline to make an effective fighting force. And what exactly they planned to do with the bodies they'd taken from the field he shuddered to think.

10

This was the fourth night the refugees had spent in the forest. They were camped on the main road with baggage wagons drawn up as a wall to the south and to the north of the site, and watch fires had been set at regular intervals under the trees. At first the people had adapted quite well to the conditions, and after the ceremony Oskan had carried out in which the soldiers of the Oak King had appeared, the terror of the forest had been replaced by a simple fear. But now, after living through the deep blackness of the forest's night, a growing dread was once more threatening to get out of hand at any time.

Thirrin had hoped to boost morale by making a great display of deploying the few soldiers she had in full battle gear along the makeshift defensive walls of the wagons and around the watch fires. But the two hundred troops only looked stretched beyond their capacity once they'd been stationed along the nearly half-mile length of the encampment.

"What can I do, Maggie?" she asked Maggiore Totus as they sat around their fire close to the southern wagon wall. Primplepuss was sitting comfortably on Thirrin's knee, basking in the warm glow and daintily accepting small morsels of chicken that the Princess held out to her. "The people are happier than they were, but at the first wolf howl they could become a screaming mob of terrified berserkers."

"There's nothing you can do, really. Just get us through this forest as quickly as possible," the neat little man replied. "Sometimes even the greatest leader has to accept the limitations of a situation and just hope for the best."

"That's not what I want to hear," she snapped unreasonably. "Can't you suggest some magical solution?"

"Not my field, I'm afraid. Perhaps you should ask Oskan."

They both turned to look at the witch's son, who was sitting and staring silently into the impenetrable black of the forest beyond the encampment.

Thirrin nudged him with her toe. "Well? What do you suggest?"

Oskan turned large unseeing eyes on her, then he blinked, and vision seemed to rekindle in his dilated pupils. "Sorry. Did you speak?"

"Yes!" Thirrin answered irritably. "What can we do to improve the people's morale? They're still afraid of the forest, and there's at least two more days of traveling before we reach its northern border. Maggie thought you might be able to use magic in some way."

"I said no such thing!" Maggiore protested, but Oskan only shrugged.

"I've told you before, I don't know what you mean by magic. My mother had some Knowledge, but I'm not her. Besides, the people have nothing to fear from the forest. It's the cavalry they should be afraid of."

"Cavalry? What cavalry?" Thirrin barked, causing Primplepuss to look at her questioningly.

"Coming from the south. There's no danger yet. They're at least a day's ride away."

"How do you know? What cavalry? Polypontian?"

"Yes, Polypontian. How do I know?" He shrugged again. "I do, that's all."

"Then my father's dead and the army wiped out?"

"I can only see the approaching cavalry. I don't know about anything else. I'm sorry."

Thirrin sat in silence for a few seconds, allowing herself to be the worried daughter of a soldier who was away fighting a war. Then she sat up and squared her shoulders as she took up the responsibility of her kingdom again. "Maggie, do you believe this? Could Oskan be right?"

"My Lady, since being in this strange northern land, I've learned that the truly rational individual keeps an open mind at all times. After all, I've seen legends walk in daylight and heard a wolfman bring news of invasion, so a simple case of clairvoyance warning of pursuing cavalry is easily believed. At the very least we should prepare for all possibilities and take what precautions we can. Dispatch a fast rider to the Hypolitan and ask them to send help as soon as they can, and position the few soldiers we have as a rear guard while the people move on as quickly as they can."

"Oskan, should we move tonight?" Thirrin asked, leaning forward and staring earnestly into his face as though she were trying to communicate with someone barely conscious.

"No," he answered in surprisingly relaxed tones. "The cavalry commander is driven by a huge ambition, but he knows the value of resting his troops, and the trail he's following is so obvious he knows he can't lose us. Basically he thinks we're fools, and expects to capture the 'Little Princess' in a day or so."

Thirrin was livid. "'Little Princess'! He's hunting the Wildcat of the North, and her teeth and claws are ready for his throat!" She leaped to her feet, depositing Primplepuss in an untidy heap on the ground, and strode around for a minute before sitting down again and muttering to herself. "How can you hide the trail of a city's entire population? It's impossible! I'd like to see him do better."

"The opinion of a moron has no value, Madam," said Maggiore. "In the meantime I suggest we keep this . . . possibility of a pursuit from the people. As you pointed out earlier, it would take very little to cause a panic."

Cassius Brontus led his cavalry through the main gate of Frostmarris. He'd ridden ahead to the city with his regiment of horses and an extra five hundred that had arrived in the Icemark soon after they'd received news of their invading army's destruction. He'd then stormed along the main highway, meeting no opposition, and had reached the capital city within two days.

At first they'd approached the towering walls with caution, but it had soon become obvious that his scout's reports were correct and the city had been abandoned. Even so, he entered the main gates with great care, all the troopers riding with pistols in hand and sabers drawn, expecting some trickery. But the city was deserted. The bitterly cold wind muttered eerily through the empty streets and here and there a door banged, the sound echoing over the intense stillness of the settlement. To the young officer's heightened imagination, every window watched them as they rode along the resonant streets and every alleyway hid an army of shadow-people. It was almost as though the ghosts of Frostmarris had come to resist their invasion. The wind carried a tangled whispering and, once, he was almost certain he heard a thin evil snickering. But whenever he looked toward the sounds, they stopped and there was nothing to be seen.

Soon the horses began to shy and blow nervously, and when one of them reared, almost throwing its rider, he was nearly convinced he saw a ragged shadow scuttling back down an alleyway. But Cassius Brontus was the product of the best education available in the colleges and training camps of the Polypontus. He was steeped in science and the belief in a rational universe. If a thing couldn't be counted, studied under a microscope, or dissected on a marble slab, he *knew* it didn't exist. Remembering this, he relegated all of his fears to mere imagination and they swiftly ebbed away. He suddenly laughed as the road ahead straightened out and he could see it climbing steadily toward the open gate of the citadel. The city was his! He raised the pace to a swift trot.

But behind the cavalry the shadows thickened like living smoke. The soldiers' fears might not get them today, but somewhere not too far ahead they lay waiting.

The troopers were soon striding across the Great Hall of the palace and having given the order to tear down the white bear insignia of the Icemark, Cassius Brontus himself climbed to the huge oaken crossbeam and replaced it with the Imperial Eagle of the Polypontus.

Leaving fifty men as a skeleton garrison in the citadel, he then set off in pursuit of the Princess. He was supremely confident. He had more than fifteen hundred well-trained cavalry troopers under his command and a trail as wide as a river to follow. They set out at a fast trot, clattering through the empty streets and sounding the battle call of the Empire on their bugles as they rode along. The city echoed with the arrogant noise of their presence, but as the last horse disappeared through the long exit tunnel and out onto the brightly sunlit plain beyond the walls, a deep haunted silence settled over Frostmarris again. The regimental color sergeant who'd been left in command of the occupying garrison somehow knew that the winter would be long and that it would take all of his considerable experience to maintain discipline.

Cassius Brontus, however, was almost excited. He felt like a young boy on a day trip to a favorite resort. He believed that his destiny lay ahead, and he couldn't help thinking it would be glorious. The great General Scipio Bellorum himself had shown the same flair and daring at the beginning of his career, and perhaps . . . just perhaps, the name of Cassius Brontus would one day be spoken with the same reverence as that of the army's commander in chief. He admitted to himself that he still had some way to go to equal the general who had added three countries and five provinces to the Empire of the Polypontus. But he, Cassius Brontus, was still a very young man, and if he managed to capture the Icemark's Princess, then he'd have made a greater beginning to his military career than even Scipio Bellorum had done.

These happy thoughts kept even the freezing wind of the Icemark at bay, and he stared eagerly ahead to the huge forest that was beginning to loom threateningly on the horizon. But the wild wood held no fears for him. To his military eye the massive living organism that was the Great Forest represented nothing more than a good source of material for ships, siege towers, and other equipment the triumphant armies of the Polypontus might need. The Empire consumed massive amounts of raw materials to keep its war machines working, and the largest, most ancient tree was nothing more to it than one more piece of fuel.

Cassius Brontus could clearly see from his position at the head of his troops that the road entered the forest, and that the trail of the Princess and her people went with it. His scouts, a hunting people from the far south of the Empire, confidently assured him that the tracks were much less than a week old and, given the slow pace at which such a huge convoy would be moving, he expected to catch up with them within two days.

They reached the eaves of the forest and rode into it without the slightest pause. The brilliance of the winter day was suddenly reduced to a green twilight, and the rattle of hooves on the flagstones of the road echoed eerily through the temple-like stillness of the trees. But any awe the troopers might have felt was ignored. In woodlands there were echoes simply because sound waves rebounded from the boles of the trees; the atmosphere seemed breathless because wind and air movement was generally hampered by the dense foliage and undergrowth. Like Cassius Brontus, they were soldiers of science and rationality, intent on their mission to bring logic and order to a world crippled by superstition. The Polypontus Empire had so far brought enlightenment to more than fifty countries and provinces, crushing the irrational beliefs of their populations whether they liked it or not.

But for the time being, all such philosophical ideals took a poor second place to their ambitions. They were as determined as their young officer to gain as much ground on their quarry as they could before dark. In the forest, night would fall early, and the winter days were short enough already, so standing in his stirrups Cassius Brontus gave the signal for greater speed, and the pace was increased to a canter. Both horse and trooper could keep this up for hours, eating up the ground before them and bearing down on the refugee column as if they had an appointment with the Goddesses of Fate that their superstitious prey probably believed in.

They'd made good time over the last couple of days. Maggiore Totus had managed to instill a sense of urgency into the column without causing panic, by claiming that the winter snows were finally on their way and would hit them before they reached the province of the Hypolitan if they didn't hurry. But they'd never be able to outrun the approaching cavalry. Oskan, in a dark and brooding mood, continued to give warnings of the enemy troopers' progress, and such was his quiet authority that even Maggiore accepted his clairvoyance without question.

"How long now, Oskan?" Thirrin asked for the fourth time that hour.

"A day or so."

"Can't you be more accurate than that?" she snapped. "I need to know exactly."

They were riding at the back of the column with the two hundred soldiers they had as a rear guard. The forest was particularly silent that day, as though holding its breath, and Oskan reflected its sense of foreboding exactly. There was an atmosphere about him, like midnight in the deserted hall of a great fortress. When he spoke, he was quiet and withdrawn, so much so that Thirrin had to strain to hear what he was saying.

But at last he seemed to rouse himself from his strange mood and, looking at her with suddenly bright eyes, said, "They will catch us in exactly one day from now. You and the housecarls will defend a narrow place in the road where they won't be able to use their numbers against you. But how it will end I don't know. I can see no more. The Sight comes and goes. I can't command it."

She stared at him, not realizing she was holding her breath until she suddenly let it go in an explosive sigh. "Tell Maggie," she ordered. "I'll speak to the captain of the guard."

Oskan nodded and then, amazingly, smiled. Now that he'd given the last of his clairvoyant warnings, it was as though a darkness had been lifted from his mind and the boy she knew returned to help her. "Do you think he'll believe me?"

"Of course he will. Our tame master of the *rational* secretly puts more faith in your powers than anyone . . . apart from me. Now go."

As the boy galloped off on his ungainly mule, Thirrin rode on alone, deep in thought. Oskan was certainly right about the type of place she'd choose to make a stand against the Polypontian cavalry. A narrow place in the road, with dense undergrowth beneath the trees to protect the flanks of her housecarls, would be an obvious choice of position. The enemy wouldn't be able to use their numbers efficiently, however great they were, and her soldiers might be able to stand up to ten deep, depending on exactly how narrow the road was. All she had to do now was keep a sharp lookout for this obvious place and speak to her soldiers.

They reached it an hour later. For some reason known only to the ancient engineers who'd made the highway, it abruptly narrowed as it climbed a low hill, and the trees crowded up to the verge in a particularly dense stand that was thick with low bushes and brambles. No horse could force its way through such an entanglement to take them in the flank, and the crest of the hill would give Thirrin and her housecarls a slight advantage over the enemy.

She tried to shake off the sense of desperation that had been creeping up on her all day. The cavalry of the Polypontian Empire had the reputation of being the finest in the known world, and she had only two hundred foot soldiers to set against it. What hope did they have? They were outnumbered with very little chance of any help or reinforcements arriving before they were wiped out, so there seemed little point in resisting. Why not simply surrender? Allow herself to be captured and beg for mercy for her people?

For a moment she almost convinced herself of this argument. But then she remembered the terrible stories of the massacres and atrocities carried out by the soldiers of the Empire. Of course, she had no way of knowing whether they were true or not. Stories like that always grew in the telling, and they were always told by the losers in the many wars the Empire had fought. And that in itself was natural enough, because the Polypontians had never lost a war yet. People hated the Empire. Of course they did: It took away their freedom and it crushed their individuality, so it was quite natural that negative stories about the way it treated defeated people should be common. Perhaps they really were exaggerated and the population would be well treated. And even if all the stories were true, what could she do? Did she really care if the populations of entire towns were enslaved and moved out to work in the Empire's mines or factories? Did she really care if those too old to be of use to the Imperial slave masters were slaughtered in a murderous act of efficiency? As long as she was safe and allowed to keep at least the trappings of royalty, why should she continue to struggle against overwhelming odds? With a secret, deeply shocking sense of relief, she imagined handing responsibility for the Icemark over to the Empire. She could become a puppet queen, doing exactly as she was told and being allowed to live in peace and comfort in Frostmarris.

And perhaps the people would simply have exchanged one system of government for another.

But then the blood of the Strong-in-the-Arm clan awoke, roaring in her brain, and the fighting spirit of the Hypolitan, her mother's people, straightened her sagging spine and sent a tingling excitement coursing through her veins. She was heir to the throne of the Icemark and she could never be certain that stories of Polypontian cruelty were untrue. She *must* defend her land and her people! This was her role and meaning in life. To betray their trust, even in the face of impossible odds, would be the most terrible of treacheries. Above all she was her father's daughter, and she must stand with her housecarls and give the column of refugees at least some chance of escaping. Or she must die trying. Even so, she trembled with the terrible responsibility of it all. For the first time in her proud young life she found herself envying other girls of her own age: young peasants, or the daughters of rich merchants and artisans. All they had to worry about was themselves and their immediate families. Would *their* young shoulders be strong enough to carry the weight of an entire country?

By this time her horse had climbed the small hill the road followed, and she drew rein. The captain of her housecarls had been stumping along stolidly behind her, but seeing her stop he held up his hand, and his command of foot soldiers stamped to a halt.

"We make our stand here, Captain Eodred," Thirrin said.

He nodded silently and, turning to the men, ordered them to fall out. Then he turned back to Thirrin. "When do we fight, Ma'am?"

"A little less than a day from now. We'll be facing cavalry, and we'll be outnumbered."

He nodded, accepting the information without question.

"A good position," he said, looking around. "We could hold ten times our number here."

"Yes, but for how long, Captain?"

He shrugged. "That's with the gods."

Later that night, Oskan, Maggiore, and Grimswald galloped back to consult with Thirrin. The refugee column was now several miles ahead and would continue to travel through the night as they tried to outrun the bad weather Maggiore had convinced them was on the way. All three of them were wearing borrowed armor, and it was all Thirrin could do not to fall into fits of giggles when she saw Grimswald. His helmet was so large the nasal plate reached to his chin, and if he turned his head suddenly, the helmet stayed staring forward, and then would slowly revolve to catch up with the face it supposedly protected. Even Maggie and Oskan looked vaguely ridiculous, like large children dressed up in their fathers' clothes. After a long struggle Thirrin managed to gain control of her features, and then asked:

"And why, exactly, are you three wearing armor?"

"Because we want at least a chance of surviving the first charge tomorrow," Oskan answered brusquely.

"Well, you don't have to worry. I can guarantee that you will. You'll all be with the wagons." Thirrin waited quietly while the protests and arguments washed over her, and then she said, "None of you are trained. None of you are natural fighters. All of you would die. Quickly.

"Maggie, you can barely use a fruit knife without cutting yourself; Grimswald, I admire your bravery, but you're far more useful to me ensuring that I have everything I need, when I need it, and Oskan . . ." She sighed, exasperated that she needed to point out the obvious. "Oskan, you're a healer among other things. You're supposed to repair the damage fighting inflicts on people, not cause it yourself."

"But me and Maggie are your advisers; the King himself appointed us. We can't just abandon you at the first sign of a fight! Redrought would expect us to be with you," Oskan said, his voice taking on a note of desperation as he realized that Thirrin was determined, too.

"The King would expect advisers to advise, not fight. You and Maggie would both serve me best by leading my people safely to the Hypolitan," Thirrin answered quietly. She was well aware that she was dealing with male pride here as much as loyalty and a sense of duty. Oskan was a boy who was standing on the threshold of manhood, and to leave a fourteen-year-old girl to fight while he rode away would be hard for him to bear. "Oskan, you must help Maggie lead the wagons to safety. You've become a symbol of hope and magical power for the people. When you're with them, they feel less afraid, and that, combined with Maggie's authority, is just what they need right now. If you abandon them in the forest, they'll panic and run amok. Your duty lies with them."

Oskan looked at his feet but eventually nodded. He knew she was right, but his self-respect had demanded he at least try to help in the coming fight. Maggiore nodded, too, though for him the gesture was more an acknowledgment that Thirrin had grown to fit the role that the war had forced her to take. She was already every inch a Queen with an air of command and a fighting spirit, but now she'd also developed a diplomacy that handled the tender pride of a growing boy to perfection. He suddenly felt enormously proud of her and, stooping, he kissed her hand. "Don't worry about your people, Ma'am. We'll look after them."

"Thanks, Maggie," she answered simply, and smiled. Then

she went on, "One more thing. My closest kin is the Basilea of the Hypolitan; she's my aunt. I name her now as my heir. If I fall tomorrow, you will serve her as loyally as you served me."

No one replied, but both Oskan and Maggiore bowed deeply, and Grimswald wiped his nose on a handkerchief he found after much rummaging under his armor.

The next day dawned bright and cold again. Good fighting weather, as Captain Eodred had said. During supper the previous night, Thirrin had asked Oskan if he could tell her exactly when the enemy cavalry would arrive, but the Sight would give no answers, and he'd shaken his head regretfully. Not long after that, he, Maggiore, and Grimswald had ridden forward to rejoin the column of refugees, leaving Thirrin feeling isolated, despite being surrounded by two hundred housecarls. She'd been almost sick with fear, but now that day had dawned she was too busy to feel lonely or even nervous. There was equipment to check, running repairs to carry out, orders to give, and scouts to send out to give her warning of the Polypontians' approach. When all of this was done, she arranged the battle order, putting the strongest and fittest soldiers in the front ranks and packing them ten files deep on the narrow section of road.

Now all they could do was wait. Thirrin took up her position at the very center of the shield-wall's front rank, while Captain Eodred controlled the left wing and his second in command the right. The soldiers cheered as Thirrin locked her shield into the wall, and the bearer of the regiment's fighting colors rolled up the flag and laid it at his feet, saying that the Princess was now their battle standard and they would all fall before she was taken. This was greeted by another cheer, then the soldiers beat their axes and swords on their shields, making a rolling rhythm of sound that slowly grew to a crashing crescendo that swelled through the surrounding trees, echoing and reechoing through the forest.

Thirrin raised her ax in acknowledgment of the salute, desperately hoping that none of the housecarls could see how afraid she was of failing them. Mastering weapons technique on the training ground was one thing, but how would she perform in battle? All these soldiers were looking to her to provide leadership and an example of ferocity and courage. What if she couldn't fulfill their expectations? For a moment a searing flame of panic flared up in the pit of her stomach and thrilled through her body.

But then a tiny ribbon of sound rippled through the trees. A horn was sounding the battle note of the Icemark! One of the scouts had spotted the enemy! Immediately the ranks of soldiers around her tightened, and the shields locked closer together.

"Housecarls of the Icemark. Here we stand or die!" Thirrin's clear voice rang out in the cold air, and as she spoke all fear left her. The die was cast; their fate lay now with the gods.

But for the next few minutes nothing happened. Thirrin stared along the road to the point where a slight bend hid it from view, but all was still. Brilliant sunshine cascaded through the naked branches of the winter trees, dappling the forest floor and the flagstones of the road in a dazzling display of light and shadow. Nearby a bird sang, the sweet tumble of notes amplified in the surrounding silence so that it filled the senses to brimming.

Nothing else stirred. The wind had dropped to a mere whisper that barely moved the slenderest twigs, and in the stillness the cold winter sun warmed up the thick carpet of leaf litter on the ground, and a rich earthy scent enveloped the waiting soldiers.

Then, like the shatter of breaking glass, the enemy burst into view. Rank upon rank of cavalry cantered along the road, all the troopers riding with pistols and sabers drawn. A murmur ran through the waiting housecarls, and then they fell deathly silent. Thirrin gazed hungrily at the cavalry; these were the first Polypontian soldiers she'd ever seen, and their appearance was both exotic and strangely beautiful.

They all wore brightly polished breastplates and helmets with cagelike face guards, but strangest of all to Thirrin were the brilliant plumes and silk sashes that blazed in the dappled sunshine. Even their thick winter coats were richly embroidered, and the officers had lace collars and cuffs. She might have laughed if she hadn't known that these were the ferocious warriors who had made the largest empire history had ever seen.

At the head of his command, Cassius Brontus saw the shield-wall of housecarls that blocked the way, and he calmly called a halt. He wasn't surprised; the warning calls of Thirrin's scouts had prepared him for such an eventuality, and his troopers had been riding in a state of high alert for more than two miles. For almost five minutes the opposing forces stared at each other, then Cassius Brontus waved up his officers.

He was painfully aware that the Icemark's commander had chosen his position well. The dense undergrowth ensured that they couldn't be outflanked, and the narrowness of the road at this point meant that he could use his meager numbers of housecarls to great effect. On top of this, the horses would have to charge uphill. The commander was obviously a wily old bird that would take some killing. Still, killed he would be — then he, Cassius Brontus, would overtake the refugees, kill the old, and enslave the rest. He should get a good price for such tough individuals. But most important of all he'd capture the Princess. She was the key to his entire future, and she was just waiting to be seized.

The conference with his officers was short. They had only one choice: Charge and sweep the Icemark's little band of foot soldiers aside. Quickly they deployed to their commands and Cassius Brontus withdrew to the side of the road.

A silence fell of such intensity that Thirrin could hear the blood whispering in her ears. She expected a herald to ride out from the Polypontian cavalry at any moment to make ritual demands that she would ritually reject — and then when that was done, they could begin the fight. But no such thing happened. A high brassy note blasted out from the ranks of the Polypontians, and they charged.

Thirrin was shocked, especially since their commander, the one with more plumes and sashes than anyone else, seemed to be watching proceedings from the roadside! But she quickly recovered and braced herself as the cavalry began to climb the hill at full gallop.

Before her was a wall of horseflesh rushing down on their thin line of shields like a tidal wave. Surely they must be swept aside. But then roaring and racing into her veins swept the combined battle fury of the Icemark and the Hypolitan. Her high-pitched voice climbed in astonishing power over the noise of the charge, and the shield-wall rose and slammed forward as one to meet the onslaught.

The screaming shock of onset made Thirrin's head reel, but after a second she recovered and swiftly looked to her right and left. The line had held. Before them horses struggled to regain their feet, and riders fell in a tangle of human and horse that writhed like a storm at sea. Those still mounted hacked with their long sabers at the housecarls before them, and a ragged volley of shots from the long cavalry pistols rang out. Thirrin swung her ax furiously as the Polypontian troopers desperately tried to surge forward over the fallen bodies and the shield-wall, and slowly the explosive shouts and curses of the housecarls consolidated into the familiar war chant.

"OUT! Out! Out! OUT! Out! Out! OUT! Out! Out!"

But then, with a suddenness that shook her, the troopers before them melted away, and Thirrin watched as they galloped back down the hill.

Cassius Brontus observed the withdrawal calmly. The enemy was densely packed into the narrow defensive position, and it would take several charges to finally dislodge them. But they were heavily outnumbered, and he'd use fresh troopers for each charge. The end was inevitable; it would just take a little longer than he'd hoped. He waved up the next squadron of cavalry and watched impassively as they exploded into a charge up the hill toward the housecarls. Once again the shield-wall surged forward to meet the attack, and the thunderous roar of onset filled the surrounding forest. The ring of saber on shield and ax against the heavy plate armor of the horses was punctuated by volley after volley of gunshot, but still the line held and again the cavalry withdrew.

Thirrin watched as the second wave cantered away, and swiftly checked the shield-wall. Already they'd had to pass many dead and injured housecarls back overhead to clear the line. At close range the long-barreled cavalry pistols were having a devastating effect. Even while she was calling out encouragement and praise to her houscarls, her quick mind was calculating that it would take only another three such charges to break their wall. She was bitterly angry. Just another five hundred soldiers and they could have held the road indefinitely and ground down the enemy. As it was, her first battle was about to end in defeat. For a moment the reality of the situation caused her to despair, and she had to struggle to hold back tears of anger and frustration. Immediately the soldiers around her sensed this and looked at their leader in alarm.

Her response was quick. Tightening her grip on shield and ax she laughed aloud, the sound creating its own power, and soon the terrible joy of battle surged through her again.

"Housecarls of the Icemark! We've made the Empire pay dearly for their attacks, but now I think we've warmed up enough to really make them suffer! After the next charge we'll send back only the horses. The riders we'll lay on the earth in tribute to our King, Redrought Strong-in-the-Arm Lindenshield, Bear of the North!"

A huge cheer greeted her words, and again the rattling rhythm of axes beating on shields rolled and swelled through the trees in tribute. Many of the veteran housecarls could hear the voice of Redrought himself echoing in the light tones of this young girl, and her fighting ferocity had given them heart in the face of overwhelming odds. But down the hill, Cassius Brontus was staring at the shield-wall in excited amazement. Judging by the clear and high voice he'd just heard, the commander of the enemy was a mere girl. But more important, he realized that only one girl in the whole of the Icemark could possibly command an infantry unit. The heir to the throne herself was standing only yards away! She was almost in his grasp! Spurring his horse forward, he called up his officers for a conference.

Up on the hill, Thirrin watched as Cassius Brontus spoke to his unit commanders. She knew that something different was about to happen and guessed it would take the form of a full-scale charge using all available troopers. She looked along her thin line of soldiers and doubted they could withstand it. If only she'd had a few more housecarls! And then, unbidden, the image of Oskan summoning the soldiers of the Oak King just before they had entered the forest came into her mind. Of course! Allies needed to be summoned. It was considered the height of diplomatic bad manners if the forces of a friendly power intervened in your war before being invited. She almost laughed aloud, and then just as quickly sobered up. She mustn't get too excited. She might not have the power or the right to call the Oak King's soldiers.

She ordered a nearby housecarl carrying a hunting horn to give the call of summons. All of her soldiers watched her step forward from the shield-wall and raise her arms. "Greetings to His Majesty the Oak King, Lord of the Forest and all wild places, from Princess Thirrin Freer Strong-in-the-Arm Lindenshield, Wildcat of the North, heir to the throne of the Icemark. Hear now my call for assistance. Soldiers of the Polypontian Empire have crossed your borders without permission and now threaten my people and my own royal person. We courteously ask your help in defending ourselves from our enemy and thank His Majesty for his friendship and alliance!"

Standing alone before the battered ranks of her soldiers she seemed incredibly fragile and vulnerable, but the housecarls now knew how strong she was in battle and they trusted her judgment and leadership implicitly. Many were already looking around for the arrival of the oak soldiers, but nothing happened. For several minutes Thirrin stood in silence. A sudden braying of bugles from the enemy ranks sounded suspiciously mocking, especially when it was followed by laughter. But then a wind sprang up, blowing and growing in strength as it howled and raged through the branches of the trees. Just as suddenly it dropped and a deathly hush followed.

Cassius Brontus had placed himself at the head of his cavalry. He intended to lead the charge and capture the Princess himself. This was his greatest political and military opportunity yet, and he didn't intend to allow a little superstitious ceremony to rob him of it. He signaled to the bugler, and the note of the charge rang out.

The entire force of cavalry leaped to the attack, storming up the hill toward the line of housecarls who stood waiting steadily. Thirrin's voice rose in power above the din of the galloping horses, shouting out the war cry of the Lindenshields: "Blood! Blast! And Fire! Blood! Blast! And Fire! Hold the line, warriors of the Icemark!" and her soldiers answered with their war chant:

"OUT! Out! Out! OUT! Out! Out! OUT! Out! Out!"

Then, with a tremendous roar, they leaped forward to meet the charge. The crashing ring of shield meeting cavalry echoed through the forest, and a volley of pistol shots rang out. The shield-wall bowed dangerously, and Thirrin screamed out the order to stand. Then into the huge calamitous roaring a new sound exploded. It was a noise like an avalanche in the mountains, and the cacophony grew as horses screamed in terror and men shouted. Thirrin stared in amazement as the very trees of the forest seemed to roll forward and smash into both flanks of the cavalry. The oak soldiers had arrived and were driving into their enemy. With a great shout of triumph the housecarls pushed forward and straightened their line, hacking at the troopers before them and dragging them from their saddles.

Cassius Brontus stared about him wildly. This could not be happening! Trees did not fight! Pieces of wood shaped like soldiers could not charge and attack his cavalry! It was madness, yet it was happening and his troopers were being outflanked. Realizing his danger, he gave orders to retreat; his words were translated into bugle calls that rang out above the din of battle. But as the horses were turned around, they found their route of escape blocked by more of the impossible wooden soldiers.

Thirrin seized her moment, and shouting out the battle cry of the Icemark, she led her housecarls in a smashing charge that drove against the trapped cavalry. The Polypontian soldiers fought with a controlled fury that showed their superb discipline. For more than half an hour the cavalry continued to fight a now defensive battle against the allied forces of the Icemark and the Oak King.

The political ambitions of Cassius Brontus were no longer of any importance to him. He simply wanted to save his command from annihilation. In very different circumstances he would have found the situation almost amusing: from arrogant certainty of success to a desperate struggle to survive in less than two hours. But he had no time to consider such ironies. As he barked out his last desperate orders, his cavalry began firing a continual rolling volley of pistol shots, and he led his troopers in a final charge against the part of the trap that had been most weakened by the earlier fighting. But Thirrin had read his thoughts perfectly, and her housecarls stood ready to receive them.

Spurred on by desperation, the Polypontian charge was a maelstrom of disciplined fury. They smashed into the shield-wall, bearing the soldiers of the Icemark back until their line was bent like a drawn bow. But at the center stood the burning figure of Thirrin Freer Strong-in-the-Arm Lindenshield,

Wildcat of the North, and she held her housecarls with a will that grew in strength the more she demanded of it. Her high-pitched voice rose like the cry of a hawk above the din of battle, and her soldiers rallied again and again as she called on them to stand and hold the line. Her battle-ax was notched and her shield was hacked and scored by the cavalry sabers of her enemies, but still she stood her ground and her soldiers stood with her.

Then a strange gasp arose from the ranks of the cavalry, and a cry of despair went up. Cassius Brontus had fallen. His exhausted horse had stumbled and immediately soldiers of the Icemark had leaped on him, hacking him to pieces where he lay. An answering cheer burst forth from the housecarls and they drove forward with renewed determination. The cavalry fell back at last, their final hope gone.

For another hour the cavalry fought on against Thirrin and her allies. Toward the end they dismounted and formed a defensive square. The ammunition for their pistols was spent, but they continued with their sabers, standing shoulder to shoulder and defending their standard to the last.

Three times Thirrin offered them terms, but each time they refused. Soldiers of the Empire had never surrendered. And so, as the last rays of the winter sunset bathed the naked trees in a glorious light of red and gold, they were all cut down where they stood around their banner.

The housecarls and soldiers of the Oak King drew back and stood in silence, staring at the fallen troopers before them. Thirrin finally removed her helmet, leaned her shield against her legs, and for a moment allowed herself to be a fourteen-year-old girl once more. She wept for the deaths all around her, she wept for her people forced from their homes into the harsh winter of the Icemark, and she wept for the young Polypontian trooper who lay at her feet, the blood seeping from the wound in his neck where her ax had bitten deep.

And as the tears streamed from her eyes, a line of steel-gray clouds drew down upon the land and released the first snows of the winter in a swirling tangle of white that would shroud the fallen and preserve their bodies for months.

11

The first of the winter storms died out during the night, and at daybreak the sun was reflected brilliantly by an unbroken blanket of snow. The people of Frostmarris looked even more ragged and dirty than usual set against the freezing, fresh white of the new day, but now that the storm was over, their mood had lightened. The snows had arrived at last, and they could begin to hope that the bad omen of their late appearance would begin to lift.

As usual, Oskan and Maggiore led the way, and soon they noticed that the trees were slowly beginning to thin out. They were coming to the end of the forest, and by midday they reached its eaves. Before them lay a wide snow-covered plain, brilliant and glittering under the winter sun. The road was only just discernible as a slight hollow in the softly undulating surface, and when the next storm hit the old highway, it would be completely lost until the spring thaw.

After a brief pause to view the sight before them, the people plodded on. Maggiore turned in his saddle to look back over the refugees and then said casually, "You don't feel a need to ride back to see how the Princess is faring, at all?"

Oskan looked at him and smiled. "No. I know she is safe. She's won her first battle, Maggie. She's proved herself the warrior we all knew she was. And besides, I don't fancy being flayed alive by her tongue for leaving the people to the mercy of the weather. The fact that we've got at least two days before the next storm won't make any difference to her."

"No. I suppose not," the neat little man answered automatically. But his mind and attention had suddenly wandered elsewhere. Thirrin had won her battle *and* they had at least two days before the next storm! After a quick calculation he realized that they would reach the main Hypolitan city before bad weather hit again. With a whoop of joy he urged his mare to a plunging gallop through the snow, throwing his hat into the air and laughing aloud while the people watched and cheered.

Then he reined to a halt and considered how he'd changed over the last few weeks: The rational man of science was now quite ready to accept without question the word of a dubiously educated peasant boy! And he really didn't mind at all! So far Oskan had always been proved right, and what sort of rationality rejects proof just because it seems a little . . . *colorful*?

Maggiore sang bright, lilting songs of the Southern Continent for the rest of the day. His voice fell completely flat in the dense silence of the snow-covered land, but he didn't seem to care, and the people added their own voices in a tangle of different songs and tunes that burst from the column of refugees like a flock of noisy birds.

It was Oskan who first spotted the splash of bright color moving steadily toward them across the white of the land. His keen eyes soon showed them to be cavalry of some sort coming from the north along the main highway.

He called Maggiore over and pointed ahead. "The Hypolitan have found us," he said simply.

* * *

Thirrin led the march through the forest at an unfaltering pace, one they could keep up for hours. She wanted to put the trees behind them as quickly as possible. They had sufficient rations to last them for three days, but if a really bad snowstorm hit, they could be forced to stop for a week or more. In truth, she hadn't expected any of them to survive the fight with the Empire cavalry, so she'd only given sketchy thought to the idea of rations to see them safely to the Hypolitan. But it was Oskan who'd insisted that she check and recheck their supplies before he'd left for the column the night before the battle. She was glad she'd listened to him now, but despite the shock of her first taste of open warfare, enough of the Princess still survived in her personality to be annoyed with him for not telling her to pack more. But, she eventually conceded, they were both novices when it came to provisions and rations; it was an easy enough mistake. Come to think of it, they were both novices at everything!

She'd actually recovered from the trauma of combat sooner than she could have ever imagined and now knew that she could lead her soldiers in battle with confidence and skill. As the housecarls themselves put it, she had "blood-proof," and the veterans of her first fight would proudly boast of it for the rest of their lives.

Within half an hour of the last Polypontian soldier falling, she'd regained enough of her composure to remember to thank the soldiers of the Oak King, and had even presented them with the spoils of war in the form of the weapons and armor of the fallen soldiers. They had bowed low in reply, then melted back into the fabric of the forest once more, their bodies absorbed by tree and earth, leaving Thirrin and her housecarls standing alone on the road.

That was more than a day ago, and since then the first snows had fallen, prompting Thirrin to order a forced march through the night in an attempt to catch up with the column of refugees. But if more snow fell before she reached them, her first victory could be her last.

Just after midday they came to a cairn of rocks piled in the center of the road. Thirrin gave orders for it to be dismantled, and inside they found sacks of nuts, berries, and other dried fruits of the forest. The Oak King had sent them supplies. The housecarls cheered and beat their swords and axes on their shields in salute, while Thirrin simply called, "Thank you — this won't be forgotten!" into the surrounding woodland.

The following night was even colder than usual for an Icemark winter. Even when they'd built huge blazing fires, the freezing winds reached icy fingers into the small domes of warmth and light that hugged the flames. Ten of the older soldiers died overnight, their gray housecarl beards white with frost and their hands frozen to the hilts of their swords. With a sense of quiet despair Thirrin realized that it wouldn't be long before the younger soldiers started to die, too, but there was nothing she could do about it. She guessed that unless they reached shelter within two days she could lose up to a quarter of the soldiers who'd survived the battle. With this thought in mind she set a punishing pace along the road, driving the housecarls along by reminding them it was not only ferocity in battle that marked a good soldier but also stamina and endurance.

They marched through the night again, their pace slowing to a crawl in the darkest hours. The forest distantly echoed with strange calls and bellows as though giant beasts were hunting them. Once, Thirrin thought she heard howling, but it was very faint and she had no way of knowing if it was the sound of ordinary wolves driven down from the hills by hunger or if they were the cries of the Wolf-folk, her allies. Then just before dawn, all fell silent as they trudged along, the only sound being the faint crunch as their feet broke through the crisp shell of frozen snow to the loose powder beneath. Thirrin was exhausted, and so were her housecarls. They would have to stop, if only for an hour or so, to eat rations and warm their frozen hands and feet at a fire.

She'd just given the order to halt when she caught the sound of hoofbeats approaching steadily. Without a word the shield-wall was raised and she took up her place at its very center. All her soldiers were staring ahead to a point in the road where it bent out of sight under the trees. Thirrin found herself wondering if they could put up much of a fight in their present condition. But she forgot all such thoughts as the horses came into view. They were about five hundred yards away, and in the cold clarity of the morning air Thirrin could see there were two columns, one made up of small sinewy animals and the other of larger horses. Both were carrying soldiers in brightly colored clothing.

One of the smaller horses was leading the columns, and its rider was wearing a scarlet cap with cheek flaps that looked somehow familiar to Thirrin. Seeing the shield-wall before them, the leader gave orders to halt before riding forward with another soldier who was on one of the larger horses. As they got nearer, Thirrin could see that the commander of the cavalry was a woman and she was holding up her hand in a gesture of peace.

"Who are you that rides armed in the forest in these times of war?" Thirrin called.

The woman didn't reply but dismounted and walked forward to within a few feet of the housecarls' shield-wall. Her face was stern and coldly beautiful, and Thirrin guessed she would be about Redrought's age. Suddenly the woman dropped to one knee.

"Hail, Princess Thirrin Freer Strong-in-the-Arm Lindenshield. I am your vassal Elemnestra Celeste, Basilea of the Hypolitan, and this," she said, indicating the huge man who stood respectfully some feet behind her, "is my consort Olememnon."

The housecarls began to cheer, but Thirrin curtly waved for silence. Something about the woman warned her not to hold herself with anything other than supreme dignity in this first meeting.

"Greetings, Elemnestra Celeste, Basilea of the Hypolitan. I would inform you that you have not given my due titles fully, as you missed the fighting epithet 'Wildcat of the North,' given to me by my father, Redrought, King of this land," she said proudly.

The woman returned her gaze steadily for a moment and then bowed her head. "Forgive me, My Lady. We had not been informed of this addition to your titles, but I will say that it is a fitting epithet for one who has just achieved her first victory with such glory." The woman then looked up and smiled, her whole face transformed into a warm and radiant beauty.

She stood up before adding, "And while we are talking of titles, you have missed one of mine, My Lady. That of *'Aunt'*; your mother was my youngest sister."

Of course Thirrin knew that the Basilea, or governor, of the Hypolitan was her aunt. But she had never met her mother's relatives before, and after the trauma of the last few days she thought she could be forgiven if it had temporarily slipped her mind.

"Greetings, then, Aunt Elemnestra. And this must be my

uncle Olememnon," Thirrin answered, nodding at the huge man who stood quietly waiting.

"Well, yes . . . I suppose so," Elemnestra answered, as though it had never occurred to her that a man could hold such a position. "Olememnon. Come forward and greet your . . . niece."

The governor's consort stepped forward and smiled as he dropped to one knee. He was massively built, with wide shoulders and a deep barrel chest, but oddly, he had no beard. Thirrin wondered if he'd had some dreadful accident, but then noticed that none of the other soldiers on the larger horses, all men, had beards, either. The common-sense answer occurred to her at last. Of course, they shaved. She was almost shocked. It was strange to look on men of the Icemark with no beards. It was almost like looking at older versions of Oskan, except that all of these soldiers had the stature of full-grown men.

The other soldiers on the smaller horses were women, and were as tall and slender as their Basilea. They carried short compound bows, spears, and crescent-shaped shields made of strengthened wicker, while the men carried round shields and axes like her own housecarls. But they all dressed the same, in brightly embroidered pants, coats, and scarlet caps with cheek flaps.

Thirrin turned her attention back to Olememnon, who was still kneeling before her, and stepping out of the shield-wall she took his hand and helped him to his feet.

"Greetings, Uncle," she said formally, and kissed his shaven cheek.

"Greetings, My Lady," he answered in a deep yet quiet voice, and smiled back at her.

Thirrin then turned to her aunt and, stepping forward,

embraced her. A huge cheer rang out from the housecarls and this time Thirrin didn't try to stop it.

Maggiore looked around him. The rooms were light and spacious, and the white-plastered walls with their murals of hills and trees reminded him of his childhood home. Except these hills were bigger, of course. And they were in the north, not far from the lands of permanent ice where the days and the nights were six months long. So how did the artists of this cold land know about the low hills and different species of trees found far to the south? How could they know of the countries where the sun is kind and the rains are well mannered enough to come at set times of the year so the people can prepare for them? It was a puzzle, though he supposed that they had simply copied works they had seen while traveling. Even so, the murals were to be found everywhere in the Basilea's palace, and they were so vivid and of such high quality that Maggiore was almost convinced that they proved some sort of link between the Hypolitan and the regions of the south.

But he was happy to let the mystery of the decor remain unsolved for a while. He was still enjoying the unusual luxury of being warm. A huge fire blazed in the log basket that sat in the center of the room, and the windows were tightly shuttered against the howling blizzard that was raging around the city of Bendis, the chief settlement of the Hypolitan. Warmth and good-sized food rations were just what he needed after that hellish journey, though he had to admit, things could have been far worse. "Thank whatever gods an agnostic like myself can believe in that the Basilea got our messages and brought help," Maggiore murmured to himself.

When the soldiers had found them on the road, they'd

immediately fed the people and, hearing of Thirrin's rear guard action, the Basilea herself had ridden on to the forest with supplies. By the time Thirrin and her escort had reached the walls of the city, the refugees had been settled in for more than a day, so most of them had joined the crowds that had lined the main highway leading to the citadel.

Thirrin's reception had been truly amazing: The Hypolitan saw the Princess as one of their own, which was hardly surprising, Maggiore conceded to himself, considering that her mother had been a member of their governing aristocracy. They'd cheered and waved and, oddly, laid furs at the feet of the horse she'd been given by the Basilea, so that Thirrin was obliged to ride over them.

Maggiore found himself fascinated by the traditions of the Hypolitan, and though he'd only been in the city for two days he'd already found out a lot. As a foreigner who'd spent most of his time in Frostmarris, he was surprised to hear words he didn't recognize sprinkled through the speech of the people. A dialect he'd expected, but these words sounded like the remnants of a language that was now almost lost. The religion, too, was different. As far as he could tell in his brief scan around, the local gods were mainly female with a dominant Mother Goddess, and this seemed to be reflected in mortal society, with few men in positions of power at any level. For a while Maggiore's male pride had been affronted, but then his brilliant scholar's mind had become fascinated, and finally he'd had to accept that the system was settled and ordered and all the people seemed happy enough.

Sitting before his fire in the comfort of his room, he'd reached the inescapable conclusion that the Hypolitan were immigrants, perhaps refugees themselves, who'd settled in the land at some point in the past. Even their names were different, with an exotic wealth of Cassandras and Iphigenias, which glowed like jewels among the background grays of Aethels and Cerdics. Maggiore's scholarly curiosity had been thoroughly aroused, and he'd ferreted out as much information as he could.

A knock at his door interrupted his thoughts, and he looked up just as Oskan and Thirrin walked in. They'd obviously been debating matters as they'd been walking along, and continued to talk after both raised their hands to acknowledge his presence.

"There's no way we can afford to sit around during the winter months and hope the Polypontians will just go away!" Thirrin snapped in her usual way, proving she'd completely recovered from the march and the battle.

"I never suggested that," Oskan answered just as forcefully. "If you'd actually listen instead of assuming I'm going to say something to annoy you, you'd have heard that I thought it was a good thing the *people* now have a chance to recover before the campaigning season begins again in the spring. I don't expect *you* will do anything even remotely like having a rest."

"No! There's the fyrd of the north to be called out, and equipped, trained, and housed. There are supplies to be secured and delivered, there are weapons to be made, repaired, and prepared! Rest is a luxury I can't afford and don't want!"

"But perhaps My Lady and her young adviser could at least sit down for now," said Maggiore quietly, and pointed to some chairs that stood against the walls.

Thirrin and Oskan fetched them and placed them next to the hearth. "I'm calling a meeting tonight with the Basilea and her council, so Oskan and I are just getting ready by airing our views. What do you have to say, Maggie?"

"About what particular aspect of the situation?"

"Any of it! All of it!"

"You seem to have the military preparations well in hand. But what of diplomacy and alliance?"

"Ah yes. I've decided —"

Oskan suddenly stood up, strode to the window, and threw open the shutters. The howling storm outside burst into the room, driving snow in a great billow toward the hearth, where it hissed and sizzled in the flames. Thirrin and Maggiore coughed and spluttered in the smoky steam and started to shout at Oskan above the roar of the wind.

"Listen!" Oskan snapped with such authority the other two fell silent. "Can't you hear it?"

"Hear what?" Thirrin demanded.

"The howling!"

All three sat quietly in the midst of the snow and raging wind and listened as slowly the thin edge of a howl separated itself from the noise of the storm.

"Wolves. So what? They're hungry and have come down from the hills!"

"No! Not wolves. The Wolf-folk. They're calling for you," he said forcefully.

Thirrin leaped to her feet. "What are they saying?"

Oskan stood listening for almost a minute, his eyes unfocused as he concentrated. Thirrin could barely contain her frustration, but she didn't dare say anything until he was ready. At last he blinked and said, "They want safe conduct into the city. They want you to meet them outside the gates."

"Right!" Thirrin hurried to the door. "Oskan, issue orders for all gate guards to let them through. No one is to harm them in any way, on pain of death! Maggie, tell the Basilea what's happening and meet us in the main hall."

* * *

As Thirrin and Oskan rode down from the citadel, the wind continued to howl and drive the snow in a stinging hail, like ice arrows that made it almost impossible to see. Oskan found himself wondering how anyone, or anything, could survive such conditions, and yet the Wolf-folk had traveled through the storm and were waiting now beyond the gates.

The guards had already received their orders and so were ready to let Thirrin and Oskan out into the blizzard. But as they opened the gates, four snow-encrusted figures stumbled in, carrying what looked like a large stretcher between them. The guards drew their swords, but Thirrin snapped out an order and they sheathed them. The tallest of the strange figures stepped forward and dropped to one knee. It raised its hideous mask of a face, and the Princess could clearly see the mingling of human and wolf in its features.

"My Lady, we must go up to the citadel of the Hypolitan Basilea. We have come to return something to you." The creature's voice boomed easily above the screaming wind.

"What is it?"

"Not here, My Lady. It would not be . . . fitting."

Thirrin glanced at the stretcher and nodded quickly. "This way."

By the time they reached the main hall, Elemnestra the Basilea and her consort, Olememnon, were waiting. They were sitting in their Thrones of State, wearing their official robes as though expecting foreign dignitaries. Beside them the ten members of the High Council of the Hypolitan stood waiting quietly, as did an anxious-looking Maggiore.

As Thirrin strode into the hall, she couldn't help noticing that Maggiore and Olememnon were the only men present, but she was so busy trying to appear calm that she had little time to think of anything else.

As Thirrin reached the dais, Elemnestra stood to offer her the throne, but she waved her to sit. The werewolves now stepped forward and placed their burden on a trestle table that stood nearby. The council members murmured at the appearance of the Wolf-folk, and the guards around the hall quietly loosened their swords in their sheaths.

Thirrin looked around her, aware of the mistrust in the hall, and felt her temper rising. "These people are my allies and have already shown me great loyalty and trust. If anyone here present mistreats them in word or deed, I will call upon my powers as heir to the throne of the Icemark and I will order their hanging out of hand!" She looked around her fiercely; none would meet her eye. "Good. Then I call on the Wolf-folk to speak now. What have you brought us?"

Once again the tallest of the werewolves stepped forward. "My Lady, our burden is heavy and we have carried it far from the battlefield of the south." A murmur ran through the hall as people realized for the first time that the creatures could speak. "But the weight has been no physical hardship. The Wolf-folk could carry ten times the weight for twice the distance and feel no effort. No, the burden has been one of sorrow, knowing what pain we must bring our ally."

Thirrin gazed at him steadily, her face pale in the light of the hall's torches. "What have you brought us?"

The wolfman bowed his head and, turning to the stretcher, he pulled aside the cover, revealing the bodies of Redrought and the Lady Theowin, packed in snow that had perfectly preserved them.

A gasp ran around the hall, and then a perfect silence returned as Thirrin stepped up to the stretcher. Redrought was still wearing his armor, though his helmet had been placed on his chest, and the Wolf-folk had also taken time to clean the bodies of any blood so that they appeared to be in a deep and dignified sleep.

Thirrin gazed at her father and remembered the huge man who'd loved cats and fluffy slippers, who'd played with her as a little girl and had told her stories when she went to bed. Her eyes filled with tears as she took the icy-cold hand in hers.

"Dad," she whispered. "I love you, Dad." She stooped and kissed his cheek. Then, standing upright, she turned to the wolfman. "What news of the battle?"

"The King defeated his enemies and took their banner. It lies now at his feet. But his army was destroyed in the act of destroying. The enemy numbers were too great, but we believe he knew what he was doing and sacrificed his army to give you time to raise a second host and call on the help of your allies. We Wolf-folk were not ready; it takes many cycles of the blessed moon to gather our people; but a few of us went to watch so that we might bring news to you, My Lady. When we saw Baroness Theowin fall and King Redrought killed just as he seized the enemy's battle standard, we ran to collect their bodies from the field before the soldiers who came on horses after the fighting could take them.

"We have brought them now to you, our ally, and also bring greetings from our king, Grishmak Blood-drinker. He says that the muster is under way and will be ready in the spring, when he will expect your call to battle."

Thirrin stood silently gazing at the body of Redrought, her face pale and her eyes bright. But then she seemed to collect herself and, looking up, said, "We return greetings and friendship to His Majesty Grishmak Blood-drinker and assure him that the call for battle will be sent with the new campaigning season." Then she looked at her father again, and added in a voice that began quietly but climbed with a rising power, "But before that, there are pyres to be built, and a hatred to be stoked up to a blazing height that will scorch the Empire of the Polypontus. It will rage and roar through its very streets until the Emperor's palace itself is an explosion of flames. Let our drive be revenge! Let our weapons be hatred! Let our anger be the power that smashes the Empire!"

At once a huge clamor broke out as the guards beat their swords on their shields, the Wolf-folk howled, and everyone cheered. Maggiore was interested to find himself shouting with the rest, and noted wryly that the power of emotion could overthrow even the most objective of minds.

12

The wide square in front of the Basilea's palace was lined with people. In the center a pyre had been built using thick stakes of oak, layered level on level so that it soared into the sky like a wooden pyramid. Soldiers were pouring oil and other flammable liquids over the already fuel-drenched wood, and draping the battle colors of the Icemark over two platforms that had been constructed at the top. One was set a yard or so below the other and had Baroness Theowin's striking hawk insignia placed before it, while the topmost one had been dressed with Redrought's personal device of the fighting bear.

The sky was a heavy, dark presence threatening more snow, and a bitter wind scythed through the silent ranks of people, causing them to draw their winter cloaks tighter about themselves. In front of the masses stood ranks of housecarls, their armor glittering redly in the light of the torches that each soldier held, and from the buildings that faced the square, long banners of mourning snapped and fluttered in the wind, their deep purple almost black against the brilliance of the snow.

The people had been waiting for more than an hour now, and despite the freezing cold they gave no impression of impatience.

All of them were aware that they were about to witness one of the most important events in the history of the Icemark. A great warrior-king and his loyal vassal were to be cremated in as spectacular a ceremony as the heir to the throne could muster, considering the circumstances of war and invasion.

In more normal times the dead monarch would have been cremated on the plain before the city of Frostmarris, and once the flames had died, a mound would have been raised over the ashes. But Princess Thirrin had decreed that the ashes of her father, mixed with those of the Lady Theowin, would be gathered in an urn and no burial mound raised until she had returned to the capital at the head of a liberating army.

A slow drift of snow began to fall, settling on the huge pile of wood in the center of the square and adding fresh layers to the frozen and impacted ice that coated every surface. Oskan Witch's Son had said there would be a light sprinkling but nothing that would interrupt the funeral, so the people put up their hoods and simply hunched their shoulders against the weather.

Suddenly a fanfare of deep-toned horns rang out, and the housecarls snapped to attention. A murmuring buzz ran through the crowds, and every head craned to see along the main road that led to the citadel. In the distance the gates of the fortress slowly opened, and a long procession filed out. Those citizens at the back where the road entered the square now had the advantage, because they could plainly see the Princess Thirrin in full armor, marching at the head of an escort of housecarls and warriors of the Hypolitan. Beside her walked the Basilea, and just behind them came the witch's son and Maggiore Totus. The soldiers marched in a square formation surrounding a wide bier that was being carried on the broad shoulders of ten werewolves.

A collective gasp rose up from the people at the sight of the Wolf-folk marching with the soldiers. Until Thirrin's alliance with King Grishmak they'd been the sworn enemies of the Icemark, and most citizens still found their presence within the walls of a city frightening and strange. But as the crowd watched the approach of the procession, the huge creatures kept perfect step with the escorting soldiers, and the sense of their restrained ferocity added a dignity to the funeral beyond that of even the most disciplined troops.

A silence descended, broken only by the slow rhythmic tramp of marching feet. None of the citizens wept. Redrought had been a good King, as far as that affected the lives of the people. He'd demanded no new taxes; he'd threatened no new tithes; and his appetites and interests hadn't put any extra burdens on the society of the Icemark. What's more, he'd died doing his job, trying to defend the country from invaders. That was something he'd been good at.

But to most of the citizens the King was a remote figure, and it was hard to relate to his death in a directly emotional way. They were more interested in the practicalities of his successor. Would Thirrin be able to defend the country, and therefore their lives, from the invading Polypontians? So far she'd done well, carrying out the evacuation of Frostmarris with skill and control, and then defeating the enemy cavalry that had pursued them. She'd also shown an amazing ability to form alliances with the most unlikely . . . people.

In many ways the ordinary citizens found it easier to accept the idea of an alliance with the Wolf-folk and with the Oak King and Holly King than the ruling aristocracy did. They were realists who were happy to accept any friendship that would save their skins. Only those who knew that one season's harvest stood between them and famine truly understood that yesterday's sworn enemy can be working beside you in the field the next day. Only fools skirmish in their backyard when war is knocking down their front door.

In the meantime they watched the slow advance of the funeral cortege. Not only was it free entertainment in the dark days of the winter but it gave the people a chance to gauge the morale of the ruling elite. If they looked worried, the people had every right to be terrified.

The procession tramped slowly into the square before marching a complete circuit of its perimeter. Thirrin's face was set in rigid lines, and both Oskan and Elemnestra, the Basilea of the Hypolitan, seemed preoccupied by other matters. Only Maggiore's scholarly curiosity caused his eyes to dart from one interesting sight to another as he observed the fascinating funeral customs of the country. The people of the Icemark collectively relaxed. There were no signs of anxiety anywhere on the part of the ruling elite.

As the bier passed close to the crowds, many heads craned to see the bodies of King Redrought and the Lady Theowin. The snow the Wolf-folk had packed around them had perfectly preserved them, and they both looked suitably stern and warriorlike. The fact that they also looked as though they were sleeping added further to the emotional distance that the people felt, and a strange carnival atmosphere developed as the crowds began to applaud. Thirrin's composure slipped for a moment, and she looked at the crowds sharply, but then her expression relaxed. Her father would have probably preferred clapping and cheering to weeping. It was, after all, a sign of appreciation.

The procession then approached the pyre, and the escort of soldiers stamped to a halt, allowing the werewolf pallbearers to march forward and slowly climb the stairway that had been built into the huge stack of wood. The crowd now fell silent as the creatures placed the bodies of King and vassal onto their respective platforms and draped them with their personal banners. As they withdrew, the housecarls began to tap sword hilt and ax haft on their shields. Gently and slowly the sound grew and swelled, rolling around the square as it rose to a massive crescendo that echoed back from the lowering clouds and stone buildings. Then slowly it died away to silence as the Wolf-folk resumed their positions among the soldiers.

Thirrin had prepared no speech and had called on no others to speak. In her silence lay her grief. In the lack of speech and oration lay the country's loss. Quietly she stepped forward and, without turning, held out her hand. The Basilea joined her and gave her a compound bow of the Hypolitan and a single arrow, the end of which had been wrapped with pitch-soaked linen. Thirrin fitted arrow to string and drew it back. She nodded, and the Basilea lit the linen-covered head and withdrew. The Princess raised the bow high and loosed the flaming arrow, and it streaked like a tiny comet against the background gray of the heavy clouds.

The crowds followed its course as it arced skyward and then fell in a graceful parabola to land deep in the piled stakes of the pyre. Immediately a small flame licked about the fuel-drenched wood and began to grow. The Basilea now gave a signal, and the female soldiers of the Hypolitan all raised their bows and loosed a rain of flaming arrows onto the pyre. After this the housecarls rushed forward and threw in the blazing torches they'd been carrying, and the pyre erupted into a huge ball of fire that sent a blast of heat against the crowds.

The housecarls resumed their positions and stood watching as the fire settled down to a steady blaze. Now the Wolf-folk threw back their heads and began the eerie and mournful howling of their kind, the notes rising up through the octaves and then slowly descending to a silence.

Thirrin watched as the flames roared up to a great height, illuminating the gray and white winter city with golds and fierce reds. She tried to keep her mind clear as the incredible heat slowly unmade the body of the man who'd been her teacher and guide from the time of her earliest memories. She tried to believe that she was watching the honorable funeral rites of a man who was no more important to her than any other great warrior. But the image of a hugely bearded, laughing face kept forcing its way into her mind's eye. His bluff and gruff kindness had comforted her through many of her childhood hurts and disappointments, but it was the memory of his ridiculous fluffy slippers that finally made her weep.

The sight of the stern young warrior-maiden with tears rolling down her rigid cheeks was an image that many of the people in the watching crowds would remember most about the funeral of Redrought Strong-in-the-Arm Lindenshield, Bear of the North, King of the Icemark.

The council chamber was surprisingly only half full, considering the importance of the meeting that Thirrin had called. At the table there was only the Basilea, the ten members of the ruling council, and five commanders, while Thirrin's contingent included herself, Oskan, Maggiore Totus, and all of the officers who had marched north with her.

The new Queen of the Icemark was still getting used to the idea of full command and power, and she'd been arguing with her aunt the Basilea for almost half an hour before the meeting had even properly begun.

"I will have *all* my commanders here at the council, including those of the Hypolitan army!" Thirrin said icily. "Not just those that Hypolitan tradition allows." And she clasped her hands behind her back in an attempt to stop them from shaking.

Basilea Elemnestra held her niece's angry gaze for a moment and then said with quiet venom, "But our men are not trained to take part in meetings such as this!"

"Men have positions of command in your army, don't they?"

"Yes. And anything they need to know will be conveyed by their immediate superiors."

Thirrin kept her voice low and measured. The slightest waver would show just how scared she was of her formidable aunt. "So they receive all news and plans at secondhand and are robbed of all immediacy. It's not good enough, Basilea. I want my orders to be heard directly, not conveyed by someone else who may not give the precise emphasis and weight that I want."

"It's not possible for all officers to be at every conference and council. Some commanders will always receive information at secondhand," the Basilea argued.

"True. That cannot be helped in armies of any great size. But you want to bar at least ten middle-ranking commanders who could easily be at this briefing simply because they're men, and I will *not* have it. It's unjust, ridiculously old-fashioned, and most important it is an inefficient way to conduct military business. Do you really think that General Scipio Bellorum would allow such hidebound traditions to compromise the workings of his war machine?"

"Bellorum is a murderous barbarian; I couldn't possibly say how he would act."

Thirrin took a deep, steadying breath. She was determined to at least look as though the Basilea didn't worry her. "He is the most successful general the known world has ever seen! He took a huge and cumbersome military monster and turned it into a deadly efficient fighting force within five years. And in the last ten years of his command he's added three countries and five new provinces to the Polypontian Empire. If we're not to become the fourth sovereign state to be turned into just another administrative area within his Imperial ambitions, we'd better learn to think and act like him. And that means efficiency, and the ability to recognize when the worst enemy we have is ourselves! Now, as Queen of the Icemark I order you to send for your commanders or I will invoke the power of my office and have you replaced by a Basilea who sees sense — aunt or not!"

Maggiore Totus watched his former pupil with a delighted satisfaction he was beginning to expect. Thirrin had already surprised him several times since the war had begun, by showing an accelerating ability to cope with situations that were beyond anything she'd experienced before. However, he thought to himself, this was a very delicate situation. She couldn't afford to alienate any part of society in this time of extreme crisis, and how she resolved this conflict could affect the outcome of the war.

The Basilea sat in silence for a moment, obviously weighing the content of her niece's threat. At last she nodded, spoke to a guard, and sent her off to fetch the male commanders.

Thirrin silently breathed a sigh of relief. Ten minutes of uncomfortable silence then followed until the first of the officers began to arrive. Thirrin greeted them with a smile and, understanding perfectly that they'd never been to such a meeting, personally directed them to their seats. She then explained why they were all there.

"This is a council of war. We have five months before the spring begins to clear the roads of ice and snow. In that time I intend to train a fighting force the like of which has never been seen in the Icemark before. It must be efficient, disciplined, and well equipped. I've already given orders for the armories to increase their output, and the fyrd has been called. In a matter of days the raw recruits will be coming in, and it is the job of the regular army to train them."

The most confident of the Hypolitan male officers raised a hand, and Thirrin nodded at him to speak.

"I presume, then, that the training methods for the fyrd are to be changed in some way, Your Highness."

"No," Thirrin answered. "They're to be added to. The period and method of basic training will be the same. But then I want each and every fyrd member to be given the same instruction as the housecarl regiments. I want no elite corps in my army; *every* soldier is to be a member of the elite!"

For the next hour Thirrin outlined her plans and answered questions on every aspect of her strategy, from instruction to housing and supply. She was horribly aware of the massive task that confronted them and the fact that everyone was relying on *her* to lead the way. Fortunately she'd already thought long and hard about the issues and had a ready solution for most potential problems.

At last, when all possibilities had been examined, she sat back and smiled. "There's one more issue that needs to be discussed. I intend to go on a Royal Progress to meet with the Vampires in The-Land-of-the-Ghosts."

She waited quietly for the uproar of objections to die down and then continued, "I intend to go for one simple reason: We need allies."

"But we've already made alliances with the Wolf-folk and

with the Holly King and Oak King," Elemnestra pointed out. "Why risk your life by going to the Blood Palace of the Vampire King and Queen?"

"I've discussed this issue with my advisers, Maggiore Totus and Oskan Witch's Son, and we all agree that if the Icemark is to survive this attack from the Polypontian Empire, then we must have more allies. In fact, the more the better. We must never forget that we're trying to defend our little country from the largest, most efficient army the world has ever seen. And you all know that it is commanded by the most successful general in all remembered history. Even with the help of the Vampire King and Queen our survival remains doubtful, but without them we are certainly lost."

"Then send a trusted ambassador in your stead. We can't risk losing our Queen at this time," cautioned the Basilea.

Maggiore Totus coughed apologetically and stood up. "That has been considered, but we decided that as relations with The-Land-of-the-Ghosts are at a particularly . . . low ebb, it would take a diplomatic mission of the highest standing to repair and reestablish proper links. Especially as we will be asking for military aid at the same time."

"Can you guarantee the safety of the Queen?" Elemnestra demanded.

"Madam, none of us can guarantee that we will be alive to take breakfast tomorrow, let alone the safety of the monarch of a war-torn country. But there are times when risks must be taken for the general good."

"Then you must take an escorting army with you."

"And make the Vampire King and Queen think we're trying to invade?" Thirrin said. "No. I will take a small escort of ten cavalry and twenty infantry."

"How can we be certain that The-Land-of-the-Ghosts won't try to invade now that we're distracted by war in the south?" one of the Hypolitan commanders asked.

"For two reasons," Thirrin answered easily. "First, none of the border fortresses has reported anything unusual in the way of troop movements, and second, we're a buffer zone between the Empire and their own lands. Added to that is the fact that the Polypontians are creatures of science and rationality. The Vampire King and Queen would be objects of complete loathing for them: things to be stamped out and purged from the earth. If the Icemark falls, their lands will be next on Scipio Bellorum's shopping list, and there'd be no option of citizenship in the greater realm of the Empire for any of their . . . people. They'd all be wiped out. This fact will be our greatest bargaining point in the coming negotiations."

She looked around the table to see if there were any more questions before going on. "I'll be taking Oskan Witch's Son with me, but Maggiore Totus will stay here. The journey may get both hard and hazardous, and I want no casualties among my advisers."

Another of the male commanders of the Hypolitan raised his hand and she turned to him.

"How will you let the Vampire King and Queen know of your intentions? Surely you can't just cross the border and expect a friendly reception?"

"Our allies the Wolf-folk will smooth the way there. I've already been in touch with King Grishmak, and he's agreed to send emissaries to the Blood Palace. By the time I reach the border, Their Vampiric Majesties will know I'm coming," Thirrin answered, more confidently than she felt.

"You could, of course, be walking into a trap of your own making," the Basilea pointed out.

"I could," Thirrin agreed. "But as we have already said, there are times when risks must be taken. And as this is the case I've decided to take as many precautions as I can." She stood up and, raising her voice so that all could hear her clearly, she announced: "I now name before you all Basilea Elemnestra, my aunt and loyal vassal, as my heir. In the event of my death or disappearance she will be declared Queen and lead you all in the struggle against the Polypontian Empire. I present to her now the Great Ring of State that will be given back to me on my return from embassy."

Thirrin took the ring from her finger and handed it to the Basilea, who took it with a look of bemusement on her face. Maggiore was as surprised as everyone else by this gesture but, smiling secretly to himself, he had to admit it was the perfect way to heal the rift that had been caused by Thirrin's insistence that the male staff officers should be present at the meeting. Her growth into her role as Queen of the Icemark was now almost complete, thought Maggiore, and perhaps her Royal Embassy to The-Land-of-the-Ghosts would add those indefinable finishing touches that would make her a truly formidable monarch.

Scipio Bellorum watched his army thoughtfully from his vantage point high on the hill. From here it was possible to follow the tactical patterns precisely as cavalry moved against the disciplined blocks of infantry. He'd ordered live rounds to be used in practice maneuvers and had allowed himself a casualty rate of ten percent. A little wasteful perhaps, but there was nothing like the threat of blood to sharpen a soldier's concentration, especially when that blood might be his own.

He was well aware of the setback his first invading army had suffered, and now that the snows had come he knew it would be several months before he could send in any substantial reinforcements. It had all been a calculated risk — the snows had been late and there had been a chance that he could have established a strong bridgehead before the spring. Well, that chance had slipped through his fingers, and now he had to make the best of the situation.

The only real problem, as he saw it, was how to keep his troops in tip-top battle readiness over the slow winter months. It was all too easy for a fighting unit to lose its edge. But if he kept them busy with war games and allowed the cannons to use live ammunition as well as the muskets, then he'd have created conditions as near to war as it was possible to get without taking the field against an actual enemy. Horribly wasteful of men and ammunition, of course, but the army could sustain it. And it would be easily justified when he led a fresh and battle-ready invasion force into the Icemark next spring.

He smiled quietly to himself: At least he would be in a state of complete preparedness when the thaw came. No need to wait for regiments to make their way along recently opened roads. They'd all be in position, just waiting for his order to advance.

A short while later he became aware of a pleasant hunger — there was nothing like maneuvers to stimulate the appetite. *A little beef for dinner tonight*, he thought, *cooked very rare, with one of those fine red wines from the latest of my conquests. The two would complement each other perfectly.*

13

Thirrin pointedly ignored the long woolen warmers that Oskan had carefully rolled down over the ears of his mule, Jenny. Even the fact that they were bright yellow with red pom-poms on the very tips didn't drag any sort of comment out of her. She was determined not to notice them or the richly colored bridalry the mule was decked in, but she was swiftly coming to the conclusion that there were times when Oskan deliberately tried to annoy her. He still refused to ride a horse that she thought more fitting for one of her most important advisers, and now he'd taken to making a naturally ridiculous-looking animal look even more ludicrous by dressing it in brightly colored knitwear!

The escort of ten Hypolitan cavalry troopers and twenty housecarls had all grinned like complete idiots when Oskan had first appeared on his mule, and she expected anyone they met on the road to do the same. It was hardly in keeping with royal or ambassadorial dignity.

"Are you ready?" she asked, looking down on him from the huge height of her war stallion with what she hoped was disdainful dignity, and Oskan smiled brightly and nodded.

The main road out of the Hypolitan city was lined with the refugees from Frostmarris, who watched them ride by in almost total silence. They knew their young Queen was taking a terrible risk, and that if she failed they were almost certainly doomed to defeat at the hands of the Polypontian Empire. Even the sight of the mule in its ear-warmers did little to lighten their mood. A few raised their hands in farewell, and one or two called blessings and little spells for safe journeys, but otherwise they were as quiet as a frozen lake.

Thirrin was relieved when they'd finally ridden through the gates and the road lay empty before them. Oskan had said they could expect at least three days of calm weather, by which time they should be close to the border. And certainly the day was bright and clear — the best sort of conditions for traveling in the winter, if it really couldn't be avoided. The frozen snow reflected the sunlight brilliantly, and the sky was the polished blue of washed enamel. Thirrin sniffed the air appreciatively. Beyond the immediate strong aromas of their horses and the leather of the soldiers' equipment, the day smelled only of the clean cold scent of snow. She felt suddenly free, and had she been on her own she would have raced through the tingling air, urging her horse to greater and greater speeds. But she was now Queen of the Icemark, and an overriding sense of her responsibilities stopped her. The realization that responsibility would color her every decision and action from now on suddenly weighed heavily on her, and her mood darkened.

"I suppose you're cold," she said grumpily to Oskan.

"Of course. It's winter," he answered blandly.

"I might've expected you to feel it more than most."

He looked at her, assessing this new mood, then he said, "Madam, I've lived all my life in a cave and walked naked in all weathers until I was seven. Yes, I'm cold, that's an obvious fact — everyone who leaves their fireside in an Icemark winter is cold. But I'm not complaining. I'm as cold and as refreshed as someone who's just plunged into a mountain lake."

She grunted moodily in answer, but she had to admit to herself that he certainly looked comfortable enough, dressed as he was in the sort of brightly colored quilted jacket and leggings that were common among the Hypolitan. In fact, Oskan matched Jenny the mule perfectly. She was only surprised he wasn't wearing ear-warmers under his scarlet cap.

His mood wasn't exactly in keeping with circumstances, either. Most people had waved them off with a gloomy air, acknowledging the desperate situation that had driven the new Queen of the land to seek an alliance with their ancient enemy. But Oskan gave the impression he was off on some holiday jaunt.

"Why are you so happy?" Thirrin asked accusingly. "Everybody else is terrified by this war, but you look like a kitten with cream."

"I am happy," he said, grinning at her hugely, "because there's no fighting at the moment. The sun's sparkling on the snow and the sky's as blue as a kingfisher's wing."

"And you think your attitude's appropriate? People have died and many more will be killed before the fighting's finished, and yet you smile as though your mouth's got an ambition to reach your ears!"

"And exactly how does a miserable face help the war effort?" he asked sharply, his mood beginning to change. "Will a frown bring back the dead or fortify a town? If I allow myself to laugh in the face of misery, I rest my mind from the stress of it all, and then it'll work the better for you and your war. And if I'm really to be one of your advisers, Your Majesty, accept this piece of advice: Take happiness where and when you find it, because there's going to be precious little of it in the next few months!"

Thirrin reined to a halt angrily and glared at him. "I don't like your tone, Mr. Royal Adviser! Perhaps my father was wrong and you'd be happier in some other role."

"Perhaps! Perhaps! You really have no idea how people feel, do you?" Oskan said sharply, his anger oddly disproportionate to the situation. "I've never wanted the job of being the voice of reason to Her Majesty of the Royal Cloth Ears. Do you really imagine that ominous warnings about losing my position are some sort of threat? There's nothing I'd like better than to go back to my cave and live as I want."

"Ha! And how would you be able to live in your cave with troops of the Empire stomping all over the Great Forest?"

"I can assure you that in the woodlands I'm seen only when I want to be. Why does Thirrin Freer Strong-in-the-Arm-Make-Enough-Noise-to-Wake-the-Dead think she never saw me until this year, when I've watched *her* ever since she first ventured into the trees on a lead rein?"

Thirrin could have screamed, she was so angry, but she steadied her voice to an icy hiss. "Then perhaps Oskan Witch's Son would be happier using his superior woodcraft by working as a scout for the fyrd! Once he's completed his basic training, of course."

"And exactly which of your regiments of iron-plated country bumpkins do you fondly imagine has the ability to hold me?" he asked, smiling viciously. Thirrin was suddenly aware of how catlike and fierce his features could be when he was angry. "Healers make the most dreadful enemies, Scion of the House of Strong-in-the-Arm. The Knowledge that saves lives can be used to do exactly the opposite. Especially when they have the blood of the Wise Ones in their veins."

Thirrin looked at him for a moment and was amazed at the transformation. His eyes were wide and wild, his lips were drawn back from his vividly white and oddly sharp teeth, and she truly believed that if she touched him, his skin would crackle with rage. And there was something else. There was an aura of power about him that was almost tangible. It seemed to thicken the air around him, rippling it like a heat haze, but retreating when the eye tried to pin it down.

He really would make the most terrible enemy, and though she was livid and would have liked nothing better at that heated moment than to draw her sword and force him to beg her forgiveness, an insistent note of caution chimed in her brain: *You need him, the country needs him. Don't drive him along dark paths because of your pride. You are Queen now, you can't allow personal anger to endanger the land.*

Somehow she knew that this was a pivotal moment. Where it had come from and how, she couldn't tell. But she knew if she lost Oskan now, something Dark would gain by it.

She breathed deeply, battling with her emotions, and slowly winning. When she looked at him again, his eyes were oddly unfocused, but they still blazed with an anger she'd unwittingly called forth. It was up to her to break the mood and win him back.

She leaned forward in her saddle and looked closely at him. "Oskan Witch's Son. Don't leave us. We need you. Would your mother, White Annis, have left us at such a time of need? Come back, Oskan."

Slowly his eyes refocused, but still he looked at Thirrin as though she were a stranger.

Long ago, White Annis had told him about his father, and how his kind always had to make a choice between the Light and the Dark. Well, now his time to choose had come. The raging, boiling anger that had erupted seemingly from nowhere had presented him with a choice. Either he could use his powers for himself in glorious selfishness, or he could use them to help others, often for little return, perhaps not even for any thanks. It was as simple as that.

The decision, of course, was obvious, and his grin broadened into an almost wolfish snarl. But then recognition of the young girl who was looking so desperately at him returned and he shook his head. What had she said? "Come back"? Why should he? Why should he give his power and strength to help others? But he already knew the answer. Thirrin Freer Strong-in-the-Arm Lindenshield needed him, and so, too, did her tiny, foolish, brave little country. Slowly he turned away from the temptation of the Dark and looked around him.

"Come back, you say! Where in the world do you think I've been? And who's leaving whom?"

"You were threatening to go back to your cave."

"Was I? No . . . I seem to remember you were the one making the threats."

"A royal prerogative. Consider them forgotten."

He seemed a little confused, but after a while he smiled with his old warmth. "What on earth got into us?"

"Who knows? But it's over. Let's forget it."

"No. Let's remember it," said Oskan mysteriously. But he smiled again, so brightly that Thirrin was reassured and deeply relieved.

During this time, the escort of soldiers had stopped and had been anxiously watching the pair battle over something they didn't understand. But now, as the Queen and her counselor relaxed and started to talk in normal tones again, they resumed their march.

* * *

The very short day of the Icemark winter meant that to put a reasonable distance behind them they had to continue marching after sunset. But there was no need to light the torches they carried. The moon was a day away from full, and when it rose into a sky of brilliant stars, its soft silver-gray light was reflected and magnified by the snow so that the entire world seemed to glow like a pearl in the dark.

But the cold was vicious, and with the setting of the sun, the already low temperatures plunged to depths that made leather brittle and breathing painful. They endured marching in the cold for four more hours. Then, as soon as Thirrin gave orders to halt, the soldiers began the task of setting up shelters by unloading long flexible poles from the packhorses and forming them into rigid dome-shaped frames over which many layers of thick woven rugs and animal hides were tied. The floors inside were also covered with rush matting, braziers were lit at the entrances, and soon the tents had reached a temperature that was at least above freezing. Even the horses had their own shelter, constructed along the same lines but with a deep bedding of straw. Carrying enough equipment to make traveling possible in the depths of winter was one of the reasons why Thirrin had wanted to keep the numbers down, but everyone was well used to the conditions and carried out their tasks efficiently.

She was still worried about the possibility of snowstorms, but Oskan had said that blizzards blowing to the south of the forest wouldn't move north until they were close to the Wolfrocks, by which time she hoped they wouldn't be too far from the Blood Palace of the Vampire King and Queen.

She and Oskan ate their meal together in the royal tent, listening to the singing coming from the housecarls' shelter pitched a little way off. The strange argument they'd had earlier in the day at first made them a little awkward, but after Oskan had dismissed it as "magic pollution" blowing on the wind from The-Land-of-the-Ghosts, they became a little easier.

"After all, what else could it have been? It came out of nowhere, reached huge heights of stupidity, then disappeared as soon as we confronted it with common sense," he said logically.

"As soon as *I* confronted it with common sense," Thirrin pointed out. "You were ready to stomp off back to your cave, like a sulky toddler."

"Yes, well, perhaps we shouldn't revive the corpse of a conflict," Oskan said. Then he added sweetly, "Maybe the royal skills of diplomacy need a little more polishing before we meet Their Vampiric Majesties in the Blood Palace. We don't want a war with two enemies."

Thirrin drew breath to answer this, then let it out slowly. He was right. She'd need to be the greatest diplomat the world had ever seen to make peace with The-Land-of-the-Ghosts, so she'd better start practicing right away. "Would you like some more stew?" she asked pleasantly, and called over the servant.

They began to discuss the mission in more detail, going over and over obstacles and difficulties until they'd exhausted every possibility they could think of.

"They have a reputation for being as tricky to pin down as eels in lard," said Oskan. "Seal every agreement you make in the only way the Vampire King and Queen will honor."

"Which is?"

"Blood, of course."

"Ah yes. Of course."

"Anything else they'll just ignore, and you'll be fighting a war thinking you can rely on them, but all you'll have will be an alliance that's as empty as a wineskin after a feast."

"Whose blood will it need to be sealed with?" Thirrin asked.

"Theirs . . . and yours, of course. In effect you'll be signing a contract, and in The-Land-of-the-Ghosts, blood has the same legal weight as the strongest oath."

"How do you know all of this?" Thirrin asked. "It almost sounds as though you've had dealings with Their Vampiric Majesties before."

Oskan shook his head. "Maggiore and I spent a very useful time in the archives of the Hypolitan while you were drawing up plans to reorganize the army. Maggie thought there might be something helpful there because the province lies so close to the border, and we struck gold." He turned to call the servant and, after his and Thirrin's mugs had been refilled, he went on.

"In the deepest vault of the archive we came across a chest labeled with the name of the Icemark's King Theobad the Bold. It dealt with the time of the arrival of the Hypolitan in the Icemark more than four hundred years ago, when, as you know, there was a war. Maggie was fascinated and kept saying things like, 'Ah, that explains so much,' and 'That's why Hypolitan culture's so different, they're from the Southern Continent,' which I didn't know, did you?"

Thirrin shook her head, regretting that her mother had died when she was so young. Maybe she, Thirrin, would have been told such things if only her Hypolitan mother had lived longer. "No. I didn't know that. But their names are different, and women rule their government, so I suppose they must have come from a very foreign place."

"Exactly," Oskan agreed. "All the old heroic tales tell of the war between King Theobad and the Hypolitan, and how they fought each other so long and so fiercely that eventually they began to admire and respect each other. But none of the tales ever mention the fact that Theobad had signed a treaty of nonaggression with The-Land-of-the-Ghosts, which gave him a free hand while he fought the Hypolitan. It makes sense if you think about it. Their Vampiric Majesties would certainly have invaded while he was fighting his war if he hadn't sealed an agreement with them beforehand."

"Why didn't you mention this before? All this time I've been thinking we're attempting the impossible, and now I find there have been treaties with The-Land-of-the-Ghosts before!" said Thirrin angrily.

"I was going to tell you tonight, anyway," Oskan explained hastily. "And I meant to tell you earlier, but with all the planning and packing it slipped my mind."

"Slipped your mind! One of the most important pieces of information I could use to persuade Their Vampiric Majesties into an agreement, and it slipped your mind!"

He shrugged. "Yes. It happens. I'm only human . . . mainly."

Thirrin counted to ten and remembered her need for diplomacy. "Just go on with your story. And don't leave out anything else!"

Oskan took a steadying drink from his mug and went on. "Well, as we know from the heroic tales, Theobad and the then Basilea of the Hypolitan finally made peace when she agreed to acknowledge the Icemark's King as her overlord, in return for the land that became the province of Hypolita. And ever since that day, the Basilea has always answered the call of the monarch of the Icemark whenever there's been a war. They're our greatest allies. *But* the archives also give details about the treaty between Theobad and The-Land-of-the-Ghosts, stating that the treaty was drawn up and sealed with the mingled blood of the King and Their Vampiric Majesties."

"And did it mention exactly how King Theobad persuaded them to sign?" Thirrin asked eagerly.

"Er . . . no."

"No?!"

"No. It just said a pact of nonaggression was agreed upon and they signed it." Oskan shrugged again uncomfortably.

"Well, marvelous!" Thirrin exploded. "So we know exactly which legal forms to use if we ever get an agreement with the Vampire King and Queen, but we have no idea how we can get it! So much for lessons from history!"

"Yes, but at least we can point out to them that there have been other treaties. We're not breaking new ground or violating any taboos," Oskan pointed out.

"True," Thirrin agreed, as she began to see some use for his information after all. "But, more important, we're letting them know that we're aware of earlier treaties. No doubt they remember signing the nonaggression pact with Theobad, but they've allowed that fact to get lost over the centuries. The immortal memory is obviously long, Oskan, but it doesn't have to reveal all its secrets to short-lived little nothings like me and you."

They continued to discuss their plans far into the freezing winter night, but eventually Oskan went to his own tent and slept for a few hours. His brain was buzzing with problems and possibilities, but he was so tired he soon drifted off. And just as he began to descend into the deep realms of sleep, his mind turned to the strange argument he and Thirrin had had earlier. It was so odd, blowing up out of nowhere like a storm in the mountains, and it had left him feeling . . . different in some way he couldn't quite pin down. But before he could analyze it further, he fell deeply asleep.

By the time the day dawned, they'd been marching for two hours. If anything, it had been colder as they packed up the shelters and set off, and Thirrin had begun to wonder if Oskan had any spare ear-warmers that she could use for her stallion. But she resisted asking him. Frostbite would have to be imminent before she'd give him that small victory.

When the sun finally rose in splendid fire, they stopped for breakfast. The homely scent of frying bacon and griddle cakes seemed completely out of place in the austere beauty of the breaking winter day. But Thirrin could remember no food being more delicious. She munched hungrily while staring out over the slowly undulating field of snow that here and there refracted the low rays of the rising sun into brilliant rainbows. The sky was a pristine polished blue from horizon to horizon, and she found it almost impossible to believe in Oskan's prediction of blizzards by the end of the next day. But she ignored her own newfound skepticism, and soon had her escort marching again as she tried to reach the border before the weather deteriorated.

They kept up a good pace throughout the day, frequently stopping for short breaks and food as they marshaled their strength against the bitter cold and the steepening gradients. At one point a herd of shaggy-coated bison ambled across their route, stopping to dig through the snow to reach lichen and grass, and watching the soldiers with a vacant curiosity as they chewed. But there was no other sign of life in the frozen lands.

The short day wore on to evening, and as the sun dipped below the horizon the temperatures once again plummeted.

But for Thirrin the extreme discomfort of the cold was almost compensated for by the beauty of the moonrise over the snow-fields. Silver light seemed to fall from the sky in a polished drizzle that transformed even the most everyday objects into subtle works of art that amazed the eye. But she wouldn't allow herself time to look at the splendor all around, and after a brief glance at the reflecting snows that seemed to breathe the light back into the sky, she directed the setting-up of the camp.

That night, clouds started to advance across the sky from the south. Thirrin and Oskan watched from the entrance of the tent as the massive bank of vapor slowly ate up the shimmering field of stars. The leading edge of the cloud bank seemed to tower for miles into the sky, its billowing hills and valleys delicately washed in moonlight.

"I'm sure we won't think them so beautiful tomorrow when the blizzards hit us," Thirrin said.

"No. But we should be in sight of the border by the time the first snow falls," Oskan answered, turning to look at the Wolfrock Mountains, whose jagged peaks rose against the sky like the broken battlements of a gigantic fortress.

"But what then? Do you know exactly how far it is from the border to the Blood Palace? We could freeze to death before we even have the pleasure of setting eyes on Their Vampiric Majesties."

"That won't happen." Oskan's eyes had become strangely empty-looking, his voice had become deeper, and his words had taken on the timbre of a chant or song as he spoke. "We'll meet them and, later, something more fantastic, more frightening than even they. An ally, Thirrin, the greatest ally we'll ever have. . . ."

Thirrin recognized the signs of the Sight on her adviser, and held her breath as she waited for him to say more. But instead his eyes cleared and he smiled.

"No more, I'm afraid. Just a small glimpse. . . ."

"What did you see? Who is this ally?" she asked eagerly.

He shrugged. "I don't know. Someone powerful and ferocious, but a loyal friend. Though not a man or a woman. . . ." He shook his head. "I can't say any more than that. Perhaps the Sight will come back and tell us more."

But it didn't happen that night, and by morning the low and heavy cloud cover occupied all of Thirrin's attention. They plodded along under the iron-gray skies as though they were carrying a huge weight. They were now climbing the foothills of the mountain range that formed the border, and snow-covered boulders like giant sheep were beginning to heave themselves out of the surrounding geography.

But even these signs that they were getting closer to their destination couldn't distract Thirrin from the lowering sky. The light had an odd, almost brown, tinge to it, and there was a sense of anticipation as though the land were holding its breath. They expected the first wisps of snow at any moment, but none fell, and this added to the rising tension. Suddenly Jenny, Oskan's mule, let out a huge bray that sounded almost muffled under the deeply gray sky. But she continued the strange, wheezy screech for almost a minute before finally falling silent.

"And what was all that about?" Thirrin asked disapprovingly from the height of her stallion.

"The wind's coming," Oskan answered simply.

"Is that all?"

Her counselor looked at her but said nothing. Then, reining in his mule, he dismounted and rummaged in his saddlebags until he found an extra coat with a deep hood and put it on. After this he unfolded a thick blanket and draped it over Jenny's back, securing it with ties at the front and back.

Thirrin took the hint and ordered the escort of soldiers to put on any extra clothing they had, and then with Oskan's help she draped a blanket over her stallion. She wasn't sure what to expect. The winter winds of the Icemark were legendary, and she'd heard tales since childhood of them freezing birds to branches and beasts to the ground. But despite riding and hunting in the wilds since she could barely walk, she'd never before been this far north, or in the open when they'd struck.

After half an hour or so she was just beginning to wonder if Oskan and his mule could have been wrong when a gentle breath stirred her stallion's mane and she heard a sound like a distant stormy sea crashing to the shore. She turned in her saddle but could see nothing. The snow was frozen, so no loose powder was being blown around, and in this area of the Icemark there were no trees to wave their branches as the storm rushed by.

But the sound grew closer and closer, rising to a high-pitched howl until, with the suddenness of a slamming door, the wind hit them. If Thirrin had had the breath, she would have gasped in shock. The temperature dropped like a lead weight, and no amount of clothing could keep the wind at bay. She pulled up her hood and hunched down in the saddle. She could almost see the leather of the reins becoming brittle as they continued to ride, and no amount of coaxing could have made her take off her gloves and touch the steel of her armor or sword. She knew that if she did, she would leave fingerprints as thick as her flesh was deep.

* * *

The terrible wind continued blowing for the rest of the day. One of the packhorses fell and refused to get up again, so they distributed its load among the others and left it to die. In such extreme conditions there was no room for compassion. It would take only one small addition of hardship and they could all freeze to death. Thirrin dreaded the night. If they failed to reach the border, or lost their way, they would have to set up camp again, and the thought of trying to pitch their tents in that howling storm was the stuff of nightmares.

By this time they were laboring up a fairly well-defined path that wound its way through the steep rocky slopes of the foothills. Ahead of them the Wolfrocks loomed out of the sky like broken teeth, and Thirrin could only pray that they didn't miss the route to the pass. Here, the snow had been scoured from the rocks, which lay strewn around the terrain in a black and broken tumble that could give no foothold for life of any kind. The entire landscape looked as dead and barren as a desert. It all seemed horribly ominous to Thirrin, and exactly appropriate for a border with a land that was ruled by the undead. But had she seen the area in summer, she would have seen that deep in crevices where the winds couldn't reach, lizards, mice, and many other creatures slept, awaiting the return of the sun.

Then, as suddenly as a fall of rocks in the mountains, the snows swept down on them, whipped to a biting frenzy by the wind. They were instantly trapped in a white and claustrophobic world where no points of reference applied. There was no north or south, no east or west, and only the pull of gravity let them know which way was up. Thirrin had tried to prepare for this, and they were already roped together so that none would get lost, or at least no more lost than the group as a whole. But now no precautions or plans were of any use. They were completely blind, each individual wrapped in a swirling cocoon of snow that reduced visibility to virtually nothing. Thirrin couldn't even see Oskan, who she knew was riding right next to her, and she could hear nothing but the screaming of the wind.

She stopped, and knew by the pull on the rope that everyone else did, too. But now she had no plan to offer: No one could do anything. If they moved forward, they could lose the path; if they stopped still, they would freeze to death, and the blizzard was so wild no one would be able to even find the tents, let alone set them up.

For several minutes they sat and waited, hoping that the snow would stop, but it continued to swirl and lash about them like vicious white silk, its deadly cold drawing away what little warmth their bodies still retained. Thirrin knew that in a very few minutes they could all be dying, and despair engulfed her. She thought of the Icemark ruled by her aunt Elemnestra. She'd named her as heir as a means of healing the rift that had opened up when she, Thirrin, had broken Hypolitan tradition by insisting that men attend the war councils. But she didn't doubt that if Elemnestra became Queen, she would try to impose the Hypolitan system on the entire land of the Icemark. Thirrin had visions of civil war as the barons and baronesses took up arms against the imposition of such a foreign culture. How Scipio Bellorum would laugh as his armies crushed the little land that was stupid enough to be fighting itself when he invaded.

Thirrin cried aloud in despair, her voice mingling with the howling of the wind that answered and echoed in mockery. This was the sound that a cold and dead throat would produce, she found herself thinking with sudden and remarkable calm. She listened, almost hearing words and a cruel melody in its noise. But then she thought it took on a different note, somehow . . . *earthier*, with more living warmth, and she turned her head toward this new sound. It came again, ululating now against the rise and fall of the wind and bursting out to right and left.

Then into her vision burst a huge and hairy face. "This way!" a powerful voice bellowed, and her horse lurched forward. They stumbled on in confusion for several minutes, then the snow seemed to stop and they almost fell into a space that was wide and smoky and filled with light and fire and blessed warmth. Thirrin brushed the snow from her frozen eyelids and looked around. They were in a cave filled with massive hairy creatures who, on seeing her, threw back their heads and howled.

The Wolf-folk had found them.

14

The werewolves ate a lot of meat. And they were not fussy about whether it was cooked or raw. But they quickly guessed Thirrin and her party preferred it when it wasn't actually bleeding, and they soon had huge piles of sizzling hot steaks heaped before them on rough platters made of flat pieces of stone.

They all ate ravenously, the warmth of the cave flowing over them and slowly thawing out frozen fingers and limbs. As soon as she felt the blood pulsing strongly through her veins again, Thirrin climbed to her feet and checked over her escort. Amazingly, none had any permanent damage apart from a few very mild cases of frostbite.

There was an inevitable nervousness among the soldiers; the werewolves may have been allies, but the friendship was very recent, and there was a history of literally centuries of conflict between the two races. But apart from a few wary glances and weapons kept close at hand, the escort conducted itself properly.

Even the horses were in good shape, standing patiently in a corral the Wolf-folk had made with branches at the back of the cave. They were eating a rough fodder made up of dried grasses, nuts, and the same sort of lichen Thirrin had noticed the bison eating earlier in their journey. At first the horses had been very nervous about the werewolves, shying and snorting whenever they came near, but when the Wolf-folk spread the fodder on the floor of the corral and then ignored them, they settled down.

Thirrin now allowed herself to look around the cave. It was huge — almost as big as the Great Hall in Frostmarris, except here there were at least eight fires, not just the one that had occupied the very center of the hall. Each of the fires burned on permanent-looking hearths, and they all had troupes of the Wolf-folk gathered around them in what Thirrin assumed were extended family groups. But the central hearth was the biggest, and here a particularly large werewolf wearing a silver collar sat surrounded by dozens of others who seemed to be receiving orders or bringing over choice cuts of meat.

This was obviously the center of power in the cave, and taking a deep steadying breath, Thirrin immediately headed for it, collecting Oskan en route. As soon as the huge werewolf noticed her approach, it stood and, incredibly, curtsied.

"Greetings, My Lady Thirrin Freer Strong-in-the-Arm Lindenshield, Wildcat of the North, Queen of the Icemark. I am Baroness Lishnok Grin-Skull of the Wolfrock Grin-Skulls. Perhaps you have heard of my family?"

Thirrin was still recovering from the sight of seeing this huge creature curtsy, and for one dangerous moment she almost giggled, but she quickly regained control and answered with extreme politeness. "Greetings, Baroness Grin-Skull. My entire party and I owe you our lives, and the House of Strong-in-the-Arm Lindenshield will forever remember this. The fact that I do not have a deep knowledge of your family is a fault that is entirely my own, and I can only plead that the hostilities that once existed between our races are to blame. But from this day forth, the House of Grin-Skull shall be known throughout the Icemark."

The Baroness simpered at this courtly reply and, extending a hugely clawed paw, she invited Thirrin to sit beside her. Thirrin gladly accepted another helping of cooked meat from the werewolf's own plate and, making room for Oskan beside her, they began to practice their skills of diplomacy.

"Tell me, Baroness, has this . . . dwelling been in your family for very long?"

The huge wolfwoman looked around the cave with pride. "Over ten generations of Grin-Skulls have been whelped in this hall. It was here that Baroness Padfoot White-pelt founded the Grin-Skull dynasty after fighting in the Blood Wars against the Vampire King and Queen more than three thousand moons ago. She took the new family name to commemorate personally flaying the skin from the face of the Vampire standard-bearer, and it's been carried with pride ever since."

"A very worthy genesis for an illustrious name," said Oskan, helping himself to a slab of meat. "But now your people are allied to Their Vampiric Majesties, are they not?"

"King Grishmak Blood-drinker, Lord of the Wolf-folk, has made alliance and equal partnership with the Vampire King and Queen, yes. And as long as the interests of our two peoples continue to follow the same paths, the agreement will no doubt survive."

Thirrin searched for the right words as she gazed around the hall and tried not to be overwhelmed by the fact that the entire future of the Icemark was relying on her and on how she conducted herself over the next few days. But at last she managed to thrust aside her fears and said, "I would imagine that your allies will know of the new alliance between the Wolf-folk and the Icemark?"

"Oh yes. And King Grishmak has been smoothing the way for your mission to Their Vampiric Majesties. They expect you tomorrow night in the throne room of the Blood Palace."

Diplomacy, Thirrin was coming to realize, meant that at times you showed delighted surprise at things you already knew, so she stood to thank the Baroness for her King's efforts. "May the sacred moon forever shine on the pelt of His Majesty Grishmak Blood-drinker," she said, using the correct werewolf blessing for such occasions. "If I do not have the pleasure of meeting His Royal Mightiness before I leave his lands, please convey my thanks to him for arranging the meeting between myself and the Vampire King and Queen. Truly it was the work of genius that could overcome the animosity of centuries and secure such agreement from Their Vampiric Majesties."

"King Grishmak is mighty in all things," the Baroness stated loyally. "But you will be able to convey your thanks in person, as His Majesty will be at the Blood Palace tomorrow night to help plead your case."

Thirrin thought only criminals had to "plead a case," but she smiled her gratitude and chewed her steak as she practiced the new skill of keeping her thoughts to herself.

Oskan, who'd been listening carefully, licked his fingers clean in the werewolf way and then asked, "Are there any . . . indications of how exactly the Vampires view our coming visit?"

"I'm told they're intrigued and curious to meet the new Queen of the Icemark," the Baroness answered. Then lowering her voice, she leaned forward and said, "You'd do well to be as interesting and as lively as you can be. Being undead is a terrible burden, I'm told; the years drag on and on with nothing really new to interest you. Can you imagine living forever with no hope of a quiet death, no hope of a gentle release from the effort of life?"

"Unless someone puts a stake through your heart, beheads you, or burns you to a crisp," Oskan pointed out.

"Well, yes, there are those options, I suppose," the Baroness admitted. "But those are hardly quiet deaths, and the knowledge that only a violent end will release them from life must add to the burden of their immortality."

"I suppose it must, " Oskan agreed. "So, we should be lively and interesting to help relieve their boredom, is that it?"

"It would be to your advantage to do so. You're more likely to get an agreement from them if they find you entertaining."

"You make us sound like a traveling company of actors, or children who are expected to amuse their grandparents," said Thirrin curtly. The trauma of the day with its cold and blizzards was beginning to catch up with her, and her diplomatic skills were starting to slip.

"Well, children you virtually are, even by the years of your own kind," the Baroness snapped. And then, remembering herself, she added, "Though no child has ever achieved such skills in battle or such political maturity. But remember, even the oldest mortal being is a child beside the Vampire King and Queen. They are ancient. Man and woman they may once have been, but how long ago and of what race, even they have forgotten."

"So, basically, you're telling us to show respect and help them through another wearisome day," said Oskan.

"Yes. Respect is always to be recommended when dealing with a foreign power, and especially so when you're in need of their help," the Baroness answered pointedly. "I say all of this with the greatest respect to yourselves, of course. We all of us need help at times. The trick is to make that clear to the Vampire King and Queen."

Thirrin and Oskan both nodded as they accepted this advice, and then by some unspoken mutual agreement they changed the subject to the safer areas of family lineage and the doings of ancestors.

Finally, after a further hour of polite conversation, the Baroness stood and, curtsying deeply, asked her guests' permission to make up her bed for the night. Thirrin, in her persona of Queen of the Icemark, graciously assented, after which she and Oskan withdrew to their own allotted hearth.

All throughout the cave, the family groups were placing huge piles of furs around the hearths. Obviously the Baroness's decision to sleep was a signal for her entire household to do the same. Roughly cured furs were distributed among the soldiers of the escort, but Thirrin and Oskan were each given beautifully soft and rich pelts that were pure white and deeply luxurious.

They were soon all asleep, exhausted as they were by the long march and the blizzard. All around the cave, torches were doused, and soon the only light came from the flickering of the fires. But as the night drew on, even this dimmed as the fires sank to glowing embers, each hearth studding the darkness of the surrounding cave like galaxies in the vastness of space.

Thirrin and her escort awoke with a start as the werewolves greeted the new day by howling in concert. The heavy hides that covered the cave entrance had been thrown back, and the brilliant, brittle light of a sunny winter day burst into the blackness. With it came the scent of new snow, and a keen fresh air that sliced through the fog of wood smoke and many furry bodies like the sharpest razor through unwashed wool.

Breakfast almost inevitably consisted of meat, and lots of it. It never occurred to the Wolf-folk that humans might eat anything else, so when one of the soldiers found a winter-stored apple in her bags and sat eating it along with a huge steak, some of the werewolves gathered around to stare.

"There are times when I think you humans are simply our hairless cousins. But at others, I can see the differences are deeper than that," said an elderly and grizzled werewolf sadly.

The soldier offered him a slice of her apple. But after sniffing at it, he sneezed explosively and scuttled off, determined to find a particularly bloody piece of meat for his breakfast.

After eating, Thirrin and Oskan went to pay their respects to Baroness Grin-Skull and found her gnawing on a haunch that had a brand of the Hypolitan herd clearly stamped on it. Thirrin raised an eyebrow at Oskan, but they were both diplomatic enough not to mention the stolen meat as they stepped up to the hearth. The Baroness stood, curtsied, and invited them to sit. "Good morning, Your Majesty and Counselor Oskan. As you can see, the snows have blown farther to the north and my nose tells me they will not return for another week."

"Six days," Oskan corrected.

The huge wolfwoman bowed her head. "I see I am in the presence of one steeped in weather lore . . . and perhaps other abilities." After gazing thoughtfully at Oskan for a few moments, she went on. "With Your Majesty's permission, I will send a guide and a guard of twenty of my people to add to your party."

"I thank the Baroness for her kindness," Thirrin answered formally. "The addition of the Wolf-folk will make my escort royal indeed."

She and Oskan now accepted a second breakfast as preparations were made for their departure. As they ate, they watched the cave become as busy as an anthill.

"What news do you have of the werewolf muster?" Thirrin asked.

"Slow, as usual. But they should all be gathered in by the time we are needed," the Baroness answered, making the army of the Wolf-folk sound like a living harvest.

"Good. We'll be facing Scipio Bellorum and his hordes before the walls of Frostmarris by then, and we'll need all of our allies if we're to survive."

"You're right to describe the army of the Polypontian Empire as 'hordes.' Their numbers are huge indeed. But, Madam . . ." The Baroness leaned toward the Queen, and her huge hairy face became deeply earnest. "Don't make the mistake of thinking the Empire's only military strength is size. Ever since the alliance between us was forged and the danger from Scipio Bellorum became obvious, our spies have been watching far beyond the borders, and we now know for sure that the Empire can call upon more soldiers than our two nations have people! But there's more even than that to fear; more even than their cannon and muskets. At the center and heart of their huge strength is intelligence. Scipio Bellorum and his officers can direct their troops with a discipline and a tactical brilliance that none have yet withstood!"

"Then we must hope that the united front of our alliance will surprise them enough to make mistakes," Thirrin answered, trying to sound brave and defiant.

"Scipio Bellorum is not just a bully who picks off small individual countries who have no friends to help them. Don't think your alliances, as clever as they are, will be enough on their own to save any of us in this coming war," the Baroness warned. "Our spies have spoken to many sources, not just the limited eyes and ears of humanity stuck within the borders of their own little lands but to the far-seeing eagle and to other birds that live in many countries and to beasts that cross continents in their migrations. And they tell of a war between the Polypontian Empire and a power far, far to the west, whose armies equaled those of Bellorum's in size and discipline. For three years they fought for the prize of a land rich in forests and slaves and iron, and the clash was like that of two giants fighting over hunting rights in the ice fields far to the north. But Bellorum and his officers were as cunning as a hungry wolf pack, and tricked and trapped their enemy so that they fell to his Imperial armies in battle after battle."

"Then what hope do we have?" Thirrin asked, aware of how young and inexperienced she was, her voice almost weary with despair.

"We must make the price of the Icemark too high. The armies we destroy, the iron we make the Empire spend on us, must be worth more than the land they would buy."

"Efficient marshaling of resources," Oskan said. Then, when he noticed the others looking at him, he explained, "In other words, we must use what we have to the greatest possible effect. No arrow must be shot, no army moved, without it being exactly the right time to do so. Our troops must be more disciplined than his and better trained, and our tactics must be superior by far."

"Otherwise we fall," Thirrin added simply.

"Yes," the Baroness agreed.

Thirrin and her party set out an hour later. The escort had spent some of the previous evening cleaning their armor and other equipment so that they gleamed in the early morning sun. As they took up their positions in the column, Thirrin felt a thrill of pride. The ten Hypolitan cavalry glowed like cock pheasants in their brilliantly embroidered surcoats and hats, and the twenty housecarls looked like well-polished cogs in a powerful machine. When the twenty werewolves from the Baroness's household added themselves to the escort, they looked like an army that could take on the entire world, or so thought their young Queen.

It had been agreed that the packhorses and tents would be left in the cave, since the Blood Palace was less than a day's ride away. So, with pennants snapping bravely in the now light wind and the personal banner of the Royal House of Strong-in-the-Arm flying in the brittle morning light, the embassy of the Icemark set off on its mission.

The Wolfrock Mountains now towered before them, and as they followed a path scoured clean of snow by the previous day's wind, Thirrin stared ahead into the far distance where the trail disappeared between two massive shoulders of the mountain range. This was the pass into The-Land-of-the-Ghosts, and cold fear seemed to breathe from it, as though from the open mouth of some undead creature.

Only the werewolves seemed unaffected by the proximity of the country ruled by the undead. Thirrin's soldiers were almost completely silent as they marched along, and even Oskan seemed nervous.

"There are witches in The-Land-of-the-Ghosts, aren't there?" Thirrin asked him.

"Evil ones, yes," he answered. "Your father expelled them after he won the Battle of the Wolfrocks. But he let the good witches, like my mother, stay."

Thirrin nodded. "I remember him telling me that. He said they were useful and loyal."

"And so they have been. They've watched the borders for years. Don't forget, not all evil is ruled by Their Vampiric Majesties. There are spirits and sprites and twisted creatures that haunt the Icemark even now, and it's the Power of the witches that keeps them in check."

"I've heard the country folk talk of such things: goblins and creatures of the night. But if the witches are so effective against them, how come they still figure in stories of blighted cattle and stolen babies?"

Oskan looked at her in annoyance. "The army of the Icemark is arguably the strongest in the known world, apart from that of the Empire, and yet your father fought constant border wars to keep the country safe. If everybody took your attitude, we'd be asking why your army doesn't stop every pirate raid on all fishing villages and every cross-border Vampire attack. There are limits to Power."

Thirrin had to accept the logic of this argument, and she smiled in agreement. "Well, I hope the witches know we're grateful."

"Don't worry. The country folk and peasants have their ways. It's only the elite of society who forget."

"Then I'll see they remember from now on," Thirrin answered forcibly.

They rode on in silence, watching as the border drew steadily nearer. The pass was now clearly visible, yawning before them like an open wound. Thirrin shuddered and immediately hoped none of her escort had noticed. They mustn't see she was afraid. But she needn't have worried. All of her soldiers were too busy with their own fears to notice anyone else's.

After less than an hour the path climbed sharply, and after a struggle with the horses they stood on the very threshold of the pass. The peaks of the Wolfrocks towered to either side, stark and snowcapped against the brilliant blue of the sky. And before them the pass opened. It was wide enough to allow a troop of twenty cavalry to ride abreast, and the path wound out of sight beyond spurs and outcrops that jutted from the flanks of the mountains. Good country for an ambush, Thirrin thought, but rather than risk her intentions being misread by anyone, she ordered all weapons to be sheathed.

The werewolves now stepped forward and, throwing back their heads, they let out a collective howl that echoed and re-echoed among the rocks. The horses shied and neighed, but the troopers kept them under control. All eyes were on the pass before them. Now was the time for treachery if it was destined to happen. But Thirrin, sensing this was on the minds of her escort, immediately spurred forward into the pass and signaled the buglers to sound the fanfare of the Royal House of the Icemark. Her presence now announced to all, she led the way along the path.

Within a few yards of entering the pass, the mouth behind them was lost to view. Narrow walls of rock loomed over them, and each boulder seemed to hide a watcher. Every now and then small stones would slither down the rock face as though dislodged by something, and the wind that had begun to moan among the outcrops seemed to mask harsh voices.

After a few minutes, dark flying shapes appeared in the sky above the escort. It was difficult to judge exactly how large they were, but they seemed too big for birds. Thirrin beckoned over the captain of the Wolf-folk and asked what they were.

"Vampires, Madam," he answered, confirming her fears. "Vampires in their shape-shifted form. They're just watching how things are progressing, and no doubt keeping Their Vampiric Majesties informed."

"No doubt," Thirrin agreed.

Occasionally one of the shapes flew low enough for its leathery wings and bat face to be clearly seen, but mainly they stayed high above the escort like a collection of black clouds.

Several of the soldiers reported shapes, sensed on the edge of sight, flitting around the rocks but disappearing as soon as they stared directly at them.

Oskan shrugged when he heard this. "Who can be surprised that there are ghosts in The-Land-of-the-Ghosts?"

About halfway through the pass, a huge Rock Troll rolled into view, slumping from an outcrop like a small landslide and blocking the route. Thirrin called a halt and signaled furiously to her troops when they started to draw swords and form a shield-wall. Reluctantly they sheathed their weapons and waited. The troll roared and, hefting a massive boulder, it strode forward. But in quick response the werewolves formed a solid phalanx and advanced on it, howling and snarling fiercely. For a moment the troll watched them come on through small stupid eyes before sullenly dropping its boulder and climbing back onto the outcrop, where it seemed to melt back into the rock. The captain of the Wolf-folk guard beckoned Thirrin on, and she led her small troop forward.

There were no more incidents of this sort, and they quickly trotted through the pass. After about an hour they reached the far end quite unexpectedly. Rounding a spur of rock, the view suddenly opened up like a huge and dramatic window on a land of dense pine forest and rocky hills that flowed down from the Wolfrocks to the hazy distance. Even though it was winter, the spicy aroma of the pines reached them, mingling with the cold scent of snow to create an exhilarating perfume that lifted all their spirits.

But fear quickly descended on them again when they

noticed a rocky watchtower, tall and black, standing on a high bluff overlooking the pass. Most of the flying vampires wheeled off to circle the tower before landing to perch on its battlements like giant black birds.

Once again the troop of werewolves threw back their heads and howled before setting foot into The-Land-of-the-Ghosts, and Thirrin likewise signaled her buglers to sound her royal fanfare. With a sense of finality she urged her horse forward, and entered the land whose rulers had been the bitterest enemies of the Icemark for centuries.

15

Maggiore Totus had spent a good part of his time since Thirrin and Oskan had left making sure the people of Frostmarris were settled in comfortably. Wherever possible they'd been housed within the Hypolitan city, but there was no way to squeeze the entire population from one very large settlement into the walls of a much smaller one, especially when the original population was still living there.

An overspill camp had been built just outside the walls, and Maggiore himself had supervised its construction, making sure that the streets were wide enough and that enough latrines had been dug, and appointing citizens to the task of clearing away garbage. He moaned and groaned about the work to anyone who'd listen, but secretly he relished it. It was almost like designing and building an entire new city from scratch, allowing him to test several theories he'd developed over the years, and he was very pleased to say that most of his ideas had worked.

There'd been one or two disasters. Nobody had wanted to join the district choirs, which he'd started as a means of quickly encouraging and developing a community spirit in the new settlement. And in the end he was quite philosophical when a football league spontaneously sprang up between the districts. But then he'd realized that the overspill camp was beginning to function like a city in its own right, and he became positively joyful when several shops sprang up.

But now the camp had begun to run itself, with several citizens being appointed as a committee to supervise the various functions, and Maggiore had resigned his post as city planner. For a while he'd busied himself finding space for the huge numbers of people that were beginning to flock to the city in answer to the calling of the fyrd. But the army had soon taken that in hand, and several new districts had been added to his overspill camp.

At one point he'd begun to wish he'd gone with Thirrin; after all, he was the one with the experience of life and the correct manners needed for diplomatic missions. But deep down he knew he'd never have been able to stand the cold of a winter's journey in the Icemark. Even in the Hypolitan city, sitting next to a blazing hearth, he felt cold, so he was almost certain a journey in the wilds would have killed him. Besides, he'd lately found a project that had finally engaged his clever mind.

He was now sitting in his room with the shutters firmly closed on the snowstorm that was howling over the city. His fire was banked high with logs, and a glass of wine was close at hand while he put the last notes he'd taken into order. Primplepuss was curled up comfortably on his knee, and he absentmindedly stroked her as his pen scribbled across the page. When the war was over, he hoped to be able to write his notes up into a scholarly work on the origins of the Hypolitan. Not that anyone would read it, he supposed, but at least it kept his mind active and ready for when the Queen returned from The-Land-of-the-Ghosts and the spring thaw allowed the war to continue.

He was waiting now for Thirrin's uncle, Olememnon, to arrive. With his help Maggiore had been compiling the notes he needed for his history, and so far he'd been a fascinating source of information, on top of which Maggiore found he enjoyed the huge man's quiet company. He had a dry sense of humor, and his deep and gentle voice could say the most outrageous things with such a sense of seriousness that it often took Maggiore several seconds to realize what he'd said. Also, as the Basilea's consort, Olememnon had the highest status of any man in the province, and apart from fighting in the Icemark's wars he had no other duties, so he'd been a brilliant ally in hunting down State papers and manuscripts to help in their research. No door was locked to him, no archive out of bounds, so Maggiore only had to mention that he had the approval of Olememnon and all objections melted away.

So far, the little scholar's studies had confirmed what was generally known, that the Hypolitan were not originally from the north. Today, he hoped to get to the more interesting bits of his investigations and find out exactly where on the Southern Continent this fascinating people had first come from. Maggiore was just savoring the idea of the investigation when a gentle knock sounded at his door.

"Come!" he called in his best schoolmaster's voice, and the door opened.

Into the room stepped one of the biggest men Maggiore had ever known. Olememnon was even taller than King Redrought had been, and was easily as broad, and yet his shaven face gave him the appearance of an overgrown boy. To

Maggiore, whose own scholar's beard almost reached his waist, a clean-shaven man was still an odd sight, especially since all the men in every other part of the Icemark grew beards as soon as they could. This was just one more difference between the Hypolitan and the other citizens of the Icemark.

The big man smiled in greeting, his face and eyes lighting up as he strode forward.

"Ah, Olememnon! Sit down, sit down. A glass of wine?" Maggiore asked, pouring the drink before getting an answer. "Are you ready for our little chat? Have you remembered any folktales and legends I haven't recorded yet?"

"I'm not sure. Perhaps. It depends what you want to hear," Olememnon answered, his deep, soft voice filling Maggiore's large chamber to capacity.

"Well, let me see," the little scholar said, picking up his notes and balancing his spectoculums on the end of his nose. "Ah yes! We were about to discuss the *genesis* of the Hypolitan. The land of their origin and the reason for their migration."

"Well, that's easy. War, and a need to escape a power that wouldn't let us live as we wanted," said Olememnon, sipping his drink and settling back into his creaking chair. Primplepuss had looked up when the huge man came into the room, and now hopped down from Maggiore and walked across the floor to take up residence on the new lap. Perhaps there was something about the Basilea's consort that reminded her of another special man who'd filled a room in the same way, and this was her way of honoring his memory. Olememnon stroked her as soon as she settled onto his lap, and to the accompaniment of her purring, looked expectantly across at Maggiore, who waited with pen poised.

"Fine, fine. Well, tell me what you know from the beginning, while I take notes," said Maggiore, who knew the big man was a natural storyteller.

"Well, now, let's see . . ." began Olememnon. "The Hypolitan once lived in the mountains of the Southern Continent, many hundreds of years ago. They were, even then, a fierce people who lived by hunting and fighting. But the other people around respected them and learned to revere the Great Mother Goddess, sending offerings to the warrior-priestesses who served her in her mountaintop shrines."

"Aha!" said Maggiore as he scribbled away. Some of his guesses had been right. In his own land there had been legends of warrior women who had served the Goddess of the Moon.

"For many generations life was good for the Hypolitan, but then a threat of war arose, and a great movement of people came from the east. Their armies were huge, and after many battles the Hypolitan retreated to the sanctuary of their mountain shrines.

"Our soldiers fought a long and bitter war but knew they couldn't win. The enemy was massive and sent army after army against our strongholds. But the Basilea of the day, Queen Athenestra, devised a plan. When the Blessed Moon was dark, the warrior-priestesses and the fighting men would carve a wide swathe through the besieging armies to allow our people to escape to other lands and find peace again.

"And this they duly did, taking the enemy by surprise and bursting through their lines. So began a great trek, taking us through many nations, until at last we came to lands we felt were home. This country had mountains and winters as fierce as those we had known in our citadels built in the clouds.

"The land was, of course, the Icemark. But here the people were the strongest we'd met since the war with the eastern invaders. We fought long and hard, never winning, never losing, neither side able to gain the final victory. Until at last the King of that time, who was called Theobad, called for a truce, and after long talks agreement was reached. Queen Athenestra would acknowledge the King of the Icemark as her overlord, and we, in return, would be allowed to stay in the lands we now hold. And ever since that day, the Hypolitan have been loyal subjects of the Icemark and her greatest ally in times of war."

Olememnon fell silent and sipped his drink while Maggiore faithfully wrote down his words in the special shorthand he had devised for his study notes. At last he laid down his pen and smiled. "Well, that's quite a tale. Some of it I'd guessed already, of course, but the details are quite fascinating. I'll need to verify and corroborate some of the finer points, but overall you've given me a wonderfully concise framework from which to expand my studies."

"One thing, Maggie," Olememnon said as he stretched his long, thickly muscled legs toward the fire. Primplepuss jumped lightly down and began to wash. "Thinking about these old tales has brought something to mind. . . . There's a similarity between the descriptions of the invading people who drove the Hypolitan out of their homeland and the Polypontian Empire."

"Really?" the little man asked. "In what way?"

"Well, mainly their method of fighting. The way they just overwhelmed the opposition with the size of their army. The way one defeated force would simply be replaced with another and then another until all opposition was ground down."

"Yes, I see what you mean. But it's probably just coincidence. After all, we're not talking subtle tactics here, are we? Really, it's just the method of a bully who's bigger and stronger than everyone else and uses his brute force to get what he wants. In the past, it was your invaders and today it's the Polypontians."

"Perhaps. But as far as I can make out, the Empire started in the south and over the years has expanded northward — particularly in the last twenty years or so while Scipio Bellorum has been the commander in chief of their army. But from where in the south did they come? How *far* south? Do you know?"

Maggiore had to admit that he didn't. It was an interesting point, and one he'd follow up.

"And as for the Polypontians being bullies," Olememnon went on, "well, you're right. And that was more than enough to get them an empire. But with General Scipio Bellorum their bullying strength is allied with a clever tactical brain, and that's a difficult combination to fight."

"Yes, I know," the little scholar said, abruptly and painfully reminded of the war that waited for them beyond the spring thaw.

"If we'd just been fighting their army without the general, we might, just *might* have had a chance. But with him . . . ?" The big man shrugged, then stood to leave. "But that's defeatist talk. And I've got a fyrd to help train. I'll see you tonight at dinner, Maggie."

And with the suddenness of the changing wind, Olememnon was gone. Maggiore had gotten used to this rapid change of pace and mood in his big friend, but any room he'd been in seemed unbearably empty for a moment, as though he'd left a vacuum behind him. Primplepuss felt it, too, and meowed plaintively, but then with the poise and balance typical of any cat, she quickly adjusted to it and meowed again to remind Maggie it was her dinnertime.

He put aside his notes and stood to fetch her bowl, noticing as he did so that the little animal was no longer a kitten. Her legs had grown and her head was losing its baby roundness as it developed the sleek lines of an adult cat. Thirrin would notice a difference when she got back from her travels.

His thoughts turned again to the young Queen and her mission. So much depended on her success, and so much could easily go wrong. It wasn't that he lacked confidence in her. In the last few weeks she'd matured at a terrifying speed; circumstances hadn't allowed anything else. But she was trying to make an alliance with the Icemark's oldest enemy. There were centuries of bitterness and hatred to overcome. And if she failed, they'd all die. He shrugged. There was nothing he could do to help her; he'd just have to hope and wait like everyone else.

16

Thirrin, and her escort of soldiers and werewolves, had been traveling through the forest of dark pines for more than an hour. It had taken them all morning to ride down from the pass and reach the tree line, thousands of feet below, and when they'd finally ridden under the eaves of the forest, it had been with a sigh of relief. At least here they had some shelter from the bitterly cold wind that had begun to blow, but now the soldiers were getting nervous. All around them the forest echoed with strange noises. Sudden screeches and distant howling would burst out, then fall silent. Now and then a glittering grayness would form far off in the shadows and keep pace with them briefly before fading away like mist before the sun.

But there was no sun here in the forest. Thirrin caught only an occasional glimpse of the sky through the tightly packed branches, and what light there was seemed to emerge in an unhealthy glow from the snow that had somehow managed to find its way through the trees to the ground all around them. This place was nothing like the forest at home. There, the trees were alive with creatures that scampered along the branches and trunks in search of food. Even in the winter when most of the trees had shed their leaves, there was a sense of life at rest, and the many animals that hadn't hibernated searched for nuts or hunted one another with an intensity made sharper by hunger. But here in this great pine forest where no tree slept through the cold months, there was only a sense of watchfulness. Even the howling and screeching that burst out here and there in the gloom seemed to have nothing to do with animal life. It was too cold, too removed from any need to communicate with other living things. Thirrin thought it sounded like sharp glittering knives being scratched over polished ice. She shivered, drew her cloak tighter about her, and stared as far ahead as the tightly packed trees would allow. The whole world seemed to have been smothered by the trunks and writhing roots and stiff needle-covered branches of these dark green-black trees.

At last they reached a clearing, and the soldiers almost ran forward to greet the space, but then checked their pace and stared. In the very center of the clearing, sitting on the broken trunk of a dead tree, was an enormous Snowy Owl. It stood at least three times taller than the white owls that lived on the northern snowfields of the Icemark, and its vivid blue eyes seemed alive with a sharp intelligence. The captain of the werewolves walked forward and saluted the creature, which stared at him, blinking slowly. A strange conversation followed as owl and wolfman snarled and hooted at each other, after which the captain saluted again and walked back across the clearing. He stood before Thirrin, but before he could speak, the owl spread its huge white wings and soared silently away, its brilliant form glowing in the gloom as it dwindled skyward over the trees.

"Their Vampiric Majesties sent their herald to greet you, Queen Thirrin Freer Strong-in-the-Arm Lindenshield, Wildcat of the North. They bid you as welcome as you deserve, and advise you to hurry, as the weather is closing in again and there will be snow before nightfall," the captain said, slipping into the formal language of the court as he reported the owl's message.

Thirrin turned to Oskan. "Is that right? Will there be snow?"

Oskan nodded. "In two hours or so." He was the only one in the entire party of humans who seemed as relaxed as the werewolves in the dark forest.

"Then we must make haste. Captain, is there a more direct route to the Blood Palace?"

"No, Your Majesty. But if we hurry, we should be there before the snows, if the Witch's Son is correct about the time."

"The Witch's Son is correct," she answered, spurring her horse across the clearing.

After another hour of hard marching, the trees began to thin and eventually their ominous presence gave way to a wide sweeping hill that descended to a valley floor. By this time the clouds had gathered, rolling and iron gray, and the light had diminished to a strange dim glow that seemed to pulse from the unbroken sweep of snow. But at least the freezing wind had dropped, and the escort crunched over the frozen land without having to unpack extra layers of clothing.

The last fitful light of the day soon faded to a deeply dark night. Thirrin ordered every second soldier to light their torch, and they continued on their way. But the werewolves didn't seem to need any such aid in the darkness; their night vision was so acute that they led the way, finding a path in what seemed a trackless waste to the humans. After a while an excited growling and snarling broke out among the Wolf-folk, and the captain appeared at Thirrin's stirrup.

"Your Majesty, the Blood Palace."

Thirrin stared ahead, following the line of his pointing finger, and there between a cleft in the distant hills she could just make out a looming shape, faintly outlined by twinkling lights.

"I see it," she answered quietly as she fought down a sudden surge of fear that threatened to engulf her. "Oskan. Do you . . . feel anything?"

The Witch's Son gazed ahead in silence for a few moments, then said, "Nothing unexpected: evil, great age, a hatred of mortal things." He shrugged. "A typical nest of Vampires."

Thirrin nodded. "No disaster, then? No sudden death?"

"Your dying lies elsewhere, Thirrin Lindenshield," he answered simply.

She glanced at him sharply to see if any insult was intended with her pared-down name, then asked, "In glory?"

"Hidden," he answered, and smiled.

"'Hidden, *Your Majesty,*'" she corrected with her usual fire, and Oskan's smile turned to a wolfish grin.

They rode on with greater speed until the palace loomed before them. Even in the dark of the cloudy night, details were easy to make out, as every one of the hundreds of windows glowed with an eerie green light and torches were set in the walls and at regular intervals along the roofline. It soared from the land around it like a miniature mountain, its dozens of spires and towers silhouetted a deeper dark against the cloudy sky. The pointed arches of its windows and doors gathered in a tangle of architecture that seemed to have grown from the land like a stony and ill-disciplined fungus. But as Thirrin and her party drew closer, they realized that what they had thought was ordinary dark stone was, in fact, polished and of the deepest red in color — almost black, in fact, like dried blood.

The huge double doors stood open, and the greenish light spilled out onto the snow like a puddle of sticky liquid. Thirrin almost expected it to bubble and hiss like some fetid swamp water, but the illusion was destroyed when the leading werewolves stepped into it, and their huge shaggy shadows were thrown back toward her. Thirrin reined to a halt and signaled for her trumpeters to sound a fanfare. Up into the black night the brittle brassy notes soared, and after they had died away there was only silence.

For a few moments they sat and waited, then the predicted snows began to fall. In effect, their decision had been made for them. After scouting around they found a huge empty stable block where they left the horses, then they strode back to the front of the palace.

Everyone was waiting for Thirrin to make the first move, and knowing this, she immediately squared her shoulders and started to climb the flight of polished steps to the open doors. At the top a wide terrace swept up to the threshold of the high arched doorway. Above it, the walls towered like a cliff and the green glowing windows stared down at them like hating eyes. Thirrin took all of this in for a moment before walking confidently forward, all the time taking deep steadying breaths as she tried to control the fear and loathing that crawled screaming through her frame.

At the doorway she stopped and turned to Oskan, who was directly behind her. "I don't suppose we can expect a welcoming committee after so many centuries of war."

"No," he agreed. "We'd better just go in and get out of the snow."

She nodded and, after a pause, stepped through into an enormously high and wide hall. The black-and-white-tiled floor stretched away for a seemingly impossible distance, and everywhere was lit by the same green glow, even though there were no torches or lanterns or any other means of lighting as far as she could see.

The rest of the party followed, and soon the rattle of their boots and armor echoed across the empty space. In the dim distance at the far end of the hall, Thirrin could just make out a raised dais, and as they approached she realized that two thrones stood on it, each carved out of the same dark red stone. But still there was no sign of any other occupants in the entire palace, either living or dead.

Thirrin was just about to order her trumpeters to sound another fanfare when the green light flared to a dazzling brilliance, and the hall was filled with tall, pale, hissing figures that stared with large unblinking eyes. Immediately Thirrin's soldiers threw up a shield-wall around her, their spears leveled.

Into the tense silence that settled over the hall a light and deadly cold voice said, "I've seen such battle formations before and know just how effective they are. I see you keep your troops as well drilled as your father ever did."

Thirrin snapped an order, and the soldiers lowered their shields. She stepped through the hedge of spears that still bristled in their protective ring, and gazed in wonder at the dais, where two figures now sat on the red thrones. They, too, were pale and thin, and Thirrin could see that, even sitting down, they were tall. Once they had been a man and a woman, but now they had an unnatural and terrible beauty that made them completely un-human. Both had snowy white skin and their lips were deep red and moist, like raw liver.

"My father always impressed upon me the need for discipline and drill among the housecarls of the army. In that way, even mortals can face and fight the undead."

The Vampire King and Queen gazed at her in silence and she continued. "But the need for allies when facing danger is equally great, and the chances of victory are increased manyfold when your friends stand with you."

She stepped aside slightly, allowing Their Vampiric Majesties to appreciate fully what she knew they must have clearly seen. The werewolves had instinctively formed a circle of their own, enclosing the shield-wall of her soldiers and facing out in readiness to fight off any attack by the Vampires.

"You have no need to display your fighting prowess here," the Vampire Queen said. "This is a palace, not a fortress. There are no soldiers here apart from your own."

Thirrin nodded and gave another order. The spears were grounded, and the escort snapped to attention.

"I believe mortals feel the cold," the Vampire King said, and casually cast a glance at the huge fireplace that stood halfway down the hall. Immediately flames belched out into the cold air, then settled down to burn steadily, quickly warming the atmosphere. Thirrin had never seen such a fireplace before. In Frostmarris, the Great Hall was warmed by a huge central hearth and the smoke found its own way out, eventually, through vents in the roof. But she had no intention of appearing a bumpkin to these cold and sophisticated creatures, so she merely nodded her thanks.

"Now, I believe this is a diplomatic visit. So shall we get down to business?" the King said, reminding Thirrin for a moment of Maggiore Totus. But this illusion was soon dispelled when she looked up and saw his sharply pointed teeth.

"Yes, by all means. I've come to warn you that the Icemark has been invaded by the Polypontian Empire, and my father has died in the act of destroying their army."

"Oh, well done," said the Queen. "You obviously don't need our help, then, if you've already defeated them."

"Unfortunately they still occupy the southern half of the Icemark, so come spring they'll be able to send another army to attack us."

"Which you will also destroy, I suppose."

"Of course!" Thirrin answered with fire.

"Then I ask again, why do you seek our help if you so obviously can deal with anything the Polypontian Empire sends against you?"

Thirrin tried to hold the cold gaze of the Vampire Queen, but she suddenly became aware of the enormous weight of time and experience that lay in the horrendous depths of the Vampire's icy blue eyes. This pale woman had existed for probably hundreds of years, murdering her way down the centuries and maintaining her inhuman nonlife with the blood of countless numbers of people. She was loathsome, hideous, and deeply evil, and Thirrin felt an overwhelming need to be away from the Blood Palace. To be anywhere but here in the sick green light, surrounded by these pale, undead courtiers.

"Well," the Queen continued, "do you or do you not still say that you need our help?"

"Well, yes, we do," Thirrin blurted out, afraid that her diplomatic mission had failed before it had properly begun. "We've destroyed one army, but they'll send another. . . . That's how they fight, they just keep coming. . . . They won't stop. Not until we're destroyed. Then they'll come for you! They'll kill you all, burn your palace, exorcise your ghosts. . . ." She stopped, feeling every one of her inadequate fourteen years, and tried not to blush.

"So you haven't defeated them. Just slowed them down a bit," said the Vampire Queen's sweetly vicious voice. "And now you want to forget nearly a thousand years of hostilities and become our friends. How convenient . . . for you."

"And also for you, Your Majesty," said Oskan, coming to Thirrin's rescue. "The Queen of the Icemark is perfectly correct when she says that if we fall you will be next. The Empire prides itself on being modern, on being *scientific* and *rational.* Monst — people like yourselves and your subjects are the exact opposite of their ideals. To them you're abominations of nature, and they'll destroy you if only to make their idea of the world tidier."

"What is this *scientific*? What does it mean?" the Vampire Queen asked.

"It means believing only what logic tells you is true. In some cases, it means believing only what you can see and what you can weigh or measure. It means denying that something exists unless it's already recognized by science, and in most cases that means only if it can be weighed, measured, or seen," said Oskan, impressing Thirrin enormously with his cool and calm approach.

"Stupid!" the Queen spat. "Doesn't it occur to them that some things can't be measured or weighed?"

"Yes, I suppose. But in that case they'd probably believe their science has not yet developed the means of measuring or weighing the thing in question."

"Then by that argument, young mortal, their science will have to accept us, because we most patently *can* be weighed and measured. *Ergo,* they will have to accept our reality and our right to exist," said the Vampire King with a triumphant smile that revealed all of his sharply pointed and glittering teeth.

"You would think so, wouldn't you," Oskan answered conversationally. "But you're forgetting the woefully mortal ability to be unfair. You see, they don't like you. They don't even like the idea of you. And when some rational people of science don't like something and believe it shouldn't exist, they either ignore it or try to destroy it. In your case, they'll try to destroy you, and not only because they don't like you but quite simply because you occupy a rich and plump country that they want." Oskan shrugged. "In my fifteen years of life and experience, I'm afraid I've had to come to the conclusion that sometimes people just aren't fair."

Their Vampiric Majesties gazed at them for a moment, then both began to giggle. Quietly at first, but then with more and more force until their cold laughter was echoing around the vastly high ceiling of the hall. "Oh, my dear, how precious! How perfectly glorious they are," said the Queen. "I'm so glad we allowed them to come. Do make them do it again, I could listen all night!"

"Now, now, sweetness," said the King in mock annoyance. "You're being most *unfair*. Please remember their ambassadorial dignity. They have every right to our respect and good manners!"

Their Vampiric Majesties looked gravely at each other, then spluttered into uncontrollable laughter again. The undead courtiers now joined in, until the hall was filled with the hideous sound of mocking laughter and the King and Queen were leaning weakly against each other wiping their eyes.

Thirrin and Oskan felt like foolish children who'd attempted to impress some sophisticated adults and had only succeeded in making complete idiots of themselves. The longer the laughter went on, the worse they felt, until eventually they could only think of running away from the humiliation. Thirrin's face blazed crimson, and Oskan stood hunched as though a weight of shame were bearing him to the ground.

"Enough!" a deep and guttural voice suddenly bellowed, rising powerfully over the laughter and snuffing it out like a candle flame. "Queen Thirrin Freer Strong-in-the-Arm Lindenshield, Wildcat of the North, is my ally and my friend, and I will not have her mocked!"

Thirrin turned toward the source of the voice and watched as a huge wolfman marched down the length of the hall. Immediately the Wolf-folk guard threw back their heads and howled in greeting and salute as their King approached.

Grishmak Blood-drinker the First raised a paw in acknowledgment as he walked by the escort of werewolves, and then stopped in front of Thirrin. As she craned back her neck to meet his eye, she realized she'd forgotten just how tall he was, and she almost flinched as the huge paw took her hand and raised it to his lips in courtly greeting.

"Your Majesty, may I be the first to welcome you correctly to the palace of Their Vampiric Majesties. They themselves seem to have forgotten the rules of etiquette and decorum that should be displayed between rulers. But some are stupid enough to believe that mere physical immortality somehow excuses them for their ill manners and boorishness." He turned to face the twin thrones where the Vampire King and Queen sat glaring at him. "Some kings and queens have made the mistake of believing that the long number of years they have sat on a throne will never end, and that nothing could topple their power. I would remind such rulers that wars have been fought for much less reason than an insult to a valued friend, and I would also remind such rulers that they lost that war and were very nearly destroyed in it, immortal or not!"

* * *

Grishmak's anger stemmed from a genuine affection for Thirrin that had grown since he'd first formed an alliance with her. Of course, at the time, accepting her offer of friendship had simply been the most sensible thing to do, especially as refusal would have meant being hanged, drawn, and quartered by Redrought's housecarls. But alongside all of the political and military good sense of having a strong alliance against the Polypontian Empire, Grishmak found that he quite simply liked Thirrin.

Grishmak glowered at the Vampire King and Queen, challenging them to say anything else insulting to the young human girl.

Thirrin, for her part, found herself warming to the Werewolf King enormously, and she was very happy to see Their Vampiric Majesties turn aside their eyes as if observing something down at the other end of the hall.

"I think it should be remembered," Grishmak Blood-drinker went on, "that the dignity of a true monarch is born, and can sometimes be found in the youngest Queen, whereas others who have ruled for centuries have yet to acquire it, and perhaps never will."

Thirrin smiled at the Werewolf King, her poise and confidence now completely restored. "I am so glad to see you, King Grishmak Blood-drinker. Baroness Grin-Skull told me you would be here, and I am most happy that she was right."

"Ah, the Baroness! How is she? I really must visit her caves when next I make Royal Progress."

"She is well, and was most courteous in giving us shelter after my party got lost in the fiercest blizzard. Her werewolves rescued us from certain death and led us to the caves of the Baroness. Her hospitality was both warm and deeply polite," Thirrin answered, not deigning to glance at the Vampire King and Queen. "She also told me the interesting origin of her family name. I only wish I could have witnessed the young Baroness Padfoot ripping the face off the standard-bearer after the defeat of the Vampire Army."

"Before my time, too," King Grishmak answered. "But it must have been a glorious sight!"

"Now that you two have exchanged pleasantries, perhaps we can get on with the business at hand," the icy-cold voice of the Vampire Queen interrupted.

The huge wolfman winked at Thirrin secretly, and then turned to face the twin thrones. "Business? Isn't it already settled? Surely none of us has any choice. In alliance we have a chance against the Empire. Alone we have no hope whatsoever."

"There are things to discuss, details to finalize," the Vampire King insisted.

"Work for clerks," Grishmak snarled. "Draw up a treaty and we'll all sign it. Now," he said, turning to Thirrin, "I've got a comfortable and warm set of caves away from this morbid labyrinth. There's plenty of space for all your party, and lots of good red meat. Oh yes, I know you people like it burn — cooked, but I can arrange that, too."

"You're so right, of course," the Vampire Queen simpered knowingly. "Alliance between us is an obvious solution. Especially when the Queen of the Icemark has such a high-ranking adviser, who is more akin to our people than to hers."

"What do you mean?" Thirrin snapped.

Their Vampiric Majesties smiled to see they'd scored a point, and the Queen continued. "The boy, Oskan Witch's

Son, I believe you call him. We have many witches in our land, so he's almost a citizen."

"His mother was a *White* Witch. They fought against you, and still protect our lands from your evil!"

"Oh, I admit there are a few rebels who resist us. But magic power is still magic power. It comes from the same source as ours. And he is strongly connected to that source; anyone can sense it."

"I'm no wizard of the Black Arts!" Oskan exploded, his face red and eyes blazing.

"Wizard? Who said anything about being a wizard?" the Queen asked, her voice heavy with contempt. "I'm not talking about all that male mathematics and mumbo jumbo. Your source of Power comes through your mother, through the female line. And as for your father — well, he was hardly what you'd call mortal, now, was he? But besides all of that, my dear Oskan Witch's Son . . . you have a Power from a very female source; you are a warlock. You are a male witch."

Now it was Thirrin's turn to rescue her adviser as he floundered in a sea of mixed emotions. "Do you really think this news is some sort of shocking revelation?" Thirrin asked, her voice as deeply contemptuous as the Vampire Queen's had been. "Any who have seen my chief adviser helping in our struggle over the last few weeks will have plainly seen his power at work. But I do have Your Vampiric Majesties to thank for giving it a name," she said, her voice steady and strong. "If Oskan Witch's Son is indeed a warlock, then we know that his abilities work for good against evil, and we all have reason to be grateful for his powers."

A silence fell, and as the atmosphere crackled with hatred and resentment, King Grishmak faced the thrones squarely. "Have we all finished scoring points now? Because I'm getting hungry and quite frankly I find your taste in palace decor cold and morbid. The sooner I get back to my cave, the better. Let's all just admit that we need one another and tell the clerks to get weaving on the treaty so that we can have it signed and be out of one another's company as soon as we can. Agreed?"

After a smoldering moment, Their Vampiric Majesties nodded, and Grishmak let out a weary sigh. "Good. Now, Thirrin . . . I mean, Your Gracious Majesty, my invitation still stands. Would you care to join me at supper?"

Thirrin smiled. "I'd love to."

The huge wolfman took her arm and, gently turning her away from the twin thrones, he led her down the hall toward the doors. "What I said earlier, by the way, about getting out of one another's company, doesn't apply to you. I was referring to Their Royal Face-aches back there."

"I know," she answered. "And I entirely agree with you about the decor. It's about as cheerful as an iceberg."

Werewolf and young Queen swept through the press of Vampire courtiers, who quickly made way for the formidable pair. The escort of soldiers and Wolf-folk followed in their wake, with Oskan at the rear. He was deep in thought, at last fitting answers to the questions he'd been asking himself for years. The Vampire Queen's statement that he was a warlock explained so much, but it would take a while to adjust to the idea. Now he knew why he could sometimes see the future, speak to wild animals, even heal without medicines and read the weather with such accuracy. He had many other skills, too, which he now realized might have their roots in magic. It would all take some thinking about.

Thirrin and King Grishmak reached the entranceway and swept out of the Blood Palace, followed by their escorts and Oskan. The massive double doors slammed shut after them with a deep boom. Oskan woke from his reverie with a shock — the slamming doors had only just missed him. Swinging around furiously, he glared at the studded and hinged woodwork with such fierce intensity that they suddenly burst open again, crashing back against the walls inside the palace and splintering deeply.

"I'm sure you didn't mean to be rude," he bellowed over the heads of the courtiers cowering just inside the entrance. "Your doors seem to have slammed shut in a draft. I'd get that fixed, if I were you."

Grishmak's grin revealed his huge teeth. "Useful sort to have around, that warlock," he said. Then he led the way down the steps of the palace and toward the surrounding forest.

17

Thirrin and Oskan gladly accepted a selection of meats. It was torn, rather than cut, into huge chunks, and smoked from the rough toasting it had been given over the nearby fire. King Grishmak ate with surprising delicacy, picking up slabs of raw flesh between his thumb and forefinger and biting off a modest mouthful before returning the rest to the flat piece of stone that served as his plate.

The caves were warm and dry and, as the Werewolf King had promised, were more than big enough to accommodate them all. In fact, they were so big that a decision was made to fetch the horses from the palace stables and house them in another of the connecting caverns rather than leave them to the uncertain care of the Vampires.

The caves lay in a rocky outcrop about a mile from the Blood Palace, and as Thirrin sat eating her meal, she could see at least six fires burning in the vast space. King Grishmak had obviously brought a large household with him on his visit to Their Vampiric Majesties. And though neither Thirrin nor Oskan could quite work out exactly what the duties of the dozens of werewolves were, they all seemed amazingly busy, bustling around from fireside to fireside and constantly arriving at Grishmak's side to whisper in his ear.

"The treaty should be ready for signing tomorrow," the King said as he politely licked the last of the blood from his plate.

"So soon?" asked Oskan. "I'd have thought there'd have been all sorts of legal wranglings and niceties to deal with first."

"No. You can bet Their Royal Face-aches have had their clerks working on it for weeks already. Tomorrow morning their people will arrive here and it'll all be ready for signing. One thing, though," and he looked at them closely. "Let *my* clerks read it through first. It's almost certain they'll try to pull a fast one in the wording somewhere, and you'll end up ceding a province here or a town there, if you're not careful."

Thirrin nodded. "We'll be glad to let your people read it first. I'm most grateful for your help."

"Happy to be of service," the King answered gruffly. "You've both done very well for such youngsters. Their Vampiric Majesties are as tricky to handle as fish in a barrel of grease, even for one as gray-pelted as I am. But come the day when the Blessed Moon has completed her cycle a few dozen times, you'll both be more than a match for them, whether they've lived for a thousand years or not."

"Have they really lived as long as that?" asked Thirrin in an awed whisper.

"Well, I suppose we should technically say *existed*," Grishmak answered. "But actually it's longer. More like twelve hundred years, but they've ruled for a thousand."

"They claim their kingdom extends to the top of the world, where the ice never melts," said Oskan. "Is that true?"

"No. They'd like it to, but there are some to the north of here far more powerful than they ever could be, even though they're mortal and live no longer than any other creature that walks beneath the sky."

"Who are they?" asked Thirrin, puzzled that Maggiore had never mentioned them in their geography lessons. "Are they people?"

"People? Well, of course they're *people*," Grishmak answered in surprise. "But if you mean are they *human* people, then no, they're not."

"Then what are they?"

Grishmak seemed reluctant to answer, but after a while he said, "They're secretive and quiet. They make no contact with others unless the outsiders make it first. Then if they don't like you, you're dead."

"Yes, but what are they?" asked Oskan, frustrated by the king's hints and riddles.

The huge werewolf stared into the nearby fire, and when he answered, his voice was quiet as though he were still thinking things through. "They're the strongest creatures I know and they'd make a formidable ally in the coming war. Perhaps . . . just perhaps, Thirrin could make a friend of them and bring them into the struggle. If anyone can do it, she can. She could make peace between night and day, between dark and light, if she wanted." He blinked and turned to face the young Queen of the Icemark. "Thirrin Freer Strong-in-the-Arm Lindenshield, Wildcat of the North, I give you a task. Your challenge is to make an alliance with Lord Tharaman-Thar of the Icesheets. He who is as white as the snows, as strong as rock, as tall at the shoulder as a man, as wise as a scholar, as gentle as a feather, and as fierce as the wildest winter storms. Bring him into our covenant and even Scipio Bellorum will be in awe of us. With Lord Tharaman on our side we will have a chance of stopping even the Empire . . . at least for a while."

"Gladly. I'll do whatever I can to try to win him over to our side. But where does he live, and how do I get there, and exactly what sort of . . . creature is he?"

"He is winter, given animal form," answered Grishmak. "He and his people are Snow Leopards. They stand as tall and as large as your horses, their teeth are like shattered stars, and their claws like cavalry sabers. With them as allies, we could hold back the Empire and live free!"

"Snow Leopards!" Oskan said, amazed. "But how can we talk to them?"

"Exactly as you talk to me: They use the language of humans."

"They talk?!"

"Oskan Witch's Son, have you walked deaf through your woods and caves?" King Grishmak asked darkly. "Do you truly believe that only human people use language and talk to one another?"

"Of course not," Oskan answered sharply. "I know the language of birds and of the four-legged ones. If I concentrate, I can even understand some of the meanings of insects and fish. But you're not saying that they use the language of animals; you're telling us that these leopards use the *words* of human speech. How can that be?"

The King shrugged. "You've spoken to the Wolf-folk on many occasions and have never seemed surprised. What's so different here?"

"Your people are at least partly human. Their language comes from the humanity in their blood. Are these leopards also part human?"

"No. They're pure cat. But their legends say that when the One made the world, it loved their power and beauty as much as it loved the mind and adaptability of humanity, and so blessed them with the gift of speech, so that its two favorite creations could one day speak each to the other. Don't you see? — that time has now come. Thirrin, take this legend to the Snow Leopards and bring them into our alliance."

"But will they obey us?"

"No! Never!" King Grishmak howled. "They are a free and thinking people who obey none but their own Lord Tharaman-Thar. But they may agree to help you."

Thirrin gazed at the Werewolf King as the information about these new people settled into her brain. "Where exactly do they live, and how do I get there?"

"Their home is on the mountain at the Hub of the World. Tharaman-Thar's palace is made of natural ice and rock, and his people live by hunting walruses and the great ice bears that roam their lands," Grishmak answered. "As for getting there, you'll need help. No horse could travel over the snows and Icesheets that shift and change day by day, and if a storm hits you, then you'll die unless you have the knowledge only a few people possess. Are you sure you're ready to take on such a trek?"

Thirrin answered quickly. "No. But I have no choice. Such an ally could shift the balance of the war and help us hold back the Empire. Who are the ones who can guide us?"

"There are tribes of the Wolf-folk who live far to the north. They hunt on the Icesheets and travel sometimes for weeks before returning home. If I send out word now, they could be here in two or three days."

Thirrin gazed silently into the fire, then said decisively, "Send for them, Grishmak. I have an alliance to make."

The next night, a herald and escort of Vampires arrived at the caves carrying a huge document made of dressed vellum. At first they demanded it should be signed immediately, but after Grishmak had laughed at them they agreed to leave it for examination and return the next night. A group of gray-pelted werewolves then took the document and went to the back of the caves, where they could be heard snarling and growling over it far into the night.

Later that day King Grishmak sent couriers to the north in search of the tribes of Wolf-folk who lived on the Icesheets. Thirrin stood quietly thoughtful as she watched the messengers run off with the odd loping gait the werewolves used when they knew they had miles to go. And her mind ran in the same way over the events of the last few months.

In less than half a year her life had been shattered and shaken into a new form that she was still trying to come to terms with. The Icemark had been invaded, her father killed, and she'd become Queen of a land that was likely to fall to the Empire within a few short months. Only her soldiers and the network of alliances she was struggling to forge could save her people. And all of it had to be coordinated by her, essentially a young girl not yet fifteen, with little or no experience of anything but the classroom and the weapons training ground.

Most of the time the sheer momentum of the emergency was enough to keep her focused, but occasionally, when she was forced to wait quietly for events to unfold, the full impact of her near-impossible situation came crashing in on her. How could they possibly win? What chance would the army of a tiny northern kingdom, with a ragbag of allies, have against the massive might and power of the Polypontian Empire? Why not just cut their losses and flee into exile where she could at least live in the comfort and safety that the wealth of the Royal Treasury would bring her?

She fought against the rising tide of panic welling up inside her and turned abruptly to walk back into the cave. Oskan followed.

"Now that you've finished scaring yourself half to death, I'd like to have a word," he said softly.

"What do you mean? Scaring myself?"

"The Empire. How does it go? *We have no chance. By this time next year we could all have been destroyed.*"

"How did you know I was . . . ?" Her question trailed off as a now familiar sense of awe washed over her.

Oskan grinned. "Oh, don't worry, I wasn't reading your mind. I just found myself in exactly the same situation as you; I've got nothing to do at the moment, and suddenly I had all the time in the world to start worrying and panicking. So I thought we'd both better keep ourselves occupied."

Thirrin groped for her royal dignity. "And what does my adviser suggest?" she asked, in a voice made haughty by the relief she felt that he hadn't been reading her thoughts.

"Well, first I think we'd better arrange to send most of the escort back to the Hypolitan. The horses certainly can't come with us to the Icesheets, and I suppose we'll have to carry all our own supplies with us, so the fewer in the party, the better."

"Yes, you're right. Give orders to the captain of the escort while I have a word with the King." Thirrin strode away to find Grishmak, ignoring Oskan's bow that was a little too playfully mocking for her liking.

She found the Werewolf King holding court around the cave's huge central fire. About twenty of the Wolf-folk stood before him, all snarling and howling in their strange language. But as soon as they saw her approach, they politely changed to human speech. The King stood to greet her and cleared a pile of bones that lay scattered on the rock next to him so that she could sit down.

Grishmak agreed that sending back some of the escort was a good plan, and he ordered some of the Wolf-folk to guide them back to the Hypolitan. "In fact, I'd send them all back if I were you. It'd be far better if just you and the Witch's Son went to the Hub of the World. Lord Tharaman-Thar would be far more impressed by the bravery of a small party than the glitter of an escort."

"Wouldn't it make the Royal House of the Icemark seem less important if only Oskan and I go?" Thirrin asked, politely accepting yet another platter of toasted meat from Grishmak's chamberlain.

The King barked a short laugh. "This nest of Vampires might be dazzled by the sight of soldiers and weapons — after all, your dad *did* beat them in battle — but the Snow Leopards are different. They understand a brave heart and think it gives more glory to a ruler than any number of soldiers."

"Oh. Doesn't Thara . . . Tharaman-Thar have many soldiers himself, then?"

Grishmak patted her knee affectionately with a huge hairy paw. "You don't have to worry about that. His Snow Leopards may not outnumber the Empire's armies, but when he calls them to fight, they're an avalanche of power; they're a blizzard of ferocity. I think even Scipio Bellorum would be daunted by the sight."

Thirrin nodded, secretly thinking that the Empire would soon be fighting the strangest army it had ever come into conflict with. Not only would humans be taking the field against them, but Wolf-folk, Vampires, and possibly even giant Snow Leopards! If she were Scipio Bellorum, she'd take one look at the ravening monsters waiting to fight her, turn right around, and run all the way back to the Polypontus.

But that wasn't going to happen. General Bellorum was a

brilliant and vicious soldier; he'd adapt, and so would his army. No miracles would win the war against him, just hard fighting and hopefully brilliant tactics. She felt suddenly weary, so after emptying her plate of meat, she politely withdrew from the werewolves and went to sit in a quiet corner at the back of the cave, where she immediately fell asleep.

Thirrin was woken by the sound of huge wings beating the air. By the cave entrance she could see King Grishmak waiting patiently with his courtiers and, scrambling to her feet, she hurried over to him.

"Ah, Thirrin, there you are. I was just about to send a chamberlain for you."

"What's that noise?" she asked as the sound of the wing beats continued to thunder on the air.

"Vampires," the King answered. "In their bat form. I think it's the King and Queen come to sign the treaty, along with most of their court, by the sound of things."

Several huge leathery creatures dropped out of the darkening evening sky and literally stepped out of flight, like fashionable ladies descending elegantly from a carriage. Vampires settled at the cave entrance, where they folded their massive wings with fussy neatness and looked around them. They were an odd gray color, like the dawn sky on a rainy day, and they had doglike faces with massive fangs. Their features began to run and blur, like pictures left in the rain, and their bodies seemed to flow like candle wax until slowly they coagulated into their human shapes.

"Ah, King Grishmak and Queen Thirrin," said the Vampire Queen as she smoothed her beautiful silk gown. "My consort and I have come to sample your hospitality . . . and while we're here we might as well sign this treaty you're so keen on."

"Your Vampiric Majesties are both welcome to the Embassy of the Wolf-folk. Please come in and be seated," said Grishmak, and he led the way to the largest fire in the cave, where a semicircle of four massive boulders had been set up as rough thrones.

The Werewolf King escorted the Vampires to their seats, then, taking Thirrin's hand, he led her to the boulder next to his. As they all sat, Thirrin couldn't help noticing that she and Grishmak were looking down on Their Vampiric Majesties. And that the Vampires' long limbs were stretched out in front of them so they looked like schoolchildren who had outgrown their desks. She smiled secretly to herself; there were obviously times when points could be scored even within the restrictions of diplomacy.

Oskan took up a position behind Thirrin's throne, and a silence fell as they all looked at one another. At last the Vampire King said, "Well, as we're obviously not going to be offered any refreshments, we might as well get this treaty signed."

"I have no blood to offer you," Grishmak explained. "And for some reason, nobody wanted to volunteer when I asked for donors."

"Werewolf blood is tainted with animal," the Vampire Queen said with a shudder. "But human, on the other hand . . ."

". . . is not being offered," Thirrin interrupted coldly.

"Then let's get down to business," the Vampire King said with a weary sigh.

Grishmak raised his paw, and five gray-pelted werewolves came forward, the foremost one holding the rolled vellum of the treaty in his hand. He bowed deeply to the figures on the thrones and, after a nod from Grishmak, he said, "My colleagues and I have studied the document in detail, and have found several . . . errors in its composition."

"Errors?" the Vampire Queen asked in a bored voice.

"Yes. Somehow a clause had been inserted that required Queen Thirrin to cede a third of her lands to Your Vampiric Majesties and to pay a tithe of twenty youths and twenty maidens per month."

"Really? I can't think how that happened," the Vampire King said with wide-eyed innocence. "Must have been a slip of the pen."

"That being the case, I am sure that Their Vampiric Majesties will raise no objection to the fact that I and my colleagues took it upon ourselves to erase this clause — and the one that required the Icemark to acknowledge its status as a vassal to The-Land-of-the-Ghosts."

The Vampires coughed and looked away. "Yes, yes. All right!" the Queen finally said into the following silence. "Let's just sign the treaty and we can get back to our palace and away from this . . . *rustic idyll.*"

Grishmak snapped his fingers, and a chamberlain appeared carrying a cushion on which lay four daggers and four quills. Thirrin followed the werewolf's lead and picked up one of the daggers and one of the quills, and waited almost breathlessly as the cushion was then carried to the royal Vampires. They, too, picked up a dagger and quill each and, without hesitation, each of them cut their forearms and dipped the point of the quills into the running blood.

The gray-pelted werewolf now presented the treaty, and Their Vampiric Majesties signed their names. Grishmak also cut his forearm, though without the same drama or depth that the Vampires had used, and dipped the quill into the small nick. He signed his name on the treaty and turned with a smile to Thirrin. Taking a deep breath, she steeled herself and cut her arm. The blade was sharp and the blood ran easily, and quickly she added her name to the other three on the treaty. In the dim light of the cave she thought the blood looked black, and she almost shuddered as she watched it trickle, shiny and thick, across the vellum.

Then Grishmak leaped to his feet, threw back his head, and howled with such bloodcurdling ferocity that all other sound fell away. The Werewolf King's deep guttural voice then boomed out, "May all the goddesses and gods of the earth and sky, all the spirits of blood and death, all the watchers and keepers of oaths see this act and hold our written names as binding. And may any and all who break this trust fall from the face of the Mother Earth and live an unending life skinned under the endless gaze of the blazing sun, mortal and immortal, Vampire, Wolf-folk, and human being!" He turned his bloodshot gaze on Their Vampiric Majesties. "By garlic, wood, and cleansing fire, *so mote it be*!"

The Vampire King and Queen leaped to their feet and hissed, drawing their moist red lips back from their pointed teeth. "You go too far, Grishmak!"

"Perhaps," he agreed, his voice mild and calm once more. "But now you're bound, and not even you would dare break this treaty."

The Vampire King and Queen hissed again and, striding to the cave exit, they and their courtiers transformed back into giant bats and flew away screeching.

"Good, that's a job well done," Grishmak said cheerfully. "Am I the only one who's hungry?"

•

18

They had been traveling for most of the short winter day. The air was freezing cold, and tiny particles of ice drifted and shimmered in the brilliant sunlight so that they seemed to be journeying through a world of polished crystal. Thirrin and Oskan were snuggled down deep under thick coverings of fur while the glittering white world rolled rapidly past. They were in a long low sleigh being pulled at breakneck speed by six enormous white werewolves, their legs pounding tirelessly through the snow, while their arms pistoned the air like parts of a living machine. Alongside them was a second sleigh packed with food and fuel and other equipment needed for their survival in the wilds of the far north. This, too, was being drawn by six of the white Wolf-folk, and as they ran they constantly raised their snouts to the air as though smelling their route to the top of the world.

The Wolf-folk had arrived the day before at King Grishmak's cave, announcing their presence with a great clamoring and baying that even Thirrin's untrained ear could tell was different from the usual werewolf language. With them was one of the King's runners, who had set out three days earlier to find them, and she saluted her leader proudly as she approached.

"They were far to the north and east, My Lord," she had explained in the human tongue. "But they answered your summons at once."

The King nodded, and turned to the newly arrived werewolves, who immediately howled in salute. "Wolf-folk of the Icesheets, I have an important task for you," he had said. "This human female is Thirrin Freer Strong-in-the-Arm Lindenshield, Wildcat of the North, Queen of the Icemark, and ally of our people. She is also my beloved friend whose safety and good health I cherish above all others."

The huge white werewolves turned to gaze at her, their ferocious faces for a moment calm as they sniffed the air, marking her scent and memorizing her form. Then, as one, they threw back their heads and howled.

"Your task, my people, is to take Queen Thirrin and her adviser to the court of the Snow Leopards at the Hub of the World, where she will invite their King to join our alliance against the Polypontian Empire. Her safety and good health are your responsibility. No blood must be spilled unless it be yours, no breath may be stilled but your own. You will set your teeth at death and you will be an enemy of failure. And you will return the Queen here to this cave in one half of the Blessed Moon's cycle. Do you understand?"

The leader of the white Wolf-folk, Grinelda Blood-tooth, then stepped forward. She stood a head taller than even the King, and to Thirrin and Oskan her mouth seemed as full of teeth as a forest of trees.

"Lord Tharaman-Thar and his Snow Leopards are a fearsome people, King Grishmak Blood-drinker," she said bluntly. "But the human Queen will be returned safely to you, or we'll die defending her."

"Thank you, Grinelda Blood-tooth. I can ask no more," Grishmak had answered after a moment's silence, then turning to Thirrin, he'd said, "You can see now how dangerous your task is. The Snow Leopards are answerable to none. If they don't like you, they'll kill you."

Here was the duty at the center of Thirrin's power. At that moment she would have liked nothing better than to give the responsibility of it all to another, but she knew she had no choice. It was for this sort of pressure and danger that she'd been born, so she simply nodded and tried to look as though riding off to meet killer leopards was an everyday event in her life.

"Before I set off on this journey, King Grishmak, I would ask you to give shelter to Oskan the Warlock until I return, or . . ." she said, after a brief pause, "until I don't return."

The changed form of his name momentarily shocked Oskan into silence, but he quickly recovered and exploded angrily, "If you dare try to leave me behind, I'll follow on foot, and when I die in the snow, I'll come back and haunt you. I'll make your life a complete misery. No ghost will ever have been as inventive in its nastiness as I'll be: I'll turn your food rancid; I'll transform your drink into blood; I'll howl and moan throughout the night; there'll be no place safe from me. And don't think I couldn't do it, Thirrin, Queen of the Icemark, because I can assure you, I could."

Thirrin looked at her young adviser, whose eyes were wide and alight with barely suppressed rage. There were times when she found his friendship terrifying, but this was soon overridden by a sense of huge relief and gratitude. At least she wouldn't have to face the Snow Leopards alone.

"I think, King Grishmak, we'll not need to impose on your hospitality any longer," she'd said. "We'll both be going to the palace of Lord Tharaman-Thar."

The wolfman had nodded. "As you wish, My Lady," he'd said, secretly relieved that he wouldn't have to contain the power of an angry warlock. "We will watch keenly for your return."

A sudden dip in the ground jolted the sleigh, and Thirrin's thoughts returned to the present. Oskan seemed engrossed by the land around them as the werewolves thundered along at an incredible pace. His face turned upward to follow the branches of a small stand of pine trees they were passing beneath, and he twisted in his seat to watch them as they left the copse behind and thundered on toward the Kingdom of the Snow Leopards.

"They were the most northerly of all trees," he said almost to himself. "From here onward the lands of humanity end, and the rule of the wild begins."

Ahead of them the land was white and featureless under its slowly undulating blanket of snow. The sun had already sunk after the brief day of the northern winter, leaving the sky stained by the pink afterglow of its light. And low over the horizon the pristine brilliance of the Even Star shone out as the day faded.

Thirrin looked at Oskan as he gazed at the star. "Why were you so determined to come with me to the Kingdom of the Snow Leopards, Oskan?"

He turned to look at her, a slight frown on his face. "If you fail, Thirrin, and you die trying to make an alliance with Tharaman-Thar, then the Icemark will be lost, and Scipio Bellorum and all he stands for will rule in the land. Rationality, science, industry, progress. All fine things in their own right and when playing their proper part in the life of a nation. But as far as I can tell, in the Empire they rule over all else. Magic and mystery have no place or worth; even nature is only a sort of huge storehouse to provide science and industry with the raw materials they need. What place could there possibly be for me in such a world? I'd be a bit of flotsam, some trash left behind by a retreating tide. Interesting enough in its own way, but with no real worth beyond some small curiosity value." He turned to look ahead at the sky that was slowly unfolding the bloom of its night stars. "I'd sooner die a quick death under the crushing paw of a Snow Leopard, a victim of some unstoppable force of nature, than dwindle away like an oil lamp low on fuel."

She nodded, understanding him perfectly. "You've obviously been thinking this through for some time, and I suspected you might say something of the sort." She suddenly smiled at him. "Look at the two of us, barely out of childhood and already we're too old-fashioned for this changing world. Is it possible to be born old? Because I certainly feel it sometimes. How can we hope to stand against unstoppable *progress*; how can we possibly win a war against the forces of science?"

Oskan snorted. "Which question do you want me to answer first? Born old? Yes, right now I feel ninety. And as for the rest, we're not fighting progress or science; they're both ideas that belong to all people — ideas that should help us to understand the beauty of our world and improve the lives of everything that lives in it. But the Empire has kidnapped them, and progress of its sort means sweeping aside everything that isn't new, whether good or bad. And to the Empire, science is just a means of creating more efficient ways of killing people."

"Do you think all scientists are bad?" she asked.

"Maggiore Totus is a scientist," he answered simply.

"Yes," she said, remembering the experiments and tests she'd sweated over only the year before — in another life. "*He'd* use science to make people happy."

"He would. And I'm sure there are many others like him."

They fell silent, listening to the hiss of the sleigh's runners as they sped over the snow. The last of the light had drained from the sky, and the stars coldly blazed above them, glittering and scintillating like ice crystals in the frozen air.

The werewolves ran on, seemingly tireless, sniffing the wind and occasionally adjusting their course as they headed for the Hub of the World. But then, as a half-moon rose over the horizon, they howled in greeting of the sacred giver of light and slowed to a halt.

Oskan and Thirrin watched as the Wolf-folk busily emptied the second sleigh of most of its contents and erected a low tent that was big enough to take them all. When everything was ready, Grinelda Blood-tooth curtsied politely and asked them if they would care to join them in the shelter.

Thirrin nodded with the proper amount of regality and accepted a fur-covered hand as she stepped from her sleigh. Made of thick layers of dressed hides, the tent was spacious, with furs piled deeply underfoot and braziers set at intervals around its wide interior. At the entrance a huge fire had been built where two of the werewolves squatted with slabs of meat on sticks, which they were attempting to toast for the human guests. After watching for a few moments, during which the meat was first burned and then dropped into the ashes, Oskan politely took the sticks and told the werewolves that he and the Queen would prefer to cook their own food.

The Wolf-folk seemed relieved, and after bowing they hurried off to help with the other tasks of setting up camp. But it soon became clear that Thirrin was no better at cooking than the werewolves, and Oskan told her to leave it to him.

"I'm pretty sick of meat, anyway," she whispered when the rest of the party seemed busy. "I'd happily kill for a loaf of bread or a bowl of carrots."

"Or even just an apple!" Oskan whispered back.

She nodded in vigorous agreement. "I never thought I'd find myself dreaming of cabbages and turnips, but right now they seem like food for the gods. My jaw aches with chewing all this half-cooked meat."

"I suppose we can expect more of the same from the Snow Leopards," said Oskan. "Assuming, of course, that we're not part of the menu ourselves."

"Well, I'll do my best to stick in their throats, if it comes to that," said Thirrin fiercely, and watched in surprise as Oskan giggled uncontrollably. There were times, she thought, when boys were just impossible to understand.

The entire party of twelve white werewolves and two humans crammed into the tent to eat their meal, and as soon as it was done, the Wolf-folk settled down to sleep. There was no ceremony and not much room, but the braziers, the fire, and the hairy bodies generated enough heat to make conditions quite comfortable. Even the intense cold of the dark hours found it impossible to penetrate the cocoon of warmth that the werewolves had made. Both Thirrin and Oskan were soon asleep, and woke with a shock to a brilliant morning light and the howling of the Wolf-folk greeting the day.

They were now so far north that daylight would last for little more than three hours, and before they reached their journey's end they would be traveling through perpetual night. Grinelda

Blood-tooth urged them all to eat, pack, and begin the trek as quickly as possible, and within a few short minutes they were again thundering over the ice on their way to the Hub of the World.

The land was now almost completely flat and featureless. Occasionally they would pass strangely contorted shapes where the wind had carved the snow into fantastic sculptures. But mostly the terrain slowly billowed and undulated toward the horizon with no landmark or feature to show they were getting anywhere.

As they approached the realm of the Snow Leopards, the weather began to change. Thirrin didn't think it could possibly get colder, but the temperatures tumbled and a thick rime of ice began to grow over everything. The outer covers of the sleigh were stiff with it, and even the pelts of the werewolves sparkled with a frosting of crystals. The air burned with a hideous cold that froze living skin within seconds of being exposed to it, and the glare of the sun, reflected from the white world around them, made their eyes ache even through their whalebone slit-goggles that let in only the barest sliver of light.

But the intense brilliance of the sun stopped being a problem when, one morning, dawn didn't come at all and they entered the world of perpetual winter's night. For Oskan the true magic of nature was encapsulated in that journey to the Hub of the World. Above him the star-encrusted sky slowly exploded across the hours of the day as the constellations rose from the horizon and gradually arced to their setting while their sleigh glided on across the snows. Very occasionally a shooting star would streak a brushstroke of light across the sky, and he'd find himself childishly making a wish that they'd win the coming war and no one would die. But then he'd cynically remind himself that the first part of the wish was unlikely and the second part impossible.

Moonrise was always greeted by the werewolves, who would stop in their tracks and howl in salute as the brilliant silver fire broached the horizon. Even half full, its light was sufficient to illuminate the snows to a breathtaking radiance that somehow contrived to be brighter and yet more subtle than daylight.

Both Oskan and Thirrin began to lose all sense of time and with it their understanding of reality. Without the regular exchange of day for night and night for day, they felt themselves to be adrift in a coldly beautiful world journeying on and on across forevers and nowheres. Neither of them minded too much. An eternal trek through beauty was preferable to any war, and slowly all sense of urgency was leached from their minds.

But one day, as the sleighs whispered over the endless snows, Oskan felt a shift in the patterns of the air. He sat up and looked out over the snowfields to the horizon, but there was nothing to be seen.

"What is it?" Thirrin asked.

"The world's making weather," he answered, without taking his eyes from the distant line where land met sky.

"Bad weather?"

"Very bad, I'd say."

Immediately Thirrin called to the werewolves, and the sleighs stopped. Grinelda Blood-tooth stepped out of the traces, walked back to the two humans, and curtsied deeply. "There's a problem, My Lady?"

"Oskan the Warlock says there's bad weather on the way."

The creature eyed the boy for a few seconds, sniffed the air, and called to the others in her own tongue. A growled conference took place, punctuated with much snuffling, squinting at the horizon, and spitting speculatively into the wind. Finally the leader turned back to them and said, "The warlock's right, but it's very faint. We should have three days before it hits us."

"Two and a half," said Oskan decisively.

"Then we'll need to make our own shelter. It's still another four days' journey to the border of the Snow Leopards' lands."

"Will these shelters take long to construct?" Thirrin asked.

Grinelda Blood-tooth shook her head. "No. An hour at the most. We still have at least two days' traveling time."

"Then let's make sure we don't waste it," Thirrin said in her best royal voice.

Grinelda curtsied again, strode back to her position at the head of the pulling team, and with a ferocious howling they shot away across the snows at a startling speed.

But no matter how fast the Wolf-folk ran over the Icesheets, they couldn't outstrip the weather. Over the following day, the stars were slowly hidden from view as a huge bank of clouds advanced across the sky. And with them came a strange whining and howling, thin-sounding in the distance and fitful, like a hunting wolf pack that has picked up a scent. This was the voice of the distant wind, icy and deadly, that hated all living things, and that would drain the life-warmth from whatever it touched.

Over the following days and hours, the wind gradually ran them down, eating up the distance between its blood-freezing cold and the teams of werewolves who ran on tirelessly through the arctic night. Soon Thirrin and Oskan could see a deep gray shadow dancing and swirling on the horizon as the blizzard bore down on them, and the moaning and keening came closer and closer.

At last, the Wolf-folk teams stopped and turned the sleighs to face the approaching storm, making a V formation by drawing their fronts together and lashing them securely with hide ropes. Quickly they cut blocks from the icesheets around them, using whalebone blades they'd made sharp and rigid by spitting on them and allowing the saliva to freeze. As one group cut the blocks, another built them into a wall, so that soon the sleighs were surrounded by a boat-shaped barrier that stood to shoulder height and sloped slightly inward. The pointed "prow" of this barrier faced into the oncoming wind and its tail tapered away to a second point.

The blizzard was now only minutes away, and Thirrin and Oskan watched in amazement as the Wolf-folk moved at an incredible speed, draping the thick pelts of the tents over both sleighs and lashing them tightly into position to make a secure shelter. The frozen floor was covered as usual with furs, and braziers were lit as they all scrambled inside and settled down to wait for the storm.

In less than an hour the werewolves had built a weatherproof refuge, and not a moment too soon. Suddenly the wind hit them, howling and screeching like an army of giant Vampires. The hide roof of their shelter flapped and shuddered crazily. Thirrin and Oskan were afraid it would be torn away, but it soon became obvious that the hide ropes that lashed it firmly to the sleighs would hold, and they began to relax.

It even became quite enjoyable as the temperature within their ice walls reached comfortable levels, and a cozy sense of safety settled over them. The meat that the Wolf-folk served out from their supplies tasted better than it had in a long time.

Even so, they still longed for the simple pleasure of a crust of bread or a dish of boiled vegetables.

After the meal, the werewolves began to tell tales and legends of their northern tribe, in which giant bears and magical whales were hunted over ice and across the seas. They told how their great hero Ukpik had fought a battle with the Demon of Darkness that had lasted half a year, but which he had finally won, and so brought the sun back to the sky to give light to the world. They told, too, how the Demon of Darkness somehow managed to steal the sun again every year, plunging the world into winter, before Ukpik would repeat his feat of strength and rescue the light of the world just in time for summer.

In the short silence that followed this epic, Thirrin decided to tell the tale of Edgar the Bold and his war against the Dragon-folk of the Wolfrock Mountains. The werewolves were hugely impressed and growled their approval when she finished. But only Oskan noticed how sad she looked. No one else knew that Thirrin was remembering the last time she'd heard the tale, sitting with her father in the cozy comfort of his rooms on Yuletide Eve while Grimswald, the Chamberlain-of-the-Royal-Paraphernalia, read from *The Book of the Ancestors*. But that was when she'd still been a child.

The storm raged for two days, screeching like a "sackful of boiled monkeys," as Oskan put it. But at last the wind slowly dropped, until its final moan drifted away over the ice and silence returned. Grinelda Blood-tooth opened the flap in the hide tent and crawled out. Downwind of the storm, snow had gathered around the wall of ice blocks in a long-tailed drift that stretched off into the darkness, but on the windward side the wall was smoothed and polished as though a giant hand had rubbed it to a sheen.

The others scrambled out, too, and stood stretching and breathing in as much as they dared of the bitterly freezing but wonderfully fresh air. Two days spent in the cramped company of twelve huge and hairy werewolves was not the most fragrant of experiences, and the pristine beauty of the frozen world was in striking contrast to being inside the tent. After a few minutes of enjoying the freedom of space, the Wolf-folk started to prepare food and soon they were all eating the inevitable meal of meat.

After that it was a matter of minutes before the tents and other equipment were stashed away, and they set off once again on their trek to the Kingdom of the Snow Leopards. Thirrin and Oskan took their usual places in one of the sleighs, and they sped over the ice as the world got steadily colder and colder.

The Wolf-folk seemed determined to make up as much of the lost time as they could, and they ran on for hours as the stars wheeled slowly in the black crystal sky. Then, as Thirrin and Oskan watched the stately theater of the night, a sudden burst of color draped itself in a long wavering streamer from horizon to horizon. They both gasped aloud, and the werewolves slowed and stopped before throwing back their heads and howling.

"What is it?" Thirrin called to them. "What are those strange lights?"

"The Veils of the Blessed Moon, My Lady," Grinelda answered as a cascading curtain of red-and-yellow flame shimmered and flickered over the sky. "They're omens of great good fortune."

The visual immensity of the display of fire was in awesome contrast to its total silence. In Thirrin's opinion, a manifestation of such brilliance and beauty should have crackled and roared like the biggest bonfire, and yet every cascading waterfall of color, every billowing banner of light, was as strangely soundless as an empty hall.

"I think I remember Maggiore talking about this in one of my geography lessons."

"You did listen sometimes, then?" Oskan whispered, as though not to disturb the display and frighten it away.

"It had a strange name . . . the aurora borealis, I think . . . Yes, that's it! The aurora borealis."

"So what is it? What causes it?"

"I can't rightly remember," Thirrin answered. "It's to do with the sun's light on the upper atmosphere, or something like that."

"That's the trouble with science. It has to *explain* beauty. It can't just let it be."

"It doesn't stop it from being beautiful."

"No, but it takes away the mystery. It takes away the magic. I prefer the Wolf-folk's name for it: the Veils of the Blessed Moon."

"But you asked me what it was. You wanted to know."

"Well, next time don't tell me. Knowing exactly what things are doesn't improve my life in any way."

"You know you don't mean that. You're just reacting against the Empire and its scientists. You've already said that science can be used for good."

"Well, yes, I suppose so," Oskan agreed grudgingly. "But leave some magic in the world. Leave us some mystery to enjoy."

The werewolves now began to pull the sleighs again, and they traveled on under the colossal and silent majesty of the northern lights until, on the horizon, a dim uplifting of the land beneath its frozen skin of ice began to appear. Gradually over the next hour or so, the hills resolved themselves into mountains that climbed in awful majesty, white and glistering against the black of the perpetual night. The aurora borealis bathed their white crags in a deep blush of blue and crimson, and a shooting star blazed over the highest peak.

"The Kingdom of the Snow Leopards," called Grinelda, and the sleighs shot forward at even greater speed as they headed toward the mountains.

19

The Wolf-folk had stopped and were staring at something in the distance. Both Thirrin and Oskan stood up in the sleigh and tried to make out exactly what was approaching. At first they could see nothing, and when they called to Grinelda she waved them to silence without taking her eyes off the horizon.

Then, after a few minutes, all the werewolves stepped out of the traces and formed a tight protective ring around their human charges. Oskan gasped and seized Thirrin's hand. "There!" he said, pointing. "A leopard, an enormous leopard!"

She followed his pointing finger, screwed her eyes against the distance, and at last saw it. It was closer than she thought. Its mainly white, black-spotted coat camouflaged it perfectly against the background of snow, ice, and shadow. And Oskan hadn't exaggerated, it *was* enormous: about the size of a war-horse at the shoulder, and its massive head was lit by eyes of vivid amber.

As it walked unhurriedly over the snow toward them, Thirrin noticed that its paws were huge and soft-looking, and despite its obvious weight they carried the animal over the loosest snow without once sinking through. But it was its mouth that held her attention: As the leopard approached, it raised its head and drew back its lips in an action that was so like Primplepuss that Thirrin knew it was scenting them. The movement revealed a row of teeth that made her shiver. They seemed whiter than the surrounding snow, the smallest of them were longer than her fingers, and the fangs looked as lethal as ivory cavalry sabers.

Thirrin squeezed Oskan's hand once for comfort, then she released it and raised her head proudly as she donned her full queenly persona.

The creature stopped about ten feet away from the nearest werewolf and sat down. After a moment of gazing at them, it licked a paw and yawned enormously, displaying its impressive teeth, and then to the amazement of the human members of the party, it spoke.

"Who are you that trespass on the lands of Tharaman, the Thar of the Snow Leopards?"

Even though both Thirrin and Oskan had been told that the leopards could talk, they had expected them to sound like the werewolves, uttering the gruntings and growlings of an animal in a way that somehow resembled speech. But this creature sounded completely human, even refined, and a little bored.

"You know well that we are Wolf-folk of the Ukpik tribe," the leader of the white werewolves replied. "And we bring with us Queen Thirrin Freer Strong-in-the-Arm Lindenshield, Wildcat of the North and Monarch of the Land of the Icemark. With her is her adviser Oskan the Warlock. They are humans who seek audience with Tharaman-Thar of the Snow Leopards."

The creature immediately stopped licking its paw and

looked up. "Humans! Here? Let me see these beings of legend."

Thirrin immediately jumped down from the sleigh and advanced toward the leopard, while Oskan scrambled behind her and tried not to look afraid.

The giant cat stared at them for a long moment, then said, "Are these puny things human beings? Well, how disappointing. I really can't believe that these small objects were blessed with the same tongue as the Leopard People. Tell them to go back where they came from."

Thirrin was so furious she forgot to be afraid and, drawing her sword, she advanced on the leopard. "Small or not, Master Pussycat, I will not go back, unless, of course, I take your head as a trophy for my wall!"

The creature laid back its ears in amazement. "They do speak our language, and with clear diction, too!"

By this time Thirrin was standing squarely beneath the leopard's chin, and she placed her sword against its broad throat. "I'd say you speak *our* language, pussycat, and quite well for an animal. But if you wish words and not blood to come gushing out of your mouth, I suggest you show a lot more respect!"

The giant leopard looked down at her and, nonchalantly raising a paw, it flexed a set of long and glittering claws. "I'd say the human being is a little underarmed and undersized to threaten me effectively. Still, I must admit it's brave — almost a pity to kill it."

"Oh yes, you could kill me," said Thirrin in a voice that hissed with rage. "But I can assure you, you'd die of your wounds before you could gloat!" And with sudden lightning speed, her sword flickered and both sets of the Snow Leopard's whiskers and the tip of his beard lay in the snow.

The giant cat let out a roar that almost flattened Thirrin, and reared up on its haunches so that it towered into the sky like a vast monolith of living ice. Both its forepaws were now glittering with enormous claws, and its open jaw was like a cave festooned with white and jagged stalactites. She waited for the beast to strike but instead it stepped back and looked at its whiskers. "Oh dear. What will the others say?" The leopard glanced at Thirrin. "Do I look too ridiculous?" Then it did something that almost made her drop her sword. The cat laughed, and the sound was so human and joyous she almost joined in.

The massive tension that had built up evaporated, and Oskan breathed a sigh of relief. Somehow, despite Thirrin and her temper, they'd survived their first meeting with a Snow Leopard.

"Madam, my name is Taradan, second in command of the armies of Tharaman-Thar of the Snow Leopards. We seem to have gotten off on the wrong foot. My fault entirely for underestimating the spirit of human beings. May we begin again?"

"We may," Thirrin agreed.

"I am forever grateful, My Lady. Then, first, as the herald of the Thar of the Leopard People, might I ask why you have come to our lands?"

"I seek an audience with Tharaman-Thar, where my business will be stated clearly for all to hear."

"I see . . . then you're not the vanguard of an invading army?"

Thirrin laughed shortly. "No. I've come to offer friendship and alliance with the Leopard People. Any more than that I will not say until I am in the presence of the Thar."

"Very well. I've asked the questions that tradition decrees, and since you're obviously not part of an invading army, I'll escort you to the royal palace of Lord Tharaman, One Hundredth Thar of the Leopard People," he said. Walking a little way off into the snows, he then raised his head and let out a series of short coughing barks that echoed over the sky.

After a few moments, Thirrin thought she heard a distant reply, followed by two others from different directions. When all had fallen silent again, the Snow Leopard turned to them and said, "Climb back into your sleigh, Thirrin-Thar, and have your Wolf-folk follow me. We still have a long journey ahead of us."

The werewolves picked up the traces of the sleighs again, and Thirrin and Oskan settled back under the furs. Soon they were hurtling over the snows, following the giant leopard as he ran ahead with the grace and beauty of muscled water.

A few hours later they approached the lower slopes of the mountains that stood at the Hub of the World. The high peaks and slopes were uniformly covered in snow, and under the light of the stars and a three-quarter moon, they gleamed and shimmered like chiseled light.

"It's beautiful," Oskan stated matter-of-factly, as though announcing the day of the week. "Beautiful and terrible. Rather like our friend the leopard."

"Yes," Thirrin agreed. "He could almost be made from the same material as the mountain."

Oskan looked ahead to where Taradan galloped over the snows. "Yes, it's hard to believe warm blood courses through that beautiful body. I'd expect quicksilver or maybe *ichor,* the blood of the gods."

"Do you think we're going to die, Oskan?" Thirrin suddenly asked in completely calm tones.

He shrugged. "I don't know. Perhaps. But Taradan seems friendly enough . . . for now."

"True, but I have a feeling that it's all surface, and if you scratched below the outer layer, you'd find an incredible savagery."

"I'm sure you would; they're wild animals, after all. Just because they sound like Maggiore Totus doesn't mean they have his attitude toward life. If in the end they decide they don't like us, you can be certain we'll just be another snack for whichever leopard gets to us first."

"Yes, I suppose so. Still, we had to try, didn't we?"

"We had to try," Oskan agreed.

A short time later Thirrin and Oskan sensed they were at last nearing the end of their journey, a wide valley opened up before them, and their pace began to slow. The cliffs that bordered each side of the valley loomed slowly closer as the road narrowed. The scattered boulders gathered around the towering walls as though their stony faces were frozen waterfalls and the rocks were the glacial spray that had flown up in some unimaginable past. It was then that Thirrin noticed figures sitting or lying on top of the rocks. Snow Leopards! Each one was at least as big as a warhorse, but their coats blended so perfectly with the background that she'd only noticed them as their sleighs passed directly beneath them.

"Oskan. Look!"

He followed her pointing finger and gasped. "There are dozens of them!"

"Dozens that we can see. There are probably hundreds or even thousands more watching us at this very minute."

The werewolves thundered on, following Taradan closely as he approached a sheer rock wall at the end of the valley. Thirrin could now see that a broad platform like a terrace lay at the foot of this towering cliff, and at its very center stood a large boulder draped in crystalline splendor, with huge icicles that glittered and shone in the starlight like carved diamonds. But this spectacle paled into insignificance as she realized that the entire platform was packed with hundreds and hundreds of Snow Leopards.

"Oskan, they're everywhere!"

"I know, I can see them," he answered in a very small voice.

They stared wonderingly at the giant cats sitting in ordered ranks around the central boulder that rose ten feet or so above them. But then Thirrin realized that something else sat at the very top of the rock. It was the largest leopard they'd seen so far. Its fur was brilliantly white and marked with spots, rosettes, and small stripes that were so black, it seemed the night sky had dripped its darkness onto the fine fur. But as their sleigh drew closer it was the magnificent head that held their gaze. The eyes were red-amber like the deeply glowing coals of a fire, and the whiskers were like fine spindles of ivory. And then, when the animal yawned, the deep red of its mouth was the perfect setting for the array of teeth that gleamed and glistened as though polished.

Taradan stopped, as did the sleighs following him. He walked slowly back to Thirrin and Oskan. "Welcome to the court of Lord Tharaman-Thar. As you can see, you are expected, and the Thar himself will listen to your request."

"Will you present us?" Thirrin asked.

"That will be my honor," he said. Then, lowering his head as though bowing, he whispered, "Show him the fire you showed me. Hide your fear and be as haughty as an empress."

"When I want your advice, Mr. Pussycat, I'll give you due notice," she answered with a cold glare.

"That's the way," said Taradan approvingly, and winked at her.

Thirrin and Oskan both stepped down from the sleigh and followed the herald to the high platform. The sight of so many huge leopards, all staring intently at them as they approached, made the short walk a very uncomfortable experience. But both managed to hide their fear, and they walked with their heads held high.

There was a flight of graded rocks that served as steps up to the natural dais, and as Thirrin and Oskan climbed these, the nearest leopards drew back and a pathway opened up to where Tharaman-Thar was waiting.

A murmur of small growls and whispers rose up as they walked through the throng of enormous cats, but otherwise they were silent and looked constantly up at the boulder as though waiting for the Thar to set the tone of their greeting. Meanwhile Tharaman-Thar was lying at his ease and washing a paw. He seemed completely unaware of the humans and slightly bored. Eventually Thirrin and Oskan arrived at the foot of his boulder-throne and stood waiting quietly.

Taradan the herald let out an enormous roar that echoed around the cliffs and proclaimed, "All hail the Lord Tharaman, great Thar of the Snow Leopards and Ruler of the Icesheets. His will brings the sun back to the sky and allows winter to reign in its due season. He is lor —"

"Yes, yes. Get on with it, Taradan. I don't want to be here all day. Who have you brought me?" asked Tharaman-Thar in a deep and refined voice.

Thirrin drew her sword, planted it firmly between her feet, and rested her hands on the hilt. She'd been warned that the Snow Leopard King would respect only bravery and confidence so, drawing a deep steadying breath, she said, "He's *brought* you no one at all. But if you allowed him to do his job properly and announce me, you'd find out that he has *escorted* a fellow monarch into your presence!" Her voice cut sharply into the cold air, and the huge leopards all stared at her in shock.

"My name is *Queen* Thirrin Freer Strong-in-the-Arm Lindenshield, Wildcat of the North, Ruler of the Icemark. My will commands no heavenly bodies, and no season waits for my permission to begin. But even so, I *do* demand a little respect from my equals and deference from my many inferiors!"

Tharaman-Thar turned his huge head to look at her, and his amber eyes glowed deeply. "So, the legends are true. Human beings do exist and they can speak our language. How amusing." He turned to wash his paw again. "I was of two minds whether to believe the reports. But now I see they were right in every way. And yes, you are puny, aren't you?"

Thirrin controlled her anger and directed it into her voice. "For my part, I'd heard nothing of the Snow Leopards until a few days ago; their fame seems to be restricted to a scant area of the frozen wastelands. But I have been warned over the last few hours or so that their ruler is arrogant and has no knowledge of how to behave in a civilized manner when receiving guests!"

A gasp rose up from the surrounding courtiers, Tharaman-Thar stopped washing his paw to glare at her, and Taradan looked intently at the ground. "It was you who sliced the whiskers and beard from my herald, wasn't it?" said Tharaman-Thar.

"It was. I found his manners needed improving. But now I see the fault was not his."

The Thar climbed to his feet and let out a huge roar at this, but gritting her teeth against her fear Thirrin ignored him, and turning to Taradan said, "Please accept my apologies, Master Herald. I realize now that the fault was not yours; your society is barely civilized, and no one has the right to expect better behavior from an individual than his homeland can teach him."

Tharaman-Thar roared again and loomed menacingly from the edge of the boulder-throne. "The lemming shouldn't squeak in a parliament of cats!"

"I've no idea what a lemming is, My Lord Tharaman-Thar, but I bet very few of them are battle-trained, tough as boiled leather, and armed with a sword that could slice open a cat's throat before it even considered leaping from a rock!" As quick as a striking heron she spun around and thrust her sword into the open mouth of a leopard that had moved up behind her. "Perhaps you don't value this individual, My Lord Thar. But if you really don't want me to skewer its brain, I suggest you order it to withdraw."

The Thar of the Leopards nodded almost imperceptibly at the huge cat, and it stepped carefully away. "Why have you come? What do you want of us?"

Thirrin turned to face the throne again and said angrily, "After a polite greeting, those should have been your first questions!"

"I can only thank you for the valuable lessons in etiquette you are giving us," the Thar said sarcastically. "But now perhaps you'll be polite enough to answer me."

"Certainly. I came to offer you friendship."

The giant leopard laughed. "A fine way you have of showing it! And why should we need or want your friendship, anyway?"

"Because the day your existence is known to humans, many people will come, but they won't be offering friendship — only war!"

"And why would they come to the Hub of the World?"

"To rule it. To enslave your people, to kill you and take your skins."

"Take our skins?" Tharaman-Thar asked incredulously. "Why would they do that? Haven't they skins of their own?"

"Oh yes, but humans feel the cold, and your skins are so beautiful they'll want to make them into clothes so they can look as lordly and as gorgeous as you."

The huge leopard fell silent, and his amber eyes looked out over the starlit ice fields. "How can I believe such a thing? You hardly seem a threat at all, being so small and insignificant. And not only that, you're the only humans I've ever seen. You're a legend to the Leopard People. How can I know that there are more than a few of you?"

"Humans inhabit almost every part of the world," said Thirrin. "I'm told we speak many different languages, we have different-colored skins, and we believe in many different gods. But in one way we are nearly all the same. We fight wars, we want power and wealth, and we want to dominate everything we see around us. We are truly terrible and terrifying if you only knew it. We may seem puny, but our numbers are overwhelming, and our weapons of war make us stronger than the most ferocious warriors of any other species. Be afraid of humans, Tharaman-Thar. Be afraid for your Snow Leopards. Once the eyes of humanity are turned on you, there will be little you can do to save yourselves and your lands. You will be hunted and killed, you will be stripped of your homes, your dignity, even your fur, and you will be left to go into the dark of death to be forgotten by the lands you once ruled."

Tharaman-Thar stared at her long and hard, then spoke in a quiet voice. "If I were to believe you, Thirrin-Thar, why should I make an alliance with such hideous monsters?"

"Because I said we are *nearly* all the same. Some of us are honorable and live with our neighbors without harm, or at least with as little harm as possible. We hunt to eat, as you do, and we take from nature what we need. But some of us take as little as we can and try always to pay back when the opportunity is given. But now even we are threatened by our own species. And if we fall, then you will, too. A great war is coming against a ruthless Empire — and I am trying to build an alliance of free peoples of many species to fight it. Already the Wolf-folk have joined with us, and even the Vampire King and Queen, but we need more allies or we'll fail. I offer you friendship and death, I offer you despair and a glimmer of hope, I offer a long struggle with no way of knowing how it will end. But alone you will definitely fall — this year or the next or the one after that, but fall you undoubtedly will. With us, you will at least have a chance."

In the silence that followed, Tharaman-Thar raised his head as though scenting the wind, and when he looked down again, he said, "I smell your spirit, Queen Thirrin. It is young but strong, and it will tell nothing but the truth. But your words are strange and terrible. How can we accept the threat and power of this Empire that we have never seen or indeed even heard of before this day? And why should we form an alliance with any people, when we have lived alone since the One made us from the ice of the land, the light of the moon, and the fire of the sun?"

Thirrin remained silent as she gathered her thoughts. Setting her shoulders in determination, she said, "Leopards of the Hub, I believe even the Great Creator holds its breath tonight. The One made us of different form but placed in our throats the same tongue and in our heads the same thoughts, so that one day its two favorites of all Creation could talk." Her voice echoed on the freezing air, the natural amphitheater of the rock walls and cliffs projecting her voice far out over the valley. She'd hoped that reminding the leopards of their creation myth — which King Grishmak of the Wolf-folk had told her about — would draw some response, but they remained silent. She almost panicked as she faced the unblinking gaze of thousands of amber eyes. But fighting for control, she drew breath and went on. "Tharaman-Thar asked who the people are who threaten my lands and your lives, so I'll attempt to explain. The Polypontian Empire is huge; it stretches from the Southern Sea to the east and west beyond our knowledge. Its rulers are cruel, unstoppable, and trample everything in their path."

"So you say," a voice called from the ranks of leopards. "How do we know they're not simply your personal enemy you want to destroy?"

"A good question," the Thar said, turning to Thirrin. "Well, how do we know?"

"You don't; you can't," Thirrin answered, feeling her battle-blood rising. "You have only my word, the word of a creature who walked out of your legends and into reality only today. But if I can't convince you that I'm telling the truth, then we'll all die, it's as simple as that. My cities will burn, my people will be enslaved, and the Polypontian Empire will ruthlessly extend its borders farther and farther to the north until they discover another land, the Hub of the World, fantastic and beautiful and unconquered. And you will then have to fight alone against a mighty enemy and, have no illusions about this, you *will* lose and you *will* die in your thousands."

Suddenly a huge anger burned up in her frame and, striding to the boulder-throne of the Thar, she climbed it and stood looking out on the massive crowd. Drawing her sword she shouted, "But if the Snow Leopards of the Hub will not help in their own war, then my people and their allies will die fighting to defend the borders of this land *you* believe to be safe. Shame on you if you do nothing in defense of the north!"

The giant leopard sighed, then strolled to where Thirrin stood. "Would you be so kind as to answer my questions without the rhetoric and insults? This Parliament of Leopards requires only facts and information to make its decision. Your personal views and jibes only cloud the issues."

Thirrin felt her face burn, but took comfort in the probability that the giant cats wouldn't recognize human embarrassment. "I stand ready to answer any questions put to me by the Parliament, but reserve the right to voice my opinion on any issue."

"Very well. Then answer me this. You mentioned our creation myth, so am I right in assuming that one of the reasons you expect help from my leopards is because our peoples were both loved by the Great Creator?"

"*One* of the reasons, yes."

"And am I also right in assuming that the people of the Polypontian Empire are human beings, too, and therefore loved equally by the Great Creator?"

"Well, yes, they are human, but —"

"But *they're* a threat and therefore we should help *you*."

"Yes."

"But why should we assume that the One wants us to kill *them*? We share the gift of speech with all human people, not just the population of the Icemark. One day, perhaps, I will be talking to envoys from the Empire, and remember, we have only your word that our conversation will be anything but friendly."

"But . . . but the people of the Polypontian Empire speak a

different language. You couldn't talk to them. You couldn't talk to them at all!" said Thirrin, her voice rising in triumph as she realized the importance of the point.

"A different . . . *language*?" the Thar said as though he found the word strange. "Do you mean that the humans of the Empire use different words when they speak?"

"Completely different. In fact, only the peoples of the Icemark and the Icesheets use the language that we're speaking now. The Wolf-folk use it as a common tongue to communicate with other species, and even Their Vampiric Majesties use it." Thirrin could scent victory now, even though it was still faint and distant. All she had to do was present her arguments with logic and precision and perhaps she could win!

But the Thar was far from finished. "Queen Thirrin, it almost sounds as if you want us to fight these people simply because they speak a different *language,* as you put it, and because they come from a different part of the world," he said with quiet determination.

Thirrin tried to suppress her frustration; she just seemed to be confusing things. "No, great Thar. The Icemark has never fought a war or taken a life for any reason other than self-defense! We judge people on their conduct and their personal spirit; the language they use and the place of their birth is of no importance to us. We are but two closely linked peoples who face a common enemy, an enemy who has set out to conquer the world with evil and aggression."

A lone voice called, "How do we know that the people of the Empire use different words? Speak some of them, let us hear how different they are."

"But I don't know any," she said, feeling horribly deflated as her chance of winning over the leopards seemed to be slipping away.

"Um . . . I know one phrase, I think," said a small voice from the shadows beneath the boulder-throne.

Thirrin peered down into the gloom and hissed, "Well, get up here, then. And be quick about it!"

Oskan scrambled up onto the boulder and stood blinking in the brilliant light of the moon. But the sight of the huge crowd of leopards cramming the lower end of the Ice Valley seemed to strike him dumb, and he stood staring at his feet like a bashful schoolboy.

"We're waiting," the Thar rumbled impatiently. "Say these words, let us hear how different their language is."

Oskan looked and felt so completely unlike a warlock that he could have cried. In fact, he very nearly did, as terrible stage fright threatened to completely overwhelm him. But then, slowly, a small spark of courage ignited in his brain and, taking a deep breath, he suddenly bellowed, "*Veni, Vidi, Vici!*"

The shrill sound of his panicking voice cut the freezing air, and a rumble broke out through the ranks of leopards.

"Yes, that's it," he said, his confidence returning with every second. "*Veni, Vidi, Vici*. Maggiore Totus, one of Queen Thirrin's advisers, once told me that the generals of the Empire use this phrase every time they invade a new land. It's a sort of ceremonial chant."

"All very interesting, I'm sure," Tharaman-Thar said. "But what does it mean?"

"It means 'I came, I saw, I conquered.' Maggiore said the Polypontians are always so certain of winning when they invade, they proclaim victory as soon as they set foot on foreign soil."

Another rumble of growling arose from the huge crowd of leopards. The arrogance of the Empire seemed to anger them.

"I see," the Thar said slowly. "And do they always win? You seem to imply they're invincible."

"If I believed that, I wouldn't be preparing for war now," said Thirrin. "I know they can be defeated. Just after Yule my father, King Redrought Strong-in-the-Arm Lindenshield, destroyed a single Polypontian army. But make no mistake, any victory against the Empire comes at great cost. The army of the Icemark was also destroyed in the clash, and my father was killed." She stopped. A strange rumble became a crescendo of sound as the huge cats let out a tumble of coughing barks that echoed and rolled around the valley before slowly dying away.

She looked questioningly at Tharaman-Thar. "A warriors' salute to the brave dead," he explained. "King Redrought and his army must have been mighty indeed."

"They were," she answered proudly, suddenly realizing that his sacrifice and her own courage were making a bigger impression on the leopards than all her arguments so far. "My father's achievement did not end the invasion attempt; it only bought us a little time. In fact, as huge as the force was, he only defeated the vanguard that had been sent to test our defenses. If they could have, they would have swept through the land and added the Icemark to the Empire then and there. But thanks to my father, they have had to reschedule that for next spring.

"If the Empire had succeeded, no mercy would have been shown. When the Empire conquers, the defeated soldiers are killed, their homes are looted and burned and, of those who are left, the very young and the very old are murdered and the strongest are enslaved. These are the people you will face — either as part of an alliance that has at least some small hope of success or, at some point in the future, standing alone, with no hope whatsoever."

"Queen Thirrin, I can see you've been completely honest

with us," said Tharaman-Thar. "You've warned us that if we don't fight, there is every possibility that the Empire will eventually seek us out and destroy us, but you've also warned us of the terrible dangers we'll face if we choose to join your alliance. As Thar of the Leopards of the Hub, I could command my people to fight in the coming war, but I will not do so. The choice must be theirs."

He looked out over his Snow Leopards, who were all listening intently to his words, then he turned back to Thirrin and Oskan. "For my own part I say we should seize the faint hope that alliance gives us and defend the Icemark in the coming offensive. But that may not be the opinion of my people." He paused. "There is a factor to be taken into account that you know nothing of, Queen Thirrin."

"And that is . . . ?"

"We're already fighting a war."

"Already fighting . . . ?" Her voice trailed away as she realized the hopelessness of her situation.

"Even if the Parliament of Leopards does agree to join your alliance, we couldn't send an army of full strength, because we need to defend our eastern borders against the Ice Trolls."

"Ice Trolls! Who exactly are they?" Thirrin asked quietly, as she realized that her mission to the Snow Leopards might have been a complete waste of time.

"They're our archenemies. They hate all warm-blooded creatures and invade our borders every winter. So far we've always driven them back, but if we deplete our forces too much, they could overrun our lands, destroy our holds, and kill our people."

Thirrin nodded resignedly. Her worst fears were being confirmed, but she listened politely as Tharaman-Thar went on.

"*However,* I think we could maintain our garrisons on the

eastern borders if I lead my own personal guard in the war against the Polypontians and call for volunteers from the hold militias of the west. None of these troops has ever figured in the army of the eastern borders, and so there'll be no weakening of our defense force."

"How many soldiers could you bring with you?" Thirrin asked eagerly as her spirit revived.

"The Royal Guard stands at one thousand leopards, and perhaps another thousand could be raised from the militias."

She almost squealed with delighted relief, and then remembered the leopards had yet to vote. "Lord Tharaman-Thar, the Icemark and all the lands of the north would be forever in debt to your people if they chose to form an alliance with us. Could you please ask them to make their decision?"

Suddenly the huge leopard reared up on his hind legs, towering over the land like the living threat of an avalanche, and he roared three times into the frozen sky. "Hear now my voice and make your decision, Leopards of the Hub. No people can stand alone against two enemies; we would be crushed between the hammer of the Empire and the anvil of the Ice Trolls. But now we are offered friendship and alliance with human beings who will stand with us in a new type of war against a people overwhelming in number and terrible in power. Consider, then, your options: alliance and possible death with Queen Thirrin of the Icemark, or isolation and certain death when the armies of the allies are destroyed and none are left to stand with us." The Thar paused to look out at the giant cats that covered the contours of the Ice Valley like a living carpet. The silence that rose from them was absolute; only the gently moaning wind and the whispering chink and crackle of the frost could be heard. Then Tharaman-Thar drew breath and boomed, "The choice, my people, can only be yours!"

Back came the answering barks, crashing into the sky in an eruption of sound that rolled again and again around the valley. Neither Thirrin nor Oskan could make out any answer or opinion in the stupendous noise. But eventually all fell silent, and Tharaman-Thar nodded.

"The Parliament has spoken, Thirrin-Thar. Have you anything to say?"

"I would have if I knew what the decision was," she said, her tone a mixture of anxiety and annoyance.

"You have won the day. The Leopards of the Hub will fight in your alliance."

20

The Basilea of the Hypolitan watched the troops maneuvering on the plain below the hill where she sat on her horse. She was secretly pleased, but she kept this fact carefully hidden from her officers who stood nearby. Before her niece Queen Thirrin had even set off on her quest for allies, it had been agreed that every soldier would receive the same training and instruction as the elite housecarls. And as a result the fyrd had been called in, and basic weapons training had been followed by war games, forced marches, and other endurance tests.

The housecarls, in an attempt to maintain their standing as the elite of the army, had voluntarily brought in their own training regime in which they marched longer, fought harder, and endured more than the fyrd. It was all going very well, and if the Basilea Elemnestra had her consort to thank for it, she certainly wouldn't say so . . . in public.

She turned in her saddle, caught her husband's eye, and gave the slightest of nods to show her pleasure. Olememnon remained stony-faced, but when no one else was looking, he winked in return. After thirty years together, they didn't need long speeches to make the other understand.

The other sections of the army were also training hard. Day after day the cavalry had practiced formations, and if the wooden practice dummies had really been Polypontian troops, then the Empire's armies would already have been several thousand soldiers short as they were hacked by cavalry sabers and spitted by lances.

The regiments of archers spent most of the daylight hours practicing in the butts, shooting wave after wave of arrows in a devastating rain down on targets drawn in the snow. Some of them were even proud that they'd trained until their fingers bled, but after several had been put on charges for "neglect of the person" by the Basilea herself, the rest made sure they always wore their leather finger-guards.

As Basilea, Elemnestra didn't often review the progress of training personally. She had enough to do with the day-to-day administration of her province and preparing for the coming campaign. But word had been received that Thirrin was returning at last and bringing allies with her. Admittedly the report had been a little garbled, and she'd had the messenger censured for being drunk on duty when he delivered it. But even so, Thirrin was coming home, and as Basilea, Elemnestra was determined not only to be in total control of all preparations when the Queen returned but also to be *seen* to be in control.

As she watched the regiments on the training ground below forming shield-walls and attacking one another with blunted swords, she ran over the exact wording of the messenger's report. She finally decided that she was quite prepared to believe in the two dozen white werewolves pulling the Queen in a sleigh; she was also happy to accept that her niece's adviser was a warlock. No surprises there at all, really. In her opinion Oskan was shifty and had an air of deviousness about him that was completely explained by the fact that he was a male witch.

But she would never believe that Thirrin had made an alliance with a species of giant white Snow Leopard that lived at the Hub of the World. It was quite obvious that the messenger had been drinking and had probably seen cavalry regiments that were all mounted on white or dappled horses. Amazing enough in its own right, without any need for embellishments. She hoped the messenger had been correct about the numbers, though; three thousand cavalry would be a very useful addition to their army.

Her mind continued to run over preparations and problems posed by the coming campaign, but after a while she found herself becoming absorbed in the mock maneuvers on the plain below. The defending troops were all made up of units of the fyrd, while the attacking soldiers were housecarls. For more than twenty minutes the conscripted soldiers had managed to hold the professional housecarls at bay, while the drums rattled and boomed over the frozen air, giving a rhythm and sense of cohesion to the defenders' efforts to hold their line. The drums had been Maggiore Totus's idea; he'd told them that the Empire used the instruments to intimidate their enemies, but he'd developed the system further by using different beats and rhythms to give instructions and orders in the heat of battle. A commanding officer could send a message to the drummers, and the regiments could then be ordered to the left, or to the right, to hold their position, advance or retreat.

Elemnestra had to admit that the little scholar sometimes had flashes of pure brilliance, but his quiet, studious nature was so alien to her fiery energetic temperament that she found it almost impossible to communicate with him. She was aware, though, that he and Olememnon had become great friends, and she often wondered what they found to talk about as they huddled for hours around the central hearth in the evenings.

Of course, she could have joined them to find out, but she was the Basilea, and she'd never demean herself by openly seeking the company of mere men.

She was suddenly aware that her consort had moved his horse and was waiting quietly for her to notice him.

"Well?" she said in tones of practiced indifference.

"Another messenger begs audience with the Basilea," Olememnon answered, not at all offended by his wife's curtness.

"Permission granted."

He beckoned a soldier forward, and she dropped to one knee, waiting for the Basilea to give her leave to speak.

"What have you to tell?" Elemnestra asked.

"My Lady, the Queen has crossed the border into the Icemark. She and her party should be here before nightfall."

"Good. And the allies the Queen brings with her, do you agree with the earlier estimate of three thousand?"

"Yes, My Lady. Their King himself leads his personal guard of one thousand, and there are two thousand volunteers from their militia."

"Excellent. Olememnon, their horses will need the best stabling. Make sure everything's ready."

But before he could move to carry out her orders, the soldier coughed apologetically and said, "I'm sorry, Ma'am, but the allies have no horses —"

"Infantry, then! The first messenger was more drunk than I thought. Olememnon, raise his punishment to twenty lashes!" Once again the soldier coughed, and Elemnestra turned to her angrily. "Young woman, is there something wrong with your throat?"

"No, My Lady," she almost whispered. "But I think you should know that our new allies are not infantry, either."

"Then what are they?"

"Leopards, Ma'am."

The Basilea gazed at her with icy blue eyes, then asked, "Have you seen these creatures yourself?"

"Yes, Ma'am. And I spoke to the second in command, Taradan. It was he who told me their exact numbers."

"Spoke to the second in command; then they have humans working with them?"

"No, My Lady. Taradan is a leopard."

"You spoke with a . . . ?" Elemnestra's voice trailed away, and she looked at her consort, who raised his shoulders slightly and remained silent. After a moment's thought, she shook her head as though to clear it of all impossibilities and said, "Olememnon, set free the first messenger and give him an extra day's pay. I could have been a little hasty."

In the warmth of his rooms, Maggiore Totus sipped gently at his beaker of mulled wine. He'd already heard the dispatches telling of Thirrin's return and had just completed his reports on the training and preparations he'd been responsible for in her absence. But unlike Basilea Elemnestra, he had no image to maintain or position he was desperate to keep, so he was altogether more relaxed in his outlook. His scholar's mind ran over some of the wilder elements of the messenger's reports. A few short weeks ago he would have dismissed them as pure fantasy, but since retreating to the north with the royal household, he'd not only witnessed, but actually conversed with, Wolf-folk and Vampires. If such creatures of legend could exist, why not giant talking leopards? Being a true scientist, his mind remained completely open to all possibilities, and he decided to await events.

The wind rattled his shutters, and a gentle powdering of

snow tumbled to the floor, where it quickly melted. He'd almost grown used to the winters of the north, and he'd even learned to appreciate the sense of coziness a warm room gave when the world outside was locked in ice. He sighed contentedly and settled his spectoculums comfortably on the bridge of his nose before leafing through the papers on his desk. He hoped at some point in a more peaceful future to present Thirrin with his history of the Hypolitan people, which he'd been compiling with the help of Olememnon. After all, her mother had been a member of the Hypolitan aristocracy, so the heritage it recorded was as much hers as it was that of the Icemark itself.

But his history was still only in note form and there was a war waiting to be fought. No doubt it would be a long time before Thirrin would have time to sit down and read anything other than battle reports and casualty lists. He sighed and felt a familiar sadness creeping over him as he thought about the young Queen and her burdens.

But then a sudden knock on his door announced the arrival of his friend Olememnon, and his room was filled with a quiet energy as the huge man came in, stamping the snow off his boots and grinning apologetically at the little scholar, who clucked and fussed around him.

"Boots, boots, Olememnon! There now, you've got snow all over the floor and it'll stand in puddles when it melts."

"Well, call a servant to wipe it up. It's what they're for," he said, his deep voice never needing to rise above its usual steady level.

"Yes, yes, I suppose I should. But they're all so busy. I don't like to bother them."

"Then give me a cloth and I'll do it."

"Certainly not! Sit down and help yourself to wine."

The Basilea's consort settled into a chair by the central hearth and filled a beaker with wine that stood warming in the ashes. "So the Queen is on her way back at last."

Maggiore paused in wiping up the now melted snow and looked at Olememnon over his shoulder. "Yes, and if the reports are to be believed, she's in the company of giant white leopards."

The Basilea's consort nodded slowly. "It's an odd one, eh? But I know both the messengers, and they're usually reliable soldiers."

The little scholar finished cleaning up the puddles and returned the mop to its proper place. "I'm keeping an open mind about this, Olememnon. Since coming to live in the Icemark I've seen too many legends walking around in the sunshine to dismiss anything as a fairy tale."

His friend nodded, then waited until Maggiore had refilled his own beaker with mulled wine and sat down. "Your health, Maggie."

"Likewise, Ollie."

The two men drank deeply and sat in companionable silence for a few moments before Olememnon said, "I suppose you've read the reports coming in from the south?"

"Yes. An unusual man, this Scipio Bellorum. How many other generals campaign in the winter?"

"None that I know of. But he's not having it all his own way. The besieged city of Inglesby still hasn't fallen, and he lost almost an entire army when they tried to march along the Great Road."

"That's true. I can only presume the much-vaunted science of the Empire doesn't include the discipline of meteorology, otherwise Bellorum would never have sent his troops marching off when a blizzard was imminent. How many survived?"

"The last werewolf report said less than a thousand made it back to their camp near the border."

"We may have had a lucky escape. Their target must have been Frostmarris. If they reach the capital before we get back there, it'll be a terrible psychological blow to our war effort."

"Well, we can't risk sending a garrison out yet. There's still bad weather brewing south of the forest, and any troops caught out in the open will die, whether Icemark or Empire."

"How long before it clears?"

"The White Witches who came in from the south last week figure another month at least. They say the forest and the region around Frostmarris is sitting under weather of its own making, something they've never seen before, but they obviously know enough about it to say it won't move just yet."

"Good," Maggie said. "That gives us time to prepare a garrison for the capital."

Thirrin and her party had been traveling south for more than a week. She felt disgustingly dirty and completely unkempt. She couldn't remember the last time she'd had a clean change of clothes, and though she'd kept her hair neatly braided, she hated to think what sort of wildlife might be living in it. She looked at Oskan, hoping to gauge by his appearance exactly how disheveled she herself must look. But apart from a few ragged patches of adolescent facial hair, he looked annoyingly neat. Close-cropped hair and simple black clothes tend to be very forgiving, no matter how long they're neglected.

She looked across to where Tharaman-Thar trotted at the head of his army of Snow Leopards. He was certainly a magnificent sight. All the giant cats were, and the only thing they needed to keep themselves scrupulously neat was a quick wash and wipe with the back of a paw. But despite her envy of their beautifully groomed appearance, she felt a warm glow of excitement as she led them to join the army that would defend the Icemark. With such formidable allies, she at last felt that they had some small chance of driving the Polypontians back to their own lands — or failing that, perhaps maintaining an independent state in the north, beyond the Great Forest.

She turned in the sleigh to look along the line of leopards that marched in double file for as far as she could see. Their coats were so well camouflaged against the snow that it was impossible to be sure where the line ended. And now that they'd entered the latitudes where the sun briefly shone in winter, their coats shimmered and glowed with a subtle shading that astonished the eye. It seemed that the gods of winter had molded soldiers from the Icesheets and armed them with formidable ivory and claws of frozen steel.

Tharaman-Thar noticed her gaze and immediately glided over to walk beside the sleigh. "I smell strange scents, Thirrin-Thar, like none in the memory of my nose."

"Describe them to me."

"Flowing blood that isn't blood. Sharp, like snow would smell if it were living. It clears the head and removes all thought of sleep."

Thirrin looked puzzled, but Oskan said, "You smell tree sap, My Lord. The sharpness is that of pine forests. The-Land-of-the-Ghosts is deeply wooded and the winds have blown over miles of trees, less than a day's march from here."

"What are trees?"

"Growing things, plants taller than some hills. Unmoving and solid," Oskan answered.

"Plants?" Tharaman-Thar said thoughtfully. "The only plants I know are the lichens that grow in the most southerly part of my lands in the summer months. But they barely rise above the ground. How can I believe in these trees that grow taller than hills?"

"Only by seeing them, I suppose," Oskan replied. "And that you'll do in a few hours' time."

"Perhaps you ask too much of my ability to believe."

"Perhaps. But didn't human beings walk out of your legends, and don't you now march south as an ally of a human Queen? Even a month ago, could you have believed in such things?"

"No," Tharaman-Thar answered shortly. "And I'm not sure I believe in them even now. My dreams can be extraordinarily vivid."

"Ah, but are we the stuff of nightmares?" Oskan asked with a grin.

The giant leopard regarded him with blazing amber eyes. "I've no doubt that some of you are, Oskan the Warlock. I can only be glad that you're on our side."

The sun set in the early afternoon, and they passed like an army of ghosts under the starry skies. No sound came from the leopards, and only the slender hiss of runners over snow-covered earth gave away the presence of Thirrin and Oskan's sleigh. On the horizon a collection of tall shapes gathered, almost shocking the sight after days of slowly undulating Icesheets and snow-covered flats. Oskan waved to Tharaman-Thar, and the Leopard King glided over to walk beside the sleigh.

"Tell me what you can see on the horizon," the warlock said.

"Tall, spreading bars of shape," the leopard answered. "Like frost patterns on the polished surface of rock, but dark rather than white."

Oskan nodded. "Those are trees," he said simply. "The first trees growing on the very borders of their northern range. You are about to enter the realms of human beings. Be prepared for cruelty and kindness, for friendship and hatred. People are made of all possibilities and conditions."

"Warlock, your words are no comfort."

"No. But they are a warning."

When Thirrin and her party reached the trees, they stopped while the Snow Leopards gathered around them, sniffing their strange scent and staring up into their branches.

"Soon we'll reach forests, huge gatherings of trees that stretch for miles," Thirrin called out to the army of giant cats. "Many animals live there, some of them dangerous, but none that should present a problem to any of you. While we travel through the trees, you will be able to hunt, and soon after that we'll enter the Icemark, where you'll be fed from the herds of beasts that we farm on our lands. In the meantime we must cross The-Land-of-the-Ghosts. The rulers of this country, the Vampire King and Queen, are our allies, and we will not be threatened."

"We hope," Oskan said quietly.

"This is the final stage of our journey," Thirrin continued, ignoring the remark. "Let us begin."

Immediately the Snow Leopards formed into their double file, and they marched off into the night.

21

Thirrin and the Snow Leopards had been in the Icemark for half a day. After a brief rest with King Grishmak and a less than courteous courtesy call on Their Vampiric Majesties in the Blood Palace, they'd left before dawn, and by midday had traveled through the pass in the Wolfrock Mountains and down into the Icemark. Thirrin still had her white werewolf guard and her sleigh, and King Grishmak had agreed that they should continue to serve her for as long as she needed them.

She soon found that rumor of her return had traveled ahead, and after two messengers had met them on the road, she knew that the news of the Snow Leopards would be all over the streets of the city. But already people were beginning to line the road. How they could possibly have heard of her return, and where they'd come from in the frozen wastes of the northernmost areas of the Icemark, she could only guess. But there they were, either gazing in amazement at the army of giant white leopards or running in panic from the sight.

And the closer they got to the regional capital, the larger were the numbers that lined the road. Soon the Hypolitan were joined by natives of Frostmarris who'd traveled out from their refugee towns that surrounded the city proper, and after gazing in wonder on the leopards, they then cheered themselves hoarse as their young Queen came home.

Tharaman-Thar trotted along beside Thirrin's sleigh and gazed at the crowds that lined the route. Turning to look at her he said, "I now begin to understand and believe what you said about the population of human people. Already I've seen numbers equal to the entire nation of Snow Leopards, and we've yet to reach the city."

"Yes, and we are one small country, My Lord Thar. Imagine, then, the population of the Polypontian Empire, whose lands stretch beyond our knowledge to all points of the horizon."

The giant leopard remained silent for a moment, then raising his head he roared with such power and ferocity that the crowds lining the route quailed. And when his three thousand soldiers answered, many people ran or threw themselves to the ground, convinced they were about to be attacked. "Thirrin-Thar, at last I fully appreciate the dangers you face. Our war will be long."

"Or very short, if we can't hold them back," Oskan said grimly.

"Oh, we'll hold them," Tharaman answered. "But I wonder if the end will be to our liking."

At last the walls of the Hypolitan capital came into view. The sunlight glinted brilliantly on the snow, throwing much of the scene into silhouette, but as they drew closer they began to make out a huge crowd spreading like a dark stain over the pristine white. Before the main gate the Basilea waited with an honor guard of cavalry and housecarls and, spilling out onto the surrounding plain, almost the entire population stood waving and cheering.

As Thirrin and her party approached, some of the horses shied nervously as they caught the unfamiliar scent of the leopards. But their riders kept control, and the cavalry stood firm as the sleigh was drawn across the wide sweep of land that led to the walls of the city. Then, when the werewolf team was within a bowshot of the waiting honor guard, they slowed to a halt, and a silence descended. All eyes were on the army of Snow Leopards, who stood silently in disciplined ranks. Thirrin stepped down from her sleigh and Tharaman-Thar joined her. Together they both walked gravely forward toward the Basilea.

Elemnestra dismounted and dropped to one knee as her niece approached. "Greetings, Queen Thirrin Freer Strong-in-the-Arm Lindenshield, Wildcat of the North. Your safe return brings joy to my heart and to the hearts of your subjects."

"Greetings, Basilea Elemnestra. What news of the war?"

"All is quiet at present. But your army is prepared to strike back when the change of season opens the roads."

"Good. We will review the troops later today," Thirrin answered formally. Then, visibly relaxing, she said, "Aunt, could you send for a loaf of bread and a bowl of apples?"

The Basilea looked at her in surprise, then, realizing she wasn't joking, she beckoned a soldier and sent her riding back into the city. In the silence that followed, Elemnestra's eyes strayed to the huge figure of Tharaman-Thar. At such close quarters, the sense of awesome power that seemed to beat from the animal in a rhythmic pulse became almost overwhelming, and despite the cold a faint dew broke out on the Basilea's upper lip.

Sensing her scrutiny, the Snow Leopard Thar turned his brilliant eyes upon Elemnestra and the warrior needed all of her fighting spirit to hold his gaze. Thirrin was secretly aware of her aunt's struggle and allowed her to suffer for a few seconds more before she spoke.

"Elemnestra, Basilea of the Hypolitan, I present to you Lord Tharaman, One Hundredth Thar of the Snow Leopards, Ruler of the Icesheets, Scourge of the Ice Trolls, and now our friend and ally in the war against the Polypontian Empire."

With her usual keen sense of etiquette and precedence, Elemnestra immediately assessed the Thar as her superior in the hierarchy of leadership, and dropped to one knee. "Hail and greetings to you, Tharaman-Thar of the Snow Leopards, you are welcome indeed to my small province and we are honored to provide shelter to you and to your army."

Tharaman continued to regard her in silence for a few seconds, the great amber eyes seeming to search for her very soul as they bored into her face. Then, at last, the beautiful, refined voice boomed into the cold air. "Greetings, Elemnestra of the Hypolitan, your offer of hospitality is accepted with gratitude and friendship."

A buzz of excitement ran through the part of the watching crowd that was near enough to hear. The rumors were proven true; Queen Thirrin had made an alliance with talking leopards!

For a moment the Basilea seemed almost shocked, but she quickly recovered and smiled in reply. Thirrin now greeted her uncle Olememnon, the formality of the royal presence soon forgotten as they embraced and chatted excitedly about the journey and the military preparations. But they were interrupted by a slight figure that stood by politely and coughed gently.

Thirrin turned toward the newcomer, and her queenly

demeanor slipped even further when she recognized who it was. "Maggie!" she squealed in delight, hugging the royal adviser closely. "Have I got some tales for you. We've always thought the lands to the north were dead and empty, but they're teeming with life and wonders. Oh, if only you could have come with us, you'd have been struck dumb with amazement."

Maggiore Totus smiled fondly at his former pupil. "I'm quite sure I would have been. But it seems you've brought some of the wonders with you. May I be presented to the King of the Snow Leopards?"

Thirrin squeezed his hand and turned toward the Thar, who'd quietly watched the reunions. "Lord Tharaman, meet Maggiore Totus, a great scholar from the Southern Continent and a valued royal adviser."

The Snow Leopard slowly blinked his huge eyes in polite cat-greetings, and Maggie bowed as low as his cold-stiffened joints would allow him. "Hail, Tharaman, One Hundredth Thar of the Snow Leopards, Lord of the Icesheets, and Scourge of the Ice Trolls," the old scholar declaimed, proving that he'd been listening very closely to all the proceedings. "May I express the gratitude of all the people of the Icemark for your help in this time of our greatest need."

"Your gratitude is noted, Maggiore Totus, and I say that the nobility of the people of the Icemark would always attract friends and allies to their cause no matter how desperate their need."

Thirrin wondered if scholar and King could ever get beyond the formality of courtly behavior, then Maggie said, "Do you know there's a species of Snow Leopard in the high mountains in the south of my country, but they're vastly inferior to your own mighty people."

"Really?" asked the Thar, deeply interested. "In what way?"

"Well, they're much smaller, for a start. Probably standing about waist height to me. And most strikingly, they cannot talk."

"Then presumably they resemble us in some other way."

"Oh yes, their coats and markings are exactly the same as your own, and apart from size, their anatomical detailing is identical. But there are other differences, too. For example, they seem to be solitary beasts, whereas your own people obviously live together in large groups."

A deep rumbling sound of pure pleasure emerged from Tharaman's chest as he warmed to the conversation.

"And that's another thing," continued Maggie. "They can't purr, either."

"Then are you quite sure they're Snow Leopards?" the Thar asked with a laugh.

"Oh yes. But perhaps they're only as similar to you as the ape creatures of the hot lands are to us."

"But are these ape creatures considered human people?"

"Well, no," Maggiore admitted. "But some scholars in the Southern Continent are beginning to put forward theories that they may be *relatives* of some sort that are not as advanced."

"Then if the ape creatures are not human, by the same token neither can your mountain cats be Snow Leopards. Perhaps they should be seen as a sort of first attempt on the part of the gods to make a new species, which later models have superseded."

"Precisely, precisely!" Maggie agreed enthusiastically. "If I may add —"

But at this point he was interrupted by the return of the soldier that Elemnestra had sent off to the city for bread and apples. The Basilea handed two large loaves and a bag of apples to Thirrin, who immediately turned and beckoned to Oskan, who'd been watching proceedings from the sleigh.

He hurried over the snow and, after a hasty bow and greeting to all the dignitaries, he seized one of the loaves and started to tear great chunks out of it with his teeth. Everybody watched in amazement, and Elemnestra seemed about to say something, when Thirrin also began to wolf down her bread. After they'd both demolished half a loaf, they each grabbed an apple, quickly ate it, then finished off the bread.

Thirrin looked at the amazed expressions around her and explained, "We've eaten nothing but meat for weeks."

"More like months," Oskan added. "I don't think I could even look at another steak or cutlet, let alone eat one!"

Thirrin nodded in agreement, and Elemnestra discreetly signaled to Olememnon, who understood perfectly what she meant and sent a rider back to the palace with orders to change the menu for that night's banquet.

The party then waited politely while the Queen and Oskan ate another apple, after which the Basilea took control of proceedings.

Slightly to the left of the welcoming party stood a large group of women, with one or two men among them. They were of all ages and their dress ranged from the rich and splendid to a pungent gathering of rags. But all seemed to be treated with respect by the soldiers and crowds that stood around them. At their head stood a tiny wizened figure, bent almost double with age. She leaned on a staff that was as thin and twisted as she was, and her fine white hair blew and streamed out in the light breeze, as though she were standing in a hurricane. Her name was Wenlock Witchmother, and she was the oldest and most respected of the White Witches of the Icemark.

The Basilea beckoned to them, and the entire group moved forward to surround Thirrin and her party.

"Greetings, Queen Thirrin," the Witchmother said in a surprisingly strong voice. "We give thanks to the Great Goddess for your safe return from The-Land-of-the-Ghosts and pledge our loyalty for the coming struggle."

Thirrin gazed at them with a mixture of wonder and respect. These were the White Witches her father had told her about. After Redrought had defeated the Vampire King and Queen at the Battle of the Wolfrocks and expelled all magical creatures from the Icemark, he'd allowed the White Witches to stay, and they'd repaid him with unswerving loyalty and service. She nodded her head in greeting to the Witchmother and thanked her for her continuing support.

"To that you're welcome, Queen," the old woman answered shortly. "But our main purpose here is to greet one of our own. Oskan the Warlock."

Oskan stepped forward and bowed to the old woman, then waited silently for her to speak.

"I remember your mother, White Annis. Had she lived, she would have taken my staff as Witchmother when I am called to the Summer Lands. But the Goddess had other plans for her, and she went home before me. The Mother knows her own mind, and we must accept it. But I have this to say to you, Oskan the Warlock: Your path won't be easy. Much of it is hidden, as was the fate of your mother, but I have been shown that as a saver of lives you may never kill, except perhaps once. And if that happens, you'll pay a heavy price. I've been told to tell you that death will come from the skies and healing from the earth."

Oskan frowned. "But what does that mean?"

The old woman laughed. "The Goddess will tell you when she's ready, and not one moment before. Be content to know this, Oskan the Warlock, you're favored by the Mother. Your powers are stronger than any I've ever known. I can *feel* the presence of them like storms in the summer air." She paused here, and her eyes turned disdainfully to the Basilea and her soldiers. "Some people think the Goddess is for women alone and that she has no time for men; well, they forget she has her husband and loves him well. And they also forget that she's the mother of us all, and a mother's love for her sons is special and strong.

"Not many men carry the burden of her powers; that's her blessing on them. Her gifts are heavy, and her sons she's happy to see carefree. But sometimes she chooses a man whose spirit is strong. You can see them among us," she said, nodding her head at the few men who stood in the group behind her. "And when she does, their Power is something to behold. But none, none at all equal you, Oskan the Warlock. And I say this now to all with ears to hear: I name you as my successor! You will carry the staff of the Witchmother when I am called at last to the Summer Lands. You will be Oskan Witchfather, only the second of your kind to carry the staff."

A gasp rose up from the group behind her and she laughed. "We do live in times of history, do we not? But I'm not dead yet, and won't be for a few years to come. The Goddess has other tasks yet for you, Oskan, son of White Annis, beloved of the Mother."

Oskan dropped to his knees and bowed his head. "Will I be strong enough?"

The old woman sniffed. "The Goddess chose you — she's never wrong. Now I'm going in; it's cold." And with that she turned and walked off toward the city.

"I think we've been dismissed," Thirrin said, bending to help Oskan to his feet. "Come on, I can hear some cheese and a hunk of bread calling."

The warlock's eyes lit up. "With pickled onions!"

"You'll have to fight me for them first." Thirrin raised her hand to Grinelda and her sleigh team, who trotted over the snow and waited while she and Oskan climbed aboard.

As the sleigh made its way toward the city gates with its escort of Snow Leopards, Thirrin waved to the cheering crowds while she and Oskan discussed the possibility of vegetable stew for supper that night and tried not to drool too noticeably.

The banquet was a "celebration of vegetables and winter-stored fruits," as Maggiore put it. Some of the housecarl officers at the top table looked a little put out when meat failed to appear, but after the beer and wine servers had been around a few times they started to cheer up. Even so, one or two of them gazed enviously at the mounds of raw flesh that the Snow Leopard soldiers and the Wolf-folk were eating down in the main body of the hall, and one much-scarred veteran of King Redrought's wars found himself watching every mouthful that Tharaman-Thar delicately selected from the wide bowl set on the table before him.

Thirrin had wondered how the leopards would react to a feast with humans, but she needn't have worried. After an initial wariness, the soldiers down in the hall soon realized the huge cats were warriors like themselves, and they were soon swapping boasts about their battle exploits and listening to tales about war with the Ice Trolls in the lands far to the north.

She'd also worried about the mix of brute strength and alcohol and had privately hoped that the leopards wouldn't like beer or wine, but they'd literally lapped it up and had begun joining in with the housecarls' more lusty songs, or simply sat purring loudly so that the hall rumbled like a benevolent thunderstorm.

Of course, not all of the soldiers, whether leopard or human, could sit in the Great Hall, but huge bonfires had been lit in the palace courtyard, and tables had been set around them so that many of the soldiers who were not on guard duty could join in the feasting.

Thirrin was quite aware that the banquet was not just a State occasion designed to welcome her as Queen back to her domain but also an ideal way of introducing the new allies to her army and its officers. She had to admit that talking leopards would be more than a bit beyond the experience of her people, but so far the initial introductions were going well. She'd noted that there were at least three phases in her people's reaction to Tharaman-Thar and his soldiers: fear at first, closely followed by amazement and wonder, and then a sort of pride of ownership as the humans vied with one another to prove that they knew the leopards better than anyone else. She'd yet to see any examples of complete familiarity, but that was hardly surprising. Given time she was sure her resourceful subjects would begin to show it.

Basilea Elemnestra was discussing tactics with Tharaman-Thar while her consort Olememnon was trying some Hypolitan jokes on Taradan, who'd been invaluable as a bridge between the two peoples in the first hour or so of the meetings. A sudden shout of laughter proved that human and cat shared the same sense of humor. Taradan then told a joke that was so rude Thirrin felt herself blushing as he reached the punch line, but Olememnon's huge booming laugh distracted attention from her, so no one noticed.

"My Lady, exactly how do you propose to integrate the Thar's army into our tactics?" Elemnestra asked.

Relieved to be on familiar ground, Thirrin answered, "Tharaman and I have been discussing this on the journey from the Icesheets, and we've decided on some ideas we'll be trying out over the next few days."

"Would you assess them as cavalry or infantry?"

"Cavalry," Thirrin answered firmly. But neither she nor Tharaman would be drawn out any further on the subject.

Over the next few days, Thirrin's head spun as she attended meetings and training sessions and discussed logistics and troop movements. Hardly an hour passed when she wasn't involved in one military problem or another, from overseeing the construction of new ballistas to the best method of transporting rockapults. But overall, the training was running with a precision that was almost faultless.

Then, one fine crisp morning, she and the Thar rode out of the city and onto the wide plain. Already waiting were the Snow Leopard army and a large contingent of the best cavalry selected from regiments of both the Icemark and the Hypolitan. The troopers had wisely led their horses to stand at a wide distance downwind of the leopards, but even so, many were shying and whickering nervously.

Thirrin, as usual, was being drawn in her sleigh by her werewolf guard, but when she and Tharaman had reached a point equidistant from the two blocs of warriors, she climbed out and sent it back to the city.

The young Queen gave a signal, and a squire led out her charger. She walked slowly to greet him, calling his name and reassuring him as he walked over the snow. When he reached her, she took the reins from the squire, and the huge stallion nuzzled her. After she'd fed him an apple, she led him over to Tharaman-Thar, who quietly watched their approach.

"So these are the creatures you call horses," the King of the Leopards said. "They seem unsteady and easily frightened to me."

Stroking the proudly arching neck of her horse, Thirrin said, "This is Osdred, my charger. The cavalry of the Icemark broke the massed ranks of the werewolves at the Battle of the Wolfrocks and has driven the Corsairs back into the sea. But, yes, horses can be easily frightened and sometimes easily driven off. A trained cavalry mount is a different thing, though. Wait, I'll show you. . . ." She climbed nimbly into the saddle and, standing in the stirrups, she drew her sword and gave the war shout of the House of Strong-in-the-Arm. Immediately the stallion screamed a fierce challenge and reared, lashing out with its forelegs.

The Thar nodded slowly, but said nothing.

"Growl at him, challenge him," Thirrin called. "Pretend to attack him."

Tharaman roared deafeningly and reared up on his hind legs. The stallion leaped forward, snorting, and fearlessly followed Thirrin's commands as she wheeled in close to the Snow Leopard, whirling around him and feinting thrusts and hacks with her saber.

She drew back and waited for the Thar's reaction. He sat in thought for a moment, before saying, "A strange beast of contradictions. Gentle warriors: eaters of grass and yet the hearts of hunters. Let me see what else horses can do."

Thirrin nodded, then cantered back to the regiment of cavalry, who had watched the first meeting of horse and Snow

Leopard with interest. She gave a sudden great shout and the troopers swept forward in a charge, across the snows to where the leopards stood waiting. Holding their line, the giant cats roared as the cavalry approached, but then at the last moment the horses turned aside, following Thirrin's pointing saber as she led them in a long, swerving arc back to where the Thar sat apart, quietly watching.

"Enough," said the King of the Leopards. "Your horses are warriors indeed, and I and my army will be proud to call your cavalry comrades."

Thirrin nodded and smiled, then she dismounted and began to discuss training methods with the Thar.

For the rest of the day each trooper's mount was introduced to the leopards and, under instruction from Thirrin, the huge cats breathed into the nostrils of the horses in a display of friendship. Then, as the short winter day was drawing to a close, she began to put her plan into action, creating a line of cavalry that alternated between horse and cat across a wide line. Any enemy they charged would face a deadly combination of lance, saber, tooth, and claw.

As the sun stained the snow a vivid crimson, Thirrin and the Thar urged forward the first canter of the new cavalry. Gradually they raised the pace until they were thundering across the snows at full gallop, the Snow Leopards letting out a strange coughing bark of challenge and the horses neighing, while the troopers sang the paean, or battle song, of the Icemark.

Thirrin laughed aloud for joy. "We'll destroy them with our noise if nothing else," she called to Tharaman, who thundered beside her.

"Let's hope not," he called back. "I prefer it when the enemy puts up a fight!"

Later, as the moon rose over the frozen land, a mixed column of horse and leopard trotted smartly back to the city: cats and humans, absorbed in singing marching songs and oblivious to the people who lined the road up to the citadel, watching them pass in admiration and hope.

22

The Imperial meteorologists had promised at least a week of quiet weather, and as Scipio Bellorum had threatened them with twenty lashes for every day of inaccuracy, he was inclined to believe them. Certainly the weather was good now, even glorious, with high blue skies and a crisp frost. Perfect riding weather.

Behind him marched twenty thousand cavalry and eighty thousand infantry made up of pikemen, shield-bearers, and musket regiments. In addition to this he had a battery of one hundred cannons and an entire rabble of engineers, carpenters, and the usual camp followers. This time there would be no mistakes. The debacle of the earlier invasion had been one of the very few defeats any Imperial army had suffered since he'd taken command of the military twenty years ago, and he was determined that there wouldn't be another.

His spies had reliably informed him that there was no defending army in the region, and that the nearest large town had only a rabble militia to defend it. The decision was therefore simple. He would take the settlement and use it as base camp for the coming campaign. His highly trained and superbly equipped Imperial troops would breach the walls and secure the town within two days, three at the most, after which the supply caravans could start moving in and they would be ready to begin the war proper with the spring thaw.

He rode at complete ease, hand on hip, highly polished boots resting in gilded stirrups. Despite the cold he wore no hat on his closely cropped head of gray hair, believing that the men should be able to recognize their commander easily. But not one of his soldiers could ever have mistaken his slight, whiplash-hard figure for anyone else. This man with the light blue eyes and thin hawklike nose had led them to victory after victory. And this same man had hanged some of them, whipped them, and sold them into slavery if he thought they'd given less than their very best. This was Scipio Bellorum, Commander of the Imperial armies, and no one — not even the Emperor himself — would deny him anything he wanted if it was within his power to give it.

As it happened, Bellorum's estimate for the fall of the town of Inglesby was over a week off. The militia and townsfolk had kept them out for ten days, despite the fact that the guns had breached the walls in more than six places. He watched now as the latest attack force came streaming back from one of the breaches. This was the third time in as many hours that the defenders had repulsed his soldiers, and he was beginning to lose his temper.

Added to this, the weather had turned for the worse more than three days ago, and in a rare act of rashness Bellorum had lost a large contingent of troops he'd sent on a mission to garrison the capital, Frostmarris. They'd been caught in a blizzard, and the general who was noted for his good luck had lost his gamble. Usually he ensured that all points were secured before he advanced farther, but the road was open and the prize was too much of a temptation. If he could have taken the city without a blow being struck in anger, the war would have been as good as over.

But for once he'd failed, and to add to his anger, the temperatures had plummeted and it had begun to blizzard, making the besiegers' camp a place of frostbite and death. It was now imperative that the town of Inglesby be taken, not only to satisfy Polypontian honor but for the sake of survival. If they didn't get under more substantial cover than Empire-issue canvas, they'd all die of the extraordinary cold.

"Colonel Marcellus, your regiment, I think," Bellorum said as the Imperial troops streamed back from the walls of the town. His voice was as cutting as the wind that scythed across the frozen land, and the shivering of the men within earshot had more cause than mere cold.

One of the officers standing in the small knot behind him shuffled forward. "Yes, sir. But they're at a disadvantage not knowing the layout of the streets, and the defending housecarls are as tough as frozen leather."

"Tougher than Imperial troops?" the general asked quietly.

"Well, no, sir. But the defenders are fighting for their homes and their loved ones; that alone gives them an added incentive."

"Colonel Marcellus, our incentives include living to see the spring and not being hanged for lack of military fervor. You will now regroup your regiment and personally lead it back into the city. You will not retreat. I expect to see you again either as a corpse or as victorious commander at the head of his adoring troops. Do you understand?"

Marcellus saluted and marched away to join his regiment, which was still falling back through the breach in the walls.

Bellorum then ordered a fresh bombardment of the city to keep the defenders occupied while he ordered up reinforcements.

Within fifteen minutes the regiment had regrouped and stormed back through the breach, at exactly the same time the other Imperial troops fought their way through the main gates and into three other breaches around the perimeter walls.

This time the defenders were pushed back slowly, fighting street by street and house by house, until finally, after more than five hours of desperate struggle in which the general himself helped to maintain the stretched lines of communication, the defenders held one barricade in the courtyard of the citadel. Here, the last of the housecarls raised their shield-wall and stood shoulder-to-shoulder with the surviving townsfolk.

Firing volley after volley at the upturned carts and old bedsteads that made up the barricades, the Imperial troops stormed a waiting hedge of spears where they were impaled by the momentum of their charge and the press of their comrades pushing from behind. Again and again they attacked, like a storming sea crashing against a rocky headland, but each time they fell back and the defense held.

Bellorum watched the struggle for almost an hour from the broken gatehouse, his face an impassive mask, until he suddenly dismounted and drew his sword. The time had come to set an example. He walked to the head of his exhausted troops, who had retreated yet again, and stared at them silently. Then, raising his sword, he turned and faced the last barricade. By this time the short winter day had drawn to a close and snow had started to fall again, drifting slowly down to settle on the debris and corpses of the besieged town.

The defenders waited silently. Nothing could be done. Earlier, their commander had tried to negotiate with Bellorum under a flag of truce, in an attempt to evacuate the noncombatants, but after listening for a few moments the general had nodded to the musketeer beside him, and the housecarl commander had been shot in the head. Even the Vampire King and Queen in the Ghost Wars had respected the flag of truce; only Bellorum, it seemed, set his own conditions.

The dull rattle of shield locking with shield was the only sound the defending line made as the Imperial troops began to advance. But this time, instead of charging, the soldiers of the Empire walked slowly forward, as unstoppable as a rising flood behind their brutal general. The surviving townsfolk picked up stones and broken roof tiles and hurled them at the Polypontian soldiers in a deadly hail, but still they came slowly on, unheeding of the resistance. Bellorum reached the barricade and began to climb, his shield raised above his head to receive the blows of ax and sword, but his face remained calm and impassive as though he were taking a stroll in a garden. At last he reached the summit of the barrier, and his sword struck at the housecarls' line, the thin blade snaking forward with deadly accuracy to pierce the eye and brain of the soldier before him. Then, glittering in the torchlight, it struck to left and right, slicing open a throat, severing a jugular. The line started to fold, and the Imperial troops drove forward, hacking and slashing in a bloody storm. And still Bellorum strolled on, killing as he went.

Within fifteen minutes most of the resistance had crumbled, and Bellorum set his victorious troops to work, eliminating the last few survivors. First, the soldiers were disarmed and beheaded, after which the townsfolk were herded against a wall and systematically shot by massed ranks of musketeers. The general smiled grimly as he walked away to direct the setting-up of his headquarters in the citadel. Halfway across the courtyard he stopped at the corpse of a Polypontian officer. It was Colonel Marcellus, just recognizable through the mask of blood that had flowed from a massive head wound. Bellorum raised his sword in salute before walking calmly on.

Later that night a howling erupted outside the town walls. Some of the soldiers securing the citadel gate heard it, and assumed scavengers had come to feed on the corpses. But the cries of the lone werewolf were forging the first vocal link in the chain that would pass the news of the fall of Inglesby, voice by voice, over the frozen land, back to the city of the Hypolitan.

Maggiore Totus watched Thirrin pace up and down his chamber. He knew she'd eventually stop and tell him what she was going to do, ask for his advice, and then ignore it completely and do exactly as she'd intended in the first place. With him sat Olememnon, looking solemn, and Oskan, looking sleepy. The only other person standing up was Elemnestra, and her body swayed backward and forward as Thirrin paced toward her, then turned and walked away.

Tharaman-Thar was sharing a rug next to the fire with Primplepuss, who was snuggled between his massive paws. Every now and then he raised his head to watch Thirrin as she paced, and would yawn enormously and lie down again, nose toward the flames.

"Bellorum *himself* is attacking! Attacking in the winter, and Inglesby's fallen, Maggie! Where is Inglesby?"

"Where it was when you last asked, five minutes ago. Ten miles from the southern pass into the Polypontus and three miles from the Great Road."

"Then he could march on Frostmarris and be there in days!"

"Not for at least another week. Oskan reliably informs us that there'll be blizzards until then. And I'm sure he won't march even then. Bellorum will need reinforcements first. The werewolves told us that he lost many troops taking the town, and even more to the weather."

"But, Maggie, we're dealing with a man here who's totally unpredictable! He not only began his invasion in winter but, when that failed, he didn't even have the good grace to sit back and wait for spring! Oh no, not Scipio Bellorum — he simply gathered another army and attacked again, even though there's at least two months of bad weather still to get through!"

"Well, if he's as brilliant as everyone says he is, he'll have learned his lesson and he'll wait. Not even the discipline of the Polypontian army can impress a snowstorm. They may die in perfect order, but die they will if they try to march anywhere for the next week or so," said Oskan, the last few words of his comment lost in an enormous yawn.

"I'm not so sure," Thirrin said darkly. "I'm beginning to wonder if this general has a secret of some sort."

"He's only a man, you know, not a Vampire," said Oskan, reading her mind perfectly. "He'll die one day, just like the rest of us mortals, and if he's not sensible, it'll be sooner than any of us dare hope." He slumped back in his seat as though the effort of talking had drained him of all energy.

"Even here, this Polypontian general's greatest weapon is working," said Tharaman-Thar, raising his huge head to gaze at them.

"And what weapon is that?" Thirrin asked.

"Fear. We're all afraid of him, or at least of his reputation. He's obviously very clever. The stories you've told me are of a man who's coldly ruthless and vicious in his cruelty. And yet none of you has said that he's a barbarian. Even beyond his borders he's managed to cultivate an image of sophisticated ruthlessness, of intelligent implacability." The huge leopard paused to compose his thoughts. "He's obviously a true genius. His weapons are both physical, in the form of his army, and psychological, in the form of the dread that precedes him. And when this is coupled with the reputation of supreme intelligence, he seems truly invincible."

"Your analysis is impeccable, My Lord Tharaman," said Maggie quietly. "But I'm afraid there is a flaw in your logic if you're implying that the stories are in some way unwarranted. You see, the facts bear out his reputation. He *is* ruthless, he *is* cruel, and so far he *has* been invincible."

"His armies *have* been defeated before."

"Yes, but never when he was in command," said Maggie. "Even when heavily outnumbered, his brilliant tactics have always won the day."

"Then it's time he learned the lessons of the vanquished," Tharaman rumbled darkly.

"I'll second that," said Oskan.

Thirrin fell silent and began pacing up and down again, then abruptly she stopped. "Right!" They all focused on her, knowing from her tone that she'd made a decision. "The werewolves have told us that Frostmarris seems empty, and the weather's going to be foul for a week, so we have time to prepare to march. When the blizzards stop, Tharaman and I will lead the cavalry back to Frostmarris and hold it. Elemnestra will follow with the infantry. Questions? No? Good. Then *move,* people! I want the cavalry training in the indoor pens, and the infantry likewise! Maggie, summon all logistics officers and tacticians. Oskan . . . go back to bed for two hours. I'll expect you to be alert and making sensible contributions from then on!"

The room emptied as thoroughly as an upturned jug, leaving Maggie in the silence with Primplepuss. "Well, I suppose I'd better do as I'm told and brief the officers," he said to the little cat that had already grown from kitten to leggy adolescent. But he finished his glass of sherry first, and then called Grimswald to fetch him another. While the blizzards of the Icemark were blowing, nothing moved around the country, and ten minutes' peace here and there would make no difference.

The weather was bright, clear, and the coldest it had been so far that winter. Oskan had strongly advised against riding out that day, but Thirrin was determined, and the streets were lined with people braving the cold to wave off the Queen and her amazing cavalry as they rode for Frostmarris. They gazed in awe at the twin columns that glittered in the brilliant sun, the breath of horse and leopard pluming on the frozen air as they waited for Thirrin and Tharaman-Thar to give the order to march.

Oskan was riding his mule, Jenny, having bravely declined the comfort of the Wolf-folk sleigh, and he sat now as easy as a boy on a sack of broken glass as he listened to Maggiore Totus, who was standing at his stirrup, talking earnestly.

"Remember to use the werewolf relay regularly. I must be informed of everything that's happening. I can't keep you properly supplied and the logistics running smoothly unless I know precisely what you need and when you need it."

"I'll send a message every night at the third hour past sundown," said Oskan.

"Good. And I'll expect a message tonight, of course."

"Of course," Oskan answered resignedly.

Thirrin turned in her saddle and looked back over the twin columns of her cavalry. Farther back stood the infantry of both the Hypolitan and the Icemark, the fyrd and the housecarls indistinguishable now that the heavy training and new equipment gave all the soldiers exactly the same appearance.

The young Queen glanced at Tharaman, who blinked slowly in agreement, and then, standing in her stirrups, she gave the order to march. Immediately a deep booming rhythm echoed over the streets as kettledrums mounted on four huge horses set the beat for the pace.

Elemnestra watched the cavalry trot ahead, then gave the order for the infantry to follow. She, too, was in command of her own personal regiment of mounted archers. The five hundred warriors were all dressed in the distinctive cap and brilliantly colored jacket and pants of the Hypolitan, and each one of them carried a compound bow and four quivers of arrows hung to either side of their saddles.

The only mounted member of the infantry was Olememnon, who was riding only because Basilea Elemnestra had insisted upon it. He'd had some odd notion that as commander of the infantry he should share the conditions of his soldiers. Sometimes, she thought, he had no concept of his own dignity as her consort, and she wasn't prepared to compromise her own standing in the eyes of the populace. It was bad enough that he'd spent most of the morning with that little foreign adviser of the Queen's, saying good-bye and probably drinking too much of that southern sherry. Sometimes his choice of friends was deplorable.

He sat slightly behind her now, on a horse big-boned enough to carry the combined weight of his muscular frame and his heavy shield and weaponry. She caught his eye and smiled, but he merely saluted in return. *Well, let him sulk,* she thought to herself. *He'll soon lower his guard when the cold creeps into his bones during the night and no amount of blankets and pelts can keep him warm.* There was nothing quite like another body to snuggle up to when the night was crackling with blood-freezing frost.

By this time the cavalry was trotting out of the citadel gates and was heading down into the city. Cheers rose up from the people lining the route, and Thirrin nodded to the right and left as she rode. Oskan was more enthusiastic in his acknowledgment of the cheering crowd and waved at them wildly. Jenny, too, laid back her long, woolly-warmer-covered ears and brayed loud and long, earning a frown of disapproval from Thirrin, but she carried on hee-hawing, anyway.

In an attempt to mask the noise, Thirrin began the cavalry paean, and soon the troopers and leopards were all singing gustily — but, rising powerfully above it all, Jenny brayed her own song. Once beyond the city gates and the need for royal dignity, Thirrin turned in her saddle.

"Did you have to let her do that?" she snapped at Oskan.

"Do what?"

"You know full well what I mean. That braying. And while I think about it, I thought we'd had words before about your mule wearing ear-warmers. We must have looked and sounded like a circus!"

"As for her braying, I know no way of stopping her once she's in full flow," Oskan replied with dignity. "And warmers are a complete necessity for an animal with ears of Jenny's length. Just imagine the delay that could be caused if she got frostbite."

"I can assure you that frostbite to any part of that animal's anatomy wouldn't delay us for a second. If she were unfit to travel, I'd personally poleax her," Thirrin said with venom. Then she added as an afterthought, "And I'd enjoy it!"

Oskan and Jenny withdrew with dignity into an offended

silence, and the journey continued with Tharaman making lighthearted remarks and observations in an attempt to improve the atmosphere. Even Taradan's jokes could make no impression on the steely silence, and he and the Thar were reduced to murmuring to each other until they stopped for the midday meal.

But before long Thirrin and Oskan had forgiven each other and were chatting together as though nothing had happened. Tharaman-Thar watched them from his enormous height and concluded that young, as-yet-unmated humans were completely unfathomable.

The cavalry had now pulled ahead of the infantry by several miles, as had been agreed. If all went well, Thirrin would reach Frostmarris and secure it within two days, and the infantry would take approximately four to five days to join her, depending on conditions. So far, the news from the Wolf-folk spies was good: The city was still unoccupied and there was no sign of any Imperial troops on the approach roads. It looked as if Scipio Bellorum was being sensible and consolidating his position before striking north. Perhaps he'd even wait for the spring, like any normal human being. But Thirrin wasn't counting on it. She preferred to expect the unexpected when dealing with the Polypontian general.

They camped that night under a brilliant starscape that glittered and shimmered as though the sky itself had frozen and was coated with frost crystals. The human soldiers all had tents of thick hide, which slept three troopers, and each one had a fire burning brightly just outside the flap. Thirrin, Oskan, Tharaman, and Taradan sat comfortably around their own campfire enjoying the mixed scents of spicy wood smoke and the clean smell of snow. They'd already discussed and analyzed their plans with a thoroughness that had satisfied even Maggiore Totus, so they were content to sit and chat. But it was while they were talking that Thirrin had an idea.

"Oskan, the Oak King rules the woodlands at the moment, doesn't he?"

"Yes, until the summer solstice, when the Holly King takes over. Why?"

"I want to thank Their Dual Majesties for their support during our retreat from Frostmarris, and I think I know just how to do it. Could you summon their soldiers again, do you think?"

"Yes, I should think so."

"Good. We'll reach the eaves of the forest early tomorrow morning. Be ready then." She would say nothing more about it and soon went to bed, leaving the others to stare after her.

"It seems human females love cultivating a mystery as much as those of the Leopard People," said Tharaman-Thar, and purred as though amused.

The next day they began their march before dawn. The crunch of frozen snow under hoof and paw seemed magnified in the silence of the early hour, and the silken chink of equipment rose around the column of six thousand like a gentle breeze through steel trees.

They were already beginning to leave behind the wild and rocky landscape of the northern Icemark, and small stands of trees began to appear on the horizon. In the spring and summer there'd be fields of wheat and barley lining their route, but winter had hidden everything under its monochrome cloak.

As they rode on, the east began to grow pale and gradually the black of night gave way to the pink and blue of dawn. Then the sun rose into the sky and the snow glowed gold, so that they seemed to be walking through cold fire. On they marched; slowly the road began to dip into a broad valley until at last they had their first glimpse of the forest in the distance. Night still held an outpost under its eaves, and a sound like the sea reached their ears as the branches stirred and waved in the wind.

"Oskan," Thirrin said, "be ready to call on the Oak King when I give the word."

The warlock urged Jenny forward from her position just behind the Queen and Thar. "I'll be ready, but what exactly do you want me to say?"

"Just call them. I'll be my own herald when the time comes."

It took another two hours of riding to reach the first trees, where Thirrin called a halt. Oskan dismounted and waited while two buglers blew a fanfare that echoed through the woodlands. Then, stepping forward, he called, "Greetings to His Majesty the Oak King, Lord of the Great Forest and all wild places after the Solstice of Wintertide. Greetings also to your brother monarch, the Holly King, Lord of the Great Forest and all wild places after the Solstice of Summertide. Queen Thirrin Freer Strong-in-the-Arm Lindenshield, Wildcat of the North, sends felicitations, as does her ally Lord Tharaman, One Hundredth Thar of the Snow Leopards, Lord of the Icesheets, and Scourge of the Ice Trolls."

His voice died away in the shadows of the trees, and a silence fell. Even the wind dropped to an unearthly calm. But just as Oskan was drawing breath to call again, a raging tempest blasted through the forest, howling and roaring as though someone had opened a door on a hurricane. Then the wind dropped again to nothing, and from the dark tangle of undergrowth a division of soldiers stepped forward. Their skin was the gray-green of bark, their eyes were the brilliant green of newly opened oak leaves, and their armor was as polished and glossy as young acorns.

A murmur rose up from the human troops and leopards, and the horses whickered nervously. Thirrin raised her hand for silence and dismounted. "Welcome, soldiers of the Oak King. Take my friendly greetings and gratitude to your lord, and add this message: Queen Thirrin of the Icemark happily cedes to Their Dual Majesties the valley that descends from the uplands to the eaves of your forest. She cordially suggests they fill it with trees and wildlife, and so extend the borders of their realm in perpetuity. Let them know that Queen Thirrin offers this in gratitude for their help against her enemies, and for the succor they gave to her people during their retreat to the north."

After a moment of silence an oak soldier stepped out of the ranks and raised his spear in salute, and the rest of the division beat spear on shield until the forest echoed with a thunderous rattling roar. Then, as the sound slowly faded away, the wind rose again to fill the forest, and the oak soldiers stepped back into the undergrowth. The wind dropped, and in the calm the beautiful and refined voice of Tharaman-Thar was heard.

"I have lived to see wonders not even dreamed of by our poets. I stand beneath giant plants that scratch the sky with their branches, I have allied my people with the humans of legend, and I have seen soldiers made and molded from the stuff of the land. What a time I have lived in! What a life I've been granted! If I die in this war, I will have no reason for sorrow. I've had wealth beyond counting, and I fight for my friends who rise over the greatest of all and who stand in the eye of the

One!" And he threw back his head and let out a roar that blasted through the trees and rose into the sky like a banner of sound streaming in the wind. Immediately his leopards answered him, and the great noise sent crows and ravens for miles around climbing the skies in their thousands.

23

Frostmarris lay on the plain before them, pristine in its blanket of snow. The white Wolf-folk who'd drawn Thirrin's sleigh during her journey to the northern lands were now acting as scouts and had been sent ahead to confirm that the city really was unoccupied, while the cavalry stayed hidden under the eaves of the forest. The werewolves had been gone for more than an hour, and Thirrin was beginning to consider sending out riders when a distance-thin howling sounded through the freezing air.

"What are they saying?" Thirrin asked Oskan impatiently, but he raised his hand to silence her while he concentrated.

At last he said, "Frostmarris is unoccupied by any living human people."

"What does that mean?" Thirrin snapped.

He shrugged. "I'm only reporting their exact phrasing. But I suppose they mean there are no soldiers of the Empire in occupation."

Tharaman-Thar stood sniffing the breeze that blew directly from Frostmarris, and after a moment said, "The city smells empty. I smell no human people, no horses, no dog-friends or cat-companions. Only rats and mice and the smaller creatures. Frostmarris is waiting to be reoccupied."

Thirrin nodded. "Then mount up. My capital awaits."

The cavalry swung out onto the plain in a double column of horse and leopard. The troopers rode smartly, their lances raised and pennants snapping in the wind, as Thirrin and the Thar stepped out with an awesome presence. Just behind them Jenny trotted along, twitching her woolly-warmer-covered ears and occasionally giving a little hiccupping bray that was quickly cut short when Oskan sharply tugged the reins.

Their pace soon ate up the distance between the forest and the city, and as they approached the main gates the tension rose. The setting sun made a fire of the great bronze Solstice Bell that hung above the barbican. Thirrin leaned forward in her saddle — only the greatest restraint stopped her from galloping ahead. Suddenly Grinelda, Leader of the white Wolf-folk, appeared in the gateway, and throwing back her head she howled in greeting. The cavalry quickly climbed the winding track that led to the huge portcullis, where they reined to a halt.

The gates stood wide open, and a cold wind blasted through the long entrance tunnel, bringing with it a surprising lack of scents. Normally, the city would have smelled, or rather reeked, of wood smoke, dung, cattle, horses, baking bread, roasting meat, beer, and general humanity. But now it only breathed the breath of winter: snow and ice and emptiness.

Oskan looked at Thirrin, expecting a long rousing speech about reclaiming her rights and the symbolism of Frostmarris reoccupied. But instead she looked pale, and after staring along the tunnel for a while she said quietly, "Come on. Let's go in."

The rattle of iron-shod hooves on the cobblestones echoed

around them as they emerged into the main thoroughfare. The streets looked the cleanest Oskan had ever seen them, under their unsullied blanket of snow. Only the almost humanlike paw prints of the Wolf-folk scouts marked it in places, clearly showing where they'd searched through the buildings and streets for any sign of occupation. But all was empty.

Thirrin led the cavalry along the slowly climbing main street to the citadel. Here, too, the main gates stood open. She dismounted to walk across the wide courtyard, leading her horse. Then she turned and barked out orders to her commanders, who scurried off to stable horses, check barrack blocks, and post sentries on the walls of city and citadel. Then she walked to the double doors of the Great Hall and, followed by Oskan and Tharaman-Thar, she pushed them open and strode inside.

After the brilliance of the bright winter day, the hall seemed as black as night. Slowly their eyes adjusted and the huge, dark, cavernlike space became clear. The hammer-beam roof was still hung with its ancient battle standards, and at the far end the massive oaken throne still stood on its dais.

Thirrin strode forward, her boots ringing loud on the flagstones, and headed for the throne. On reaching the dais she quickly climbed it, and with an unconscious sense of ceremony, she sat down.

"Bring me light and life into this darkness!" Her voice boomed into the hall, and the space filled with scurrying soldiers and servants who lit the torches that lined the walls. One group of housecarls dragged a log through the doors and laid it in the central hearth. Then, bowing to Thirrin, they threw torches and glowing coals into the kindling and a great blaze leaped up. "Bring food into this hall! Bring bread and meat, bring beer and mead! Bring the salt and set it on a table before me!" Thirrin called again, not knowing where the words that leaped into her mind came from but happy to let them flow.

More and more servants hurried in, setting a table before the throne and rushing through the corridors beyond the Great Hall as they searched for the items and utensils of a living household. And as they hurried on their quests they opened doors and cupboards, shutters and windows, letting in the air, letting in the light of the day.

Now human and leopard soldiers spontaneously crowded into the hall from the courtyard. Before them sat their Queen on the Throne of the Icemark; beside her sat the mighty form of her ally Lord Tharaman-Thar of the Icesheets, and on the steps of the dais sat her chief adviser, Oskan the Warlock. An awed silence fell on the soldiers as they stared at the young warrior-queen, the towering leopard, and the powerful young warlock, but then a mighty cheer rose up, mingled with roaring and howling.

"We have returned! We have returned, my soldiers and beloved allies. And while we live, we will never leave again!" Thirrin called into the hall, her voice as high and as fierce as a hunting hawk's cry. "Close the gates against the winter and our enemies, and with the spring let us be ready to defend the Icemark!"

Again the cheering rose into the rafters, and over it all, a high-pitched braying could be heard from the courtyard as Jenny joined in the celebration.

Out in the shadows of the city, in the houses and cellars, in the secret rooms and locked attics, a stirring could be sensed. The ghosts and spirits-of-place whispered and muttered on the edge of hearing, glided and flowed on the edge of sight. They were pleased with the turn of events; it was they who had driven the small garrison of Polypontian troops out to die in the snow. It was they who'd haunted their movements through the city. And it was they who had joined them on watch in the dark of the night, filling their minds with a slow-growing fear, which had evolved into a terror that had driven them mad.

Several had been shot by their own comrades, who had quite rightly been convinced that they were possessed, and others had thrown themselves from the battlements in the dead of night rather than face the horror of what they knew stood just behind them. And when the surviving members of the garrison had finally decided to risk sheltering in the forest, it was the ghosts who had followed them down to the gates, whispering and laughing on the edge of their minds, watching them set out into the storm that raged and howled beyond the barbican.

The ghosts and spirits-of-place were pleased with events. The Queen had returned, and some of the people, and the rest of the folk would one day come back and they could slip back into their minds, becoming the warp and the weft of legend and stories — becoming the fireside companions of long winter nights, living their lives for a while in the minds of the breathing, in the blood that still flowed, in the feelings that still thrilled to nerves that still sensed.

For a night and a night, the ghosts flowed through the streets, being careful not to frighten these soldiers of the land and their allies. For a night and a night, the guards on the walls were aware only of a light now and then or a sound like laughter caught on the wind. But then the ghosts settled back into their shadows, and waited again in the dark of the city, in the cellars and attics and lost secret rooms — waited for their people to return and give back the strength to their legends.

* * *

Elemnestra arrived in the city two days later. There were now thirty thousand soldiers garrisoned in the barrack blocks and in the houses throughout Frostmarris. The north road became a lifeline of supplies from the province of the Hypolitan, and was patrolled daily by cavalry. Over the next few weeks the plans of defense were put in place. It had early been decided not to stand siege locked up in Frostmarris, and so a series of deep trenches and embankments of earth were painstakingly dug from the frozen land of the plain. Concentric defensive rings surrounded the city, extending out to the eaves of the forest at the point where the road entered it. The thirty thousand soldiers were stretched a little thin in some places, but it was hoped that in the spring the fyrds from different parts of the country would come to help. There was also the question of the allies. The Wolf-folk gathering was continuing, it was reported, but progress was slow. It could be well into spring before the muster was complete. And the Vampire King and Queen remained as elusive and enigmatic as ever. They were a law unto themselves, and would arrive to help if and when they chose.

In the meantime the Wolf-folk scouts continued to spy on Scipio Bellorum, and reported massive troop movement coming through the pass from the Empire. In the south of the country where the general was based in the city of Inglesby, the first breath of spring could be felt. There wasn't exactly a thaw, but at night the stones of the houses no longer cracked in freezing temperatures, and during the warmest parts of the day the ice and snow looked as though it just might start melting, given a little more encouragement.

Bellorum, like all brilliant generals, was well attuned to his surroundings and felt the change in the air. He smiled his grim smile and sent more messengers through the pass. His armies were gathering, and soon he'd be ready to unleash his attack.

Before him lay a four-day march to the capital of this little land, but he was too sensible to strike north without first securing his rear. He'd learned his lesson during the winter when he'd lost thousands of troops in a blizzard on a reckless mission to seize the capital. But now he was once again in full command of his instincts. There were two cities and three major towns in this Southern Riding, as it was so uncouthly called by its inhabitants, and *they* needed to be captured and garrisoned before he moved on Frostmarris. Nothing would be left to chance this time. The Icemark needed a war that was precisely planned and ruthlessly executed, and both precision and ruthlessness were his forte.

He stretched his elegant legs out to the fire burning in the hearth before him and called the servant for wine. There were at least another ten days or so before things really got under way, and like many old campaigners, he was determined to enjoy the luxury of rest while it was still available. His general staff officers could handle the bread and butter of the logistics; as a true artist of war, he'd wait until the canvas was ready for the master's hand.

Thirrin and Oskan looked out over the plain from the highest point of the city's battlements. The moon was half full, and the frozen land glittered under the subtle light like a tray of frosted diamonds.

"Do you remember the journey to the Hub of the World?" Thirrin asked. "It's odd, but it seems as if it happened only yesterday, and then again in another life, both at the same time."

"Yes," Oskan agreed. "Yesterday and years ago. I'd never have believed it while it was happening, but now I feel that it was one of the best times of my life. Nothing to think about but the journey ahead. Nothing else to fear but the fact that we might die, which somehow helped to make everything else seem completely unimportant."

Thirrin snuggled down farther into her cloak, then said, "Do you know, there was one point when I could have wished the journey would last for all time. We'd just seen the northern lights, the sky seemed on fire, and the werewolves were pounding on through the dark, and I felt completely . . . at peace. There's no other way of putting it. I'm sure if we'd died then, we'd have just traveled on into forever. . . ."

Oskan looked at her. "Hey, where's my warrior-queen, ready to fight for her place in Valhalla?"

"She's just a bit tired, Oskan. And scared."

He stopped his jaw from dropping open just in time, but then recovered quickly. "Well, as to that, I bet the most seasoned housecarls are wetting themselves. We're facing Scipio Bellorum and his disciplined madmen. You've got a right to be scared; we all have."

Thirrin didn't answer for a while, then when she finally spoke, some of the usual steel had crept back into her voice. "I don't want you to think I'm scared of dying. It's not that. It's not that at all. It's more that I'm afraid of failing, of letting down the House of Lindenshield. I'm carrying centuries of expectations and responsibilities. Everybody wants me to tell them what to do, and at the same time they want me to live up to the legacy of all the Ironsides, Bears of the North, and Spear Maidens. And sometimes it's just too much. . . ."

Unable to think of anything constructive to say, Oskan put his arm around her shoulder and said, "I'm happy for you just to be Thirrin."

At that moment the heavy tread of a housecarl sounded

outside, and they leaped apart as though scolded. Approaching along the narrow walkway was the captain of the guard, and with him walked Tharaman-Thar.

"Report, Captain Osgood," Thirrin barked a little too sharply.

"All's quiet, My Lady. Apart from one idiot who slipped on the steps and has probably broken his wrist. If My Lord, Oskan, could have a look at him —"

"My Lord Oskan has enough to do without tending to every half-drunken housecarl who misses his footing on the ice."

"It was a cavalry trooper, actually, Ma'am," Captain Osgood answered.

"Well, whoever!" Thirrin snapped again. "My adviser's too busy."

The captain saluted silently and moved on to complete his rounds, leaving Tharaman-Thar to look searchingly at his ally.

"I've been thinking about the healing side of things, Thirrin. Captain Osgood has just reminded me," said Oskan. "We've got most of it organized, but the witches with their healers' skills aren't here yet, and we've still got a way to go before the infirmary's ready. Converting an old stable to a place of healing takes a lot of work, and I've been shirking my share of the effort. I think I'd better go and help."

"Whatever you think is necessary," Thirrin answered, recognizing the good sense of his words but still in an uncertain mood after Oskan's embrace.

"Good, I'll get on to that now, then. And while I'm at it, I'll take a look at that trooper's wrist," he said, and scurried off as though feeling guilty about something.

"The Queen and her Warlock seem uneasy," said Tharaman-Thar when they were alone.

Thirrin looked at him, annoyed. "It's quite bad enough being only fourteen without having to fight a war and run a country as well. Do you wonder that 'the Queen and her Warlock seem uneasy'?"

"No, I suppose not," said the leopard. "But sometimes even warriors have to admit they're just people before all else. And queens who are still girls, and warlocks who are still boys, should allow themselves to be young once in a while."

"We haven't the time, Tharaman."

"No, I suppose not. There are many who are looking to a time after the war to start living their lives again."

"If that's an unsubtle attempt to tell me there are people worse off than myself, save yourself the effort. I'm well aware of that, but it doesn't make it one bit easier to deal with my own problems," Thirrin answered irritably. "To be really honest, I think if anybody did derive comfort from the fact that 'there's always someone worse off than yourself,' they'd have to be a pretty sad and sick individual. If I've sprained my wrist, I'm not made happier by the thought that someone somewhere has broken their leg!"

"Well, that's telling me," said Tharaman humorously. "Now that I've been put thoroughly in my place, might I humbly suggest that we go inside and have some more of that delicious mulled wine we had earlier with Olememnon?"

Thirrin suddenly smiled and hugged the huge leopard. "Oh, I'm sorry, Tharaman. I've been snappy with everyone recently. I suppose I'm fed up with waiting for things to start happening. I just want to get on with it and reach whatever conclusion is destined."

"Well, that goes for me, too. But while we've got a breathing space, let's try and enjoy it." A deep rumbling purr vibrated through his chest, and he laughed. "Olememnon has challenged me to a drinking contest. The first one to fall asleep is the loser. I think I'll take him up on it now."

"Is that a good idea? Elemnestra won't be pleased."

"Won't she? Good. Come on, you can be referee."

24

Spring slowly awoke from its winter sleep, stretching out its greenery and new life from the south. Rivers and streams started to flow fiercely with snowmelt, and the earth began to emerge from the deep layer of ice as the cold released its iron grip.

On the battlements of Frostmarris, sentries could smell the rich soil of the forest and the green of new growth when the wind was in the right direction, and everywhere wildflowers were raising delicate petaled heads to the sun. At first the contours of the land were blurred under a shimmering white haze of snow flowers, but gradually, as the temperatures began to rise, other colors seeped from the earth: cool blues, brilliant yellows, and rich, fiery reds. Soon the woodlands and plains around Frostmarris were steeped in a weaver's workbag of colors and lay open beneath the sun like the page of a beautifully illuminated manuscript. From the walls of the city, the housecarls would watch as the Snow Leopards, unaccustomed to a world without ice, raced and capered over the fields of dazzling color, the height and distance making them look like kittens playing on a richly woven carpet. Out on the plain, the engineers could now dig the defensive embankments and trenches with much greater ease as the frozen land thawed. The protective rings around the capital now reached in three rows from the Great Road and the eaves of the forest in the south, then swept in a large unbroken arc east, before slowly turning back on themselves to flow west to a point north of the city and higher up the Great Road. The engineers, under instruction from Queen Thirrin, extended the ditches and embankments only a matter of a few yards into the Great Forest but, oddly, the undergrowth around and between the open ends of the defensive rings seemed to grow to an incredible density in a matter of days.

Now that travel was so much easier, the fyrd began to march in from the outlying towns and villages, boosting the Icemark's defending armies to almost sixty thousand. The city and citadel were soon loud with orders and marching as the fyrd was retrained to reach the new standard that was now expected. And once again the Snow Leopards had to get used to the open-mouthed awe of people who had never seen such amazing creatures.

But with the new season and hope came ominous reminders of Scipio Bellorum. The road from the south was soon crowded with refugees fleeing from his soldiers. His war had begun, and the land was being ravaged. The first town had already fallen in the new campaign, and among the civilians were several contingents of housecarls who'd withdrawn in the face of hopeless odds to act as a rear guard for the refugees and to fight again in the army of the Queen. These soldiers gave valuable information to the commanders of the defense force, and Thirrin, hearing their news, sent out calls for archers, particularly those who used the longbow.

After being rested for a few days, the refugees were sent north to the Hypolitan province away from the immediate danger of attack, and the defenders looked grimly to the south. The Wolf-folk spies continued their relay of information and it made uncomfortable news. Polypontian troops were moving through the pass in massive numbers, and though the besieged cities and towns resisted fiercely, news was soon coming in of their capture, one by one.

This was the hardest part for Thirrin. She wanted to take her army and strike south at the invaders, but common sense told her that the only hope was to fight from their strong defensive position and wait for the allies to arrive. And that was another problem: Rumors were beginning to circulate among the soldiers that the werewolves and Vampires would never come, that their hatred for humans was too great and they would gladly watch the Icemark destroyed. Thirrin and Oskan did their best to quash this scare-mongering, pointing out the loyal white Wolf-folk who were working as scouts and as part of the message relay. But it was no good; most thought they were just a decoy on the part of the Werewolf King, offered up as a sacrifice to the greater good of seeing the Icemark finally fall. If the defenders believed the allies really were on the way, they'd stand and fight more confidently and effectively.

But despite all of this pessimism, most of the army was resigned and even eager to fight. They wanted to do as much damage to the Polypontian war machine as they could. There was pride to be gained in bravely facing the best army the known world could field, and if they could bloody their noses, they'd be remembered long after the war was over.

Thirrin and her advisers came to the conclusion that this

attitude was the best they could hope for, and worked to stoke up a will for revenge that would add fury to the resistance. Elemnestra was particularly good at instilling bloodlust in the soldiers, leading out her squadrons of mounted archers in a display that had any spectators baying and cheering as though they were watching a race. Sweeping in at an angle, the archers would bear down on a line of target stakes driven into the earth, guiding their horses with their knees and shooting a hail of arrows as they came on. As they neared the targets they would gallop parallel to them, again loosing a devastating flight of arrows into the stakes as they thundered by. The squadron would then turn to sweep by from the opposite direction before galloping away, turning in their saddles to loose yet more arrows into the targets. This was how to stop the Polypontians! This was how to show them that the soil of the Icemark cost dear! Every soldier who watched the displays was set alight with a need to strike hard at the Empire and push it back through the mountain pass to its own lands.

But the regiment of Hypolitan women, under their commander Elemnestra, never once acknowledged the adoration they received from the soldiers who watched them. Whenever they returned to the city and trotted through the streets, their faces were always sternly set and they looked neither right nor left as they made their way to the citadel. These soldiers were the elite of the Hypolitan army. They had dedicated their lives to serving the Goddess in the military field, and as such only their commander, the Basilea of the province, was allowed to marry.

At least half of the Hypolitan army was made up of women, usually fighting alongside the men in mixed regiments or in companies twinned with male divisions that complemented the others' fighting skills. But it was the exclusively female squadrons of mounted archers that were considered the greatest of the great. They had kept alive the purity of the Hypolitan culture and lived as their people had first lived in the mountain strongholds of their long-ago home. They were proud and powerful, and their brightly embroidered uniform of pants, quilted jackets, and scarlet caps with cheek flaps had remained unchanged for hundreds of years. And as the housecarls of the Icemark watched them trot by, many could see the familiar features of their own Queen Thirrin in the stern young faces with their high cheekbones and ice-gray eyes.

But despite the dark elation the soldiers felt as they prepared for the coming clash, many still muttered that the allies would never come and that the Polypontian forces would overwhelm them. And as though to confirm the military prowess of their enemy, the refugees from the south continued to flood into Frostmarris with tales of cruelty and vast armies.

It was one particularly bright day of late spring when the last exiles staggered in. They'd come from Barrowby, the final city of the Southern Riding that had been holding out against Scipio Bellorum. Before the Imperial soldiers had driven the assault home, the governor of the city had opened a secret postern gate in the walls, and the civilians, along with an escort of housecarls, had crept out under cover of darkness. Even so, all would have gone badly if they hadn't been picked up by a party of werewolf scouts and led to the safety of Frostmarris.

Thirrin had spent the morning with Oskan, interviewing the exiles and trying to gain every last detail about the Empire's army. But they learned little that was new, and rode back from the refugees' temporary encampment feeling disappointed and worried.

"Bellorum has control of the south now. His rear is secured, and he can march on us whenever he likes," Thirrin said bitterly.

"Nothing different to worry about, then," Oskan answered, determined to offset Thirrin's glum mood by being as optimistic as he could.

"No, I suppose not. Just the usual impossible odds against a general who's never been defeated, and a highly trained, hugely motivated army, against which we're pitting a semi-trained militia. Nothing to worry about at all, really."

Oskan suddenly kicked his legs in frustration, causing Jenny to hiccup in surprise. "Look, the housecarls and the Hypolitan are hardly 'semi-trained militia,' as you put it! The one set battle that's been fought between the Empire and Icemark armies ended in a draw when your father wiped them out just after Yule. And the real half-trained militias defending the cities and the towns of the Southern Riding made such a fight of it, they've delayed Bellorum's campaign by weeks! Just imagine what we can do with our trained army and new allies!"

Thirrin remained quiet as horse and mule walked slowly back toward Frostmarris. Finally she said, "I know you're right. We've got at least half a chance. I just need a place to say what everybody else is saying. And you're it, I'm afraid. And if you ever repeat anything you hear from me, I'll personally cut out your tongue."

She stopped and looked across the plain to the Great Road. "There's another supply train arriving from the north. Come on, I'll race you to it."

Her warhorse thundered off, leaving Oskan standing, but then Jenny leaped forward, taking him by surprise, and galloped after them. The determined mule had almost caught up with Thirrin and her charger when they reined to a halt at the road. Thirrin smiled at Oskan in approval, until she saw him grimly hanging on to Jenny's mane with his eyes squeezed shut.

"I was going to congratulate you on your brilliant horsemanship, but I see all of the credit belongs to your mule."

Jenny brayed loudly in acceptance of the compliment and started to graze on the carpet of wild spring flowers.

Thirrin acknowledged the salutes of the cavalry escort that led the supply train, and watched as it headed for Frostmarris. Then she noticed a small figure sitting in one of the wagons. "Maggie!" she called. "What are you doing here?"

She urged her horse forward and drew up alongside the vehicle, which seemed to be carrying a load of turnips for cattle feed. The old man smiled and waved. "What am I doing here? Well, I'm joining you in preparation for the arrival of the dreaded Scipio Bellorum. Any day now, judging by the werewolf reports."

"And what exactly do you intend to do when he does arrive?"

"Observe, make notes, and prepare to write my history of the war. Somebody has to record the facts for posterity."

"You're convinced it won't be a Polypontian scholar, then?"

"Quite convinced. The alliance will sweep the Empire from the land!"

"Maggie, I do believe you sound rather fierce," said Oskan with a grin.

"I am fierce," the old man replied with energy. "If I were twenty years younger, I'd be fighting alongside Olememnon and reveling in the glory!"

"There's not much glory to be had in killing the young men and women of any country, Maggie," said Thirrin quietly as she remembered the battle in the forest against the Empire's cavalry.

"No," Maggiore agreed. "But there are times when, perhaps, it's best to pretend otherwise. Especially when war has already started, and the most successful and ruthless general ever known is intent on destroying your people and stealing your land."

"You're right, as usual, Maggie. I'm glad you're with us," said Thirrin.

They rode toward the city through a multicolored ocean of spring flowers, the lumbering wagons pitching and rolling over the ruts like flat-bottomed ships.

The next day, one of the last convoys from the north traveled down the Great Road. The engineers waiting to cut the ditches and embankments through its wide paved surface — and so finally close the defensive ring — watched in awe as it passed. Many of the workmen even bowed and called for blessings from the travelers, and some of the younger ones smiled and waved back at the engineers. These were the Witches of the Icemark, answering the call for help from Oskan the Warlock. At their head strode Wenlock Witchmother, still bent double over her staff, but moving along at a tremendous rate; with them lumbered wagons carrying the herbs, medicinal plants, and equipment for the healing part of their deep and intricate craft.

The witches arrived in the city to be greeted by streets lined with soldiers, who watched in silence as they passed. In many ways the arrival of the witches was the real final closing of the defense against the advancing enemy. Usually they were the Wise Women and Cunning Men who worked quietly in their communities, healing the sick and helping with blighted crops and barren animals. They performed the important ceremonies of the turning year and acted as go-betweens who connected the physical and spiritual worlds. But the very fact that they'd been summoned all together somehow confirmed the terrible emergency they all faced.

One or two of the soldiers plucked up enough courage to step forward and present the prettiest and youngest witches with some hastily picked spring flowers, and in return they received brilliant smiles and kisses. But the overwhelming mood was somber. The witches had been called to help the wounded and dying that the coming war would bring, and many of the soldiers couldn't help wondering if they themselves would soon be among their patients.

When they reached the citadel, Oskan was waiting to greet them with Thirrin and Tharaman-Thar. But Wenlock Witchmother seemed interested only in the presence of the warlock, and he soon led the party to their new quarters, a large stable block that had been scrubbed out and converted to an infirmary.

"I feel completely unneeded," said Thirrin in irritable tones after they'd gone. "How many other Queens can expect to be ignored by their own people?"

"They are a little . . . self-contained, these witches, aren't they?" Tharaman answered. "I got the impression that the Witchmother thought I was nothing more than an overgrown palace cat being allowed time off from mousing in the kitchens."

"Thank the Goddess they're better healers than diplomats. Come on, Tharaman, let's go where we're appreciated. I think the unit needs a good shakedown. A gallop over the plain will clear a few cobwebs, and the better we know the ground we'll be fighting on, the greater our chances of success."

Within half an hour the cavalry were making their way

through the city streets, troopers and leopards all singing the battle paean while Tharaman, Thirrin, and Taradan discussed tactics.

On reaching the plain and passing through the defenses, the Thar gave the order to charge and they thundered over the land, the leopards giving the strange coughing bark that was their battle cry. After more than two hours of charging, redressing their lines, wheeling, and breaking and reforming ranks, Thirrin and Tharaman felt their moods lighten. The witches might not consider them to be of any particular importance in the grand scheme of the Goddess's plans, but their leopards and troopers adored them, and even the housecarls and Hypolitan army considered them their greatest military asset.

"Field Marshal Taradan!" the Thar called to his second in command, who in the quiet after the maneuvers was rolling luxuriantly in the color and fragrance of the spring flowers. "Is that really an example of proper military bearing to display before our warriors?"

Taradan immediately leaped to his feet. "No, My Lord! I'm sorry, My Lord!"

The Thar drew himself up to his full height and walked slowly along the line of leopards and mounted troopers, his amber eyes blazing. "Cavalry of the Icemark and the Icesheets. You will at all times follow the orders of your superior officers, human and leopard; you will unquestioningly act on their commands and do so willingly! Do you understand?"

"Yes, Lord Tharaman!" six thousand voices answered.

"Good! Then follow this order: Cavalry! Cavalry, play!" And with that he thundered away over the field of wildflowers, closely chased by Taradan. The rest of the leopards then tumbled and rolled together while their Thar and field marshal wrestled and the human troopers laughed aloud at the sight.

Thirrin watched from her warhorse, completely unable to lower her guard enough to join in. The royal dignity of humans was less easily set aside, and she watched enviously as the Thar jumped around Taradan like a playful kitten. But then something drew her attention away from the leopards. A faint sound, mournful and ghostly, reached her ears. She sat upright. A werewolf message, and sent in daylight when the sound traveled less well. It must be incredibly urgent! Not only that, but all the other Wolf-folk were out on patrol, so only Oskan could interpret it.

Drawing her sword, she stood in her stirrups and gave a shrill war cry that echoed over the field. Immediately silence fell, and the thin keening sound could be heard a little more clearly. "You!" she said, pointing to a leopard that stood nearby. "Go quickly back to the city and tell the Lord Oskan a message is coming in."

The leopard shot away across the plain, while the cavalry reformed ranks and trotted swiftly after. By the time Thirrin and Tharaman had hurried into the Great Hall of the citadel, Oskan and Maggiore were deep in conversation.

"Well?" Thirrin demanded as soon as she saw them.

"Bellorum's on the march. He'll be here in two days," Oskan answered calmly.

"How many in his army?" the Thar asked.

Oskan shook his head and shrugged. "Huge, massive, uncountable. Take your pick. The werewolves say at least five times bigger than the original invading force King Redrought faced, and there's more coming through the pass all the time."

Thirrin quietly sat down on the throne and placed her

hands on the huge carved paws of its arms. "At least five hundred thousand, then. How can we fight such a number? That's not an army; it's an entire country on the march! We need our allies *now*, we need them desperately!"

"We do," Maggie agreed. "But there's no sign of them anywhere. We're going to have to hold Bellorum's army on our own until they get here."

"But will they ever get here, Maggie?"

"Yes," he answered simply. "They will."

25

The city was put on an immediate war footing. Oskan didn't think it was possible for Frostmarris to become any more prepared than it was already, but he was wrong. Regiments trotted through the streets on their way to long-designated points on the ditches and ramparts of the defensive rings. And he constantly had to dodge teams of mules hauling gigantic wheel-mounted crossbows called ballistas as they were maneuvered to different points on the walls, or taken through the gates and down onto the plain as part of the outer batteries. Rockapults, with throwing arms higher than the nearby houses, were also being hauled through the streets, ready to take up their positions in the defense of the city. Armorers' shops rang with the sound of hammers and roared with the din of bellows as production was stepped up, and everywhere messengers bustled backward and forward from plain to walls and from walls to citadel.

The warlock went across to the infirmary and helped the witches to prepare for the coming offensive. The long wards had already been scrubbed spotlessly clean, and in smaller side rooms large tables waited with a grim selection of knives and saws lined up on smaller tables beside them. He wound what seemed like miles of clean bandages and fetched enough buckets of water to float a fleet of war galleys. But then everything went quiet. All was finally ready, and they had only to wait for the arrival of Scipio Bellorum.

After more than two hours of walking around the wards and talking to the witches, Oskan eventually took himself off to the citadel, where a completely unexpected and eerie silence hung over everything. The guards on the gate challenged him for the first time ever, and wouldn't let him in until an officer had verified his identity. At the double doors to the Great Hall another set of guards challenged him but let him through when they saw the mood he was in. No point in antagonizing a warlock when you don't have to.

The massive space beyond the doors was completely empty. Only the day before, Snow Leopards and the royal hunting pack of boar hounds, wolfhounds, and deerhounds had all slept together in a glorious tangle around the central hearth. But now the floor was swept clean of its usual covering of rushes, and the fire had sunk to a glowing bank of embers. Feeling suddenly superstitious, Oskan threw several logs onto the ashes and waited until they'd burst into flames. Then he shouted loud and long until a scullery drudge came along and he gave him clear instructions that the fire was never to be allowed to go out.

After that he strode across the flagstones, reached the dais, and dodged around the throne to the small door that led to the royal apartments. As he walked in, the clatter of weapons echoed across the Great Hall as Thirrin, Tharaman, Elemnestra, and Olememnon, having agreed upon final plans, prepared to take up their positions on the walls and defenses. Maggiore stood in the background furiously taking notes, and servants bustled around bringing last items of equipment and taking messages.

"Ah, Oskan!" Thirrin shouted. "Come with me, we're going up to the walls!" She led the way with Tharaman, while Elemnestra and Olememnon hurried off in a different direction to join their divisions. Oskan fell into step with Maggie, who scurried along in the monarchs' wake like an elderly mouse, and grinned at him. "Still preparing your history?"

The scholar turned eyes that blazed with excitement through his magnifying spectoculums. "Yes! Just imagine, Oskan, my work will be the source material for possibly thousands of learned works down the centuries. If I thought too closely about what I'm recording, I don't think I'd have the nerve to carry on."

"Well, don't think too much, then. Just write."

By this time they'd reached the long flight of stone steps that led to the battlements, and they all ran up to the top. Before them, the open plain lay bathed in brilliant sunshine, its millions of wildflowers a blaze of color beneath the clear blue sky. The long sweep of the defenses could be clearly seen curving from the forest that guarded the northern and western approaches and away out of sight, as it made its long triple circuit of ditch and embankment around the city. And all along its ramparts thousands of soldiers scurried, as tiny as moving grains of sand.

To the east rose the high rocky ground that formed the boundary of the farmland surrounding Frostmarris, and at a distance of two miles the southern limit of the plain was marked by hills that reached up into the sky. It was here that Scipio Bellorum would take his position when he arrived, marching his massive army along the road that led to Frostmarris and its defending forces. To take the rest of the

Icemark, the general of the Polypontian Empire must first defeat Thirrin, her soldiers, and the allies that she had managed to muster so far.

As Oskan looked out across the plain he felt an odd mixing of elation and fear. How long would they need to hang on before their other allies arrived? He'd questioned the werewolf scouts several times, but all they could or would say was that the mustering of the Wolf-folk took a long time. And as for the Vampires . . . well, they were a law unto themselves.

Then, as his eyes traveled along the ribbon of road to the south, he caught a faint glitter on the horizon. He drew breath sharply. At the same time a great clamor of howling broke out as the werewolf scouts, who'd all now returned to Frostmarris, announced the first sighting of the enemy.

An odd baying and jeering arose from the soldiers as they watched the faint metallic glitter on the horizon grow into the recognizable form of a massive army. Soon it was possible to make out ranks of the pike phalanx, made up of soldiers who carried sixteen-foot-long spears. Behind them marched countless numbers of musketeers; the ordinary foot soldiers of the infantry, armed with shield and sword, came next; and farther back still, on the very edge of sight, came the cavalry.

After a while the sound of shrill pipes and drums playing marching tunes grew and wavered on the wind, until eventually the air pulsated and rattled with the rhythm of the military band. The music was intended to intimidate the enemy, but Thirrin had an answer for this. Turning to a soldier behind her she gave a quick command, and the sound of a bugle rang out.

Oskan looked out over the walls to see what would happen. At first he was disappointed; all he could see were the defending soldiers staring at the arriving Polypontian troops. But then he caught sight of Elemnestra and her regiment of mounted archers trotting swiftly along the path that wound its way through the barriers of the defenses and out on to the plain. As the last of the female archers trotted through the narrow offset gap that was covered by an overlapping embankment, a party of soldiers repositioned the barrier of sharpened stakes that blocked it.

At a signal from Elemnestra, her regiment leaped to the gallop, and Oskan watched as in one fluid motion each of the troopers drew an arrow and fitted it to the string of her compound bow. A great shout rose up from the watching defenders as they thundered away toward the advancing army, and soon the brilliant colors of their embroidered jackets and caps made it look as though a field of flowers had taken up arms in the fight against the Empire.

As they approached the vanguard of the enemy, they swiftly altered course and, riding parallel to the pike phalanx, they loosed a rain of arrows. Immediately gaps appeared in the ranks as Polypontian soldiers crumpled to the ground, but before they could react, another flight of arrows cut into them and more men fell.

Elemnestra then signaled her archers to alter course and the regiment thundered down on the military band, silencing drum and fife with just one devastating pass. The musketeers fired in reply, rank after rank of guns sending a volley of lead shot at the regiment of mounted archers, but they'd already galloped out of range. Rapidly turning again, the Hypolitan charged down on the musketeers, who were still struggling to reload their weapons, and sent another savage hail of arrows into them, killing almost three hundred soldiers.

Again and again, Elemnestra and her archers swept down on the steadily advancing army, killing and killing, but still the Polypontians advanced, as unstoppable as the sea. The soldiers on the defenses around the city cheered and called encouragement, but gradually they fell silent as they began to realize that even a weapon as effective as the Hypolitan archers couldn't stop the Empire's advance. There were just too many of them, and this, combined with their superb discipline and unwavering courage in the face of such deadly marksmanship, made them truly formidable.

Music was once again rattling and shrilling over the plain as a band was sent up the ranks to replace those who'd been killed. But when Elemnestra swept down to wipe them out once more, she suddenly signaled to abort the attack and swerved by to loose her arrows into the ranks of the following infantry. Her close pass had shown her that most of the drummers were only boys, their faces set and determined, ready to die in their Empire's wars.

For almost an hour the archers attacked the vanguard of the Polypontian army, but then Elemnestra turned and led her regiment from the field; their arrows had run out and their horses were snorting and foaming with exhaustion. First blood had been drawn by the defenders, but Scipio Bellorum was always content to allow the enemy a little killing just as long as he struck the final blow. The soldiers watching from the defenses cheered the women as they trotted back to the city, but the cries rang hollow. What should have been a success for the defenders and a devastating strike against the Empire had been neither of these things. The Polypontians had effectively proved their overwhelming power, and at the same time the Icemark had been shown how futile their attempts to defend their small land really were.

Up on the battlements, Thirrin brooded: This was the reality of war with the Empire. They could afford to lose literally thousands of soldiers, because there were always more to call to the front. In the first hour Elemnestra and her archers had killed almost the same number as a quarter of Thirrin's entire defending army, and that represented only a tiny fraction of the enemy's vanguard. She watched now as the Polypontian standard was raised on the southern hills. Already their engineers were digging trenches to protect their front line, and wooden planking was being laid down to create firing platforms for their cannons.

"Tomorrow will be the test," she said quietly.

"Tomorrow will probably be the biggest test," said Tharaman-Thar. "If they fight like the Ice Trolls, they'll throw everything into the attack in the hope of ending us quickly. If we can survive that, they'll settle down into a more regular, sustainable fight, and we can hope to hang on until our allies arrive."

Thirrin felt the first whisperings of doubt about the Wolf-folk and Vampire armies ever arriving, but in the interest of morale she said nothing. Turning, she beckoned to a staff officer. "Send orders to dismount the cavalry. They'll fight on the ramparts under my and the Thar's joint command." The officer saluted and hurried away.

"I suggest we all get some rest," Tharaman said. "Who knows when we'll be able to sleep peacefully again?"

"One of the few advantages of age is the need for less sleep," said Maggie, who stood nearby. "I think I'll go down to the stables and see if I can get one of Elemnestra's stern young warrior women to talk to me. There's nothing like a firsthand account for clarity in historical narrative."

"As you wish," said Thirrin and, beckoning to Oskan, she and Tharaman made their way down to the royal apartments.

26

Scipio Bellorum arrived the next morning. By this time the Polypontian camp had been established, with streets of tents laid out in their usual grid pattern and every regiment in its allotted place. Wherever the general campaigned, the encampment was always set out in the same way. The routine was also always identical, with half of the army arriving first to establish its position and beat off any resistance. Some units would then man defensive outposts in case the enemy was suicidal enough to attempt an attack, and the rest would parade in their finest to welcome the general, who arrived once everything was ready.

So it was that Bellorum himself led the second half of the army into camp as usual, riding among his staff officers and making himself immediately identifiable as the only one without an elaborately plumed hat, his close-cropped gray hair glinting like steel in the spring sunshine. His armor was gilded and etched with intricate patterns of ferns and birds in flight, but his boots were the plain black of a cavalry trooper. This was the general's trademark, a mixing of the flamboyant and the ordinary.

The cheering from the soldiers who lined the central road of the tent city was enthusiastic and genuine. This was the man whose tactics had saved countless Polypontian lives in the Empire's wars. Every soldier loved a general who made his life easier and safer. But it was also sensible to give a full and proper show of your appreciation when the general arrived in camp. His eyes were sharp and he was a stickler for detail; a sloppy turnout could mean twenty lashes, and any lack of enthusiasm for his leadership could mean your regiment found itself in the most dangerous part of the battle or storming the most strongly held walls.

He had a precise memory, too. Once, during a particularly difficult campaign in the hot lands of the southern Empire, a soldier had been a little slow in saluting as Bellorum rode past. Nothing happened until the battle had been won and the campaign victoriously completed, then Bellorum gave the exact regiment, rank, and personal insignia of the soldier and inquired whether he'd survived the wars. When he was told that he had, the general had him paraded in front of his unit and he was whipped, demoted, and transferred to another regiment.

Bellorum's reputation preceded him with a threat of the strictest possible discipline and a promise of the greatest obtainable victory. He was loved and feared in almost equal measure by his men, but fear had the edge. It was said his soldiers would do anything for him. It was also said that they wouldn't dare do otherwise.

After inspecting the regiments, he dismissed them, but not before he'd had two men flogged for their poor turnout and rewarded three others with promotion for their gallantry during the winter campaign. He dismounted and walked slowly across to his tent, which was pitched, as usual, on the edge of the camp facing the enemy position. His staff officers clustered around him like eager and frightened children, but Commander Titus Aurelius seemed the most worried.

Bellorum entered his tent, sat at the table that stood in the center of the richly carpeted floor, then raised the index finger of his right hand. Immediately the canvas wall that looked out over the plain toward Frostmarris was drawn up and they all scrutinized their latest target.

"The capital of the Icemark, gentlemen. When it falls, the land is ours." He spoke quietly, in a tone that suggested he was about to laugh. "Commander Aurelius. I hear that you met with resistance when establishing the camp."

"Yes, sir. Mounted archers, women. Shockingly fine shots."

"Casualties?"

"Three thousand, sir. Two thousand musketeers, one thousand pike. Oh, and a military band."

"Well, we can't have that, can we? We'll have to see what we can do to put a stop to them."

"Yes, sir."

"What were their casualty figures?"

"Er, none, sir."

"None?"

"That's right, sir," Commander Aurelius replied, a faint dew of sweat making his upper lip shine.

"I see. What action was taken against them?"

"The muskets returned fire, but they skipped out of range, as it were."

"Then skipped back in again to kill more of my men?"

"Yes, sir."

"No cavalry was sent in pursuit?"

"Their shooting rate was phenomenal, and I didn't want to risk any more men than was necessary."

"Very commendable, Commander Aurelius. So what *exactly* finally drove them from the field?"

"Er . . . they seemed to run out of arrows, sir."

"So, lack of ammunition was more effective than any of our highly trained soldiers. Is that right, Commander?"

Aurelius looked supremely uncomfortable but eventually said, "They wouldn't have dared to attack us if we'd been dug into proper positions. They took advantage of the fact that we weren't ready for them."

"Well, well, what a revolutionary concept. An enemy that takes advantage of an army's weaknesses. Whatever next? Perhaps they'll even try to kill us. What shall we do?" The general's voice was light and playful, but the officers around the table had fallen completely silent. None of them wanted to distract Bellorum's attention from Commander Aurelius; after all, he might recall some of *their* shortcomings.

Bellorum stood up and, motioning his staff officers to remain seated, he strolled to the open wall of the tent and looked out at Frostmarris riding like a huge stone ship on a sea of brilliant wildflowers. "Perhaps I'm being a little unfair, Aurelius. We all of us know that these people are as tough as boiled leather. Our casualties in taking the cities of the Icemark have never been higher, and no sieges have ever been so long and drawn out. And here on this plain we're not facing a half-trained militia, but a Royal Army of the House of Strong-in-the-Arm. What an incredible addition they'll make to the ranks of the Imperial forces, once we've killed their Queen, of course."

The staff officers visibly relaxed as the general seemed to have forgiven the casualty rate of the previous day. "I've ordered an additional four full-sized armies to be sent from the Polypontus." He turned and smiled at the murmurs that greeted this statement. "Oh yes, I know. Three Imperial armies are usually more than enough to conquer new territory, no matter how large. But I'm afraid, gentlemen, that this little land has already stretched us to capacity. So watch and learn; a good general is never too proud to acknowledge the strength of the enemy. The Icemark has been underestimated by our tacticians and logistical experts, but I will put that right."

He walked back to the table and sat down. "With this in mind, I intend to open proceedings tomorrow with a full-scale assault by the Red Army, with the Black Army in support." He waited quietly until the burst of conversation died down. "Now, I know this is a little unconventional and that the White and Blue armies usually deepen their experience of warfare in these opening assaults, *but*, as I've already said, these people are tough, and I, for one, am completely resolved not to underestimate them. The Reds have the experience necessary to face such martial ability. And be aware of this, gentlemen: I want to be through those outer defenses by tomorrow evening and besieging the walls of Frostmarris itself by nightfall. And you, Commander Aurelius, will lead the first assault."

The commander saluted briskly. "It will be an honor, General."

"I'm *so* glad you see it that way," Bellorum replied smoothly. Then he said, "Right, down to reports. What can you tell me about their dispositions?"

Maps and charts were quickly laid out on the table, and Aurelius stood up to point out details. "Well, sir, they have their artillery positioned at several points around their perimeter. Nothing to worry about, just primitive ballistas and trebuchets, and they have their housecarls and units of the fyrd positioned equally around the defensive embankments. There is one odd thing, though. Our scouts have reported seeing giant leopards on the defenses, too. They must be tame, because they seem to be completely unrestrained, and the largest of them all is the constant companion of the young Queen."

"Giant leopards, eh? Well, I shouldn't imagine they'll be fighting tomorrow. Perhaps when we've captured the city, we can send some to the Imperial Zoo," Bellorum said, smiling softly as his officers laughed.

At dawn Thirrin and Tharaman-Thar led their dismounted cavalry down to the defenses out on the plain. The streets of Frostmarris had been alive with the noises of preparation: shouted orders, tramping feet, the clink of weapons and armor. Many of the housecarls seemed almost happy — elated, even — laughing and joking as though they were off on some exciting trip. But Thirrin felt sick with fear and kept her voice low whenever she spoke, in case she betrayed herself with a quaver or tremble.

She and Tharaman had left Oskan and Maggiore in the courtyard of the citadel, and she'd even allowed herself to hug them both, her face set in the rigid mask of martial resolve. Oskan had held her hand for a few seconds longer than was strictly necessary, and she had to steel herself not to snatch it back in front of her soldiers. But then they'd turned and marched away through the streets.

Tharaman sensed her emotional turmoil and said quietly, "Don't be fooled by this excitement the housecarls are showing. They're just relieved to be doing something after waiting and training for so long. If any allowed themselves time to think, they'd probably be terrified."

Thirrin merely nodded in reply but ran her hands deep into his thick fur.

"I suppose they're following the age-old trick of mentally running through training drills and remembering the commands of attack. I know it always calms me down," the Thar went on.

"Do you need to?" she asked incredulously.

"Oh yes. Anyone who goes into battle without fear must either be froth-at-the-mouth mad or drunk as a troll."

Thirrin grinned despite herself. "And are you running through your drills now?"

"Close ranks; brace for onset; wheel your battle to the right; wheel your battle to the left; advance; stand; withdraw. I know them all by heart."

"You old fraud," she said, and laughed, all of her tension blissfully melting away as the sound of her laughter raised itself over the rooftops and rippled through the streets.

The nearby soldiers spontaneously beat swords and axes on their shields in acknowledgment of the lucky omen, and cheers rose from the troopers and leopards of her dismounted cavalry.

Once down on the plain, Thirrin and Tharaman led their regiment to where they'd calculated the first attack would begin. The white Wolf-folk, under the command of their huge leader, were already in position and greeted the arrival of the Queen with a tumbling cacophony of howls. Thirrin smiled in acknowledgment and looked out toward the Empire's camp. Something was obviously about to happen: Bugles could just be heard, and huge blocks of soldiers were milling around in a chaos that Thirrin knew was meticulously organized.

After a few moments a small party of Polypontian horsemen rode out carrying a flag of truce, and the defenders waited quietly as they approached. Their dark red uniforms glittered in the brilliant sunshine, so that the Imperial troops looked like droplets of blood trickling over the wildflowers of the plain. When they were within earshot of the palisades they stopped, and a single horseman rode a few paces farther forward. Two buglers then sounded a fanfare, and as they fell silent the powerful voice of the Imperial herald rose into the air.

"In the name of the Emperor Tristus Angellius Lycurnum of the House of Cicero, I bring now the terms of your surrender as designated by General Scipio Bellorum of the Imperial armies. You will lay down your arms and submit to the will of the Empire and give into our keeping Thirrin Lindenshield, styled 'Queen' of this insignificant land. The slavery of your independence is at an end, and the freedom of your servitude to the Empire has begun. Accept now your fate and your warriors will be allowed to fight in the Emperor's future wars, and your people will live as citizens within his newly made borders. But if you refuse these terms, you will die, your lands will be razed, and your people enslaved, and the name of the Icemark will be wiped from the face of the earth forever."

The herald fell silent and waited with quiet arrogance for the reply. Thirrin looked around her until she saw the smallest, dirtiest drummer boy. She beckoned to him, and when he stamped to attention before her, she stooped and whispered in his ear. He saluted and turned to face the herald.

"My Queen says she won't waste her voice on you, but tells me to deliver this reply." He paused dramatically, stuck his thumb to his nose, and blew a very loud raspberry.

The herald nodded once, curtly, and the horsemen turned around and trotted back to their lines. The formalities over, the fighting could begin.

All movement in the enemy camp had ceased as the regiments had taken up their positions and were waiting quietly for orders. Then, suddenly, several teams of horses burst away and galloped across the plain toward the city.

The battle for Frostmarris had finally begun. Thirrin drew a deep breath and they all waited grimly. As the enemy horsemen approached, it was clear that they were hauling cannons. Thirrin ordered her artillery to stop them from establishing a new battery position, and immediately her ballistas fired a volley of giant steel bolts into the Polypontian gun teams. The rockapults followed, with a bombardment of graded rocks that were flung high into the air before arcing downward to smash into the gun carriages. The bombardment continued for ten minutes or so until their captains ordered a cessation. Before the cannons could fire a single shot, they'd been destroyed, and a huge cheer erupted from the defenders.

But they didn't have long to celebrate; Scipio Bellorum ordered the experienced troops of the Red Army to advance, and they came on singing. Musket, pike, and shield-bearers marched forward in vast numbers. Longbow men from the East Riding of the Icemark waited until the enemy was within four hundred yards of the first defensive embankment before loosing a hail of arrows. They fell from the sky like hundreds of hawks stooping on their prey, and the Empire soldiers dropped in appalling numbers. But still they advanced and still they sang, never wavering despite the added assault from the ballistas and rockapults. Their drums rattled out a stirring rhythm and shrill pipes set the pace. At their head an officer in a hugely plumed hat raised his sword, and the musket lines halted — they were in range at last, and they presented arms and fired a salvo. The first casualties of the defenders fell as the solid lead musket balls smashed into their lines. But the enemy had little time to celebrate as the shooting rate of the Icemark's archers increased and they concentrated particularly on the musketeers.

The Polypontian officer raised his sword again and the advance continued, the massively tall spears of the pikemen lowering into the engage position, the brightly honed metal heads glittering viciously in the spring sunshine. Then the enemy's commander threw back his head and gave a great shout, his soldiers yelled in reply, and they charged.

Thirrin's voice also rose above the din. In reply, drummer boys and girls all along the defenses rattled out their own fighting rhythm. Tharaman-Thar reared and roared, and his warriors answered, sending out a great wall of animal noise. Then the enemy was upon them.

For the briefest moment the Polypontian line wavered as the soldiers realized that the Snow Leopards were fighting alongside the human defenders. But then the Empire officers raised their swords and strode forward to meet the new threat, drawing the ranks of the army with them. Polypontian soldiers had fought before this against beasts with tusks and trunks that stood as high as houses. Fighting leopards were just one more wonder to add to their experience.

The housecarls locked their shields, and the crescendo of onset rolled out over the plain. Thirrin strode forward, her sword swinging in huge shattering arcs, and the Thar struck out again and again with his massive claws. Longbows and the compound bows of Elemnestra's regiment continued to rain devastation down on the enemy, while Olememnon and his infantry hacked and chopped at the enemy front with their axes. Some of the braver defenders forced their way through the menacing barrier of pikes to hack at the soldiers wielding them.

For fully half an hour the struggle continued with neither side giving ground, but then the massive numbers of the Empire's army began to tell, and slowly the defenders were pushed back. Step by step, they were borne irresistibly down into the ditch of the first embankment, then slowly up the slope of the second. For an hour the defenders held the ridge of the second embankment, but once again the sheer weight of numbers began to tell and they were forced back, contesting every foot of ground. Desperately Thirrin called out orders to hold, but still the enemy came on, hacking and killing as they advanced.

Then she suddenly grabbed at Tharaman's dense fur and climbed onto his shoulders, and holding her sword aloft she gave the war cry of the House of Strong-in-the-Arm, her voice as high and fierce as a hunting hawk's: "Blood! Blast! And Fire! Blood! Blast! And Fire! Hold them, soldiers of the Icemark! Hold them, Host of the Hypolitan! Hold them, Leopards of the Icesheets and White Wolf-folk of King Grishmak! Blood! Blast! And Fire!"

Her voice rose high and pure above the raging din of the battle, and immediately her soldiers drove their feet deep into the ground beneath them, locked their shields, and refused to give another inch. The Thar and his warrior-leopards roared out a ferocious challenge and smote all before them with terrible savagery, and the werewolves howled in a bloodcurdling chorus as they smashed at the lines of spears before them. Gradually, with a barely noticeable movement forward, the line started to straighten. Slowly, slowly, the soldiers of the Icemark and the Hypolitan redressed their position, while the youngsters on the drums beat out a relentless rhythm, sweat streaming down their faces. The banners of the housecarls slowly inched forward as over and over they bawled out a fighting chant: "Thirrin-Thar, Thirrin-Thar, Thirrin-Thar."

Beneath their feet the ground was slick with blood. Several housecarls fell, to be hacked where they lay, but the tide was slowly turning and the experienced warriors of the Red Army were being pushed back. Thirrin continued to fight from the Thar's shoulders, hacking and chopping at the enemy as he struck out with the devastating power of his paws or dropped forward to use his enormous teeth.

After another hour of fighting, the allies regained the crest of the first embankment. Before them the enemy still swarmed and still pushed on, singing their war anthems. But their numbers were much reduced. Out on the plain, the supporting Black Army seemed to be preparing to join in, but they didn't move forward, and now that the Hypolitan archers had a clear firing platform, they began again to rain arrows down on the Empire's troops. The enemy was taking terrible losses, but still they came on, until finally their commanding officer raised his sword and they started to withdraw in good order.

The archers, and now the ballistas and rockapults, continued to bombard them, and when the defenders turned their attention to the Black Army, the enemy finally conceded the field and retreated, their drums and fife still playing bravely.

Thirrin climbed slowly down from Tharaman's shoulders and hugged him in relief and elation as they watched the enemy march back to their camp. But when she looked out at the dead and dying, tears ran down her face. "We can't take losses like that again, Tharaman."

"Neither can they, my dear. Neither can they," he answered wearily, cleaning the blood from his huge paws. "And I can assure you they won't risk it again, either. If they're anything like the Ice Trolls, they would have expected us to fold under the ferocity of their first attack, and as we didn't, they'll show us much more respect in the future. From now on, General Bellorum will show prudence and no doubt display some of his brilliant tactical skills."

"Then we'd better be ready for him, Tharaman."

Scipio Bellorum followed the progress of the battle through his telescopic monocular. He was still seething with anger about the destruction of his cannon by what Commander Aurelius had called "primitive artillery," but he was sure he would be revenged by a swift victory for his Red Army. He could clearly see his troops advancing in their usual overwhelming surge, and he could also see the young Queen standing among her troops on the first embankment. This surprised him at first, but then he remembered he was dealing with a barbaric race of people who expected their leaders to stand with them in battle. He was also amazed to see quite so many of the reported giant leopards, as well as one or two other creatures that looked like hideously deformed bears, standing among the defenders, but he couldn't quite bring himself to believe they would fight. And if the barbaric Queen really thought that troops of the Empire could be intimidated by wild animals, then she had a shocking lesson to learn.

The roar of onset reached his ears a second after he saw it happen through his monocular. And immediately he was forced to revise his belief that the animals wouldn't fight.

"How absolutely marvelous," he said aloud. "What a wonderful addition they will be to the Imperial army."

For the next three hours he watched the battle, impatient for his troops to deliver the knockout blow that would send the defenders streaming back to their city. But it never happened.

He was about to give the order to send in the Black Army, the towering elite of his entire force, but something stopped him. As he watched the defenders forcing his troops back down onto the plain, he had the sudden premonition that if he committed his support units, they, too, would be defeated, and such a loss would be too much for his men's morale. Better by far to withdraw and prepare for battle the next day. He considered himself a patient man, and he was quite prepared to whittle away at the Icemark's strength until they were ripe for the final blow. He gave the order to pull back, his face a careful mask of unconcern.

He almost believed himself, but not quite. A niggling doubt on the very edge of his conscious mind continued to annoy him even as he mounted his horse and prepared to meet his soldiers as they returned from the field. His officers followed at a respectful distance, their faces as blank as Bellorum's. Wounded soldiers were being ferried to the hospital tents while their comrades were paraded before the dreaded figure of their general. A near-perfect hush descended on them; only the ragged breathing of exhausted men challenged the fearful quiet.

"Soldiers of the Empire, you fought well against a determined and, may I add, desperate enemy," said Bellorum in a voice that was warm and encouraging. "However, you were led by incompetents, with little martial spirit and no flair for leadership. Commander Aurelius, step forward."

The officer stepped out into the enormous silence and stood to attention.

"Explain your actions."

Aurelius looked up at the general as a sudden gust of wind brought the scent of crushed wildflowers into his nostrils. Breathing deeply he relaxed, amazingly, and said clearly, "I lost a battle against superb soldiers and an army of giant leopards."

"Have you nothing more to add?" Bellorum asked in dangerously quiet tones.

Aurelius had heard the general interrogating others who had failed in battle, and he knew exactly the tone that would condemn a man to the firing squad. He heard it now. Realizing he no longer needed caution, he spoke his mind. "I lost a battle for the first time in my career, but I feel no shame. The soldiers of the Icemark are worthy opponents who outfought one of our strongest armies. I fully understand that I will suffer the supreme penalty for failure, but I would caution the general: If you continue to execute your experienced officers, you will soon have none to lead your men or carry out your orders." A gasp rose up from the ranks of tired soldiers. None had ever spoken to the general in this way before. "I would also add that I truly believe that if the general himself had led the attack, the result would have been the same. And, I would respectfully inquire, who then would be the executioner?"

The silence that followed was so complete that the movement of troops on the defenses around Frostmarris could clearly be heard.

At last, Bellorum spoke.

"You're a brave man, Commander Aurelius, and because of this your family will receive the full rewards and rights of the fallen veteran, and your execution will be swift."

Then Scipio drew the pistols from the holsters on his saddle and shot him.

27

The noise was dreadful. Wounded soldiers were screaming, and witches shouting to one another so that they could be heard. But worse still was the smell: blood and body parts not meant to be exposed to the light of day, and over even that, urine and feces as soldiers lost control of their functions in the face of unimaginable pain and fear. Oskan helped one of the healers to stop a severed artery in a soldier's leg from spurting its precious contents all over the floor. Nearby, a young drummer boy with a dreadful stomach wound, inflicted by a spear, managed to smile as the poppy mixture one of the witches had given him started to work. Later, Oskan helped her to mix enough to keep him unconscious until he died.

There were wounded leopards and werewolves, too, their huge bodies needing many new calculations for drug and potion doses as the healers stitched and cleaned their wounds or helped them to the Goddess's peace.

Wenlock Witchmother stood in the middle of the stable ward watching all around her, giving strength to her people as they fought to save as many lives as they could. Meanwhile, out in the smaller side wards where the surgeons worked, impossibly damaged limbs were amputated with incredible speed as the rough morphine of poppy kept the pain and shock at bay. Blood was everywhere, swimming across the floors, spurting over the walls and even the ceilings in bright crimson swathes. Yet in all this chaos, lives were being saved, and those beyond treatment were helped to peace with the herbs and drugs the witches had prepared.

For more than ten hours the witches, warlocks, and the few doctors considered skilled enough to help labored to reconstruct the bodies and lives that had been shattered by their first engagement with the Polypontians. But at last all that could be done was finished, and a peace descended on the wards. The wounded lay on clean mattresses along the walls, under the watchful eyes of healers who walked quietly around, while out in the treatment areas, teams of cleaners started to scrub away the blood and filth in readiness for those who would inevitably follow.

Finally Oskan left, taking his leave from a quiet Wenlock, who merely nodded when he said good-bye and told her he'd be back the next day. He almost ran from the converted stable block that was the infirmary and out across the yard of the citadel.

Outside, the area was full of jubilant housecarls, leopards, and other soldiers who were busy celebrating the victory. Campfires were dotted at regular intervals across the cobblestones, and Oskan had to dodge from one group to the next, all of whom wanted to tell him about the battle. But at last he reached the doors of the Great Hall and was admitted by the housecarl guards. Oskan already knew that Thirrin and Tharaman were safe, but he still wanted to see them and talk with them, so he hurried across the wide flagstones of the hall and quickly dodged around the throne and through the door into the royal private rooms. Inside, Thirrin was sitting quietly with Primplepuss on her lap, while Tharaman lay sprawled in front of the fire like a huge lumpy hearthrug. Maggiore Totus was busily scribbling away at his notes, adding more to his history of the war and straining to make himself heard as he tried to question Thirrin over the cavernous snores and grunts of the sleeping Tharaman.

Thirrin stood up when she saw Oskan, depositing an annoyed Primplepuss into the deep fur of the Snow Leopard King. "Where have you been?" she snapped. "I've been waiting here for hours and not even a message."

"I'm sorry," Oskan replied quietly. "But when a soldier's work is finished, a healer's is often only just beginning. Those who could be saved are resting now, and those who couldn't have been helped gently on their way."

"Oh," Thirrin said. "I'm sorry, Oskan, I forgot. Selfish of me."

"No. You're just tired, like everyone else. Perhaps we should join Tharaman by the fire."

She smiled gently. "No room, I'm afraid."

Primplepuss started to struggle her way out of the Snow Leopard's thick fur, and he awoke with an enormous snort.

"Ah! Oskan, how are my wounded warriors?"

"Fine, most of them. Just deep flesh wounds, really. They should be back on duty within a week. Only one has died. Another is giving us real worries. Turadon, he said his name was, before we managed to put him under with some poppy. He has a punctured lung and broken ribs, but I think we'll get him back from the brink."

"Good! Good!" the Thar boomed, stretching luxuriously and filling the room with his massive bulk.

"Tharaman, now that you're awake, I'd like your perspective on the battle," said Maggiore earnestly, his stylus poised over the wax-covered boards he used for his notes.

"Um . . . perhaps later, Maggie. At the moment I'm so hungry I could eat a whole herd of caribou." He turned to Thirrin. "Shall we see if dinner's ready?"

"I don't think it will be, but we can go out into the hall and hurry things along a little."

"Good idea," he said eagerly, and led the way.

As they emerged from the royal quarters they could see the servants setting up the trestle tables that would seat the housecarls and leopards who were not on duty at the defenses. Everything was noise and bustle, but around the central hearth two figures sat quietly, seemingly unaware of the activities around them. As Thirrin and her party approached they could see that it was Elemnestra and Olememnon sitting next to each other on a simple bench. They were quiet, and the Basilea was leaning against her consort, while he rested his huge hand on her knee.

Maggie coughed diplomatically, and Elemnestra sat bolt upright and removed Olememnon's hand. "I'm sorry, Your Majesty, we were a little tired."

"There's no need to apologize, Aunt. We're all tired," Thirrin answered quietly.

"Got your notes with you, I see, Maggie," Olememnon said, and grinned hugely. "Who's for a grilling next?"

"Well, *you,* if you're amenable."

"Hungry work, talking to you. After dinner, perhaps."

"Oh, very well." The little scholar sighed and sat next to him on the bench.

"Don't keep him up too late, Maggiore Totus," said Elemnestra. "He's got a battle to fight tomorrow, no doubt, and you'll have me to answer to if he's made slow through lack of sleep."

"Rather than risk your displeasure, Madam, I will allow your consort a night of peace," Maggie replied with a deep bow.

Elemnestra looked at him, trying to decide whether or not he was being sarcastic, but in the end she decided he was beneath her dignity and she ignored him.

"The wine's good, Maggie," said Olememnon, raising a flask that had stood by his feet. "Here, have some. You, too, Tharaman, find a bowl."

A servant brought an extra cup and a bowl and soon all three were drinking deeply. "Not too much," Elemnestra said, placing her hand over her consort's. "You must have a clear head tomorrow, I want no . . . injuries because you're wine-fuddled."

He smiled at her affectionately and, despite her protests, kissed her cheek. "I'll be fine, we're eating soon, and I intend to scoff enough to soak up a barrel of booze."

By the time the food arrived, the hall had filled up with warriors of all three races, though the numbers were noticeably fewer as most of the army was on guard, patrolling the barricades down on the plain. As promised, Olememnon ate an enormous amount, beaten only by Tharaman-Thar, who ate an entire ox, bones and all. He sat with a hugely distended belly, groaning slightly, but still found enough room to lap up another three bowls of wine, after which he started to purr loudly.

"Such a pity that grape bushes won't grow in the snows," he said sadly. "I'd be more than happy to set up a wine yard on the Icesheets."

"*Vines*, Tharaman, grape bushes are called vines," said Maggie in his best teacher's voice.

"Vines, then. Are you sure there's no hardy variety that could stand the cold?"

"Certain."

"You'll have to set up an importing company, Maggie," said Oskan. "You'd make a comfortable living out of Tharaman alone."

"Perhaps I will. My fortune would soon be made."

"Not from Olememnon, it wouldn't," said Elemnestra. "He's had more than enough and he's about to go to bed."

"Is he?" asked Olememnon in surprise.

"Yes," his wife answered and, taking his hand, she bowed to Thirrin and Tharaman, ignored Maggie and Oskan, and walked from the hall. Olememnon waved and smiled as he was led off, and Tharaman muttered into his bowl as he lapped his wine.

"What was that?" Thirrin asked him.

"I said, that woman's about as much fun as a toothache. And she treats Olememnon like a servant."

"Oh, I don't think he minds too much. In fact, I think he's as happy as any man in the land," she answered.

"I can't imagine why," said Tharaman, licking the last drops from his bowl.

"Can't you? I'd have thought it was pretty obvious. They love each other."

"Oh, that! Yes, well, I dare say they do, but that's no reason to treat him like he can't think for himself."

"It's just her way of showing she cares," said Thirrin. "Oskan, you should get some sleep now. It's going to be a very long day tomorrow."

Scipio Bellorum again followed the progress of the battle through his telescopic monoculum. As usual, his army was following his orders to the letter and was attacking the defenses at three different points over a two-mile front. They'd been fighting for more than an hour now, and he thought he could detect a weakening of the central assault just as he had instructed. He smiled and turned his monoculum to the left and then to the right wing of the attack, and noted with pleasure that their fighting rate had increased.

For the next two hours the central assault continued to weaken, while the left and right wings gradually increased the pressure on the defenders and, as Bellorum had hoped, Thirrin sent more and more of her best troops from the center to the wings in an attempt to strengthen them.

"There's my good little tactician," he murmured as he watched the housecarls and Hypolitan infantry hurrying to the threatened sections of the defenses. "Commanders Anthonius and Hadrian, prepare your troops and wait for my orders!" he snapped crisply to the group of staff officers who clustered nearby. The two men saluted and hurried off.

"Now, where is that devil-woman and her mounted archers? I'm waiting for you, my dear. Everything is ready."

The battle raged on, more and more Polypontian troops pouring in to maintain the pressure on the wings, and more and more of the allies' best fighters in the center being drawn off to help.

Just three units of housecarls remained at the point where the Empire's attack was apparently failing, along with ten thousand inexperienced soldiers of the fyrd. More than enough to hold off the Polypontian assault, which seemed to be fading with every passing minute. But the old housecarl commander was uncomfortable about the situation. He was beginning to think there was something suspicious about the way the regiments of pike and musketeers seething around the slope of the defenses before him were unable to push forward. He gave orders for his soldiers to hold their position and not be drawn out. Then he sent his second in command with some of his best housecarls to shore up his right, where there were mainly fyrd soldiers. Gunhilda was the best second he'd ever had. She'd once held off an attack by more than five hundred werewolves with only half as many housecarls and brought most of her command back alive. But that was in the bad old days, and this time, it looked as though the Empire's troops were getting ready to run.

"Hold your positions," the commander shouted, but his words were drowned as the Polypontian troops before him turned and fled. With a wild yell the soldiers of the fyrd broke ranks and chased after them, leaving only the thousand housecarls maintaining their shield-wall.

Cursing loudly, the commander ordered his few remaining troops to spread out in an attempt to plug the gap in the line, then he sent an urgent message to Thirrin.

Bellorum was pleased. So far everything was going according to plan; now he needed help from good luck and chance, a general's two best friends. "Captain Aeneas, prepare your teams and await orders." He turned in his saddle and calmly beckoned to two riders who were waiting nearby. They galloped away with their messages, and soon two encircling arms of the Imperial troops started to advance onto the plain, while in the center, the soldiers of the fyrd continued to chase the retreating Polypontian army straight into the trap.

"Come along, my dear, react as you should, there's a good little Queen," muttered Bellorum as he scanned the Icemark's defensive positions before him. "Your soldiers are in danger, they'll need to be rescued by something fast and deadly — like mounted archers."

The shrill squeal of fife and the metallic rattle of drums leading both encircling arms of the pincer movement were intended to signal the position of the advancing soldiers, just in case Thirrin and her army hadn't noticed them. Bellorum was wondering ironically if he needed to add a firework display, when a movement drew his monoculum to the earthworks of the defenses.

"Aha! There she is, right on cue and, if I'm not mistaken, she's with that oaf of a consort of hers," Bellorum said happily as the Basilea led out her mounted archers and the Hypolitan infantry on their rescue mission. "Now, which wing will she take?" Suddenly the archers galloped away, and Olememnon led his infantry at a swift trot in the opposite direction. Bellorum nodded. "The right! Captain Aeneas, you will lead your teams to the right!"

Out on the plain, Elemnestra sent a rider to warn the fyrd troops of their danger and led the rest of her archers to intercept the advancing right wing of the enemy. She would engage them before Olememnon and his infantry even reached the left arm of the pincer movement. Then if she wiped out her target quickly, she could gallop back across the plain to his aid.

On her signal, the women of her troop fitted the first arrows to their bowstrings in one fluid movement. Ahead, Elemnestra could clearly see the enemy advancing and hear the fife and drums of their band. As the Hypolitan archers thundered down on them, the enemy soldiers leveled their muskets and waited grimly. Elemnestra swung around to sweep past, and the musketeers fired; several of the saddles were emptied, but now the enemy was vulnerable and the archers shot their arrows. Hundreds fell, and the women fitted their next arrows as they galloped by, then turned, guiding their mounts with their knees. Again they swept by before the musketeers had had time to reload, and again hundreds of the Empire's soldiers fell, but none fled. Instead they continued to doggedly reload their weapons, following orders to the letter.

Elemnestra suddenly became aware of six heavy covered wagons lumbering into view in the distance. They were enormously long and being pulled by huge draft horses and were obviously a massive weight, but rather than be distracted she turned her attention to the enemy pikemen, thinning their ranks with flight after flight of arrows. But still they marched on, singing the battle hymn of the Empire. The Basilea found herself admiring the bravery of these soldiers who refused to be intimidated by her archers' arrows.

By the time she focused on the heavy wagons again, they had rolled up the plain and turned parallel to her own sweep, but facing in the opposite direction. She was wary but couldn't ignore the possible threat, and so attacked. As her women plunged into shooting range the covered sides of the wagons suddenly dropped, revealing cannons. Their firing teams stood at the "ready" position and as Elemnestra and her women raised their bows, an officer in the lead wagon drew his sword and shouted an order. The cannons fired simultaneously, spewing out a broadside of chain shot and broken metal, which ripped into the galloping archers. Three hundred horses fell, disintegrating in a crimson explosion of flailing limbs and riders.

A huge cheer erupted from the Imperial troops. The devilwomen were no more.

* * *

Up on the defensive earthworks, Thirrin screamed in horror as she watched the slaughter of the archers. She turned and ran, calling for her cavalry as she went. Beside her ran Tharaman-Thar and Taradan, each roaring out a summons to their warriors. The horses of the cavalry were quickly assembled, their troopers mounted, and the leopards in position. In a blazing fury, Thirrin led the cavalry of the Icemark and the Icesheets out onto the plain. Tharaman-Thar kept perfect pace beside her stallion as his leopards let out the strange coughing bark of their war cry.

Aware of their approach, the enemy stood quietly, their cannons reloaded with chain shot. Theirs would be the greatest prize of all; they would kill the warrior-queen of the Icemark and her tame fighting leopards. The soldiers sang as Thirrin and her cavalry thundered toward them, certain this action would signal the end of the hard-fought war.

But among the scattered and broken bodies of the fallen Hypolitan archers, Elemnestra eased her badly wounded frame to lean against the corpse of her horse. She barked orders to the thirty or so women of the three hundred who were still able to shoot, and encouraged them to hurry. She knew she must destroy the cannons before Thirrin and Tharaman-Thar were in range. Her women quickly tied rags to their arrows and set them alight, laying them carefully among the flattened mat of bloodied wildflowers at their feet. Then, as Elemnestra struggled to her knees, they raised their bows, and on her orders shot their first flight. Thirty burning arrows rained down among the gunpowder barrels of the cannons. The Polypontian officer shouted orders to his musketeers, and they raised their weapons. With Thirrin's six-thousand-strong cavalry bearing down on them, he couldn't waste any more cannon shot on the fallen archers; he just wouldn't have time to reload and fire again before they were hacked to pieces by sabers and claws. But by now the second and third flight of flaming arrows had already fallen among the barrels. With desperate speed the gun teams snatched the burning rags away and stamped on them, but more fell, faster than they could move.

At last the muskets fired, but the women had dived for cover and now stood ready again to shoot their deadly rain. With a desperate scream a young soldier tried to smother a burning barrel with his body, but then a vicious screaming crack erupted into the air and the wagon was blown apart. Almost simultaneously the remaining five wagons burst skyward on a blooming forest of flame. Broken cannon and shot burst outward in a deadly driving hail, killing and wounding hundreds of the soldiers who stood nearby. The survivors of Elemnestra's mounted archers were also blown aside by a killing hand of fire that finally ended the elite regiment of the Hypolitan.

Thirrin cried out in grief and rage when she realized what had happened and, rising out of her saddle, she drew her saber and shouted out the battle paean of the Icemark. The six thousand warriors of her cavalry, human and leopard, answered, their voices ferocious and deadly. They swept down on the disrupted ranks of the Empire's soldiers, killing and killing in an attempt to avenge the loss of Elemnestra and her archers, and when at last the iron discipline of the Polypontian army was broken, they rode after them, cutting them down as they ran.

When the few hundred who'd survived her attack scrambled to the safety of their lines, Thirrin led her cavalry in a charge across the plain to smash into the Empire's units, who'd drawn out the fyrd with their sham retreat. By now the soldiers of the Icemark had remembered their training and had formed a shield-wall as they fought an ordered withdrawal back toward the ditches and ramparts of the defenses.

The cavalry sliced through the Polypontian soldiers like a razor through stubble and, bursting through their ranks, they turned to slice back through them again. Soon their resistance had collapsed, too, and this time their retreat was real. After the cavalry had chased the last of the Polypontians from the field, Thirrin returned to the fyrd, now standing at a loss watching the fleeing enemy.

"Go back to your positions and hold them!" Thirrin blazed, her eyes brilliant with fury. "If you'd followed your orders and heeded your training, none of this would have happened. You will stand to until I return! You will *not* stand down, no matter how long you have to wait. Anyone who disobeys this order will be hanged!"

Turning her stallion, she led a charge across to where Olememnon and his Hypolitan infantry were fighting against the left arm of the enemy's failed pincer movement. They'd been making good progress, first halting the advance of the Empire's soldiers and then slowly forcing them back toward their own lines. Now Thirrin and Tharaman-Thar fell upon the flanks of the Empire's army, driving through their lines as the coughing bark of the Snow Leopards and the paean of the human troopers sounded over the field. The pike regiments tried to make a stand against the fury unleashed upon them, driving the butts of their pikes deep into the ground and holding them at graded angles that should have made them impregnable to cavalry. But Tharaman-Thar and Taradan led their leopards against the long spears, beating them down with their paws, then diving between them to savage the soldiers they were supposed to protect.

Eventually the discipline and courage of the Polypontian soldiers was broken and they fled, many of them dying beneath the sabers and claws of the pursuing cavalry. But Thirrin's fury was not yet spent, and she galloped to just beyond cannon range at the enemy's lines and waited, openly challenging the rest of their army to come out and fight.

From behind the lines, Scipio Bellorum had viewed it all, and his original elation at the destruction of Elemnestra and her mounted archers gave way to frustration as he watched Thirrin and her "trained leopards" destroying his Yellow and Orange armies. Only his elite Black Army was totally intact, and with the support of the remnants of the Reds, he hurriedly sent them to hold the front line, come what may, against the barbarian Queen.

He scanned Thirrin and her cavalry, as close to panic as he'd ever come in his long military career, but then breathed a sigh of relief. The young Queen seemed to have slumped in her saddle, and one of the leopards had his face close to hers, for all the world as though he were talking to her — an illusion made all the more believable since she seemed to be holding a conversation with it, listening, then apparently replying as it looked at her.

Bellorum squinted through his monoculum, watching her mouth moving silently, and wishing desperately that there was some way of hearing what was being said. Then she hugged the huge beast and, slipping across from her saddle, she climbed onto its back and they trotted back to Frostmarris. The rest of the cavalry followed, and Bellorum sat back in relief.

The crisis was over, and luckily two of the four reinforcing armies were less than half a day's march away. Turning to his staff officers, who sat on their horses with carefully expressionless faces, he beckoned to the youngest. "How long do you estimate it would take you to ride back to the pass through the Dancing Maidens?"

"Two days, sir!" the young officer answered stoutly.

"Which means three, at least. I want you to take orders to the reserve armies you'll find camped just inside the border, and tell them to come here at all speed. The time has come to crush this queenling and her little country. Their arrogance is beginning to annoy me."

28

One hundred soldiers stood tied to stakes in the courtyard of the citadel. One in every hundred from the ten thousand members of the fyrd regiments who'd broken ranks and left their positions. They'd been chosen by drawing lots, and now were to be flogged.

One hundred housecarls had also been chosen to carry out the sentences of twenty lashes for each soldier, and stood waiting for Thirrin to give the order to begin. It was the first really warm day of the spring, and the sound of birdsong tumbled into the otherwise silent courtyard where almost two thousand of the fyrd regiment had been crammed to witness the punishment.

Thirrin was mounted on her warhorse and, urging him forward, she pitched her voice at a level everyone could hear. "Soldiers of the fyrd, you are here to witness the punishment of your comrades for disobeying orders." She glared at the ranks before her, the rage she had felt during the battle rekindling as he spoke. "The guilt belongs to all of you! By breaking ranks, you not only endangered your comrades but also put in jeopardy the entire defense of Frostmarris and therefore the country and people of the Icemark!"

Her stallion began to sidestep and snort, ready for battle as he heard the anger in Thirrin's voice. "But above even this, you are all guilty of bringing about the death of Basilea Elemnestra of the Hypolitan and her mounted archers! It was their brave sacrifice that saved you from certain destruction. A sacrifice that wouldn't have been necessary if you had obeyed orders and the most basic rules of engagement! You do *not* break ranks! You do *not* pursue the enemy unless ordered to do so! Anyone, of whatever rank, who commits such crimes again will be hanged, and his body left to the crows." She turned to nod at a lone drummer, who began to beat out a slow rhythm that would set the pace of the strokes. "May you all feel the pain of your comrades. May you all feel the disgrace of your crime." She nodded again, and the housecarls drew back their whips and began the punishment.

The crack of the lashes cutting into flesh echoed across the courtyard, mingling with the screams of the soldiers. But the watching regiments remained deathly quiet. After less than two minutes the punishment was complete, and the soldiers were cut down and carried to the hospital block where the healers were ready to receive them. Then, with a silent nod from Thirrin, the fyrd was dismissed and they were marched back down to the defenses to resume their duties.

When the last rank had filed through the gates, Thirrin dismounted and, giving her horse to a waiting groom, she walked through the huge doors that led into the Great Hall. The cavernous space was empty, and for a moment she leaned against the cool stone of the walls and closed her eyes. But then a soft step approaching across the flagstones made her open them again and straighten up. Somehow she wasn't surprised to see Oskan walking slowly toward her.

"And what do you imagine was achieved by that horrendous display of cruelty?" he asked quietly.

"Discipline and a good lesson learned!" she snapped in reply.

"Don't you think these soldiers are carrying enough of a burden without the added threat of a flogging if they make mistakes?" His tone remained even and level, but Thirrin could see him shaking with a suppressed rage that seemed to shimmer in the very air around him.

"Oskan, do you really believe that I don't understand exactly what my soldiers are going through? Do you really think I'm a stranger to burdens?" She almost laughed at the bitter absurdity of it all, but she controlled herself, knowing that if she started, she wouldn't be able to stop.

"They're lucky, they only have to worry about a flogging if they break ranks and endanger their own lives again. But if I make a mistake, thousands could die, a country could be lost, and who knows what else could be inflicted on those unlucky enough to survive!" Her voice had slowly risen in strength as she spoke, and suddenly she let everything go in a glorious outpouring of emotion.

"Don't talk to me about burdens, I drew up the plans for them! How many fourteen-year-olds do you know who rule a kingdom at war, who command an army, who keep together an alliance of more species than she can remember, who's killed more people than she can count, who waits desperately day in, day out, every living blessed second, for the arrival of allies she's terrified are going to let her down? Please tell me, Oskan, tell me her name. I'd like to have a cozy chat with her and compare notes! I'd like that, it might make me feel just a little less isolated, and just a little less afraid that at any minute the whole sorry, ludicrous, deadly, hellish mess is going to collapse around me, and everyone will finally find out that I don't know what I'm doing and that I'm making it up as I go along!"

She drew a deep, shuddering breath and fell silent, but her voice reverberated in the vast empty space of the Great Hall as though they were standing inside a huge bell that had just finished ringing.

Oskan blinked in amazement at the passionate outburst, almost smiled, thought better of it, and then finally gave her a hug that made her gasp. After a moment's hesitation she returned his embrace, gently at first, then more and more fiercely as she reached out for his help and comfort. They stood there rocking from side to side while the war raged on and the world and all its woes continued without them. But after a while she disentangled herself. Oskan grinned when he saw her red cheeks, then he said, "I'm sorry, but I must go. I've got some soldiers to patch up."

She nodded. "And I have to find a lost commander of infantry." He frowned in puzzlement, but she shook her head. "I'll explain later."

They stood in silence for a few uncertain seconds, then finally walked away in opposite directions.

Her boots echoed in the silence as she strode across the flagstone floor and into the tangle of corridors that wound and writhed around the interior of the royal palace like veins and arteries. She took a few steadying breaths as she walked along and slowly regained her composure. By the time she reached the first junction of corridor and walkway, she'd become Queen Thirrin once again, and she concentrated her mind on the task at hand.

She knew exactly where she was going and who she'd find

there. Earlier that morning she'd sent some of the quieter chamberlains to discreetly find out where he'd gone, and after they'd reported back she'd made up her mind to talk to him.

She came to a small, low door, and when she opened it, sunlight and the scent of flowers flowed around her in a warm rising wave. Before her lay the citadel garden. She walked out into the small space that was enclosed by the battlemented walls, and closed her eyes. The short Icemark spring was already evolving into summer, and the hum of bees filled the air as they shuttled like living sparks between the blooms that blazed their confusion of color into the air.

Thirrin breathed the heady mix of perfumes deep into her tired frame, and for the briefest of moments was almost able to forget the war. But then a warm gust of wind brought with it the sound of shouted orders and the tramp of marching feet, and she opened her eyes to reality and her task.

In the center of the garden tall rosebushes were already coming into flower, their deep reds, icy whites, and delicate pinks making a tangled tapestry of pigments and velvety textures on the warm air. Instinctively she walked toward them, and found Olememnon sitting on a bench surrounded by blooms and bees. He hadn't heard her arrive and he sat, eyes closed, with petals in his hair and a butterfly sitting on his shoulder. He looked like one of the many minor Gods of Nature, tired out by the effort of spring and resting in his own creation before the tasks of summer began.

Thirrin almost walked away, leaving him to whatever peace he could find, but he stirred and opened his eyes. He smiled in greeting, the expression making the grief and sadness in his eyes all the more obvious.

"Hello, Uncle Ollie," she said quietly. "Can I join you?"

In answer, he moved along the bench and patted the space

next to him. She sat and, closing her eyes, she raised her face to the sun. "I don't know what to say, Uncle Ollie. I'm only a girl, I don't know what it's like to lose someone you've chosen to love rather than someone you're born to love, like a father or mother." She opened her eyes and looked at him. "But when Dad died, I felt I'd been robbed of time . . . robbed of the times we would have had together."

Olememnon took her hand and squeezed it gently.

"And there are others . . . particularly one other, whom I don't think I could go on without," she continued. "I mean, I suppose the world, my world, would go on, but if he were killed, I don't quite know how it could."

"It doesn't seem possible," Olememnon answered at last, his low voice quietly mingling with the drone of the bees. "Even the light seems darker."

"I sometimes think it's too much of a risk to rely on someone else so much for your happiness," Thirrin went on. "But without sharing at least some of your life, everything else seems less worthwhile, less *valuable* somehow."

"The risk is worth it, Thirrin. Even when fate calls your bluff and you lose them, the risk's worth it."

Thirrin nodded, as though he'd just confirmed what she suspected. Then she said, "I can't say anything to help, of course. Nothing at all, but I need you, Uncle. I can't do this on my own. Come back to us and lead the Hypolitan infantry, at least until the new Basilea gets used to her role."

She almost gasped aloud at her own insensitivity and blushed a deep, mortified crimson, but Olememnon raised her hand to his lips and kissed it. "Don't worry, Thirrin, I'm perfectly well aware that the Convocation of Women has chosen a new leader. But any power that I had as an officer depended on Elemnestra. I was only the commander of the infantry because I was her consort. Without her, I'm just another soldier in the army of the Hypolitan."

"We live in the oddest of times, Uncle. Therefore we may act oddly, and so I, as Queen of the Icemark, appoint you Commander of the Hypolitan Infantry. And you don't have to worry, the new Basilea is a sensible woman and agrees with me. We can't lose one of our best officers just when we need him most."

"But what if he has nothing left to give? How can I lead troops in battle when I don't even have the strength to think straight? I almost have to remember to breathe; blinking has become a matter for consideration: Do I do it now or wait until my eyes sting? This is what I've become now that I no longer have Elemnestra."

Thirrin looked at him in wonder. Is this what grief could do, make almost a comedy of your life? Reduce grown people to the position of helpless babies? If it weren't so serious, she could almost laugh. "But the living still need you, Uncle Ollie. Help us, please. If you don't, then the entire population could suffer what you feel now, or at least those who survive."

He smiled sadly. "They will anyway, at some point in their lives. Better to surrender to it now. The cause is lost, anyway. Where are the allies? At heart the Vampires and Wolf-folk hate us; they won't come. And without them how long can we hold out against the vast numbers the Empire sends against us? We've had some successes, yes. But with every victory our numbers are less, and with every defeat Scipio Bellorum's army grows as he sends for more and more reinforcements. The struggle is no longer worth the effort."

A rage suddenly burned in Thirrin's body, and she stood up, almost incandescent with fury. "Olememnon Stagapoulos, Son of the Mother, one-time Consort of the Basilea of the

Hypolitan, Commander of the Infantry of the Moon, your duty awaits you. It is not yours to understand the actions of the Goddess; you can only carry out your role to the best of your mortal ability, and if you must die, then you will do it safe in the knowledge that your small tragedy had some part in a divine plan beyond your knowing!" Her voice echoed around the garden, sending a flight of sparrows into the sky and driving away the sense of torpor that had settled over the huge man before her. He looked at her now, a small puzzled frown on his face as though he were trying to remember something.

"Olememnon Stagapoulos, you will come with me now and take up your role within the design of the Mother, or your name will forever be disgraced throughout the land!"

"Those who are left to remember it," he answered defiantly, but his tone had changed and a new energy seemed to be returning to his huge frame.

"There will be many left to remember it, linked in glory to the name of Elemnestra Celeste, Basilea of the Hypolitan and Commander of the Sacred Regiment, who died defending her Queen. The Goddess has chosen that you should live, Commander Olememnon. Obviously you are still part of her design, and it remains your duty to fulfill your role." Slowly the rage abated, and Thirrin looked at the soldier who now sat, head bowed, before her. She stooped and took his hand in hers. "Come on, Uncle Ollie, your people need you, and so do I."

As she watched, the massive shoulders seemed almost to inflate as he drew a deep steadying breath and released it in an explosive sigh. After a few moments he climbed to his feet and smiled, uncertainly at first, then slowly broadening it into a brilliant grin that seemed to split his face. "Elemnestra wouldn't let me rest, anyway. 'There are things to be done and we're the ones to do them,' she'd say. Let's go and see what needs doing."

Thirrin hugged him fiercely, relief and happiness flooding through her, then taking his hand she led him back to the small doorway, each step seeming to add strength to the consort of the fallen Basilea.

The first two of the reinforcing armies had arrived, and Scipio Bellorum had personally overseen their settling into camp. Talk among the soldiers would have soon let them know just how difficult this stage of the war was proving to be, and he wanted to put the stamp of his authority and personality on them before morale could slip too far.

He'd already announced two rest days, which would allow the other two armies to arrive, and also let his men get well and truly drunk, with a day for recovery before they continued the campaign in earnest again. It also wouldn't be lost on the soldiers that the Empire was sufficiently in control to dictate the pace of the war. There would be fighting when *they* chose, and not before. The barbarians would have to wait until the Empire was good and ready.

The army hadn't been totally inactive, though. Bellorum had questioned some of the survivors from the earlier attacks on the Icemark's defenses, and there seemed to be some evidence that the ditch-and-embankment system didn't extend very far into the forest. There might even be a gap in the defenses. With this in mind he'd sent in several armed scouting parties, but so far none had returned. He sat now in his tent, its viewing wall raised, and watched through his monoculum as a much larger skirmishing party entered the eaves of the forest.

This time they had orders to send back messengers at

regular intervals to give reports. As he watched, the last of the soldiers disappeared from view, and for the next hour he waited patiently, nibbling from a silver dish of exotic fruits that had been sent from all parts of the massive Polypontian Empire.

Bellorum then heard the unmistakable sound of a musket volley, followed by the scattered, sporadic firing of soldiers under pressure. Obviously whatever the defenses were in the forest, they were strong. For the next hour he continued to scan the trees. Once, he thought he caught sight of soldiers in oddly designed and colored armor, green and brown like the surrounding foliage, but not one member of the skirmishing party emerged.

"No weak point there, then," he said to himself, and decisively snapping his eyeglass shut he sent an orderly to call his staff officers together so he could begin planning the next move.

For the rest of the day Bellorum discussed the tactics of the "endgame," as he insisted on calling the stage of the war they were about to enter.

"I've decided to make these backward people use their own barbarity against themselves." He smiled charmingly around the table where his officers sat watching him attentively. "The rational sciences are virtually unknown to them, so superstition rules their every moment. The night, therefore, probably holds an entire pantheon of terrors for the soldiers of the Icemark — and I intend to exploit that foolishness."

Bellorum walked to an easel where a large chart of complicated equations and diagrams was drawn. "You've probably all noticed over the past few days that the moon is almost full, and that in these latitudes it's remarkably large and bright." A murmur of agreement drifted around the table. "Well, gentlemen," he continued, pointing to the chart, "in two days' time the moon will be at its largest and brightest; in the eyes of the barbaric and backward, it is a time of power and magic, a time of fear and dread, and a time, gentlemen, when we will attack!"

The murmur rose to a babble, which abruptly stopped as the general laughed. "Yes, we will attack by moonlight. Already the nights are almost as bright as day, and when the moon is full, it will be brighter still. Our greatest ally has always been fear, but as soldiers of the night, we will be truly dreadful. These uneducated savages will run before us like frightened children!"

The officers broke into spontaneous applause, and Bellorum smiled.

"Permission to speak, sir," requested a young commander, taking everyone by surprise.

"Of course," the general said, recovering quickly.

"I'd like to report a rumor I've heard among the men. It's at least interesting, and could be important."

"Well?" said Bellorum, his pleasant tones edged with the slightest ice.

"Several of the pikemen and shield-bearers have reported that . . . well, that the giant leopards use human speech, in fact, the same language as the enemy soldiers."

A stunned silence fell, until Bellorum threw back his head and laughed. Immediately the other officers joined in, only stopping when the general did. "I suggest you charge those men with being drunk on duty."

The young commander smiled nervously but continued. "Then I would need to charge over five hundred men."

Bellorum stared at him for several seconds, but his gaze was returned with frank respect. "And do you believe these rumors?"

"I believe that the men who report them believe them to be true."

"Young recruits, no doubt inexperienced and easily inflamed by the heat of battle."

"No, sir. Veterans of the Red Army, some with more than twenty years' service behind them."

Bellorum sat down, his eyes staring into the middle distance as he remembered watching Thirrin and the largest leopard through his monoculum after the Basilea had been eliminated. He'd thought then that they seemed to be talking together but had dismissed the idea as ludicrous. The truth of it suddenly flared up in his mind, and with it grew a terrible sense of outrage. Man was the pinnacle of a rational universe! He alone used coherent language! He alone used coherent thought! Anything that challenged this order was an abomination!

"This cannot be allowed," he said, his voice still and cold. "Talking beasts are an insult to the Cosmos. Gentlemen, we have a duty to destroy these freaks of nature in the name of all that's rational. In two days we will be at full strength again, and we will sweep aside this petty queenling and her circus of fighting, talking beasts!"

29

Thirrin stood on the battlements looking out toward the enemy's positions. It was obvious they were receiving reinforcements, and Grinelda and her party of white werewolves had reported more troop movements on the Great Road to the south. But what really worried her was the fact that information from the other werewolf spies had stopped. A few weeks ago they'd been receiving daily messages telling of the Empire's troop movements and other news. Now there was only silence, and she was beginning to wonder if the rumors about the allies not coming to help in the war were right after all. Had Their Vampiric Majesties and Grishmak the Wolf-folk King lied when they'd sworn to help against Bellorum?

No! Not Grishmak! He hadn't lied, she was almost sure. But the Vampire King and Queen were another matter. They hated human beings. Perhaps they were hoping that the armies of the Icemark would damage Bellorum enough to stop him from going farther north.

Leaning against the battlements, she looked over the defenses; the weaknesses were plain to see. Troop numbers were dwindling by the day, with every attack the casualties mounted, and they had no reserves to draw on. If help didn't come soon, Bellorum, as usual, would win through sheer weight of numbers.

"They'll come," said a voice behind her, and she whirled around to see Oskan smiling at her.

"Is nowhere private?" she snapped. "Not even my head?"

"Oh, I don't need a warlock's powers to know what you're thinking. But they'll come, I feel it in my bones," he said, deepening his voice and rolling his eyes like a fairground fortune-teller.

"Don't joke about it, Oskan. Things are getting desperate."

"*Getting* desperate? When has it been anything else? I tell you what, though, we've bloodied Bellorum's nose. I bet he thought he'd have this little war all done and dusted by now, and that he'd be sitting back in his villa on the coast of the Southern Sea. Ha! Serves the murderous old bastard right! Perhaps next time he'll think twice before he decides he wants to add some other little land to the Empire."

Thirrin grinned despite herself. There was something comforting about Oskan's odd mixing of adult analysis and schoolroom language. "Yes, but will we be able to hold him off until the allies come?"

For some reason Oskan wouldn't look at her, and instead gazed out over the plain. "Oh yes. I'm sure of it."

"Warlock, do you know something I should hear about, something bad?" she barked, assuming her full queenly persona.

"No," he replied after a moment's silence. "I know nothing at all. That's just it, I've tried and I can't see a thing. We're obviously not meant to know, yet."

"Great," she said, her shoulders sagging. "Well, the suspense is literally killing my soldiers."

A sudden blast of bugles made her snap upright, and she peered over the battlements. Bellorum was sending his daily raid. She was well aware that he was trying to exhaust her troops by keeping them constantly on their toes, while he used a rotation system for his own soldiers that allowed the majority of them to rest. The trouble was, it was working. The defenders were all physically and mentally drained, and they had to keep fighting fresh, well-rested enemy soldiers with every attack.

"I've got to go. Have you seen Tharaman?"

"Down at the main gates," Oskan answered, and hurried off to the infirmary to prepare for the casualties that would soon be flooding in.

Scipio Bellorum watched as his soldiers charged. It was all getting rather routine now. The designated regiments of the day would march off and keep the enemy busy, while the remainder of his army rested and prepared for the final assault in two days' time.

He almost felt that he could leave this part of the war to his undergenerals — almost, but not quite, because the fighters of the Icemark were never predictable. With a sigh he snapped open his monoculum and stood at the raised wall of his tent, watching progress. As usual, the defenders were proving difficult to crack, and his shield-bearers and pikemen were being beaten back. And then he noticed movement farther along the system of ditch and rampart. Quickly he refocused his monoculum and watched as Thirrin and Tharaman-Thar led out their cavalry. He could clearly see the queenling standing in her stirrups, drawing her sword, and the unnatural giant leopard throwing back its head and sending out that bizarre coughing bark. Then the Queen's cavalry leaped forward and thundered down on his troops, smashing into their flank.

"General Fortune and Commander Chance are indeed my greatest allies!" Bellorum said, and laughed aloud. Sending for his orderly he gave precise commands, then feverishly watched the struggle on the defenses. Soon a great wave of Imperial troops was sweeping across the plain toward Thirrin and her cavalry.

"I have her! I have her!" Bellorum cried out excitedly as his soldiers took a wide sweeping arc toward the Queen of the Icemark, cutting off her retreat back to the gate in the defenses. "Not even this barbarian woman and her talking leopards can cut their way through one hundred thousand Polypontian men." He quickly calculated the odds and crowed. "Outnumbered by more than sixteen to one is too much even for her!"

Up on the battlements of Frostmarris, Oskan looked out over the plain. The wounded hadn't started to arrive in any numbers yet, and he'd taken the chance to go back to the high point and get some air. He watched as the Polypontian soldiers attacked the defenses in the segment close to the forest, then his eye was drawn to Thirrin and her cavalry riding down to the gate in the system of ditches and embankments. They rode through and headed directly for the Empire's troops. After a few moments he heard the cavalry paean and the barking of the leopards, followed by the sound of onset.

The wounded would soon be arriving in the infirmary, and he was just about to turn from the walls and head back down into the citadel when he noticed movement in the Polypontian camp. In horror he watched as thousands upon thousands of enemy soldiers burst across the plain like a flood. Nobody down on the defenses was high enough to see the danger, and he gripped the stone of the battlements in a rising panic. They were trying to cut off Thirrin and Tharaman! They'd be trapped before anything could be done.

"NO!" he shouted despairingly into the unheeding sky, his small voice lost in the clamor of battle. What could be done? By the time the defenders were given orders and had begun to react, it would be too late. Armies moved only as fast as their slowest parts. Then gradually a determination and a certainty grew within him. *He* must act, and he must act *now*! He pushed himself away from the wall and raced down the stone steps into the citadel, shouting as he went. He rushed to the stables and found Jenny munching a bag of carrots. She hiccupped in surprise as he leaped on her back without saddle or reins.

Grabbing her mane, he tugged her head around, and she trotted obediently toward the gate of the citadel. Then suddenly she caught the terrible sense of urgency that was beating in waves from Oskan, and she let out a great squealing bray that echoed around the walls. Laying back her long ears, she thrust her head forward and galloped down through the town, hee-hawing as she went. Soon they reached the gateway to the city, where the party of white werewolves was preparing to join the battle on the defenses.

"To me! To me! The Queen is in danger!" Oskan bellowed at them as he thundered by, desperately clinging to Jenny's neck. The Wolf-folk instantly fell in behind, easily keeping pace with the wildly galloping mule. Down on the level they hurtled toward the gate in the defenses, the werewolves pulling ahead and bursting through the guard that would have barred their way. Then they were through and out onto the plain. Ahead, Oskan could see the enemy bearing down on the rear of Thirrin's cavalry, and the alarm was being sounded at last all along the embankments. Olememnon was already leading his infantry out through the gateway, frantically trying to catch up with the mule and the small party of werewolves that were swiftly drawing ahead.

But the Polypontian army was winning the race. Thirrin and Tharaman would soon be cut off. Oskan shouted and screamed in an attempt to warn the cavalry, but even with Jenny and the werewolves joining in, their voices were lost.

On they galloped, heading for the rapidly closing area of open plain between the advancing Imperial troops and the defenses. Soon Oskan and the werewolves were fighting their way through enemy soldiers. Jenny lashed out like a trained warhorse and the Wolf-folk struck and beat at the soldiers. Such was their ferocity that they hardly slowed, and still they howled and screamed.

At last, Tharaman seemed to realize the danger and, looking back, he let out a huge roar. The cavalry turned around and re-formed. Thirrin circled her sword above her head and they charged back toward Oskan and his party, but it was too late. The enemy soldiers closed the escape route, and Jenny and the werewolves broke through only to join the cavalry in certain death.

"No!" screamed Oskan in total and utter despair, then all went black as he was knocked to the ground. He came to seconds later. Jenny stood over him, kicking out with her powerful back legs and sending enemy soldiers flying through the air. Grinelda, the huge captain of the white werewolves, stooped down, and carrying him in her arms she ran to clearer ground, her warriors around her. She set Oskan down, and he watched as the enemy bore down on them. In the background, the thunder of cavalry hooves drew closer as Thirrin and

Tharaman galloped toward them. But it was too late; the Imperial troops had surrounded them.

Oskan wept in despair, his frame racked with sobs as he realized they were finished. But then, oddly, two voices sounded in his head, a conversation from his and Thirrin's past.

"Can you draw down lightning?"

"I've never tried. Seems a silly idea to me. You could be hit."

Could he draw down lightning? Would it be enough? Wenlock Witchmother had said he was the most powerful warlock in generations. Now was the time to find out. He opened his arms wide and threw back his head, staring deep into the clear blue sky. He called on all his strength and forced his mind far and wide questing for power. He ranged over the realms of the four winds, and slowly ions began to gather and accumulate in the air high, high above him. The sky seemed to thicken and roll like muscled water, and then the power started to fall through the sky, crackling and snapping as it tumbled toward the small figure of the boy who stood on the plain, thousands of feet below. It hit him with shocking force, but his thin frame withstood it, shaking and vibrating as the power filled him to the uttermost brim. Opening his arms wide, he held his hands above his head and pointed them, palms open, at the enemy soldiers. With a terrible bursting crash, lightning erupted from his hands and struck the troops before him, blasting them aside, burning and scorching, blackening skin and igniting cloth, hair, and gunpowder.

Turning slowly, Oskan directed the terrible scything force to carve a swath through the Imperial troops, until an escape route stood open. Then he fell. Every piece of cloth and every hair had been burned from his body. Smoke trickled from his mouth and nose, and his skin was charred black. The cavalry reached him, Thirrin screaming in horror as she looked down on Oskan's body. Tharaman stooped and picked him up in his mouth as gently as if he were a kitten. Taradan roared, and the cavalry leaped forward, joined by the werewolves and Jenny. They burst through the gap Oskan had punched, and galloped toward the gate in the defenses. But still the enemy came on, snapping at their heels.

Advancing at a steady trot toward them, Olememnon and his infantry slung their shields, and as Thirrin and her cavalry rode by, the Hypolitan foot soldiers hit the Empire's troops with a huge roar. The impact echoed over the plain, but the Hypolitans were borne backward by the massive weight of the enemy's numbers and by their desperation to catch and kill the Queen of the Icemark.

Olememnon bellowed out the order to stand, and slowly the advance of the Imperial army lost its momentum as the soldiers of the Hypolitan drove their feet into the earth and pushed back against the impossible odds. By this time, Thirrin and the cavalry had reached the gateway and ridden through, but their pace didn't slacken. Instead, they thundered on to the city, heading for the infirmary and its healers.

Up on the defenses the ballistas and archers loosed flight after flight of bolts and arrows into the enemy ranks, and slowly the intensity of their attack slackened, allowing Olememnon and his soldiers to fight a retreat back to the gate in the defenses.

Sensing their advantage was finally lost and that the queenling had escaped, the Empire's commanders ordered their soldiers back to camp. They withdrew across the plain, arrogant and swaggering in the lack of concern they showed to the arrows and ballista bolts that continued to rain down on them.

30

Thirrin ran into the infirmary ahead of Tharaman-Thar, roughly thrusting aside anyone who got in her way and shouting for Wenlock Witchmother. But the leader of the witches was already waiting for her, leaning quietly on her stick, and with two healers in attendance.

"He's dead, Mother! He's dead!" Thirrin shrieked as she caught sight of her.

The old lady stepped forward and motioned to Tharaman-Thar to lay Oskan down before her. She nodded slowly as she looked at his burned and disfigured body. "He has paid a high price to save you, Thirrin Lindenshield."

"I know that! He's paid with his life!"

"Shut up, foolish girl! If you really thought that, why did you bring him to me? Do you really think I can raise the dead? Those who are called into the peace of the Goddess stay there until *she* decides otherwise."

The Witchmother turned to one of the healers. "Mirror," she demanded, and waited with her hand open until a small circular piece of polished metal had been placed in her palm. Then, stooping, she held it before the blackened hole that was

Oskan's mouth. A faint mist gathered on its bright surface. "He lives, of course. He has other duties to perform in this life. Take him to the place prepared."

"He's alive?" said Thirrin, caught between amazement and a knowledge that she'd always believed it from the moment Tharaman-Thar had lifted him from the battlefield. "But even if he survives, he'll be horribly scarred. Would he want to live that way?"

"However he survives is the will of the Mother. Do you think she's so blind that she can't see the unblemished soul of her son beneath the scarring of his body?" Wenlock said sharply. "Be grateful that his life is destined to continue at the same time as your own."

Thirrin looked down on the blackened and oozing body of the boy who'd been through so much with her. His face was unrecognizable, his hands had been completely burned away, his wrists mere stumps that smoked gently, and the rest of his body was charred and twisted beyond any recognition. He looked and smelled like a mutton carcass that had been left far too long on a spit roast.

She wept silently, the tears trickling down her tightly drawn face. "Where are you going to take him?"

"To the deepest cellar. A place has been prepared for him," the Witchmother answered, clapping her hands and watching as two orderlies hurried in with a stretcher and bundled Oskan onto it.

"'A place has been prepared' . . . ? Did you know this was going to happen?" Thirrin asked in quiet awe.

"Yes, and so did he, at heart. Oh, he didn't know the precise details, but he knew that he would fall defending you. Not all brave people are soldiers or warriors, Thirrin Strong-in-the-Arm."

"I know that, old woman!" Thirrin snapped back with a return of her fighting spirit. "I may be young, but I'm not stupid. Don't patronize me. I've faced death more times in the last few months than you probably have in your entire wizened life, and I'm still here. And if I survive this war, I'll still be here when the Goddess is unfortunate enough to have your company in the Summer Lands!"

"That's for the Mother to decide, not you! Don't presume that you know *her* will!"

"Oh, I assure you I don't. How could I possibly compete with a woman who seems to have just had a conversation with *her*? Perhaps you should call *her* in and we can ask *her* ourselves. Oh, but I'm forgetting, you're obviously *her* private secretary; perhaps you should just have a quick look at *her* diary and see if it's convenient."

"That's a terrible blasphemy!" Wenlock Witchmother hissed angrily.

"Oh no, it most certainly is not! I meant it only as an insult for you alone and your arrogance. Do you think you're the only one created by the Mother? Or perhaps even you couldn't be that big-headed. Perhaps you just think you're the most important of her creations!"

The two terrible women faced each other for a blazing moment or two while Tharaman-Thar and the others looked on. Then the giant leopard coughed gently.

"Perhaps now isn't the best time for this . . . discussion. The boy is dying before us."

Then, amazingly, with much creaking and groaning of stiffened joints, the Witchmother fell to her knees before the young Queen. "The Goddess has chosen with her usual wisdom. This small land is blessed with a very powerful monarch indeed."

The two orderlies now seized their opportunity to lift Oskan and head toward the doorway, where a broad flight of steps led down to the cellars. The others followed into the darkness, the healers holding torches to light the way.

The smell of wet earth enfolded them as they descended into the undercroft. When they reached the bottom of the steps, the orderlies didn't stop but hurried over to a small doorway almost hidden behind a pillar. Here, another narrower flight of steps plunged deeply into pitch-black where the rich scent of earth billowed around them. The steps were wet, and the hollow sound of dripping water echoed around them; they trod warily as they wound down the spiraling stairway to the very bottom. Here, a natural cave opened up around them and beneath their feet a rich red mud glistened in the light of their torches. Against one of the irregular walls, a small bed had been placed with no mattress or coverings of any sort, and on this the orderlies placed the burned and broken body of Oskan the Warlock.

He was suspended above the wet earth on a rough trellis of ropes, and as Thirrin looked on, small droplets of water dripped onto his blackened skin. This was a place she'd never been to, hadn't even known existed, and yet she knew she'd remember it for as long as she was allowed to live.

The Witchmother walked forward and, after mumbling to herself for a moment, she spoke up clearly. "Remember what you have been told, Oskan, Beloved of the Mother. Death would fall from the sky and healing would rise from the earth. Call now on the Goddess and be made whole."

Turning to the others, she said, "We must leave him now. Let the will of the Goddess be done."

"How long do we leave him like this?" Thirrin asked, her voice a mere whisper as she fought for control of herself.

"Until he walks from here alone and unaided."

"I see," said Thirrin simply and, taking a torch from one of the healers, she stood looking down at the disfigured body of her friend. Then she stooped and kissed his forehead.

"We must return to the war, Tharaman," she said and, wiping her eyes, Thirrin turned and led the way back up the steps.

The Polypontian losses had been minimal in real terms — two thousand or so soldiers from the one hundred thousand who had attacked — but the effect on the army had been devastating. They were openly saying that the war against the Icemark couldn't be won, that the boy warlock would return with hundreds more like him to turn the very power of the heavens against them. Even though their numbers now stood at more than five hundred thousand, with two more full armies on the way, the Imperial soldiers now genuinely believed that they couldn't crush the tiny defense force that stood between them and victory. Scipio Bellorum had hanged more than three hundred of the loudest mutineers before any semblance of order was regained, and he'd flogged more than a thousand more. Eventually the soldiers were more afraid of him than they were of an enemy who could use lightning against them. This was the way Bellorum controlled his armies. They had to believe the consequences of failure were far worse than anything the enemy could do to them. Only then would they march into the worst kind of horror and fight their way clear, rather than anger their general.

Once Bellorum had reestablished his control, he called a parade and rode his horse to a low hill where he sat looking down on the massive congregation of fighting men. Pikes bristled like a wintertime forest, pennants and banners snapped and rattled in the breeze, and armor glittered like sparks in the forge of the gods. No army in all of history had ever been assembled that matched its size and discipline, and it wasn't even at full strength yet!

Bellorum knew he had reached the peak of his powers, and yet still this tiny barbarian army was holding him at bay. Every move he'd made against them had been countered with a skill and ferocity he reluctantly found admirable. And now his army was wavering on the very brink of mutiny. He looked out at them, knowing that if they chose, they could ride him down and crush him before he'd even have time to express mild surprise. But equally, he knew they would never dare to move against him. He was the general, and they knew their place.

"The warlock is dead!" he suddenly shouted without any preamble or introduction. "Killed by his own weapon. I watched them carry his blackened body from the field."

The army remained deathly quiet.

"There are no others who have the ability to call down lightning. If there were, don't you think they'd have used them already? Don't you think they'd have used them to save the mounted bow-women? No! He was the only one, and he died protecting his Queen. A brave man. He met his death well."

Still the silence seethed, and Bellorum knew that the time had come for the *grand gesture* to restore the morale of his soldiers. "But I intend to make his sacrifice an empty act. *I* will lead the combined cavalry against the queenling and her ragged troopers and tame leopards. We are one hundred thousand of the world's best horsemen against six thousand members of a circus act!"

Overhead a skylark soared into the sky, its triumphant song erupting into the air and falling on the ears of the silent army. This was something new to Bellorum: His soldiers actually felt sympathy for the enemy, even admiration. The sudden realization made him almost choke with fury.

"The army will remain on parade to witness the destruction of the barbarian Queen!" His voice cut through the silence with a deadly assurance. Then he turned his horse and rode away to the assembly point to await the cavalry. Once the victory was won, they'd cheer and their good morale would once again be another tool to be used to further his plans. This hard-fought war would be won, and the Empire extended to the north, where the natural resources of timber, iron, and brilliant soldiers would help in the future campaigns he was already planning.

Pain! Deep, tearing, throbbing, needle-sharp, hammer-blunt pain — ripping through his body and through his mind, twisting deep in his guts and slicing at his skin with razors and broken glass. Oskan wanted to scream, but his vocal cords had burned away. He was desperate for water and he could hear it dripping all around him, but his charred tongue found nothing in his mouth but blisters and scorched flesh. For hours he lay on the ropes of the low bed, unable to move, the pressure of the hemp on his destroyed skin sending new agonies deep into his body.

At last he found the strength to tear his mind from the searing pain, and he prayed to the Goddess for release. And slowly, slowly, his mind faded into the dark, away from the torture of his burns, and he fell into the blessed release of the coma his overloaded nervous system had so far denied him.

The smell of him filled the cavern, like the ashes of a bonfire that have cooled in the morning dew. His skin oozed pus and clear serum that dripped through the ropes of his bed and onto the mud of the wet floor. Long, sticky tendrils gradually dangled and lengthened down to the glutinous, saturated earth. Eventually, after many long hours, the pendulous stalactites of bodily juices made contact with the thick, rich mud, and at the same time a small spark of consciousness returned to the warlock's mind.

He shrank from the agony, but before he could flee, a voice echoed faintly in his head: *"Remember what you have been told, Oskan, Beloved of the Mother. Death would fall from the sky and healing would rise from the earth. Call now on the Goddess and be made whole."*

His mind rose through the torture of his body, and he tried to look around him. But his eyelids were sealed shut over the jelly-filled orbs that had been boiled to blindness. He screamed silently, then, as he gathered what strength remained to him, his muscles convulsed and he sat upright, the crisped flesh cracking and snapping as his mind screamed into the blackness of the cave:

"GODDESS!"

Oskan crashed back onto the ropes of his bed, and his mind fled into unconsciousness.

But rising through the dangling tendrils of serum and mucus, power flowed from the earth. Nutrients and minerals were being drawn into his body, like the flow of oxygen and the other essentials of life between mother and unborn child through an umbilical cord.

Slowly his body began the process of repair, and as the hours passed, the rate increased, as new skin cells were forged and the layers damaged beyond healing sloughed away to mix with the mud of the cave floor.

Up above him in the infirmary, Maggiore Totus stood at the head of the first flight of steps that led down to the cave.

Wenlock Witchmother had already refused to let him go down to see Oskan, so he stood as close as he could get to the boy he'd grown to love like a nephew, if not quite a son. The old scholar fully expected Oskan to die; his injuries were so severe that recovery was surely impossible. He was also convinced that leaving him alone in a cold and wet cave would probably accelerate the process. Maggie shook his head sadly; Oskan was so young and with such fabulous potential that would now never be realized. And, he thought to himself, what would Thirrin do without her friend, without the boy who would probably have become her consort one day?

Maggiore sighed loudly, and was startled to hear the sound echo around the empty cellar. Only then did he realize that he was completely alone. The witches and other healers were busy attending to their patients on the upper levels, so, seizing his opportunity, he scurried down the steps. He didn't really know what he intended to do, other than say good-bye to the boy with the strange powers and beautiful winning smile.

The way was steep and the torch he carried burned badly, throwing an uncertain light on the steps before him. But at last he reached the bottom safely and stepped out into the mud of the cave. He was struck instantly by the cold and the earthy scent. It was so strong he coughed once or twice. It wasn't a bad smell, exactly, just very strong, like a forest after a rainstorm, but richer and with a sharp underscoring of minerals.

Maggiore raised the torch and could just make out the low bed over by the cave wall. He walked tentatively toward it, and then with a sudden rush of disgust and pity he saw the tendrils of mucus that had dripped from Oskan's ravaged skin. He stopped and peered through his spectoculums, unable to believe what he saw. Hastily he rubbed the small lenses of glass on his sleeve and looked again.

Oskan's hands lay folded on his chest, the bones gleaming through a thin covering of flesh, and his lips shone moistly in the light of the torch. Maggiore dropped to his knees and started to weep. He was now certain. He knew he was witnessing a miracle. When the boy had been brought into the cave, his hands had been burned completely away and his face had been a mask of black skin without lips, nose, or any other feature.

The old scholar placed his hands on the mud and tried to find the words he wanted. It had been many years since he had prayed, but at last he found them.

"Thank you, Goddess," he said simply, and bowed his forehead to the floor until he felt the cold, wet mud cooling his flesh.

31

Out on the plain, General Scipio Bellorum rode at the head of his cavalry. In Frostmarris the alarms were sounding as the vast hordes of more than one hundred thousand Polypontian horsemen walked slowly out over the grasslands. From the walls of the city they looked like a dark stain creeping across the once pristine green of a beautifully dyed but now battle-ragged cloth. Bugles sounded again and again through the streets, and any troops that were not already on the defenses were hurrying down to take up their positions. There wasn't exactly a panic, but there was a tautness of atmosphere and a below-surface hysteria that affected everyone.

The general had taken to the field!

General Scipio Bellorum himself had come out to fight!

On the defenses, Thirrin stood with Tharaman-Thar and Taradan watching the slow advance of the enemy cavalry. "He wants me, Tharaman. He wants me to meet him on the battlefield."

"I do believe you're right, my dear. You must have made him very angry indeed!" the beautifully clipped tones of the

Leopard King answered. "But you don't have to take up the challenge. Let him wait as long as he likes, or better still, let him come within range of the ballistas and archers, and then let's see then how long he'll sit on his tall horse with his hand so elegantly on hip."

"No, I must go out, Tharaman. I must accept his invitation to battle. He wants to end it now. We've stretched his famous army to the breaking point, and he wants us defeated and swept away. And what better way of doing that than killing me in combat?" Her voice remained even and calm, but a burning hatred blazed within her. "That man alone is responsible for this war. Every dead soldier, every dead civilian, every burned city is his responsibility, and I want to make him pay."

Tharaman's deep golden eyes regarded her for a few moments. He knew she was thinking of her father and Oskan. "But your people must have a reason to continue the struggle. If you die now, the war will be lost and the Icemark will become just another province in the Empire."

"I could have died in any one of the battles I've fought, Tharaman. That is the fate of the House of Lindenshield, that is the fate of any warrior-monarch, as well you know. But if I don't accept Bellorum's challenge, then my authority and standing will be lost, as well *he* knows. I must go."

Tharaman bowed his head, accepting her words. "Then the cavalry will ride! Taradan, send orders to the lines!"

But before the Thar's second in command could move, Thirrin raised her hand. "Wait." She paused, gathering her thoughts. "I can't ask you to join me in this battle. You've done enough in this war and now I must accept that no other help is coming from either Vampire or Wolf-folk. Whether I fall today or next week makes little difference." She drew herself up, and with tears in her eyes she said, "I release you from the alliance, you're free to go home to the Icesheets. Go with my thanks and friendship."

Tharaman-Thar gazed at her for a moment before suddenly rearing up on his hind legs, becoming a tower of brilliance and ferocity. He roared a huge challenge into the sky that echoed over the plain, and immediately three thousand Snow Leopards answered him.

Dropping back to all fours he said, "Let me remind you, Queen Thirrin of the Icemark, that I am your equal as Thar of the Icesheets and you have neither the power nor the right to dismiss me from the alliance. In the law of the Snow Leopards, agreements are binding for life. Call your warriors, friend and ally, we go to war!"

Thirrin stepped forward and hugged the huge leopard, burying her face in the deep fur of his chest, and for a moment let his purring rumble through her. "Thank you, Tharaman," she said simply. Then, turning to the Thar's second in command, she said, "Taradan, call the cavalry."

The leopard bowed his head, then stood to bark the call to arms. Behind the defenses, the human troopers and the leopards prepared for action.

Scipio Bellorum watched the defenses before him with confidence. The queenling would come out to do battle. She really had no choice. And he would annihilate her and her circus of a cavalry. He was certain the abominations of nature that took the form of talking leopards could never withstand a full volley from two hundred thousand cavalry pistols and carbines. Each of his troopers carried two long-barreled guns, and at his orders they would fire them into the enemy ranks. That alone should be enough to wipe out her combined force of six thousand, and any leopards that did survive would probably turn their spotted tails and flee.

No action that Scipio Bellorum had personally led had ever been lost, and he was fully confident that the coming battle would last only a matter of a few minutes. Back behind their lines, the Polypontian army watched as their general prepared to destroy the enemy cavalry. Many of them had fought through this long campaign with a growing sense of admiration for the soldiers of the Icemark and their young Queen. Some of the officers had privately started to say that the Icemark should be embraced as an ally rather than fought against, and that it should be granted the status of a Client Kingdom under the protection of the Emperor and Senate. But their general was determined to defeat them in the field.

He could be clearly seen watching the defenses of Frostmarris through his monoculum, waiting for the enemy cavalry to emerge. Suddenly he pointed, and all eyes turned to the gate in the system of ditches and ramparts. Queen Thirrin and her combined cavalry of humans and leopards were walking slowly out onto the plain.

They came on in twin columns, and as the Imperial soldiers watched they fanned out to form a fighting front that alternated between horse and leopard. At their head rode the girl Queen and the largest of the leopards. A murmur rose up from the Polypontian soldiers, and Bellorum gave orders for his cavalry to advance. As the two sides trotted toward each other, a trooper in the Icemark cavalry unfurled a banner. The device on it showed a galloping horse and a running leopard, and over both rose the fighting white bear of the House of Lindenshield.

Scipio Bellorum rode hand on hip, a smile on his lips. Soon, the queenling would be dead and the war all but over. He raised his hand, and his troopers drew their long-barreled pistols from the holsters on their saddles. They rode on, guiding their mounts with their knees.

Thirrin stood up in her stirrups, drew her sword, and circled it over her head. Immediately the cavalry of the Icemark broke into a controlled gallop, the human troopers singing their fierce battle paean and the leopards letting out the coughing bark of their challenge. Bellorum maintained his trot and leveled his pistols. One hundred thousand troopers followed suit and awaited his order to fire.

Again Thirrin's voice rose into the air, high and fierce, and the leopards lowered the thick domes of their skulls as the human troopers hunched down behind their shields. Bellorum stood his ground calmly as the smashing force of Thirrin's cavalry bore down on him, then as the thunder of their hooves filled the air he fired his pistols. There was a crack of two hundred thousand other pieces, and their solid shot hit the charging cavalry. It hardly faltered as Thirrin screamed out the war cry of the Icemark: "Blood! Blast! And Fire! Blood! Blast! And Fire!"

The leopards threw up their heads, and the Queen's human troopers took up the war cry. The pistol shot had been turned by the thick fur and skulls of the leopards, and by the shields and surcoats of the troopers. They smashed as a solid wedge into the Polypontian cavalry and drove through them, slashing and hacking with their sabers and striking out with their claws.

The roar of onset echoed over the field, and the Polypontian army in their camp and the defenders around Frostmarris screamed and shouted as though they were watching a race. Up on the battlements, Maggiore Totus watched as Thirrin and the cavalry fought their way through the Empire's troopers, before galloping on in a wide arc as they wheeled to charge again.

Scipio Bellorum bellowed orders, and his cavalry turned to meet the attack. They drew their sabers, settled their shields on their arms, and charged the enemy. Once again, the roar of onset rose into the air, and the Polypontian left and right flanks closed in at the rear to completely surround the Icemark cavalry.

Thirrin and her warriors fought with a dedicated ruthlessness that slowly cut a path through the enemy. She hacked and thrust at the Polypontian soldiers who swam into her view. Her horse struck out with its hooves, and Tharaman-Thar beat aside Polypontian horses and riders with smashing blows from his massive paws. Nearby, the banner of the Icemark and Icesheets fluttered in the wind, giving a focus and a rallying point for leopard and human trooper. Then, with a final heave, they were through the enclosing ranks of the enemy. Once again, they rode on in a wide arc as they slowly turned to charge once more.

A great cheer erupted from the defenses around Frostmarris as they saw their young Queen at the head of her cavalry break free along with Tharaman-Thar. But the ranks had been thinned: Both human and leopard troopers had taken casualties, and few of those who remained were without injuries.

Scipio Bellorum was furious; twice now his cavalry had failed to hold a force of vastly inferior numbers who, even as he watched, were preparing to charge again. He rallied his men and galloped to meet the enemy.

To Maggiore Totus from his vantage point on the walls, the cavalry of the Icemark and Icesheets looked like a deadly stiletto blade thrusting through a cumbersome many-headed creature that was slowly losing strength. The dead of the

Empire's cavalry lay all over the battlefield, the greater density of their bodies showing accurately where Thirrin's route had cut through.

But something new was happening. Maggie saw that the Polypontian troopers were slowing to a trot, and bugles were braying over the land, their brassy notes thinned by distance to a lonely and wistful wail. The Icemark cavalry came on but it, too, began to slow, and soon both forces had stopped and were gazing at each other over the plain. Then Thirrin and Tharaman-Thar could be seen walking slowly forward, as two figures detached themselves from the enemy ranks and advanced to meet them.

Thirrin watched as the man approached on his tall horse. His hair was steel gray and his eyes a deadly cold blue, but he rode with an elegance that suggested refinement and civilization. With him was a young officer, who saluted her smartly when they all drew to a halt and faced one another. She returned the salute and waited quietly.

"I see you have brought one of your talking leopards with you," Bellorum said with only the slightest trace of an Empire accent. These were the first words Thirrin had ever heard him utter and he'd obviously learned her language well.

"I have 'brought' nobody. However, Lord Tharaman, One Hundredth Thar of the Icesheets, has been good enough to accompany me to this meeting."

"Oh, it has a title," Bellorum said sarcastically. "Does it do tricks as well?"

"I perform only one trick, General, the killing of Polypontian soldiers, and I'm rather good at it, don't you think?" Tharaman answered.

Thirrin was enormously gratified to see the general's eyes widen slightly as the full truth of the rumors hit home. Yes, the leopards could talk, and Bellorum was shocked at the natural ease with which the words emerged from the great toothed mouth.

The young Imperial officer was visibly shaken, then, remembering the rules of etiquette, he saluted Tharaman as was due to even an enemy monarch. The huge leopard Thar inclined his head slightly in reply and said, "Is there some purpose to this meeting other than the exchange of insults? Otherwise, might I suggest we get on with the fighting? Our cavalry has some business to finish, and as there are so many of you it may take some time."

Bellorum recovered himself sufficiently to answer. "Yes, there is a purpose. I propose single combat between myself and Queen Thirrin, here and now, on this field."

"I accept," she answered immediately.

"Wait, you don't have to do this, Thirrin," said Tharaman softly. "We're slicing his carthorses and fancily dressed farm boys to ribbons. Why else do you think he's offering single combat? His cavalry's losing and he knows it. He's hoping to turn the tide by beating you in a duel. Order the charge now and we'll drive them from the field."

"I said, *I accept,* Tharaman," she answered, without taking her eyes off the general. Then, glancing at her ally, she said, "Don't oppose me in this. I want the duel! I can kill him and avenge all those who've died!" She blazed with a barely controlled fury and an insatiable need to make the man who was responsible for all the death and destruction pay with his life.

Bellorum laughed. "Come now, my dear leopard, be a good little pet and don't question your owner's decisions. Can't you see she's eager to die?"

Tharaman's eyes burned into the general and held his chilling gaze. "If the Queen of the Icemark doesn't kill you, I'll make it my personal task to seek you out and kill you myself. A slow disembowelment should be entertaining and will make some small amends for your impertinence. Can you sing, General? Because I do so like to hear my victims give voice when I play with them."

Bellorum's gaze didn't waver, but neither did he reply to the leopard. Instead he drew his saber and said, "I assume swords are acceptable? Normally the choice of weapon is the right of the one challenged, but that is the etiquette of *civilized* lands, so you will understand why I waive such niceties."

"On what terms do we fight this duel?" Thirrin asked coldly.

"Terms? What other terms can there be? If you are killed, the Icemark's resistance will end and a new province is added to the Empire. If I am killed, the army will withdraw in disarray . . . at least until the next campaigning season and the appointment of a new general."

"So, at best we'll get a breathing space."

Bellorum shrugged. "But of course. Such is the role of the victim."

"Let us fight, General."

Both forces drew back to form an arena for the combatants, leaving Thirrin and Bellorum at the center. A breathless hush descended as they each sat watching the other. Then the general began to slowly circle, while Thirrin's horse turned to keep him in sight. For several long moments Bellorum moved in a wide arc around her, then suddenly he struck, his horse crashing shoulder to shoulder with Thirrin's mount, while his saber struck down like lightning made steel.

Her shield parried the blow and she stabbed at his throat, where his sword swept her blade aside. The horses kicked and slashed at each other with their teeth as their riders continued to trade cut for thrust. The ring of saber on shield resounded over the plain like discordant bells, as the combatants circled and struck. Both were deadly accurate in their attacks, and both were skilled in their defensive blocks.

Bellorum's eyes were alight as though with laughter. He was strong and confident, his natural fighting skill polished by years of battle experience, while the young girl before him was a mere talented novice. Abruptly he leaned in close and struck her across the face with the hilt of his sword, but she hardly flinched, and replied by drawing blood from his lip with the rim of her shield. He feinted a strike at her midriff but then struck savagely upward, cutting her chin. She replied with a vicious chop at his head that he parried. And then, smiling pleasantly, he ran his sword up to its hilt into her horse.

Screaming, the animal reared and fell dead. A huge despairing cry rose up from the Icemark cavalry, but Thirrin rolled clear and regained her feet in time to take a rain of blows on her shield. From the advantage of his height Bellorum now pushed and harried her, forcing her to defend herself from his attacks and also from the vicious kicks and bites of his horse. The Imperial troops cheered excitedly; the end was near, the young Queen must surely be killed.

For several long minutes Thirrin fought a dogged defense, but she was getting tired. Sweat was trickling into her eyes, and she couldn't risk even a moment's break in concentration to wipe it away. She almost screamed aloud in frustration and anger. If she fell, so did the Icemark. She would have failed her people. Tharaman-Thar and the rest of her cavalry watched in growing fear as she weakened. The huge leopard was itching to leap into the fighting area and smash Bellorum to a quivering pulp of broken bones and ripped flesh, but the rules of dueling held him back. And not only that, this was Thirrin's personal battle, and she would hate him as surely as the enemy if he intervened.

The general's horse struck out with its hooves once more, catching Thirrin's shield squarely in the center and knocking her flat. Bellorum sensed the final triumph. Now was the moment! Now was the end of the Icemark! Raising his sword, he smiled at his troopers and hacked down at Thirrin, who had struggled to one knee before him. At the last moment, she swayed aside and the blow went wide, forcing him to overextend his reach. Immediately, she chopped at his wrist with her saber, and his hand fell into the dust, still clutching his sword.

Bellorum screamed and reeled in his saddle, a fountain of blood pumping into the air. Thirrin leaped to her feet and, grabbing the reins of his horse, she struck at his head. But even now, the general had enough strength to deflect the strike with his shield, and the blade sliced open his cheek. With a wild yell, the Imperial cavalry leaped forward, breaking the laws of the duel and threatening to trample Thirrin, but the troopers and leopards of the Icemark crashed into them, while Tharaman-Thar stood over her and killed all who dared come near.

Bellorum was surrounded by his soldiers as they bundled him away from the field. Thirrin leaped up onto Tharaman's back and led her cavalry in pursuit. Thousands of the enemy fell to the sabers and claws of the Icemark's cavalry before they reached the safety of their cannon range. Then, leading her troopers in a slow parade across the plain, Thirrin retrieved Bellorum's hand and saber and, tying them to a lance, she led her cavalry in a victorious procession past the Polypontian lines.

The fierce warrior blood of the House of Lindenshield and that of the fighting women of the Hypolitan pounded through her veins and arteries. She had defeated her enemy, and he'd escaped death only by the intervention of his entire cavalry. At last she felt she'd struck back at the Empire in a way that would sorely hurt it. Tharaman-Thar sensed her elation and roared mightily as Thirrin leaned forward and buried her face deep in the thick fur of his neck. "We got him, Tharaman! We got him!"

"*You* got him, my dear. You got him very nicely."

The Polypontians fired warning cannon shots as she rode by, sounding almost like a salute as cheers rang out over the plain. Thirrin was amazed to note that not all of them came from the defenses around Frostmarris.

But as she turned to look at the walls of the city, the ever-present memory of Oskan crowded in, and she lowered her head. "Let's go back to Frostmarris, Tharaman," she said quietly, and the cavalry turned for home.

32

Maggiore Totus sat quietly at his desk. At his elbow was a glass of wine and, despite the warmth and brilliance of the early summer day, a candle burned in the stick next to his papers and a fire danced in the hearth. Grimswald, the ancient Chamberlain-of-the-Royal-Paraphernalia, had "adopted" Maggie as his own personal charge and made sure that the old scholar always had everything he needed, even if sometimes he did overdo things. Maggie was tidying the notes he'd made while watching the cavalry battle from the walls of Frostmarris, and adding to them the eyewitness accounts of Thirrin's duel with General Bellorum.

"All very exciting and satisfactory, Primplepuss," he murmured to the small cat, who lay in a patch of sunlight on his desk. She meowed quietly and had a quick wash.

"The Queen came close to killing the old devil, and she's certainly put him out of action for the foreseeable future. But even so, it's his mind we need to fear more than his fighting ability, and I suppose that's as sharp and as ruthless as ever."

The army of the Polypontian Empire still held its position on the rising ground to the south of the plain around

Frostmarris and showed no signs of leaving, despite the defeat and severe wounding of their general. In fact, they were being reinforced on a daily basis, according to Thirrin's white werewolf guards, who continued to act as spies.

"I think we can expect a renewed attack at any time, and if our other allies don't arrive soon, they'll have nothing to do but bury our dead," Maggie continued to his audience of one small cat. Unlike Thirrin and Tharaman, he still believed that Grishmak and his werewolves would honor their agreement and that even the Vampires would fulfill their obligations to their treaty with the Icemark — but timing was all-important, and the Empire might yet deliver its final blow before they were ready.

"We can only hope for miracles, Primplepuss," he went on. "Speaking of which, I have an appointment." Climbing to his feet, he stroked the cat until she purred, then left his room and headed out along the twisting corridors of the palace. He was on his way to the infirmary.

Over the last two days he'd become very good at avoiding the witches as he made his way down to the cellar in the infirmary building. They were often far too busy to notice one old man walking quietly along, and it was a simple business to reach the cellar, collect a torch from one of the sconces on the wall, and then carefully descend the wet and broken steps that led to the cave.

Now, as he held the torch high over his head, he could see the pitted and worn treads that corkscrewed sharply to the right as the spiral stairwell disappeared into the black depths. The now familiar scent of damp earth rose up to meet him, as did the constant drip and splash of water. He was smiling to himself as he picked his way carefully down the steps. During his visits he'd been watching the progress of a miracle, and he fully expected to be further astonished when he once more raised his torch over Oskan. But even though it was an incredibly happy event occurring at a time of so much fear and destruction, he hadn't told anyone else about it. Not even Thirrin, who probably had more right than anyone else to know. He wasn't entirely sure why he'd kept it secret, and if his logical scientist's brain analyzed his motives, it shied away from drawing the most obvious conclusion: Maggiore Totus had a superstitious dread that if too many people knew, then the miracle would stop and Oskan would die.

At last he reached the bottom of the broken stairwell and stepped out across the muddy floor. He knew the way perfectly by now and hardly needed the torch; its light would be used purely to observe the wonder. Over against the far wall he could just make out the low bed, and he hurried forward. He splashed to a halt before the prone figure of the injured warlock and held up his torch; as the shadows fled, he gasped aloud. The long tendrils of mucus and serum that hung from Oskan's body had developed into ropes of skin that buried themselves deep into the thick, rich mud of the cave floor, and they pulsed slightly as he looked at them. But most astonishing of all was Oskan himself. He was almost perfect. All of the burned skin had sloughed away, to be replaced with healthy pink flesh that seemed to glow under the torchlight. His hands, lying folded on his chest, were shapely and smooth, and his facial features had been completely rebuilt so that the familiar expression of faint amusement presented itself to the world once more. Not only that, but Oskan actually seemed to have grown taller, his legs reaching much farther down the bed than when the healers had first left him in the cave. And even his hair was growing back, a dark fuzz clouding the new skin, like down on a hatchling.

Maggiore laughed aloud for joy, but then when Oskan's eyelids twitched and he seemed about to wake, he clamped his hand over his mouth. The old scholar knew that the healing sleep was not yet finished and he quietly withdrew so as not to disturb it. He paused only to sink his hands into the mineral-rich mud and thank the Goddess for her gift of healing. Then, taking up his torch, he hurried back up the steps.

Scipio Bellorum sat in his chair rather than lying in bed as the surgeons had wanted. The stump of his wrist still throbbed where they'd cauterized the arteries with red-hot irons and sealed the wound by dipping it in boiling pitch. The pain that had erupted along his arm from the outraged nerve endings had been received in stony silence by the general, who'd redirected the agony to feed a massive rage and determination for revenge. And after the best doctors the Empire could furnish had finished butchering him, he'd willed himself to stand and walk to the entrance of his tent, where he'd presented himself to the waiting army.

There'd been no cheering from the soldiers at his bravery and pure undiluted willpower, just a low buzz of respect. Every one of his men knew that he was one of the toughest in the army; this little display had merely confirmed it, and had also begun a slow realization that Scipio Bellorum was quite mad. His many enemies had known this for years, but it was an insanity that was happily and knowingly embraced by Bellorum himself. He hid it behind a facade of rationality and control that had allowed him to use its energy to reach the heights of his ambitions. What other psychopath had killed as many as he in his long campaigns, or reached the levels of personal power that placed him second only to the Emperor in the world's greatest Empire? Madness was a handicap only if you couldn't control its irrationalities. If, like Bellorum, you could, the potential was almost limitless.

He'd returned from his presentation to the army safe in the knowledge that he still retained their respect — their love he'd have had no use for — and to drive home his standing, he'd had the officers whose squadrons had performed poorly in the battle whipped in front of their men. It was silently acknowledged by all that his own shortcomings had been punished enough by the loss of his hand.

Within hours, he'd begun training with the weapons master to learn how to use a saber with his left hand. Riding would be easy; cavalry mounts were mostly guided by the rider's knees, anyway, and a shield could easily be modified to his needs. He'd returned from his training alight with the possibilities. All defensive and fighting methods were geared toward a right-handed opponent. What glorious confusion he could cause! That night he'd gone to bed far from disappointed; the army was still his to dominate and manipulate as he chose, and soon even the supreme abilities of the Icemark's defenders would be swept aside. Even they couldn't resist a host of more than half a million; it was simply impossible.

His experiences had also forced him to reach a conclusion about the people of the Icemark. They were clearly ungovernable, so when the war was won, he'd convince the Emperor to allow him to "cleanse" the land and repopulate it with model citizens from south of the border. The true potential of the new country could then be opened up, and the huge mineral reserves and timber stocks more fully exploited for the good of the Empire. And when he'd finally tidied up this annoyingly drawn-out campaign, he'd rest the army for six months before beginning another action somewhere to the south, where the opposition wouldn't be too stiff and the soldiers could regain their pride.

Only the ache and throb in his injured wrist reminded him of the failure of the day. Somewhere, deep in his mind, his madness glowed like a banked-down fire, waiting for the opportunity to blaze into raging life. But for now, Scipio Bellorum kept it under control and bided his time.

Thirrin hadn't been back to the infirmary since they'd taken Oskan down to the cave. She was afraid of what they might tell her. She knew that if anything happened to him, they would bring her news of it, but when it came, she expected it to be bad. For the past few days every servant and housecarl who'd approached her had been held in her steely glare until they'd walked by saluting or had given her an unrelated message of one sort or another.

She now sat in the Great Hall polishing Bellorum's saber, while Tharaman-Thar slept by the fire with Primplepuss. Down on the defenses the nuisance raids continued as the Polypontians kept the defenders busy, but there was no immediate danger. It was well known that the enemy was preparing for a final assault, and when it came, everyone would know about it.

She was resigned to the coming defeat. But not one of her soldiers suspected that their Queen believed the coming assault would sweep them aside, to end the nation of the Icemark and the ruling House of Lindenshield. Outwardly Thirrin appeared as confident and as strong as ever, but she had despaired of help ever arriving. She had only one ambition left, and that was to live long enough to kill Bellorum, the man who was responsible for all the disasters of the last few months.

Her father was dead, her kingdom was as good as lost, and her greatest friend lay burned beyond recognition and was probably dying even now, if he wasn't already dead. Only the discipline of her military training, her pride, and her towering hatred of Bellorum kept her going.

She added a final glittering sheen to the saber, and prayed that she might use it to cut out the heart of General Scipio Bellorum. Then she rammed it back into the scabbard she'd found for it in the armory, the metallic ring of the blade immediately waking Tharaman-Thar, who raised his mighty head and glared around the hall in search of enemies. Finding none, he yawned enormously, his teeth gleaming in the torchlight.

"Has the assault begun?" he asked.

"No, there's still time for something to eat if you're hungry," Thirrin answered, knowing that he would be.

"Well, perhaps a small ox would suffice," he answered, and nodded at a watchful chamberlain, who hurried over. "Beef, my good man, and perhaps a little something for the Queen?" he said, and looked questioningly at her.

"Why not," she answered decisively. "A cold meat pie and some bread."

The chamberlain headed for the kitchens, and Tharaman nodded approvingly at her. "That's right, my dear. You must keep up your strength."

She smiled despite the desperation of their position. There were times when the giant leopard reminded her of her father, but with a more refined accent. "Don't worry, I'm not going to starve myself. I want to be fit and well when I next meet Bellorum," she said.

"If he dares show his face in battle again."

"He'd better. Otherwise I'll go looking for him. We have unfinished business."

"Yes," Tharaman agreed, and bent his head to help Primplepuss wash herself. "But you have to accept that he may die from his injuries. The Empire doesn't have the advantage of witchcraft to help heal the wounded." He rose to his feet and fetched Primplepuss back from the middle of the floor, where his cleaning tongue had sent her flying. "I'm sorry, my sweeting," he said to the little cat as he bent and gently picked her up in his giant jaws.

"Perhaps we could send Wenlock Witchmother over to their lines under truce," Thirrin suggested, only half joking.

"Unacceptable cruelty," the leopard said after a few moments' thought.

The arrival of the food interrupted their conversation for a while, but after they'd been served and the scullions had withdrawn, Thirrin said, "The werewolves think they'll attack tonight."

"Really? Isn't that rather unusual for humans?" asked Tharaman, who was used to the Ice Troll Wars fought in the long night of the northern winter.

"Yes, very. I think they hope to unnerve us."

"How refreshingly naive of Bellorum. There's hope yet."

Thirrin smiled sadly. "No, there's not."

A commotion at the great double doors of the hall drew their attention, and they watched as Olememnon made his way across the floor toward them. "Ah, food!" he called, and smiled. "I could eat an ox, and I see Tharaman already has."

Thirrin waved at the chamberlain, who nodded and hurried off to the kitchens. "How are the defenses?" she asked automatically.

"Fine, fine. Bellorum's sent the usual party of pike and musket across to keep us busy, but nothing too worrying. The Basilea sent me off to get some food and a rest before it all starts tonight."

Thirrin glanced at him sharply, but he smiled. "Don't worry, I'm not going to have a nervous breakdown because a new Basilea is giving me orders. I've been working with her for days now; she's good. And anyway, I've known Iffi since she was a girl. Though now I have to call her *Iphigenia*, and when any of the troops are nearby, I address her as *Ma'am*. It's all she can do not to giggle sometimes."

"How's morale?" Tharaman asked.

"Good. At least on the surface it is. Have you noticed how none of the troops mention the arrival of the allies anymore?"

"Yes," Tharaman answered quietly. "They seem to have acquired a strength and dignity in their despair."

"I think we all have," said Thirrin, confident enough in her uncle's recovery from his earlier grief to reveal her own feelings.

"You, too, eh?" Olememnon said in surprise. "Funny, but only myself and Maggie still expect them to turn up." He reached across and patted her knee. "Don't worry, they're on their way. They're just cutting it a little close, that's all."

The chamberlain then returned with Olememnon's meal, and her uncle turned his undivided attention to the slabs of meat and loaves of bread.

33

General Bellorum sat astride his tall horse and rested the stump of his wrist against his hip in his characteristically arrogant riding style. Pain coursed up his arm and through his frame in agonizing waves, but it was important that the men believed he was unaffected by his injury, so he urged his horse on and trotted along the ranks with his staff officers.

The moon would rise in less than an hour, by which time his soldiers would have flooded the plain of Frostmarris and would have risen over the defensive banks and ditches around the city, as unstoppable as the sea. He had drawn reinforcements from every point of the Empire, and when the order to advance was given, it would be repeated in more than twenty different languages.

Earlier, batteries of cannons had been positioned under cover of darkness, their wheels muffled in rags, their gun crews dressed in dark clothing and with blackened faces. Then, before the army started its advance, the huge guns began their bombardment. Brilliant flashes of orange and crimson light erupted into the night sky as salvos of ball and chain shot slammed into the ditches and ramparts of the defenses, sending up fountains of earth and smashing through palisades.

But then the defenders' artillery began its reply, and the giant crossbows of the ballistas shot steel bolts down at the flashes of light that revealed the gun emplacements. The deep thrum of the ballistas' released bowstrings was followed by the silken hiss of the bolts as they flew toward their targets. And farther behind the lines, the rockapults hurled a rain of boulders high into the sky and down onto the gun teams as the Empire's soldiers bravely worked to maintain their bombardment.

For more than an hour the Polypontian artillery tried to smash the defenses of Frostmarris while most of the soldiers of the Icemark sheltered behind their ramparts. But the ballista and rockapult teams fought back with deadly accuracy, until eventually the guns fell silent and the order to withdraw was given to the survivors. Rocks and boulders continued to rain from the sky, and the steel bolts scythed into the bombardiers, sometimes pinning together two or even three soldiers in a hideous reminder of a child's paper chain.

When the bombardment stopped, almost a minute of deathly quiet followed before a single cheer rose up from the defenses, and soon others joined in until the sound swelled and rolled around the ramparts. Now the Icemark's soldiers emerged from their shelters and took up their positions on the defenses again. Soon, rock-filled barrels were rolled into the pits and craters made by the cannon fire, and teams of engineers swarmed over the palisades, lashing together the broken wood with ropes and filling in gaps with huge logs dragged from the forest.

Bellorum made a mental note to call the commander of artillery to account after the victory, then he put the next phase of the battle into action. The enemy must not be allowed any more time to recover from the bombardment. He drew his saber and, holding it aloft in his left hand, he looked out over the shadowy mass of his army and felt a cruel pride swell up in his breast. Here, more than twenty nations had come together under the guiding power of the Empire to smash and destroy the resistance of the Icemark, and his was the strength that wielded this formidable weapon. He smiled to himself as the steel of his saber glittered in the starlight above his head, then he chopped it downward viciously. "Forward, soldiers of the Empire! Forward to victory!"

The order was taken up by the officers and field commanders throughout the ranks, and the massive Polypontian war machine rolled down onto the plain of Frostmarris.

On the defenses, Thirrin watched with Tharaman-Thar as the final battle began. Each of the enemy soldiers carried a torch, and as they advanced toward them it seemed that a universe of stars had taken up arms, each separate regiment clearly defined like a galaxy in the vastness of the army's firmament.

"What a beautiful sight, Tharaman," she whispered.

"Yes," he agreed. "It's almost possible to forget why they're here."

"Almost, but not quite," she answered, turning to issue orders to her officers. Drums all along the defenses began to rattle out a stirring beat, and the housecarls began their traditional chant: "OUT! Out! Out! OUT! Out! Out! OUT! Out! Out!" The rhythm echoed along the lines, swelling to a crescendo as more and more soldiers took it up. The leopards and human troopers of the cavalry stood with Thirrin and the Thar, as did the white werewolves, who had been through so much with the human Queen that they'd come to regard her as their own. Farther along the line, the Hypolitan, under their new

Basilea, readied themselves for the onslaught, the deep voice of Olememnon shouting out orders and steadying the line. And still the housecarls chanted their challenge, "OUT! Out! Out! OUT! Out! Out! OUT! Out! Out!" mingling with a synchronized rattle as the young boys and girls of the drum corps beat a fighting rhythm for the coming attack.

Out on the plain, the enemy came on, the fife and drums of their own military bands echoing eerily in the dark. As soon as they came within range, the Icemark's ballistas and rockapults launched an attack against the advancing horde, but they never wavered in their advance. Within a few paces, longbows began to hiss all along the defenses as flights of arrows were shot into the dark sky, causing the advancing line of torches to dance and sink as the Imperial soldiers fell under the onslaught of the terrible rain. But still they came on, unstoppable in their thousands, those in the forefront pushed on by the press of soldiers behind.

Soon they were within range of the javelins thrown by regiments of fighting women in the Hypolitan army, who carried crescent-shaped shields and were deadly accurate with their throwing spears. The high-pitched crack of the opening musket volley sounded in reply, and the solid lead shot smashed into the defenders, bringing down the first casualties on the Icemark's side.

Thirrin now drew her sword and called out the war cry of the House of Lindenshield: "The enemy is upon us! Blood! Blast! And Fire! Blood! Blast! And Fire!"

A great shout rose up from her soldiers, and they surged forward to meet the first ranks of the enemy. The roar of battle could be heard across the plain, and immediately the sheer weight of the Imperial army bore the defenders back. Soon they were being forced back up the slope of the second embankment in the triple line of defenses. Thirrin called aloud the first note of the cavalry paean, and immediately her troopers, leopard and human, answered, singing out the war hymn with a growing ferocity as they drove their feet into the earth and refused to retreat farther. The werewolf guard clustered around her, howling and snarling viciously as they struck out at the Imperial soldiers or leaped on them to rip out their throats.

Farther along the line, Olememnon and the Hypolitans were being pushed hard by a massive phalanx of pikes, the giant spears thrusting through and over their shield-wall, slashing throats, piercing eyes, and splitting skulls. Time and again the warriors dived between the long spears to hack at the soldiers who wielded them, but as soon as they fell, others took their place. The Hypolitans rained javelins down into the press of enemy soldiers, and the new Basilea led countercharges into the phalanx, driving them back briefly before fighting a controlled retreat as the Imperial regiments came on again in overwhelming numbers.

Meanwhile, all along the line, the fyrd soldiers fought as well as the housecarls, but they lacked the experience and stamina of the professional soldiers and gradually their shield-wall began to buckle under the enormous pressure of the enemy's numbers. Thirrin sent as many housecarls as could be spared to shore up their line, but soon her own position was too hard pressed to send any more help, and the line buckled further.

Bellorum watched as much as he could through his monoculum, but the light provided by the torches was only fitful and everything was a seething mass of confusion. He lowered his spyglass in exasperation and turned to look at the horizon, where the full moon would rise. Sure enough, a faint glow was strengthening, and as he watched, a sliver of brilliant light rose into the sky. He smiled faintly; now his troops would be able to see exactly who they were slaughtering.

Slowly the brilliant disc sailed into the field of stars. It was so bright that Bellorum could easily read the hands on his chronometer as he checked the time to mark the moment for posterity in his memory. He turned back to watch the plain and saw the shadows withdrawing before the power of the subtle light. Soon the battlefield was almost as light as day, and he raised his eyeglass to watch his army forcing its way over the defenses.

As he followed the action, he clearly saw the barbarian Queen raising the rag of a banner she'd unfurled at the head of her cavalry, and he heard her high-pitched voice rising fiercely over the noise of battle, encouraging her troops.

"Too late, dear child. I do believe your shield-wall is broken," he said with quiet glee.

"*To me! To me!*" Thirrin called to her troops, unfurling the battle banner of the cavalry, and watching helplessly as the Hypolitan and regiments of housecarls were cut off by a seething mass of the enemy as the fyrd line finally broke. Tharaman-Thar stood up on his hind legs, towering over the battle, and roared into the sky.

"Quickly, Thirrin, climb on my back. We must bring them in!" he shouted.

Without hesitating she leaped onto his shoulders and called out the war cry as the giant leopard crashed down into the enemy lines. With her charged her human troopers, who'd followed her example and leaped onto the backs of their leopard comrades. With her, too, came the white werewolves, ferocious as they smashed into the Imperial soldiers. Thirrin and her cavalry sliced through the enemy, cutting them down with saber and claw, driving toward the Hypolitan and housecarls. Soon they reached the beleaguered soldiers and, fighting alongside them, they fought their way back to the highest point of the defenses, forming a shield-wall facing outward in all directions. The enemy surrounded them, and they were completely cut off from the city. The tiny garrison left holding the walls closed the gates and prepared to defend Frostmarris to the last.

Down on what was left of the defenses, the new Basilea and Olememnon barked orders at their soldiers and the housecarls, shoring up the shield-wall, while Thirrin and her troopers took up their position around their banner.

"Here we stand and die, Tharaman," said Thirrin.

"Here we stand. But let's see what the fates will send us. I won't say we die yet."

An eerie silence fell over the battlefield, and the defenders watched in amazement as the enemy drew back and stood watching them. The army of the Empire stretched as far as the eye could see under the silver-gray light of the moon, and for a moment they looked like ghosts, insubstantial and impotent, as though the merest breath of wind could blow them away. But then the illusion was shattered as they began to chant. The sound was raw and stirring, swelling and rolling over the plain as first one regiment and then another took up the refrain.

"What are they doing?" Thirrin asked, puzzled.

"I do believe they're singing your praises," Tharaman said. "Yes, if you listen carefully, you can occasionally hear your name among all the other foreign words."

"Well, how nice," she said sarcastically, but deep within herself she secretly found the salute oddly moving. "Does that mean they'll go away now and leave us in peace?"

The Thar laughed bitterly. "Somehow I doubt it."

The chanting stopped suddenly, and then a low drumming began as the massive army beat spear, sword, and ax on shield. Steadily the sound rose into a thunderous crescendo before dying away to silence. Orders then rang out from the officers of each of the many regiments, and the soldiers parted ranks, making a corridor down which a dark mass of soldiers could be seen moving. They carried no torches and their armor and uniforms were entirely black. As they marched, they unfurled banners of black cloth that had no insignia or marking of any sort on them. This was the elite Black Army of Bellorum's invasion force. They carried the name of "The Undefeated and Invincible," and none stood in their way.

"Here we go, then, Tharaman," Thirrin said quietly. Then, raising her voice to battle pitch, she shouted, "Prepare to receive unwelcome guests!"

Deep, deep in the dark, a small suggestion of self began to form. A broken grain, a shard of personality that placed itself with certainty within his head. He rose toward it, toward the thing that was himself, and as he approached, it expanded, filling more of the space he'd left empty. Soon, he filled the entire dome of his skull and then spread down into the rest of his body and beyond, via his senses, into his surroundings.

The name *Oskan* occurred to him and it seemed to fit, so he quickly grasped it and made it his own. This was the key, he somehow knew, to memory. But before he could use it, something else plucked and worried at the edge of his newly found mind. "*They're here!*" it said.

Who are here? he wondered. Then, realizing he couldn't know without his memory, he allowed it to return, and it flooded through him in a tumble and jar of childhood, adolescence, mother, Thirrin, war, and pain! Terrible pain!

He screamed and sat up, expecting charred flesh and finding instead smoothness and wholeness. Then with a shock he grasped his hands. He had hands! Quickly he explored; he had a face and legs and every other part he'd had before the pain had come! But he couldn't see. He was blind!

No, he was in darkness. From a point over to his right, a faint glimmer of light framed itself within a doorway. He placed his feet on the ground and found wet mud, and as he stood, strange tubes of flesh fell from his body and landed with a splash on the ground. He walked forward; he had no weakness, but even so he fell to his knees and shouted aloud for joy. "Goddess! I am healed! I am cured!" He offered a silent prayer of thanks, rocking backward and forward on his knees.

Then, on the edge of his rejoicing mind, the words came back: *They're here!*

He gasped as the full memory of the war came crashing in on him. "They're here!" he shouted aloud, and jumping to his feet he ran toward the door. Through it he found a stairwell, and climbed by degrees back to the light.

The going was slow because the steps were worn and broken, and he was often forced to crawl forward, groping his way over the stonework. At last, he emerged blinking in the dim light of a single torch.

The brilliance of it seemed to scorch his eyes, causing tears to stream down his cheeks, but gradually he was able to open his eyelids a fraction and look around him. He had no idea where he was. It was obviously a vaulted cellar, probably somewhere within the citadel, but exactly where remained a mystery. Across the empty floor, more steps led to an upper level, and he made his way toward it. As he climbed, the low murmur of voices reached him and he paused. He couldn't afford to be delayed by anyone, and as though to confirm this, the voice in his head came again.

They're here! Tell Thirrin now!

Quickly he made up his mind, and as soon as the voices moved away he ran swiftly up the steps, his bare feet making no sound. He found himself in one of the infirmary's healing rooms. Now he knew exactly where he was, and after getting his bearings he ran through the nearest door and along a corridor, then out into the cool moonlit night. The courtyard was empty; the few soldiers of the garrison were all on the wall, watching the struggle on the defenses far below.

On he ran into the streets, and down to the southern gate. Few saw him, and those who did thought his pale form in the moonlight was one of the city ghosts, disturbed by the disastrous turn the battle was taking.

He reached the portcullis, found the stairway that led up to the battlements, and ran up to the very top. Before him the plain opened out, beautiful and glowing under the full moon. But his attention was immediately drawn to where Thirrin, Tharaman, and the remaining defenders stood, surrounded by the huge Imperial army. The sound of the fighting rose to his ears, oddly faint and unreal as though he were experiencing a particularly vivid mirage.

Soldiers on the battlements were shouting and groaning, and some even threw their spears in a futile attempt to help the hopelessly outnumbered defenders. Oskan looked around, a strange sense of power settling over him. The sky began to seethe and writhe as ions gathered, just as they had when he'd called down lightning to save Thirrin. But this time the power was benign, it would hurt no one. Its purpose was simply to magnify.

At last Oskan's eyes settled on the huge Solstice Bell that hung in its scaffolding above the gate. *They're here! Tell Thirrin now!*

He ran forward and grabbed the rope that hung from its huge form, and with a massive effort he pulled. The bell swung slowly, but remained silent. He pulled harder and at last the clapper struck the rim and a deep, mellow tone boomed out into the night. He hauled on the rope again, and stared wildly out over the plain as the power that writhed and boiled in the night sky above him fell, crackling and snapping through the dark, and struck him. This time there was no pain, only a tremendous sense of strength that filled his thin frame to brimming. His throat seemed to expand, pushing at the flesh until he thought his neck would burst, and he opened his mouth and drew breath deep, deep into his lungs, and still the bell rang on, booming and booming deeply into the night.

"They're here!" he bellowed, the words soaring out as though he had a hundred voices. "They're here! Thirrin! They're here!"

Down on the defenses, Thirrin heard his cry and turned to look up at the bell. "*Oskan?*" she whispered, unable to believe what she saw. "OSKAN!" she screamed. "Look, Tharaman, it's Oskan!"

The Snow Leopard Thar looked to where she was pointing. "Yes . . . yes! But what's he shouting?"

"They're here, Thirrin! They're here!"

"Who's here?" the Thar asked.

Still the bell boomed out into the night, filling every defending soldier with a hope they didn't understand. A stillness fell that was broken only by the bell's sonorous note.

But then, in the distance, a single howling voice rose into the air, thin and mournful, and tattered to sound-ribbons by the wind.

A great joy swelled in Thirrin's frame and she screamed, "They're here! The *allies* are here!"

Then into the sky erupted the howling of countless voices, and all eyes turned to the hills that rose to the west of the plain. They shone clearly in the moonlight and as the exhausted defenders watched, a vast shadow flowed over them. The strange darkness had thousands of glowing red eyes, and was made up of a huge gathering of werewolves, specters, and zombies from The-Land-of-the-Ghosts. At its head strode the gold-collared figure of King Grishmak of the Wolf-folk.

Beside him were dozens of silver-collared barons and baronesses, and behind them came the hordes of the werewolf army. King Grishmak threw back his head and howled again, and out crashed the reply from his warriors.

"They're here, the allies are here!" Thirrin wept as the bell rang on and on. And now, a new note was added as deep-toned horns sounded through the air, and the defenders turned to watch as from the eaves of the forest a great host emerged. At its head were the Holly King and the Oak King riding tall antlered stags. Thirrin gazed in wonder on these monarchs of the Great Forest. They seemed as old and yet as strong and formidable as ancient trees; their heads were crowned with circlets of acorns and holly berries, their armor gleamed like newly opened leaves, and in their hands they carried huge maces. Behind them came their soldiers, carrying long spears and swords made of what looked like massive thorns, wicked and slightly curved like the thorns of gigantic brambles.

With them came the wild figures of Green Men and Women, naked and ferocious, tusks of polished wood bursting from their mouths. And among them came the fighting creatures of the wild wood: boars and stags, bears and wolves, all answering the summons of their kings.

Tharaman-Thar rose up on his hind legs and roared a warrior's welcome, and Thirrin wiped her eyes and laughed aloud for joy. "They're here! The allies are here! Fight now, my people, and clear this land of the enemy!"

But there were still more wonders: Now the bright face of the moon seemed to dim and grow dusky, and all watched in silence as a cloud slowly writhed and coalesced until gradually new shapes evolved. Rank upon rank of flying forms could be seen, their huge wings black and leathery against the beautiful remote brilliance of the moon. The Vampires had come, too, and with them flew the giant Snowy Owls of the northern snowfields.

"Forward, my people!" Thirrin shouted into the air, which was still reverberating with the sound of the bell. "Blood! Blast! And Fire! Blood! Blast! And Fire!"

The commanders of the Empire's army watched the arrival of the Icemark's allies in horror. How could they fight such atrocities, such abominations of nature? The undead were marching against them, and even the creatures of the woodland were forming themselves into ranks and fighting! It was painfully obvious that the tide of battle had turned, but even now they were determined to snatch victory from the barbarians. Orders were shouted, the superb Polypontian discipline asserted itself, and the soldiers fought on.

On the left flank the Wolf-folk fell on the Imperial soldiers with a mighty howl, tearing the opposition limb from limb as they smashed into their ranks. Monsters, scaled and fanged and armed with razor claws, howled and roared, literally ripping the Polypontian troops to pieces as they raged through their ranks. And zombies charged on, no matter how many sword thrusts or musket balls ripped into their bodies. Only complete dismemberment could stop them. Even decapitation wasn't enough; they'd simply tuck their head under one arm and fight on, crushing the Imperial soldiers with clubs that broke arms through upraised shields.

On the right wing, the Holly King and the Oak King advanced toward the Imperial troops. Huge and menacing, they rode forward on their antlered stags, their woodland soldiers close behind, and hammered at the enemy with heavy maces as the Polypontian troops closed ranks against them.

Then, falling from the sky with hideous shrieks, came the Vampires ripping out enemy throats and drinking their blood, and with them the giant Snowy Owls, stooping on the Empire's soldiers and tearing at them with talons.

Thirrin climbed onto Tharaman-Thar's back and, raising her sword, she gave the note for the paean and led a charge of her cavalry, human troopers mounted on their leopard comrades. Forward they drove into the enemy ranks, hacking and tearing a wedge deep into the army that still fought doggedly on, every one of the Polypontian soldiers horribly aware that if they broke ranks, turned their back, and fled, then death was certain. But behind Thirrin's charge came the Hypolitan and housecarls, and they hit the ranks of the enemy with a fury that drove them steadily back.

Many of the Vampires now assumed their human shape and appeared as soldiers dressed in black armor carrying long black swords that flowed and writhed through the air in a complex pattern of attack. Their faces were dead-white and their lips bloodred, and as they killed they bit deep into the throats of their victims. Fear began to consume the Empire's horrified soldiers; they were fighting legends and nightmares, not mere humans. All around them were monsters, and the air was filled with the wails of ghosts and other terrifying creatures of the underworld.

Slowly they began to give ground, yet their discipline was holding even in the face of the hideous mincing Vampires that swirled and danced before them, and the giant werewolves that tore them to pieces. And then the barbarian Queen herself burst upon them, leading her cavalry, who were all mounted on giant leopards, and with her came more of the terrible white Wolf-folk.

At last the Polypontian discipline failed, and a great despairing cry rose into the sky as the Empire's army suddenly broke and fled. On drove the terrible alliance of nightmare creatures, hacking and biting at them as they ran, pulling them down and ripping out their throats, drinking their blood, and tearing their bodies apart. Countless thousands died in the first few minutes of the rout, and as the night wore on, more than half the invading army was killed as they tried to reach the Great Road and the safety of the south.

From his position on the hills overlooking the plain, Scipio Bellorum watched the arrival of the terrible allies in amazement and growing rage. This could not be! Such creatures had no place in his rational universe. Nevertheless, his army was giving ground before them, and now the queenling herself was leading an attack that drove all before it. Slowly he bowed his head; this was a new experience for the great general of the Polypontian Empire. He may have lost battles before, and none so many as in this terrible struggle, but he'd never lost a war. The experience was bitter and terrible, but already his general's resourcefulness was reasserting itself. He knew he had no choice but to cut his losses. Pulling sharply on his reins, he turned his horse and trotted away.

His staff officers watched in puzzlement. "But, My Lord, what are you doing?" one of them called.

"I believe the term is 'making good my escape,'" Scipio Bellorum answered without looking back. "I suggest you do the same." Then, drawing a whip, he sent his horse at a wild gallop down toward the Great Road before it could be blocked by his fleeing army.

34

Oskan watched as Thirrin and her allies drove the army of the Polypontian Empire from the field. He continued ringing the huge Solstice Bell, its deep note sweeping over the night and adding a melodious counterpoint to the awful sounds of battle. But then, gradually, he allowed the ringing to stop as he looked out over the plain, feeling small and unwanted. Even the soldiers who'd been left on garrison duty had run down to join the battle, and his sense of loneliness was increased by the melancholy sighing of a gentle wind that stirred his newly grown hair and brought with it a scent of the forest.

But then he noticed a distant and dark flying figure that had detached itself from the black of the night. It circled slowly as though looking for something, then it dived toward the city. Soon it was flying overhead and screeching a hideous call. One of the Vampires had decided to pay him a visit for some reason, and Oskan shuddered in the warm night. He watched as the creature folded its leathery wings and landed a few feet from where he stood.

The giant bat was awkward on the ground; its small, clawed

feet minced over the stonework of the parapet and its wings rattled and billowed as it tried to keep its balance. Its face was pointed, with a wide mouth that bristled needle-sharp teeth and two huge fangs, which glittered in the moonlight.

"Oskan the Warlock," a feminine voice said mockingly.

"Do I know you?"

"Oh yes. Just a moment and I'll make things clearer," the bat answered, and as Oskan watched, the vicious foxlike face trickled and ran like wax before a flame. The ears and fur retracted and new features gradually began to form. Soon a tall and loathsomely beautiful woman stood before him, dressed in elegant black armor. "Do you recognize me now, Oskan the Warlock?"

"Your Majesty," he said in greeting, bowing his head to the Vampire Queen.

"My, haven't you grown?" she said, running her eyes appreciatively over him and licking her fangs. "Still, I'm much stronger than I look. I'll easily be able to carry you."

"Carry me?"

"To your beloved. She's reached the enemy camp and is having a conference with her allies. Surely you want to be there?"

"Well . . . yes."

"Good." Her Vampiric Majesty then turned her back on him and, peering over her shoulder, said, "Then climb aboard."

As Oskan watched, she resumed her bat form, the black armor flowing into the leathery wings and her long hair somehow metamorphosing into pointed ears. After a moment's hesitation, Oskan stepped forward and placed his arms around her neck.

"Oh, what a strong grip for such a young man. What

delightful promise the years must hold," came the mocking voice as she leaped into the air and her wings beat down powerfully. They surged skyward, and wheeled out over the plain. The battlements of Frostmarris fell dizzyingly away, and the ground ran and flowed below them as they sped toward the enemy camp.

Oskan hardly dared open his eyes after the takeoff, but eventually he peered out at the sky, its dense field of glittering stars subdued by the power of the full moon that drenched the night with the glory of its subtle light. Then he looked over Her Vampiric Majesty's shoulder and stared down at the ground. The sight was grim. Everywhere he looked, bodies lay in heaps where the army of the Empire had been broken and the rout had begun. Under the light of the moon, the armor and weapons gleamed and flashed as Oskan flew overhead, and the dead soldiers lying in their tangled and broken heaps looked like the abstract patterns that marked the pages of illuminated books. It was almost as though the night were mocking his horror with an unlooked-for beauty, and he closed his eyes on the sight.

They'd soon crossed the plain and were circling in long spirals down to the ground. The Vampire Queen landed softly outside Bellorum's campaign tent. She resumed her human form, took Oskan's hand, then stepped elegantly through the entrance and into the wide space where the general had discussed tactics. Inside, Thirrin sat at a large table with Tharaman-Thar, Basilea Iphigenia, King Grishmak of the Wolf-folk, and His Vampiric Majesty. Behind them stood Olememnon, Thirrin's bodyguard of white werewolves, and other high-ranking officers.

Waiting until she had the attention of all present, the Vampire Queen stepped forward and smiled.

Immediately Thirrin jumped to her feet.

"Oskan!" she whispered. The drama of the battle had forced her to put aside all memory of the fact that it was the warlock who'd told of the allies' arrival, and now she gazed in amazement at his uninjured form. She strode across the tent and hugged him.

"Well, how perfectly *sweet*. If I could remember how, I'm sure I might weep," said the Vampire Queen.

Thirrin released him, and holding him at arm's length she looked him up and down. "How . . . ?"

"The blessing of the Goddess," Oskan answered and smiled.

"You're perfect!" she said.

"Yes, *isn't he*!" said Her Vampiric Majesty, running her eyes appreciatively over his body.

Only then did Thirrin realize that her friend was naked. He'd run from the cave with neither thought nor time for clothes. Quickly Thirrin unpinned her cloak and draped it over his shoulders. "Cover yourself up. Remember who you are," she said, and turned to scowl at the Vampire.

"Oh, don't worry, my dear. He's a little young for my taste," she answered and smiled, revealing her fangs.

"Ah, the warlock!" Grishmak bellowed from the table. "Join us! Join us!"

Thirrin led him over to the others, where Tharaman-Thar nuzzled him and purred deeply. "Welcome back to the world of the living, Oskan. All of our lives would have been emptier without you."

Oskan hugged him, burying his face in his thick fur. "The Goddess obviously didn't want me yet."

Thirrin became suddenly brisk, and filled in missing details of the battle. "The enemy is in full retreat. The Holly King and the Oak King are still in pursuit, as are all our other allies under the command of field officers. But Scipio Bellorum seems to have escaped."

"Our Vampires are flying over the road, but so far there've been no sightings," His Vampiric Majesty said in a voice of tired silk. "And, to be honest, we intend withdrawing our forces soon. We're all perfectly glutted, aren't we, dearest?" he said, turning to his coruler and burping discreetly behind gloved fingers.

"Oh, I'm sure I could manage another regiment or two," she answered. "Some of those southern soldiers have such *exotic* blood. *So* spicy."

Thirrin did her best not to show her revulsion and almost succeeded. "How long will your forces be available to us, Your Majesties?"

"Only for another hour or so, despite the culinary temptations, wouldn't you say, dear heart?" Her Vampiric Majesty said, turning to the Vampire King for confirmation. "Then we simply must be flying home. These summer nights are so short, and I really couldn't bear being caught in the sun."

"And you, Grishmak. How long will your werewolves be staying?" Thirrin asked.

"As long as you need us. It may take months to muster a Wolf-folk army, but once it's gathered, it's as steady and loyal as any fyrd."

Thirrin smiled in relief. "You have no idea how good it is to hear you say that, Grishmak. It could take almost a year to get the country back to anything like a defensible position again."

"All we ask is board and lodgings," the wolfman growled happily. "Speaking of which, is there any food available? The Vampires may have gorged themselves, but I could eat a horse! I don't suppose there's a spare one hereabouts?"

While orderlies were sent off to find food, the commanders and rulers discussed what would follow in the next few days. Throughout the meeting, Thirrin directed operations and sent out orders with all the skill of a veteran, while she discreetly held Oskan's beautifully regenerated hand under the table.

For the next two days the enemy was pursued toward the south, until they were finally brought to battle at the very mouth of the pass that led to the Polypontian Empire. The werewolf army had taken a route through the hills and woodlands and managed to get ahead of the Empire's fleeing soldiers, a force that was still dangerously large, and had blocked their final escape route through the mountains so they were forced to stand and fight. Realizing that the soldiers and allies of a country they had ravaged would show no mercy, the Imperial troops asked for none, and had fought with discipline and bravery to the last before finally being overwhelmed by Thirrin and her allies.

Of the entire invasion army only a few thousand soldiers escaped to return home, and they were mainly garrisons left in the southern cities who had immediately fled when they heard of Bellorum's defeat. The general himself was never captured.

Maggiore Totus put down his pen and removed his spectoculums. He had dotted the final *i* and crossed the last *t* of his history. He'd worked with a speed that had surprised even himself, and he was very pleased with the results. Of course, it would be months before it would be read by anyone; after all, the manuscript had to be sent to the Holy Brothers in the Southern Continent, who would copy and illuminate it with decorative letters and pictures. Also, Thirrin wanted at least one *History of the War* for every city in the land, and one each for all the rulers of the allies, and so the process would take even longer.

Still, *his* work was done, and he poured himself a large glass of sherry. Then he got up from his desk and moved closer to the fire. The winter was particularly cold that year, and the snows so deep that Thirrin had been forced to permanently assign an entire regiment of housecarls to the job of clearing the city streets. Maggie reached his favorite chair, picked up Primplepuss, who was asleep there, and placed her on his knees as he sat down. She mewed sleepily and settled again as he stroked her.

Outside his door he could hear chamberlains and other servants rushing to and fro as they hurried to prepare for the coming celebrations. "Yule again, Primplepuss. Where does the time go?"

The little cat mewed without opening her eyes.

"And so many great people coming to share it with us. The Basilea and Olememnon, and Tharaman-Thar and Taradan. And we mustn't forget King Grishmak, even though he's become something of a permanent fixture recently."

The delicious scent of baking solstice pie crept into the room, and the old scholar sniffed appreciatively. "Now, I wonder if they're looking for tasters for the latest batch in the kitchens. Yes . . . yes. I might just go and volunteer my services."

He drained his glass of sherry, placed Primplepuss on the chair as he stood up, and went in search of some early Yule treats. Out in the corridor he was immediately caught up in a tidal rush of people carrying baskets and barrels, boxes and bushels of differing foodstuffs. Rightly assuming they must be heading for the kitchens, Maggiore was content to allow himself to be bundled along.

* * *

The small party of Thirrin, Oskan, Grimswald, and the bodyguard of white werewolves stood for a moment of silent respect by the side of the newly raised funeral mound that stood on the plain of Frostmarris. It was deeply buried under a layer of frozen snow, and beneath the pristine brilliance of the icy covering, the earth was still bare and grassless. But come the springtime it would be glorious with the tumbled colors of wildflowers, for when King Redrought's funeral urn had been placed in the central chamber, Thirrin had personally scattered seeds over the loose soil.

The raising of her father's burial mound had been for Thirrin the final act of the war with the Polypontus. She'd kept her promise and brought Redrought's ashes home from the Hypolitan, and now he lay at peace with his ancestors, close to the city he had loved.

Grimswald blew his nose loudly on an enormous handkerchief and smiled sadly. It was almost a year ago that the Empire had invaded and Redrought had marched off to destroy the first of their armies. And now that that fateful date had been commemorated, Grimswald felt that his master had finally been laid to rest.

Thirrin looked up at last and gazed around her, scrutinizing every detail of the defensive walls before slowly taking in the broad sweep of the panorama to the eaves of the forest. Beside her, Oskan waited patiently, using the time to adjust Jenny's ear-warmers and secretly feed her a carrot. Thirrin had been doing a lot of this sort of thing recently. It was as though she couldn't quite believe the war was over and the land was still free, so she had to reassure herself by looking at things long and hard, just to make sure there were no Polypontian soldiers patrolling the walls, roads, or wherever else she was staring.

"Everything all right?" Oskan asked at last, when she took a little longer than usual.

"Yes, why?" she snapped.

"Oh, no reason. I just wondered if you were looking for anything in particular."

"No, just . . . looking."

"Fine. Shall we . . . ?" Oskan nodded his head toward the forest, their intended destination.

In answer, Thirrin trotted her horse forward, and the escort of cavalry and her bodyguard of white werewolves followed. "Have you got everything?"

"Well, no, *I* haven't, but the werewolves have," Oskan answered, pointing back to her bodyguard, who each carried a barrel or a box of some sort.

"Good. Do you think they'll answer your summons? It is winter, after all."

"They don't hibernate, you know. They're not bears. If they hear me, I'm sure they'll come. They always have before."

Thirrin nodded and rode on in silence. The trees drew slowly nearer until they filled the horizon, their colonies of crows and ravens rising to tumble around the sky like black ash, their harsh calls giving winter a voice.

At last they rode under the eaves of the Great Forest, the ring of the horses' hooves on the frozen ground echoing through the woodland. "This'll do," said Oskan as they entered a small glade where a giant oak tree slept and a holly tree blazed in a glory of polished leaves and fiery berries.

Thirrin signaled to the Wolf-folk guards, who then placed the boxes and barrels they carried on the ground in a neat pile, and withdrew to stand with the cavalry troopers nearby. A fanfare was sounded, the brassy notes rebounding through the woodlands until they died away to silence. Oskan dismounted and stood quietly for a moment. His usual collection of black clothing was overlaid by a rich scarlet cloak with a green lining, an early solstice present from Thirrin, who was determined to make his wardrobe a little more colorful.

He blazed like a flame against the snow, then he raised his hands and called into the dark forest: "Greetings to Their Royal Highnesses the Holly King and the Oak King, Rulers of the Wild Wood, Monarchs of the Beasts. Felicitations from Queen Thirrin Freer Strong-in-the-Arm Lindenshield, Wildcat of the North, Monarch of the Icemark."

His voice died away, and only the sound of a gentle breeze moaning through the naked branches broke the silence. They waited for almost five minutes, and Thirrin was just about to suggest another fanfare when a sudden blast of wind exploded through the trees, sending a great billow of snow over the clearing and causing the branches to thrash and writhe against the gray sky.

The wind suddenly dropped, and when the snow had settled again, a line of twenty soldiers stood facing them. Ten were dressed in armor that was fashioned like polished holly leaves, and ten in oak; both kings had sent a guard to greet their ally.

Thirrin urged her horse forward and looked at them closely. Even after all their help in the war against the Empire, she still found them fascinating. Here before her stood the stuff of legends. These soldiers had marched through her childhood in the form of nursery rhymes and songs, and yet they were real, and had answered her call for help when Scipio Bellorum had invaded. She shook herself, brought her thoughts back to the present and addressed the soldiers of the Great Forest.

"Take my heartfelt thanks and greetings to your rulers and my fellow monarchs, the Holly King and the Oak King. Convey to them my continuing friendship, and ask them to share in our celebration of the winter solstice with these gifts of wine, mead, and beer. Take also this box," she continued, pointing to a slender polished container. "It contains the sword of General Scipio Bellorum of the Polypontian Empire, taken by me along with his hand in single combat. Receive it in acknowledgment of your monarchs' help in the war of freedom just lately won. Our victory could not have been secured without the people and the animals of the wild wood.

"Know also that no living creature will be hunted by the humans of this land while they remain within the borders of the forest, and no wood or any other material will be taken without the paying of due thanks."

Thirrin fell silent, and the gentle breeze rustled through the branches of the trees. Then one holly and one oak soldier stepped forward from the ranks, and saluting her, took Bellorum's sword. Other soldiers came forward and took up the barrels, and when they stepped back in line, the huge blast of wind boomed through the forest again and they were gone.

"Well, that went quite well, I think," said Oskan, brushing the powdered snow off his new cloak. "Shall we go back now? I'm getting quite hungry."

Thirrin glared at him. There were times when she was certain he made light of every occasion just to annoy her. But she controlled herself and nodded curtly.

By the time they were out on the plain again her mood had softened and she smiled. "I love Yuletide! I can't wait for solstice morning, with all its singing and good things to eat. Tharaman will have arrived with Taradan, and he'll have all sorts of tales about the Ice Troll Wars. And of course there'll be presents; I particularly love the presents. What will you give me this year? It had better be good."

"What could I give that you don't already have?" Oskan asked. "It's an impossible task. So I admitted defeat and got you a loaf of bread. It's a cleverly symbolic gift, as bread represents life, and you're nothing if not lively."

"Why, Oskan, how sweet," she teased in return. "Does that mean *you'll* be with me for life?"

But the warlock had fallen silent, and his eyes stared into the middle distance as though he could see things beyond human sight. Thirrin knew the signs and held her breath. He was about to prophesy.

"Thirrin Freer Strong-in-the-Arm Lindenshield, Wildcat of the North, Taker of the Hand of Bellorum . . ." His voice was strangely hollow and his breath rattled in his throat. "You ask the Old Ones about your servant Oskan the Warlock. Will he be with you for life?"

"Yes, yes!" Thirrin urged breathlessly.

"The Old Ones answer you thus . . . You'll just have to bloody well wait and see," he said, and grinned so wickedly that she cuffed him around the head.

But then a howling sounded on the frozen air and they all stopped to listen. The werewolf escort answered in a tumble of voices and then trotted on.

"Well?" Thirrin demanded.

"Tharaman-Thar and his escort have just crossed the northern border. They'll be here tomorrow night," Oskan explained.

She nodded and smiled contentedly. This was going to be a wonderful Yule. "Do you know what?"

"What?"

"The last one back has a face like Jenny's arse," she said, and galloped away toward Frostmarris with Oskan, werewolves, and cavalry escort following in wild pursuit.

ACKNOWLEDGMENTS

I would like to acknowledge the support and help of my work colleagues: Lesley, Jackie, Jon (big and small), Amy, Matt, The Stoat, Sonia, Mariam, Monica, Dipesh, Andrea, Andrew, Steve, and all of the Saturday and Sunday plebs. Also to Trace (the manager and bazooka specialist), as well as Louse, second-in-command and collector of hoofcoverings.

Family and friends who are as excited as I am can't be left out, either, and Nigel must get a mention for many years of past listening without getting too impatient!

I must also thank The Chicken House for being brave enough to publish my books. Particular thanks to Barry, Imogen, Rachel, and Esther, but also to those nice people who pick up the phone and say "Is that Stuart?" before I even have a chance to get beyond the opening remarks. It must be the accent or the neurotic way I gabble!

Finally, my heartfelt thanks go to Margaret York, writer, teacher, actress, and complete inspiration; when reading *King Solomon's Mines*, you gave a voice to Gagool I've never forgotten — I'm sure Rider Haggard would have approved!

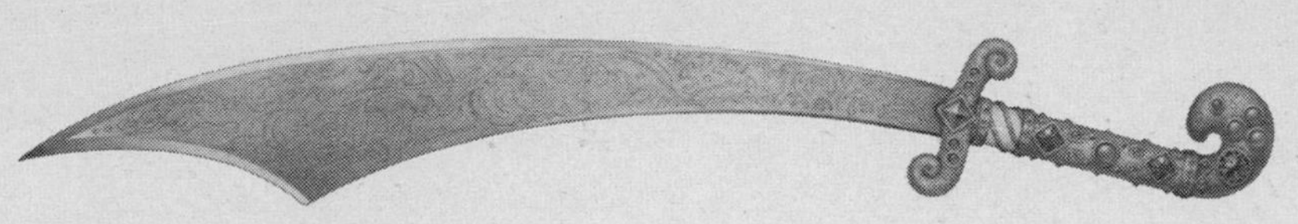

Special Sneak Preview of

Blade of Fire

The Second Book

in the

Icemark

Chronicles

Coming in Spring 2007!

SEVENTEEN YEARS HAVE PASSED. *Somewhere on the snowy borders of the Empire, just out of sight of werewolf scouts, Scipio Bellorum is planning his revenge. Soon he will hit the Kingdom of Icemark with a ferocity never before witnessed by Thirrin and her allies: for this time he has his cruel, uncontrollable sons with him, and a mighty fleet of "sky ships" at his command.*

Meanwhile, in the Icemark, Thirrin and Oskan are returning victorious from a war with the Ice Trolls. Eagerly awaiting their arrival is their youngest child, Charlemagne ("Sharley"). Little does he suspect the fateful role he will play in the struggle to come. . . .

Out in the garden, Charlemagne stopped in his tracks and listened. He understood the language of the Wolf-folk as well as human speech, having played with the palace werewolf guards since before he could crawl. He suddenly grinned as the final, drawn-out syllables became clear. His mom and dad, Thirrin and Oskan, would be home within a few hours. Giving a yelp of joy, he leaped into the air despite his withered leg and hurried back into the palace.

Watching him, Maggiore Totus rapped on the window with his stick, but Charlemagne didn't hear. The old scholar sighed. Now he'd have to wait until someone thought to come and tell him the news. Charlemagne's skill with the Wolf-folk's speech, and languages in general, was his greatest gift, and Maggie had tried to establish it within a scholarly framework. But the young prince wasn't interested. He saw the differences in the words he heard around him as a sort of mental game that he played with ease. He could speak the language of the Southern Continent almost as well as a native, and his accent was near perfect. And all this skill was based on nothing more than simple conversation and a quick ear. The old scholar almost despaired. Language-learning should be an academic discipline founded on well-tried formulae of grammatic structures and rigid exercises, not this casual method of listening and then almost perfect repetition that Charlemagne had developed! The boy had even picked up a good understanding of Polypontian after hearing the ambassadorial delegations on their annual visits to politely threaten the Icemark.

The tutor's thoughts were interrupted by a loud thump on his door, followed by Charlemagne leaping excitedly into the room. "Get dressed in your best, Maggie, Mom and Dad are coming home. They'll be here by tonight!"

"Any news of the war?" the old scholar asked eagerly.

"Well, we already knew that they'd won days ago. What more do you need to know?"

"Numbers, dispositions, tactics, casualties," Maggie listed.

"Those sorts of details you'll have to get directly from Mom tonight. They're not going to risk information like that on a relay that can be heard by anyone."

Maggie shook his head in tired amusement. Youth always assumed the world had access to its skills. "Not everyone speaks the language of the Wolf-folk, Charlemagne."

"No? No, I guess not. Well, whatever, there were no details in the report."

At this point a member of the werewolf guard arrived, saluted smartly, and then Maggie listened in fascination as he and the prince quickly spoke to each other in the strange snarls and guttural grunts of the Wolf-folk tongue.

"Captain Blood-Lapper wants to know if a full guard of honor will be needed tonight," Charlemagne translated, after politely waiting to see if Maggiore had understood.

"Yes, I think so, Captain," the old scholar answered in his role as Senior Royal Advisor. "After such a significant victory, the Queen should be greeted with full ceremonial."

"Yes, My Lord," the werewolf replied in the language of

the Icemark, his voice booming around the small room. Then saluting once more, he withdrew to pass on the order to the human housecarls and his own warriors.

Maggie sighed in sudden contentment. Charlemagne's mood had changed for the better and he also seemed to have forgiven his old tutor's earlier bluntness. "Well, there are enough of the Yule supplies left to make a scratch feast in honor of your parents' return. Though I wish they'd given us a little more warning: What's the point of setting up an efficient werewolf message system if they don't use it?"

"Maybe they were preoccupied and just forgot," Charlemagne said. "They *have* just fought a war, you know." Then, grinning, he added: "Mom was right. She warned me you can be a bit of an old woman when you get going."

"'Old woman'! What do you mean?"

"Always fussing and nagging."

Maggiore sniffed and drew his enormous dignity around him like a large cloak. "I'll treat that remark with the contempt it deserves."

Charlemagne had been standing on the battlements of the citadel for almost an hour, listening to the werewolf messages coming in. And despite several layers of furs and the blazing brazier he was standing next to, he was freezing. Even so, there were compensations. Not only would he be among the first to see the Queen and her army come into view, but the sight of the nearly full moon rising over the frozen land of the Icemark was exquisitely beautiful. The subtle light was reflected by the snows and defused through the myriad ice crystals hanging in the frigid air. It seemed the entire world had been steeped in misted silver and smoky shadow.

"'A night for magic,' Dad would say," Charlemagne mumbled to himself as he remembered the times from his early childhood when Oskan would conjure little images from the "muscle and texture of light itself" and set them skipping and dancing on his bedcovers just before he fell asleep. Once his father had built an entire miniature castle, gleaming and shimmering on the shadows, and peopled it with soldiers and a cavalry mounted on flying horses that had galloped around the towers and turrets of their citadel. Charlemagne had tried for days after to copy his dad's skills, but nothing happened. In the end he'd reluctantly come to the conclusion that he was about as magical as a chair leg. Of all his brothers and sisters only Medea had shown any magical ability.

It had been weak and unimpressive at first, just a fuzzy materialization of a mouse scuttling across her bed, or a sudden certainty about what they were going to have for dinner that night. But at fourteen her powers had grown, and under Oskan's guidance they'd developed into . . . into, well, what? Charlemagne hardly knew, his sister kept her skills and much of her life under close and mysterious wraps, letting very few into the secret world she'd made for herself. Their mother had dismissed her mysteries as teenage moods, but Oskan had taken great trouble to spend time with her, and Charlemagne wondered if there was a problem of some sort. A magical *complication* that only the Gifted would truly understand. He shrugged. Whatever it was, it only underlined his own sense of isolation. Three of his siblings had their fighting and training to keep them occupied, Medea had her magic, and he had precisely nothing.

His thoughts were interrupted by the lonely sound of another werewolf howling into the cold night air. It was nearer than the last couple of calls, which was hardly surprising: The Wolf-folk were reporting the progress of the royal army, and each time it passed a lookout point a message was sent.

An acknowledging call was relayed back from one of the werewolves at the main gatehouse and Charlemagne quickly calculated how long it would be before the army came into sight. Twenty minutes, he guessed, judging by the average marching pace of one of Thirrin's expeditions. He turned and beckoned a housecarl who stood nearby.

"Tell the kitchens the army'll be here in less than an hour, and then tell Maggiore."

The soldier saluted and hurried away. Then a sudden noise on the spiral stairway that rose through the nearby turret told him his brothers and Cressida were on the way. All of them could understand werewolf speech and so would have heard the relay, but only he, Charlemagne, could actually speak the werewolf tongue. He happily placed his language skills in, as Maggie would call it, the "credit column" of his life and, for once, refused to even think about the debit of his weak leg, his hated name, and other frustrations.

Cressida emerged first from the narrow doorway of the turret and she smiled upon seeing him. "Ah, there you are,

Sharley. I knew you'd have heard the werewolves. How long before Mom and Dad get back?"

"Another hour or so. But they should emerge from the forest in about twenty minutes."

His brothers, twins Cerdic and Eodred, then struggled through the narrow doorway. At sixteen they were already larger than most housecarls, and Maggiore said that they took after their granddad, King Redrought, except they both had jet-black hair. Redrought's had been as flame-red as Cressida's and Charlemagne's—indeed as his daughter's, Queen Thirrin herself. But as though to compensate for the difference in hair color, the twins both had their granddad's inability to say anything quietly. They boomed and bellowed and laughed with the volume of a thunderstorm in the mountains. Added to this they also had Redrought's slapstick sense of humor, and when they lay aside their axes and swords, they were as boisterous and fun-loving as kittens. Even now, as they stretched their huge frames after being confined by the spiral staircase, each nudged the other, trying to make him slip on the ice. Then Cerdic impetuously scooped up a double handful of snow from the battlements and stuffed it down Eodred's neck. The following squawking and giggling echoed over the silent citadel as though someone had released a pack of manic hens into the night.

"Stop it, you two!" said Cressida with all the authority of her seventeen years and her position as heir to the throne. "We won't be able to hear any Wolf-folk messages if you keep mucking about."

The two boys immediately settled down, despite the fact that they towered over their slightly built sister, but they continued to poke and nudge each other when she wasn't watching. "So, Sharley!" Eodred boomed, finally turning his attention to his younger brother. "When will Mom and Dad get back?"

"I've already asked that, thickhead!" said Cressida. "In about an hour. Where's Medea?" she suddenly added.

Charlemagne shrugged. "Who knows? Doing whatever it is that fills so much of her time. She'll turn up when she's ready, I suppose."

Cressida frowned. "She could at least have made an effort for Mom and Dad."

"Do you think they'll bring us something back from the ice-sheets?" Cerdic asked excitedly. "Perhaps a troll's war-hammer or maybe a piece of one of those falling stars Tharaman told us about last time he visited."

"That's Tharaman-*Thar* to you," said Cressida sharply. "And don't you think you're getting a little old to expect presents every time Mom and Dad go away?"

"No, in fact, I don't!" Cerdic answered forcibly. "It's traditional for monarchs to present their friends and allies with gifts."

"But not their small-minded offspring," his sister answered in a dangerously quiet tone that made both twins subside immediately.

"I bet they *will* bring us presents, anyway," Cerdic

muttered rebelliously, then quickly closed his mouth when Cressida shot him a warning look.

After a few minutes a chamberlain brought them all mulled ale, and they gratefully warmed their hands on the thick mugs that steamed a delicious scent of herbs and spices into the freezing air.

"You don't have to wait out here in the cold if you don't want to, Sharley," Cressida suddenly declared. "We can send word as soon as the army comes into sight."

Charlemagne sighed quietly. Even his older sister, the most sensible young woman he knew, treated him as though he was constantly on the verge of collapse. Everyone thought he was *delicate*, and yet he knew for a fact that he had fewer colds and general illnesses than anyone else in the family. He was as hale and hearty as the toughest housecarl, he just happened to have a limp.

"I'm fine," he said defensively and frowned. "At least I'm wearing furs. You lot are likely to freeze if you don't get something warm over your armor. I suppose you've been training in the lists."

"With the Weapons Master, yes," Cressida answered, deciding to overlook her youngest brother's attitude. "We're perfecting some of the finer points of the shield wall technique. I think we've got the hang of it now."

Charlemagne nodded, silent. He sometimes watched them training, but his need to join in had become almost too much to bear and he'd reduced the time he spent spectating on the sidelines. Instead, he'd taken to moping around in his room when they were due to be in the lists, resentfully aware of the time and what they'd be doing.

Cressida knew the root cause of Charlemagne's silence and put her arm around his shoulders. She was taller than him by just about two inches, and their bright red hair and green eyes would have proven to any onlooking strangers that they were brother and sister. "Come on, Sharley. We have to accept what we're given, don't we? Make the most of what you have and rise above the disabilities."

"You sound just like Maggiore Totus," he answered sullenly.

"Do I?"

"Yes. He said exactly the same this afternoon."

"Well, he's right. Look at old Carnwulf, the porter. He was a housecarl, one of the best, until he lost his leg to the green rot after he was wounded. But you don't hear him moaning or going on about the unfairness of life. He just accepted his changed circumstances and got on with it. He's one of the cheeriest faces in the palace and is liked by everyone."

"Meaning I'm not, I suppose."

"That's not what I meant, Sharley, and you know it," Cressida answered sharply. "Not all warriors carry swords and shields. Some of the bravest hearts I know are to be found among the gentlest of people. They are the ones who face up to the difficulties of life and refuse to be broken or twisted. They earn the respect of everyone and lay as few burdens as possible on those around them. Remember that, Sharley, and perhaps even the toughest housecarls will be pleased to call you friend."

Charlemagne felt his face redden in a confusion of embarrassment and anger, but before he could say anything a call rose up from the werewolves at the gatehouse. Immediately all four children of Queen Thirrin Freer Strong-in-the-Arm Lindenshield, Wildcat of the North, looked out over the snows to the dark and glowering eaves of the distant forest. For a moment it seemed that the very trees had begun to march out over the plain, but the sharp eyes of the siblings slowly distinguished cavalry horses and the raised spears of marching infantry. The army had come home.

As they watched, the softly diffused moonlight seemed to coalesce and gather about a tall figure riding a long-eared mule, and suddenly a brilliant shooting star of light illuminated the front ranks of marching housecarls and the distinctive white forms of the Queen's Ukpik werewolf bodyguard. Oskan Witchfather knew that his children would be watching from the walls, and he was sending them a signal.

A call rang out from the Wolf-folk down at the main gatehouse, and after a few moments the faint reply from the Ukpik bodyguard spread itself over the cold night air. In an instant all four siblings scrambled for the stairway, eager to be the first to greet their parents.

In one of the highest towers of the citadel, Medea looked out over the snows beyond the city walls and watched as her parents marched home. Her feelings were a tangled knot of contradictions. She was happy that they'd returned safely, but she was angry that everyone would be greeted before her. A generalized resentment seemed to fill her to the brim.

She was a year older than Charlemagne, and of the same slender build, but where he had the red hair and green eyes of his mother and Cressida, she had the same coloring as Oskan. Once, on her thirteenth birthday, a court poet had compared her white complexion and black hair to snowfall in a shadowed forest, but her silence had ensured that no other social-climbing artist had ever again tried to win her support with flattering verse or song. In her own mind she was as quiet as a winter's dawn. And her coldness was as deadly.

With her thirteenth birthday had come a focusing of the jealousies she felt for her sister and her entire brood of brothers, Charlemagne in particular. She had been six years old when the terrible plague that nearly killed him had struck, and she'd been forced then to acknowledge she had little to give to others in the way of love and compassion. She'd only been glad that at last her closest rival for her parents' attention was about to be removed by a convenient death. And then, when he'd survived, her disappointment found at least some consolation in his crippled leg.

It was only weeks later that it occurred to her the attention and pampering he received from their mother and father would be his for life, now that he would never be strong enough to fulfill his role as a fighting prince in the Lindenshield household. She felt she'd been forever demoted in the pecking order of the family, and rising above them all, even above the Crown Princess Cressida herself, was Charlemagne. Untouchable in his disability, forever sheltered by his parents' love.

But at least her Gift still ensured she had her father's attention for some of the time, as he put her through her magical paces and devised different training regimes for her. For several nights a week before she'd "come of magical age" at fourteen, he'd joined her in her tower and together they'd created landscapes and cities from the ectoplasm of moonlight and shadow, or sent their Sight far out into the night, viewing the world around and even spying on the housecarls in their mess hall. She'd been thrilled to find that she had Far-Seeing abilities stronger than her father's, and he'd encouraged her to range to the outermost edges of her Sight, until she could even see the distant coastline and watch the fishing fleet setting out for the rich hunting grounds.

"What do you see, Medea?" he'd asked, and she'd reveled in the fact that he was relying on her to describe the scene that was as sharp as polished crystal to her.

"The moon has laid a path of silver over the calm sea, and the boats are following it," she'd answered.

"Can you see the crews?"

She pushed her abilities to the very edge of their limit, but the focus broke up and became grainy. With disappointment she shook her head. "No, they're too far away."

He'd smiled and hugged her then. "Never mind, Medea.

It's just a matter of practice. Your Gift will grow and soon you'll be able to see far out over the oceans and probably count the hairs in the fishermen's hairy nostrils!"

She'd giggled, taking both of them by surprise, and her father had tightened his hug. That was the last time she remembered being happy. Not long after, Oskan had stopped his regular training regimes. He would still occasionally help in her attempts to reach her full potential but, in the magical world, the Gifted were expected to find their own way.

All of that seemed so long ago, a time when she had been so young and had yet to be disappointed by the rise of Sharley in her parents' affections. Now, with all of the lamps and candles extinguished in her tower room and the shutters wide open on the freezing night, she watched her oblivious siblings standing on the walls waiting for the return of Thirrin and Oskan. She had no intention of joining them. Instead she'd wait until the sickening screeches and tears of greeting had been performed, and then she'd go down, knowing that Oskan at least would be looking for her.

She turned back into her moonlit room and settled into the high-backed chair that stood in the center of the floor. As her eyes focused on a point in the middle distance and her ears heard the soft, sibilant whisper of snow blowing through her open window and settling in a drift against the wall, her fingers turned the faint milky blue of freezing flesh. Her body was motionless, but her mind walked the shadows of her plans. Watching, waiting, building her strength . . .